The Chronicles of Danevitch of the Russian Secret Service

Dick Donovan

Alpha Editions

This edition published in 2024

ISBN : 9789367241448

Design and Setting By
Alpha Editions
www.alphaedis.com
Email - info@alphaedis.com

As per information held with us this book is in Public Domain.
This book is a reproduction of an important historical work. Alpha Editions uses the best technology to reproduce historical work in the same manner it was first published to preserve its original nature. Any marks or number seen are left intentionally to preserve its true form.

Contents

MICHAEL DANEVITCH .... - 1 -
INTRODUCTION. .... - 3 -
THE MYSTERIOUS DISAPPEARANCE OF A MILLION ROUBLES. .... - 7 -
A MODERN BORGIA. .... - 27 -
THE STRANGE STORY OF AN ATTACHÉ .... - 48 -
THE FATE OF VASSILO IVANOFF. .... - 71 -
THE MERCHANT OF RIGA. .... - 90 -
THE GREAT CONSPIRACY. .... - 110 -
THE CROWN JEWELS. .... - 127 -
THE STRANGE STORY OF A SECRET TREATY .... - 148 -
HOW PETER TRESKIN WAS LURED TO DOOM. .... - 175 -
THE CLUE OF THE DEAD HAND THE STORY OF AN EDINBURGH MYSTERY .... - 203 -
CHAPTER I. NEW YEAR'S EVE: THE MYSTERY BEGINS. .... - 205 -
CHAPTER II. THE MYSTERY DEEPENS.—THE NARRATIVE CONTINUED BY PETER BRODIE, OF THE DETECTIVE SERVICE. .... - 216 -
CHAPTER III. THE DEAD HAND SMITES .... - 226 -
FOOTNOTES: .... - 239 -

MICHAEL DANEVITCH

INTRODUCTION.

A YEAR or two before the outbreak of the Franco Prussian War a daring attempt was made upon the life of the Emperor of Russia. He had been out shooting in the neighbourhood of St. Petersburg, and was returning at dusk in company with numerous friends and a large suite. As the Royal carriage passed an isolated house on a country road, which was bordered on each side by a dense pine forest, a bomb was hurled from an upper window of the house. Fortunately it did not strike the carriage, as was intended, but, going over it, fell between the horses of two of the Royal Guard. The horses were blown to pieces, the riders were killed on the spot, and several other men were more or less injured. For some minutes a panic ensued. The Emperor's driver whipped his horses into a gallop, and everybody seemed at a loss what to do. The house, however, was soon surrounded, and a man and woman were seized as they were in the very act of escaping. It was soon made evident that this man and woman were mere tools, and the arch-conspirators had availed themselves of the confusion caused by the bursting bomb to get off. Darkness favoured the fugitives, and though the forest was scoured they were not captured. Subsequent investigation brought to light that the plot for the Emperor's taking off had been the work chiefly of a daring and notorious Nihilist, whose capture the Russian Government had long been trying to effect. His connection with this dastardly attempt caused a heavy price to be set upon his head, and every effort was made to arrest him. But, extraordinary as it seems, he succeeded in evading his pursuers, and, after travelling many hundreds of miles through the country in various disguises, he managed to get on board of a vessel bound to Constantinople—so much of his flight was subsequently learnt when it was too late; but at Constantinople all trace of him was lost, though there was reason to believe that he had escaped to either France or England, and a large staff of the most able Russian and Polish detectives were sent out to scour Europe.

One winter night of that memorable year, I was on my way from Paris to London viâ Calais. It had been a wild and stormy day; a high wind, bitter cold, snow, sleet, hail, rain—such were the atmospheric conditions. We had had an assortment of the worst samples of weather, and as night approached it was only too evident we were in for 'a buster.' There were very few passengers by the night train from Paris. It was not a night when anyone was likely to be travelling for pleasure. On our reaching Calais Station the wind had attained the force of a heavy gale, causing a tremendous sea to run in the Channel, and we who were pressed for time heard with dismay that the boat was not likely to attempt the crossing before the morning.

The cramped and starved passengers made a rush for the buffet, but I had to see the guard of the train, owing to a hand-bag of mine having gone astray.

This bit of business occupied me for quite twenty minutes, and then, almost frozen to the marrow, I made my way to the buffet. The large stove in the centre of the room was surrounded by the passengers, so I seated myself at one of the long tables and called for hot soup. It was not until I had finished the steaming bouillon, and had begun to thaw, that I became conscious I had a *vis-à-vis*. On the opposite side of the table, on the carpeted settee in a corner next the wall, sat a man with his legs upon the settee, his arms folded on his breast. The place was lighted by lamps. The light was dim, and the man was in partial shadow; but I noted that he wore a heavy fur coat, he had a peakless fur cap on his head, and was puffing away at a long and strong cigar. At his elbow on the table was a large basin of tea, and floating in the tea were three or four slices of lemon.

I really don't know how it was that I was suddenly attracted to this stranger. Some people may try to explain it by saying it was animal magnetism, odic force, or something of the kind. I shall offer no explanation myself; I merely state the bare fact. My eyes having got accustomed to the semi-gloom, I was enabled to observe that he had a clean-shaven face, with a rather prominent nose, a clean-cut mouth, which, taken in connection with the formation of the chin and jaw generally, indicated an iron will, a dogged determination. It was altogether a very striking face, full of character, and with points that removed it far from the category of the commonplace.

Having partaken of the rest of my supper, and feeling more comfortable and cheerful, I lit a cigar, called for coffee and a *petit verre*, assumed an easier position at the end of the seat, so that I was enabled to lean my back against the wall, my shoulders being thus parallel with the stranger's, the table separating us; then I spoke to him in French—made some ordinary remarks about the weather, and expressed a fear that we were doomed to pass the night there in the buffet. He answered me very affably, and in a rich, well-modulated voice. Fancying that I detected a foreign accent in his French, I politely asked him if he was a Frenchman. He smiled pleasantly, and expressed a wish to know why I doubted his being French. I told him frankly, whereupon he laughed again, and in perfect English, except that it betrayed a foreign tongue in its pronunciation, he said:

'I guess *you* are an Englishman.'

I admitted that I was, and we chatted away first in French and then in English for a long time; we exchanged cigars; he drank with me, I with him. Now, throughout the conversation there was one thing I was conscious of—the whole drift of his talk was to elicit information. This was done so delicately and skilfully that the majority of people would not have been aware of it. But I was. It was part of my business to know when I was being pumped, to use a vulgar but expressive phrase; I was also, even as he was, a seeker after knowledge, and I fancy I framed my questions perhaps not much less skilfully than he. At any rate, we seemed to become *en rapport*, and it is safe to say we interested each other. There was a reciprocal attraction between us. After a time the conversation flagged; tired nature was overcome, and we slept where we sat. At about seven in the morning a porter with stentorian lungs came in and aroused us from our uneasy slumber by bawling out that we were all to get on board the boat, as she was about to start. Confusion at once reigned; there was a hasty gathering up of bags, wraps, rugs, and other impedimenta, and a stampede was made for the steamer, each man trying to be first, in order that he might secure the best place in view of the stormy passage we were likely to have. For myself, I went leisurely; I was too case-hardened a traveller by land and sea to concern myself even about the Channel in its anger. I had, in the confusion, lost sight of my acquaintance of the night, and for the moment had forgotten him, when suddenly I heard his voice behind me. He had caught me up.

'You, like me, don't give yourself much concern,' he remarked. 'We shall have a rough crossing, no doubt, but it doesn't alarm me; I have been sodden with salt water too often.'

This struck a keynote again; we passed on board. As we reached the deck, he asked me if I was going below; I said no, I preferred to remain on deck. So did he. We therefore secured two camp-stools, placed them so that we sat with our backs to the funnel for the sake of the warmth, enveloped our knees in rugs, buttoned up our coats, battened our caps down, and made ourselves as snug as it was possible to do under the circumstances.

It was a wild and wicked morning, and still very dark, though in the far east there was an angry gleam of glary light. The crossing was a rough one—as rough a one as I ever remember to have experienced. When we reached Dover we were all bedraggled and weary-looking, and thankful indeed for the hot coffee that was served out to us at the refreshment-bar. It was now broad daylight, and for the first time I was enabled to distinctly see my companion's face. It was altogether a remarkable face. A more pliable and mobile one I never saw. It never seemed to be quite alike for five minutes at a time. His eyes were small, but with, as it seemed, an almost unnatural brilliancy; and there was a suggestiveness about them that they were looking you through and through. His complexion was olive; his eyes were black. In stature he was about the middle height, with a well-knit frame. I noted that his hands and wrists indicated great muscular strength. He trod with a firm step; he walked upright; he was a man whose presence asserted itself. None but a fool would be likely to overlook him even in a crowd. There is one other thing I must mention: his manner was that of an exceedingly well-bred man; he was the pink of politeness.

The 'something'—call it by what name you will—that had drawn us together, kept us together, and we became the sole occupants of a first-class compartment, in which we journeyed to London. Long before our destination was reached, I had made up my mind that my *compagnon de voyage* was no ordinary man, and from certain things I made a guess at his profession, and wishing to put my opinion to the test, I alluded to the attempt that had been made some time before on the Czar's life. At this his eyes transfixed me, as it were. Question and answer followed, and at last, when I was sure that I should not make any mistake, I led him to understand that my visit to France had indirectly been in connection with the crime in Russia. When we reached London, I found he was going to stay at a hotel close to Trafalgar Square. I gave him my card. He gave me his, which simply bore the name

MICHAEL DANEVITCH.

I knew then from the name that I had formed the acquaintance of one of the foremost detectives in the world—a man who had had more to do with unravelling political crimes than any living being; and there was hardly a civilized Government that had not, at some time or other, availed itself of his services. He was endowed with wonderful gifts, and having once got on to the track of a criminal the criminal was to a certainty doomed. Danevitch's visit to England on this occasion was in connection with the attempt on the Czar's life. He ultimately succeeded in unearthing one of the criminals in London, and though the English Government would not give the rascal up, Danevitch lured him to France by a wonderfully clever ruse. There he was arrested; in due course the French handed him over to Russia, and he expiated his wickedness on the scaffold. The story of this thrilling capture will be told in the course of this series. The acquaintance which I struck up with Danevitch on that ever-to-be-remembered night ripened into a very warm friendship, which continued for many years. The result was he promised me that if he predeceased me he would leave me all his notes and papers that had any reference to his professional career, and give me full permission to do what I liked with them. Subsequently he was in a terrible railway accident in Russia: the train by which he was travelling came into collision with another train, and there was an awful smash. Poor Danevitch was so injured that both his legs had to be amputated. For several weeks he seemed to be doing well, but a change took place, and he realized that his fate was sealed. He sent for me, and during the fortnight that passed after my arrival he told me his history to a large extent, and handed me the promised records of the extraordinary cases in which he had played so important a part. It is from these records that I now compile this series of stories.

THE MYSTERIOUS DISAPPEARANCE OF A MILLION ROUBLES.

ONE evening, towards the end of summer, four Government officials left Moscow for St. Petersburg in charge of an enormous amount of money, partly in specie, but for the most part in Russian rouble notes. The money was consigned to the Treasury in St. Petersburg. All the officials had been in the Government service for a long time, and were selected for this special duty on account of their trustworthiness and the confidence reposed in them by the heads of the department to which they belonged. The oldest man, and the one in command of the little party, was upwards of seventy years of age. He had been in the Government service for forty years, and was greatly trusted and respected. His name was Popoff. The next in seniority was Ivan Basilovitch, who had been thirty-three years in the service. Then came Strogonoff, with twenty-eight years' service, and lastly a young man named Briazga, with ten years and a half to his credit in the service of the Government. In addition to these four Government officers, four gendarmes, fully armed, accompanied the treasure as a guard of safety. The party travelled by the ordinary train, but had a special saloon carriage, the packages of money being placed at one end. The only doors to the carriage were at the opposite end, one on each side, the off-side door being locked by means of a secret lock, which could not be opened except with the proper key.

The bullion was carried in oak boxes fastened with iron bands. The notes were in small square boxes, sewn up in strong canvas. In addition they were securely corded with fine but extraordinarily tough cord, which was made especially for the Government, and could not be used except for Government purposes. Every package bore the State seal. Anyone unlawfully breaking the seal was guilty, according to the law of Russia, of treason, and liable to death or banishment to Siberia. In due course the train reached St. Petersburg, where the packages of money were examined, counted in the train, and found correct. They were then loaded into a covered Government waggon, counted and examined again, and also found correct; and all being ready, the waggon drove off, accompanied by the four officials and the gendarmes. At the Treasury the packages were once again counted, examined, and found correct, and the deputy of the Minister of Finance himself gave the necessary receipt to the head-officer. The important duty being thus completed, the gendarmes were dismissed to their quarters, and the officers went to their respective homes. In the course of the next day Danevitch received a sudden command to attend without a moment's delay at the bureau of the chief of the police. He found that important functionary looking very grave and serious, and it was obvious he was disturbed by something of more than ordinary importance. With official brevity he told Danevitch about the money having been removed from Moscow to St. Petersburg the previous night, and added:

'This morning, in the presence of the Minister of Finance himself and the official staff, the various packages were opened. Two of the note boxes, although intact as regards seals and cords, and which ought to have contained five hundred thousand rouble notes each, were found to be stuffed with blank paper. There has been some clever hanky-panky business, and you are wanted at the Treasury immediately. Now, it strikes me, Danevitch, that though you've cracked some very hard nuts in your time, this one will prove too much for you.'

'Why do you think so?'

'Why do I think so! Well, because the whole business has been managed so cleverly that the thieves have calculated every chance, and are not likely to have left any trail behind them that can be followed up. However, see what you can do. You may succeed, but I'm afraid you won't.'

Danevitch made no comment on his chief's remark, but at once betook himself to the Treasury, where he found everybody in a state of great excitement. He was at once conducted into the presence of the Minister of Finance, with whom he had a long interview, and from whom he learnt all the details of the transit of the money. Necessarily the detective sifted these details, examined them one by one, and took such measures as occurred to him to prove that they were absolutely correct. In the end he was satisfied that they were. The Minister then showed him a long telegram he had received from the Treasury Office in Moscow, in which it was stated that the money was packed in the usual way in the presence of the cashier-in-chief, six of his subordinates, and a large staff, all of them proved and tried servants. Every box was numbered, registered, and sealed, and there was not the shadow of a doubt that when the boxes left Moscow each contained the full sum marked against it in the books of the department. Danevitch saw at once that if that was correct it proved that the robbery must have occurred in transit, which obviously necessitated a prearranged plan of a very ingenious nature; moreover, it pointed to the confederacy of every man, including the gendarmes, engaged in safe-guarding the treasure. It was difficult to believe in such a conspiracy; but on the first blush it seemed the only rational conclusion that one could come to, otherwise the officers and the police must have been culpably negligent of their duty to have allowed a stranger to have walked off the boxes, leaving dummy facsimiles in their place. However, Danevitch would express no opinion then, although the Minister was anxious that he should do so; but it was the detective's invariable rule to keep his opinions to himself until he was in a position to speak with something like certainty. As he himself was in the habit of saying, he never prophesied until he knew. It was a safe rule, and it saved him from many an error.

Having completed his investigations in St. Petersburg so far as he could at that stage, he proceeded without loss of time to Moscow, where he satisfied himself, from the evidence laid before him, that the money really left the Moscow Treasury all right; and it was impossible the boxes could have been exchanged between the Treasury and the station. The treasure was conveyed in a closed waggon, which was locked and barred, and in its passage through the city it was guarded by twelve mounted soldiers specially told off for the duty. At the station the waggon was backed right up to the railway-carriage, and was unpacked in the presence of quite a little army of officials. Again, unless there had been a huge conspiracy, the boxes could not have been abstracted there. This narrowed the inquiry somewhat, because it made it clear that the exchange must have been effected while the train was on its journey between the two cities. But admitting that to be the case, it at once suggested that the eight men, that is, the four officers and four gendarmes, were in league together. To that, however, was opposed the fact that the gendarmes were only told off for the duty an hour before they started, and up to that time had had no intimation they were going. Therefore, assuming the four clerks had prearranged the matter, they must have corrupted the gendarmes *en route*. That, however, was such a far-fetched theory that Danevitch would not entertain it.

The next phase of inquiry upon which Danevitch entered was that of ascertaining as much as possible about the four Government officials who travelled in charge of the treasure. These inquiries elicited the fact that they bore irreproachable characters, and were held in high esteem in the department. Popoff was a married man with a family. He was in receipt of a good salary, and appeared to be free from financial worries of any kind. The same remarks applied to Basilovitch and Strogonoff. They were both married and family men, and to all appearances in comfortable circumstances. Briazga was unmarried, but he was regarded as a very steady, well-to-do young fellow, and was known to be the main support of his father, mother, and an only sister, whose name was Olga. She was younger than her brother, and, owing to an injury to the spine when she was a child, she had been more or less an invalid all her life.

Danevitch realized at this stage, even as the chief of the police predicted he would, that he was called upon to crack a very hard nut indeed, and he did not feel confident about being able to crack it at all. The minutest investigation had failed so far to elicit anything that would have justified a suspicion of a conspiracy amongst the eight men. And yet without the connivance of them all it seemed impossible that the boxes could have been changed. But there was the indisputable fact that they had been changed;

nevertheless, there was not a single item in the list of circumstances that supported the hypothesis of a conspiracy. How, then, had the robbery been worked? Of course the Treasury people, as well as everyone connected with the Finance Department, to say nothing of the higher authorities themselves, were in a very perturbed state of mind, for apart from the largeness of the sum carried off, the robbery proved that, in spite of the safeguards employed when money was being conveyed from one town to another, there was a risk which up to that time had not been suspected. It was decided at last by the head officials to offer a reward of ten thousand roubles for any information that would lead to the capture of the thieves and the recovery of the stolen money. Danevitch was opposed to the offering of a reward, and pointed out the absurdity of it; as he said, even supposing the whole of the eight men of the escort had been concerned, they were not likely to betray each other for the sake of ten thousand roubles, when they had a million to divide amongst themselves. And if anyone else had come to know who the thieves were, he would not be blind to the fact that he could blackmail them to the tune of a much greater sum than ten thousand roubles to induce him to hold his tongue. Therefore, as Danevitch anticipated, the reward brought forth no informer. In the meantime he had been working on his own lines, and had satisfied himself the money had been put into the train all right at Moscow, and that, unless with the connivance of ever so many people, the boxes could not have been changed between the St. Petersburg station and the Treasury Office; consequently, the business must have been done while the money was in transit between the two towns. Further than that, it was as clear as daylight that the robbery had been prearranged, because the facsimile boxes had been prepared beforehand; the cord used to bind the false boxes was Government cord, and the Government seal was so cleverly imitated that the forgery could only be detected after close inspection. All this proved unmistakably that there was a traitor in the camp.

In one of many interviews that Danevitch had with the Minister of Finance, that gentleman said:

'Danevitch, you must bring the thief to light. It is absolutely necessary that an example should be made of him as a deterrent. Although the loss of the money would be a serious one, we would rather lose it than let the thief escape.'

'I think, sir, that the thief will not escape; and it is possible, even probable, that the money may be recovered.'

'Have you any clue?' asked the Minister quickly.

'None whatever.'

'Then, why do you speak so hopefully?'

'Because it seems to me that sooner or later I am sure to find a clue, and then—well, then I shall succeed in bringing the criminal to justice.'

His belief that sooner or later he was sure to find a clue was quite justified, although he had been doubtful at first. It was pretty clear now, however, that the thief had an accomplice, otherwise it would have been impossible for him to have carried out the robbery. Now, Danevitch knew too much of human nature to suppose that two or three men and more than likely a woman, as he shrewdly suspected, would be able for all time to conceal the fact that they had suddenly acquired wealth. A something would leak out—a something that would betray them to the keen eyes that were watching for the sign. Danevitch had learnt the great lesson of patience. He did not aim at accomplishing the impossible, but he knew where it was a case of human ingenuity he had the best chance, inasmuch as he was an expert in the ways of criminals. From the moment that he had gathered up all the details of the robbery, he had set a watch upon the movements of every one of the eight men who had travelled with the treasure from Moscow to St. Petersburg. The gendarmes belonged to Moscow, and had returned, but they were watched, nevertheless; though not a movement of theirs was calculated to arouse suspicion. The four Government officials were also watched, but no sign came from them. But of course they knew they were being watched; they would have been dolts indeed if they had remained in ignorance of what everyone else knew; for Government treasure to the tune of one million roubles could not be abstracted without causing a sensation and setting the populace on the tip-toe of expectation and the tenter-hooks of curiosity. The theory by which Danevitch was guided was this, that one or more of the eight men who travelled that night when the money was stolen between Moscow and St. Petersburg must certainly be in a position to throw some light on the robbery. On the other hand, every one of the eight knew for a fact, or by instinct, that he was suspected of some complicity, consequently he would take particular care not to do anything calculated to give emphasis to that suspicion, and justify active legal measures being taken against him.

Although Danevitch, by reason of the eminence he had attained in his calling and the originality of mind he had displayed in dealing with some of the most notorious crimes of his day, was allowed more latitude than his confrères, he was nevertheless subordinate at this time to the chief of the police, and that functionary, having an eye to a decoration or promotion if the mystery should be cleared up, strongly advocated the wholesale arrest of the eight men, and flinging them into a dungeon in the infamous fortress of Peter and Paul, or the still more infamous Schlusselburgh in Lake Ladoga, there to remain until misery and madness loosened their tongues. Against this inartistic and brutal measure Danevitch set his face, and he asked to be allowed to work out the problem in his own way. The Minister of Finance, and it was said even the Czar himself, supported Danevitch, so that he was not hampered with the red-tapeism of the bureau.

A month passed; no arrest had been made, and apparently not a trace of the criminal discovered. The Treasury officers were in despair, and the chief of the police showed a tendency to lower Danevitch from the high standard of estimation to which he had previously elevated him. It is true that Danevitch had many big successes credited to his score, but even a successful man cannot afford to make a big failure. The chief told him this, and Danevitch replied quietly:

'I have not yet made a failure.'

'But you have not recovered the money; you've brought nobody to book.'

'No, not yet.'

'Not yet! Are you still sanguine, then?'

'Certainly.'

The chief laughed a little bitterly as he replied:

'Well, perhaps it is good to be sanguine, even in a hopeless cause. It keeps a man's spirits up, doesn't it?'

The chief was comparatively new to his office; that is, he had only held it two years. He had received very rapid promotion owing to strong influence at Court, and influence in Russia often counts a good deal more than merit; indeed, it does in most countries. It was said that the chief had certain friends of his own he was anxious to move into the front rank, hence he was not averse to see Danevitch go down a bit.

About a week after this conversation between the chief and Danevitch, an old peasant woman left St. Petersburg by the Moscow train. She did not book to Moscow, however, but to a place called Vishni Volotchok, about midway between the two cities. She was an uncouth, clumsy, burly-looking woman, wearing the big mob frilled cap, the heavy woollen wrap crossed over the breast, the short homespun linsey-woolsey gray skirt, coarse gray stockings, and big shoes of her class. She bore with her a ponderous basket, containing a stock of slippers, boots, shoes and sabots, and, being a travelling pedlar, she was furnished with an official license, a formidable-looking document, stamped and viséd. In due course she reached her destination. Vishni Volotchok is a small town of some importance. The station is the principal refreshment place between St. Petersburg and Moscow, and a long wait is generally made by the trains going and coming. The old woman's license having been duly examined and viséd, she was allowed to go her ways, and soon after she proceeded to a fairly large house situated close to the railway, and facing a road that crossed the track. It was a detached house, built for the most part of wood. There were numerous outbuildings—a large barn, stables, cowsheds, and similar places. It was the residence of a landed proprietor named Ivan Golovnin. It was almost dark when the old woman reached the house; she tried to sell some of her wares to the servants, but was not successful. Then she pleaded illness, and begged, as she was a stranger in the town, to be allowed to pass the night in the barn. With true Russian hospitality, the servants took her into the great kitchen, and made her up a bed by the stove. As she had not recovered her health the next day, she was allowed to remain, and, in fact, finding herself in comfortable quarters, she stayed for three days; then she took her departure, before doing so presenting the three principal servants with a pair of shoes each. Being market-day, she went into the market, disposed of the rest of her stock-in-trade, and returned at once to St. Petersburg.

It chanced that a couple of days after the old woman's return to the capital, Danevitch was at the Bureau of Police, having some business to transact with the chief, who was excessively busy and excessively bad-tempered.

'By the way,' said Danevitch, as he was on the point of leaving, when he had transacted his affairs, 'concerning the robbery of the Treasury notes, I shall *succeed* in bringing the criminals to justice.'

The chief glanced at the detective and smiled. It was not a smile of satisfaction, but of doubt; and yet he knew that Danevitch had the reputation of never speaking with anything like certainty unless he felt absolutely sure. But the chief was somewhat sceptical; it was even possible he was not altogether free from jealousy, knowing as he did that Danevitch was looked upon with great favour in high quarters.

'There's a cocksureness in your statement,' said the chief brusquely. 'I suppose you've discovered something?'

'Yes.'

'What?'

'You must pardon me, but I am not justified in disclosing even to you at present what I know.'

The chief's face darkened. He was aware that, though Danevitch was nominally his subordinate, he had but little control over him. Nevertheless, it galled him to think that he, the chief of his department—in Russia it is a very influential and important position—should not be considered worthy of the confidence of Danevitch the detective, high as he was in his calling. He was weak enough to display his chagrin, and remarked with some warmth:

'Well, you have your own way of working, of course; and perhaps you are right, though on the other hand you may be wrong. But since you do not choose to take me into your confidence, and as the authorities expect that my department will unravel the mystery, I must now inform you that unless you produce evidence within the next twenty-four hours that you really are on the track of the criminal or criminals, I shall take the business out of your hands, and put it into the hands of others.'

Danevitch was not the man to be affected by any such empty threat as this. Conscious of his own strength, and firm in the resolve to pursue his own undeviating course, as he had done for years, uninfluenced by jealousy, criticism, or the opinions of others, he bowed to the chief and merely remarked:

'If in the course of the next twenty-four hours I am in a position to reveal anything, I will do so. If I am not you are at liberty to act according to your own views. Permit me also to remark that, though you are pleased to doubt my abilities, people in high quarters do not.'

This galled the chief, though he had sufficient tact to refrain from provoking further argument, which would not only be profitless, but beget ill-feeling, so he allowed Danevitch to withdraw.

A fortnight later a wedding was celebrated at the Church of St. Sophia. It was rather a stylish wedding, and a good many minor Government officials were present, principally from the Treasury office. During that intervening fortnight Danevitch had not given any sign to the chief that he was making progress; nor had the chief taken any steps to put his threat into execution. Nevertheless, he had displayed some impatience, and one day, during an interview with the Minister of Finance, he said:

'I am sorry, your Excellency, that we have made no progress in the Treasury robbery business; but the fact is, Danevitch's self-assurance and enthusiasm somewhat misled him. He speaks confidently where he ought to doubt, and is hopeful where other men would despair.'

'Hopefulness is rather a good trait in his character, isn't it? You know the old saying, "He who despairs never succeeds."'

'True, your Excellency,' answered the chief, somewhat crestfallen. 'But light-heartedness does not always command success.'

'No, perhaps not; but it deserves it.'

'Well, the fact is this, your Excellency, I am of opinion myself that more active steps should be taken to bring the culprits to justice. Now, we have to deal with facts, not fancies. A very ingenious robbery has been committed, and the Treasury of the State is a heavy loser. The thieves must still be in existence, and, being in existence, it ought not to be beyond the ingenuity of a trained mind used to working out criminal problems to discover where they are.'

'I admit the force of your argument,' answered the Minister sedately.

The chief bowed. He was pleased with himself. He believed he had made an impression.

'Of course,' he went on, 'it is most desirable that the culprits should be brought to book, and punished in such an exemplary manner that it would stand out as a warning for all time, and deter others who might feel tempted to tamper with the coffers of the State. But desirable as this is, it is even more desirable that the whole of the stolen money should be recovered. Your Excellency, however, will readily see that every day that passes lessens the chances of that, because the rascals will be revelling in their ill-gotten gains, and squandering them with the recklessness peculiar to criminals who enrich themselves dishonestly.'

'That is not Danevitch's opinion,' answered the Minister.

'Possibly; but presumably he has no warrant for his opinion. It is a mere expression of opinion, after all—nothing more.'

'Let us grant that. Now, what do you suggest?'

What the chief wanted was to have all the credit for unravelling the mystery. It meant to him promotion, and strengthening his influence in high quarters. As matters then stood, there was no confidence between him and Danevitch, who had so consolidated his position as to be independent. The chief therefore suggested that Danevitch should be put upon a case of secondary importance then occupying the attention of the authorities, and another man of the chief's choosing should be selected for Danevitch's work. This other man was a creature of the chief, though he kept that little fact strictly to himself.

The Minister was not deceived by the specious arguments of his visitor; nor was he so obtuse as to fail to see the jealousy and ill-will underlying those arguments.

'Personally, I should object to anyone else taking up the matter at this stage,' he said, 'and as far as my influence goes I should use it to prevent any change being made. For myself, I have confidence in Danevitch. He is an able man, and until I find that my confidence is misplaced I shall continue to believe in him.'

The chief was nonplussed, and he felt that it would be imprudent to pursue the subject any further. He therefore took his leave. But just as he was in the act of bowing himself out, the Minister exclaimed:

'Oh, by the way, on Thursday next there is to be a marriage in the Church of St. Sophia. A daughter of one of my subordinates is to wed one Peter Golovnin, the son, as I understand, of a wealthy landed proprietor. Curiously enough, I met Danevitch last night by chance, and he asked me if I was going to the wedding. I told him no, I had had no invitation; whereupon he expressed surprise that my subordinate had not paid me the compliment of inviting me. At the moment there did not seem to me anything out of the way in the remark, but subsequently, on pondering over it, I could not help feeling that it was full of significance. Danevitch had a deep motive in what he said. Have you any idea what the motive was?'

The chief was not only utterly amazed, but deeply annoyed. He tried, however, to conceal his annoyance, though it was very hard to do so. In his own mind he was perfectly sure that Danevitch had a motive, though what that motive was he could not possibly guess, and his annoyance was occasioned by having to confess his ignorance.

'And does your Excellency intend to go?' he asked.

'Well, yes, I think I shall. I fancy developments may take place.'

As the chief went away, he resolved that he, too, would be present at St. Sophia, for he knew Danevitch too well to suppose for a moment that his remark to the Minister of Finance was a meaningless one.

The marriage was rather a grand affair. The bridegroom was a good-looking young man, about six or seven and twenty; but he had the appearance of one who had led a reckless and dissipated life. There were incipient lines in his face, and a want of brightness about the eyes that was not good in one so young. The bride was, perhaps, two years younger, with rather pretty features and an abundance of dark hair. Some affection of the spine, however, had cruelly distorted her figure, and she was twisted out of shape. Her name was Olga, and she was the only sister of Briazga, the Government clerk in the Finance Department, who was present during the ceremony. The Minister of Finance was also present, thinking from Danevitch's remark that something was to happen. The wedding went off all right, however, and the whole party seemed very jolly and happy, until Briazga, suddenly espying the Minister, went up to him and, looking very confused and a little excited, said:

'You do us an honour, sir, by gracing the ceremony with your delightful presence. I scarcely expected you would have been here.'

'I suppose not,' answered the Minister dryly; 'but as you did not honour me with an invitation, nor even condescend to mention that your sister was to be married, I thought I would be a witness on my own account.'

Briazga grew more confused, and stammered out a lame apology, adding:

'The fact is, sir, I have endeavoured to keep the matter secret from all except my most intimate friends, for the simple reason that, as we are comparatively poor people, we could not afford to have much ceremony, and I felt it was too humble an affair to ask you to come to it. But since you have come, may I venture to hope that you will now do us the supreme honour of joining the luncheon-party at my house?'

The Minister excused himself on the score of business engagements; but five minutes later, when Briazga had left him, and he was going out of the church, Danevitch came up to him.

'I saw you talking to Briazga,' the detective remarked.

'Did you? Where were you? I didn't notice you in the church.'

'Perhaps not; but I haven't been far off. Briazga has invited you to the luncheon?'

'How do you know?' asked the Minister, in surprise.

'I guess it.'

'Then, you must have the power of a seer.'

'Not at all, your Excellency. Nothing could be simpler. You being here, your subordinate would have been guilty of an unpardonable rudeness and affront if he had not paid you the compliment to invite you. But, of course, it was a mere formality. He doesn't wish and does not intend you to go if he can prevent it.'

'I suppose not; nor do I wish to go.'

'But I should like you to go,' answered Danevitch. 'Indeed, I consider it of some importance that you should go. A little drama may be enacted in which you can play a part.'

The Minister looked hard at Danevitch, as if trying to read his thoughts, and asked pointedly:

'Do you suspect Briazga of having stolen the Treasury notes?'

'Will you pardon me for simply saying at this moment that it would be imprudent for me to answer your question?'

'Will you be there?'

'Again I must respectfully decline to answer the question.'

'But you have an object in wishing me to be present.'

'Undoubtedly.'

'Then I will go.'

Whereupon the Minister hastily pencilled a note on a slip of paper torn from his note-book, and sent it by one of the church attendants to Briazga. In the note he simply said he had changed his mind, and would do himself the pleasure of being present at the wedding-feast, as he found he had a couple of spare hours on his hands. Danevitch moved off, and had not got far away, when he was accosted by the chief of the police, who remarked sarcastically:

'I understood there were to be some developments at this wedding.'

'From whom did you understand that?' asked Danevitch, without any attempt to conceal the annoyance he felt.

'It is not necessary to mention names. I heard that you were to be here, and the Minister of Finance was to be here. The information was significant, so I came too. You suspect somebody amongst this marriage-party?'

'Yes.'

'Who is it?'

'Pardon me, I decline to state at the present moment.'

'Why?'

'Because I have no proof.'

'You are seeking a proof, then?'

'I am.'

'Do you expect to find it?'

'Yes.'

'Where and when?'

'I cannot say. It's problematical. A few hours will decide. As soon as I am sure of my ground I will report to you.'

The chief recognised the uselessness of further questioning, and left, while Danevitch withdrew into the background as the wedding-party left the church and drove to Briazga's house. He lived in what was known as the English quarter, near the English quay. There were no English living there then. Bad times and oppressive restrictions had ruined most of them, and they had gone away. The house inhabited by Briazga had been formerly occupied by an English merchant; it had many conveniences and improvements not usually found in the average Russian house. Here the Government clerk had lived very comfortably with his father, mother, and sister Olga. The father and mother were well advanced in years. They had a small income of their own to live upon.

Soon after the wedding-party had arrived at the house, an old woman, a professional fortune-teller, presented herself and begged to be admitted. There was nothing unusual in this. Vagrants of both sexes make a good living in Russia by attending wedding-parties and forecasting the future of the bride and bridegroom. As the Russians are a superstitious people, they encourage these fortune-tellers, who are feasted, and generally add to the entertainment by story and jest. Having been treated well in the servants' quarter, the woman was introduced to the company. The bridegroom, who was hilarious and full of vodka and wine, immediately presented himself to have his fortune told; but when the woman had looked at his hand and peered into his eyes, while the company waited in breathless expectancy, she said:

'I cannot tell you your fortune.'

At this there was considerable laughing and jeering, and on all sides arose the question, 'Why, why?'

'Oh, ladies and gentlemen,' exclaimed the seer, 'pray don't laugh. I can read all your fortunes—better, perhaps, than you would like me to do.'

'Then, why don't you begin with the bridegroom?' was asked by several. 'He is anxious to know what is before him.'

'Good; it shall be told,' answered the woman sharply. 'Give me a pack of cards.'

The pack of cards was brought. She spread the cards on the table in several rows. Next she shifted them about, and placed them in squares and circles, and all the time the company gathered round and waited in eager expectancy for what was coming. Presently the woman jumbled the cards up together, then repacked them and told the bridegroom to cut them four times, and the bride three. That done, the fortune-teller seemed absorbed in some abstruse calculation as she slowly sorted the cards out in four rows.

'You are a precious long time,' exclaimed the bridegroom irritably. 'It strikes me you are a humbug.'

'Patience, patience,' murmured the woman. 'There is something wrong about the cards. They won't come right.'

'Because you don't understand them,' suggested somebody.

'Possibly; but patience, patience; I shall understand them directly. Ah! I see something now. It's strange, very strange!'

The curiosity and interest of the company were fully aroused by the mysterious manner of the old woman, who seemed deeply absorbed in what she was doing; but Briazga was annoyed, and he called out:

'Ladies and gentlemen, let us stop this nonsense. The woman is an impostor, and is only wasting our time, which can be more joyfully and pleasurably employed. It is an auspicious occasion, this, and we don't want it marred by any unpleasant incident. Let us banish the woman to the kitchen.'

At these words the old fortune-teller drew herself up with a certain dignity, and remarked:

'It is customary for my people to be kindly and hospitably entertained at these festive gatherings; and I myself have the reputation of being a most successful fortune-teller; it is not my fault now that the cards will not come right. But I read certain things about the bridegroom which I am sure he would like to know. Say, shall I proceed?'

The bridegroom himself answered.

'Certainly,' he exclaimed, and there was a curious look on his wine-flushed face. 'I want to know my future; let the woman go on.'

Briazga appeared to be very greatly irritated, but as there arose a murmured assent from the assembly he yielded to the evident desire of his guests, who now crowded round the table and urged the fortune-teller to rearrange the cards. This she did, and having laid them out again in five rows, she uttered an ejaculatory 'Ah!' and after a pause added:

'It is better; but still there is a block somewhere. Can you, sir'—this to the bridegroom—'place on the table five thousand rouble notes? That will perhaps break the spell.'

It was a common thing for these fortune-tellers to request that small sums of money might be produced; but five thousand roubles was a large sum, and there was a general murmur of surprise, while Briazga appeared to be particularly uneasy and troubled. He was trying to push his way through the crowd to get at his brother-in-law, for there was such a hubbub and din of voices that he could not make himself heard; but before he succeeded in accomplishing his purpose, Peter Golovnin, with a boastful air and a drunken leer on his red face, pulled from his pocket a leather wallet, which, on opening, was found to be stuffed full of notes. With an unsteady hand he proceeded to count out five notes of the value of one thousand roubles each. Having done so, he laid the notes upon the table, and once more there was breathless silence as the company craned their necks in their eagerness to see what the old woman would now do. The bridegroom himself seemed the least concerned of anyone, and, with a coarse, drunken laugh, remarked:

'I suppose the old fool thought I did not possess so much money. It shows what an impostor she is, otherwise she would have been able to tell you exactly how much I have in my wallet. However, let her go on, and if she fails this time I will kick her out.'

The fortune-teller seemed in no ways affected by the threat, but busied herself in rearranging the cards. She spread out the five bank-notes. On each of four she placed a knave from the pack, and on the fifth she put a queen. Suspicious eyes watched her every movement, as more than one person present was of opinion that she wanted to purloin the money by some hanky-panky business.

'There is a lot of knavery here,' she remarked thoughtfully. 'The queen, as you will see, is the victim of knaves, and I am afraid will come to grief.'

'Who does the queen represent?' asked someone.

'The bride,' answered the fortune-teller.

At this there was a strong murmur of disapproval, and the bridegroom, with an angry cry, put out his hand to sweep up the notes, but the woman, quicker than he, gathered them in a heap, and said sternly:

'Do not touch them for a moment, or you will break the spell.' Then suddenly she snatched them up, and exclaimed: 'These notes are forged ones. That accounts for my difficulty.'

This was the signal for a general uproar, and the company, believing that the woman wished to steal the money, seized her, and she would have been roughly handled had she not shaken herself free, and energetically forced her way to the Minister of Finance, who was present, and, thrusting the notes into his hand, said:

'Sir, I know you; you are the Minister of Finance. Look at those notes. They are forged! I give them into your keeping. No man has a right to have false notes in his possession. You, sir, as an officer of the State, have it in your power to demand an explanation. Ask the bridegroom, your Excellency, why he carries forged notes in his purse.'

The Minister took the notes, though he seemed distressed and puzzled.

'The wretched hag lies!' thundered the bridegroom. 'The notes are perfectly good. My brother-in-law, if he respects me and the good name of his family, and loves his sister, my wife, will order his servants to whip this lying fortune-teller, who has broken up our party and destroyed our pleasure.'

There was a disposition on the part of some of those present to act on the suggestion made, and subject the old woman to rough treatment; but the Minister, holding up his hand in a deprecatory manner, said:

'Ladies and gentlemen, control yourselves, please. Keep quiet. The woman is quite right. These notes are not genuine ones. But no doubt Mr. Golovnin can offer some explanation as to how they came into his possession.'

'Yes,' cried Golovnin excitedly. 'They were given to me by my father, and I cannot believe they are false. If they are, then he himself has been cheated, and it will break his heart.'

'That the notes are not genuine, there can be no possible doubt,' said the Minister gravely; 'and that you or your father should be in possession of forged notes representing so large a sum is extraordinary.'

'I pray you return them to me,' wailed the bridegroom, looking very sorrowful and sad, while his trembling bride stood beside him the picture of puzzled distress. She seemed scarcely able to realize the situation, and her tearful eyes wandered from her husband to her brother, and from him to the Minister of Finance, as if in dumb entreaty to clear the mystery up, and not mar the pleasure of her wedding-day. But the Minister, although not there in any judicial position, clearly recognised that, as a servant of the State, he had a duty to perform, and, despite the painfulness of the situation in which he thus found himself, he felt forced to that duty.

'I cannot return the notes,' he said gravely, 'and I must ask you to let me examine the other notes in your wallet.'

At this request, Golovnin pulled out his pocket-book without the slightest hesitation, and, producing a packet of notes, handed them—with the air of a man conscious of his own rectitude—to the Minister, who, having subjected them to a close scrutiny, pronounced them to be forgeries also.

The company were startled by this into a united cry of astonishment and alarm, while the unhappy bride, with a low moan, fell to the floor in a swoon.

'Surely, sir, there is some mistake,' suggested Briazga, pallid and pale as a corpse.

'Of course it's a mistake,' shouted the bridegroom; 'his Excellency is wrong—entirely wrong. It is impossible the notes can be forged. I am sure they are genuine.'

'Briazga,' said the Minister sternly, 'you have been handling notes long enough in the Treasury to be able to tell a genuine one from a false one. Look at these, and give me your honest opinion.'

The Minister placed the notes on the table. Briazga took them up with a trembling hand one by one, and examined them, holding them to the light, and subjecting them to other tests, while the amazed guests held their breath in anxious suspense, as they waited for his verdict. Slowly and deliberately, notwithstanding that he was suffering from intense nervous emotion, Briazga went through the notes one by one, while his superior watched him intently and curiously. At last, when he had finished his task, he said:

'Sir, I am forced to confess that every note there is nothing more than a clever imitation. But my brother-in-law must surely be the dupe of a knavish trick. The matter is capable of explanation.'

'It must certainly be investigated,' answered the Minister. 'It is far too serious to be lightly passed over. I shall have to carry the notes away, and consult with the authorities as to the steps to be taken.'

'Stay,' exclaimed the bridegroom, with a pitiful wail of despair; 'this may mean for me utter and irretrievable ruin. Remember, sir, it is my wedding-day, and my ruin involves also the ruin, and perhaps the death, of my wife, who has been my wife not yet a day; to say nothing of the ruin, dishonour, disgrace of those near and dear to me. Let me beseech of you, therefore, to delay taking any action until I myself have made inquiries. I am convinced—absolutely convinced—there is some hideous mistake somewhere. I am the victim of a cowardly trick. I will swear on oath that when I left home the notes I put into my pocket were good ones. Is it not possible that the hag of a fortune-teller has brought this about by her devilish art?'

At this everybody looked to see where the 'hag' was, but she had made herself invisible. In the hubbub and confusion consequent on the discovery that the notes were forged, she had managed to slip away unperceived, and had left the house.

'I regret very much indeed,' answered the Minister, 'that such an unhappy affair as this should have occurred on your wedding-day; but it is far too grave a circumstance for me to adopt the course you suggest. In fact, I should not be justified in doing so. I repeat, I have a duty to perform, and I must do it, however unpleasant the consequences may be. Of course, as you say, the matter is capable of explanation, and any explanation you may offer will receive due attention; but a very serious official inquiry will have to be made, and the origin of these notes must be traced.'

With a dignified bow to the dumfounded company, the Minister passed out of the room and left the house, carrying the notes with him. On reaching his official residence, he found a letter waiting for him. It was from Danevitch, and read as follows:

'YOUR EXCELLENCY,

'I am suddenly called away from St. Petersburg, but shall be back in three days' time. I am happy to say I can restore the whole of the stolen notes to the Treasury. I hope your Excellency enjoyed yourself at the house of Briazga on the occasion of the wedding-feast.'

The Minister was a little mystified by this letter; and though he knew that Danevitch was not the man to make a rash statement, he sent for the chief of the police and questioned him. But that worthy had to confess that he himself was no less mystified. He said some harsh things about Danevitch, and even went so far as to express some doubt whether Danevitch was capable of fulfilling his undertaking to restore the whole of the stolen money.

'I've faith in Danevitch,' said the Minister. 'What he says he means; and though he puzzles me very much, I feel certain that all will come right in the end.'

The chief had no answer to this, so he simply bowed and took his leave.

True to his promise, Danevitch returned to St. Petersburg in three days' time, and, to the amazement of the officials and all concerned, he duly delivered to the Treasury the whole of the missing million roubles, and was enabled to lay such information before the authorities that Briazga and Ivan and Peter Golovnin were immediately arrested.

Ivan Golovnin lived at Vishni Volotchok, where he owned some property. He was an old man, and had been married twice. By his first wife he had had a large family, and they were nearly all scattered. By his second wife he had one son, Peter. This young fellow had been a managing clerk in a fur store in St. Petersburg, and had known Briazga's family some years. Olga Briazga had fallen desperately in love with him, but her deformity prevented him reciprocating her passion. Between Olga and her brother an extraordinary affection existed—an affection unusual even between brother and sister. He idolized her; and when he saw she was breaking her heart about Peter, and that her life was in danger, he told Peter he would enrich him if he would marry her. From this a conspiracy was hatched, in which Briazga, Peter and Peter's father joined interests. The old man was induced to enter into it for his son's sake. It was prearranged that when Briazga was next engaged in the duty of conveying treasure from Moscow to St. Petersburg, an attempt should be made to purloin some of it; but from the first he gave his co-conspirators distinctly to understand that, while he would do all he possibly could to assist them, he would not keep a single rouble himself. The opportunity came at last with the removal of treasure from Moscow. Briazga knew a week beforehand that he would be employed upon the duty, and he also knew what money would be removed. Everything, therefore, seemed to favour him, and he lost no time in communicating the intelligence to the Golovnins. Peter at once set to work to prepare two facsimile boxes, and to fill them with paper, the whole being the exact weight of the Government boxes when filled with a million's worth of rouble notes. The Government cord and the forged seal were supplied by Briazga. The train conveying the treasure stopped for a long time at Vishni Volotchok, that being a buffet station where passengers usually dined or supped. The night of the robbery happened to be very dark and very hot. On arriving at Vishni Volotchok, the treasure escort went four at a time to the buffet to eat and drink. Briazga was included in the first four. When they had finished they relieved the other four; but the night being sultry, Briazga's party sauntered about the platform smoking, the door of the treasure waggon being locked. On the plea of getting some tobacco, Briazga returned to the waggon; he was not absent more than ten minutes—indeed, not so long; but during the time he was enabled to open the off-side door with a secret key, and to hand out the two boxes to Peter, who was lying in wait with the dummies. Thus was the robbery cleverly committed, as proved by the evidence twisted and wormed out of the culprits themselves by the inquisitorial nature of the Russian law.

The sequel of the remarkable story has yet to be told. When Danevitch took the matter up, he came to the conclusion after a time that the robbery had taken place at Vishni Volotchok. There were numerous and obvious reasons for that conclusion. It was no less obvious that one or more of the eight persons composing the escort must have had some hand in the robbery. He soon determined in his own mind that the gendarmes were guiltless. This reduced the suspects to the four Government officials. Now, assuming that the deduction was a correct one, it was no less clear that there must have been a confederate at Vishni Volotchok; so Danevitch set to work to find out which of the officials had any connection with that place, and he soon ascertained that the Briazgas and the Golovnins were acquainted. That stage of the inquiry reached, he began to feel that he would ultimately succeed in unravelling the mystery. The means that he employed to track down his quarry Danevitch was careful never to make public, for very obvious reasons, but he had a habit of setting them forth fully in his diary, and from that source I am able to give them here.

It was known almost throughout Russia that this remarkable man had a protean-like faculty for changing his appearance. He could so alter his voice and features that, in combination with change of dress, he could defy detection even by those who were well acquainted with him. His most favourite disguise was that of an old woman, whom he could imitate to the life. In the character of a female, therefore, he penetrated into the Golovnins' home. He found, by close watching, that Peter made frequent journeys backwards and forwards between the house and a small plantation of firs, about a quarter of a mile away. As there was no apparent reason why the young man should go to the plantation so often, Danevitch was induced to search it, with the result that he found the two stolen boxes artfully concealed in an old quarry, which was almost entirely hidden by creepers and brambles. The boxes had been opened, but the contents were intact. This find was a great triumph for Danevitch, but his work was far from complete. It was necessary that he should spread a net that would capture all the culprits, and he carried this out with singular ingenuity. That one or both of the Golovnins had had a hand in the robbery was pretty evident, but others must also have been concerned, and they might escape if caution was not observed. When he ascertained that Peter Golovnin and Olga Briazga were on the eve of marriage, the plot seemed to make itself clear to him, and when he gained entrance to the marriage-feast in the rôle of fortune-teller, his triumph was complete. In the boxes hidden in the wood at Vishni Volotchok he had placed a large number of cleverly imitated notes, taking the genuine ones away. The imitations had been lying at one of the police bureaus for a very long time. They had been seized on the premises of a notorious note-forger. Danevitch was sure that Peter Golovnin, the bridegroom, would liberally supply himself with money from the boxes for his marriage, and if the forged notes were found in his possession, the evidence would be overwhelming.

It remains to say that the guilt was brought home to all concerned. They were condemned to death, as they had committed a crime against the State, but the sentence was commuted to banishment for life to Siberia. Poor Olga Briazga, whose love for Peter Golovnin had been the cause of the crime, accompanied her unhappy husband to Northern Siberia, where he was doomed to pass the first ten years of his sentence.

A MODERN BORGIA.

DURING his long and remarkable career, Danevitch was called upon to solve problems of a very varied nature, and, while his efforts were not always crowned with success—and he never hesitates in his journals to confess his failures—the percentage of his triumphs was very large. Necessarily, of course, his work lay amongst the by-ways and alleys of life, so to speak; for so long as there are crimes and criminals—and that will be as long as the world lasts—men must be found who will endeavour to lessen the one and bring the other to book. In his own particular way, Danevitch was a genius; and it almost seemed sometimes as if Nature had endowed him with an eighth sense, for he saw and grasped points which no one else could see. Although a born detective, there are many other callings in which he might have risen to eminence, notably that of the stage. He was a perfect actor, and his powers of mimicry and of changing his expression and personal appearance were little short of marvellous. He could with ease assume the rôle of an ambassador or a peasant market woman, and he possessed to a remarkable degree the faculty of patience, which is indispensable to anyone who wishes to distinguish himself in the detective's art. Moreover, he was well educated, and a fluent linguist, and these accomplishments helped him immensely. In referring to the case which I am now about to relate, he himself speaks of it as 'a remarkable and complicated one,' which all but baffled him; and he cites it as an example of the depths of depravity to which human nature is capable of descending.

It appeared that one summer night Colonel Ignatof, who was in command of an infantry regiment of the line, temporarily stationed in Moscow, returned to his barracks after being out all the evening, and, complaining of being very ill, ordered that the regimental doctor should be immediately sent for. From the time that the order was given to the arrival of the doctor in the commanding officer's room not more than ten minutes elapsed. But during that short space the Colonel had vomited violently, and the doctor found him lying on the bed, cold, pallid, and collapsed. The soldier-servant who was with him said that his master had suffered awfully, and had described his feelings as if a fire was raging in his inside. The doctor administered remedies, which so far had a good effect that the patient rallied, and on being asked if he could account for his sudden illness—he had always been an exceedingly robust and healthy man—he faintly murmured that he believed it was attributable to some iced fish soup (a favourite Russian dish), of which he had partaken freely. He thought it probable that the fish from which the soup had been concocted were not quite fresh. It seemed a natural supposition, for the intense heat of the short Russian summer makes it very difficult to keep meat and fish fresh for many hours.

He was next asked where he had partaken of the soup, but before he could give an answer he was again seized with violent retching. When the spasm had passed, he collapsed once more, and all the remedies that were tried failed to restore him. He continued, however, to breathe for two hours, and then died. As the symptoms from which the unfortunate man had suffered were identical with those set up by irritant poison, an order was received that a post-mortem examination was to be made. In due course this order was carried out, and resulted in the discovery that death was due to an irritant poison that had set up violent inflammation of the stomach. This seemed to be quite consistent with the unfortunate man's own theory that his illness was due to unwholesome soup.

The fish soup is a very common dish in Russia. It is made from various kinds of fish boiled to a pulp. It is then highly seasoned, thickened with rich, luscious cream; a quantity of olive-oil is next added, and the mess is iced until it is nearly frozen. It is a singularly seductive dish, but only those who have strong stomachs can stand it. As it is only partaken of in the summer, great care has to be exercised that the fish is quite fresh. Any carelessness in this respect is apt to produce serious illness. The peasantry, who cannot afford cream, and enrich the soup with large quantities of inferior oil, often suffer severely, and not infrequently die, after a hearty meal of this national soup, for as often as not the fish used is stale, and, as most people know, decaying fish is a virulent poison.

It was a knowledge of these facts which no doubt led the medical men to jump to the conclusion that the Colonel's death was entirely due to the soup, a conclusion that seemed quite justified by what the dying man himself had said. Some attempt was made to discover where he had dined, but as this was not successful, the doctors certified that the deceased had died from internal inflammation after partaking of soup which was probably not fresh. Here the matter ended. The dead man was buried with military pomp and ceremony, and many eulogies were uttered over his grave. It was known amongst his intimate friends that he was a married man, but owing to 'incompatibility' he and his wife had long lived apart. All his effects he left by will to a nephew named Peter Baranoff, who was a Captain in an artillery regiment, which was also stationed in Moscow.

It was generally supposed that Colonel Ignatof was well off, if not wealthy, but it became known after his death that he died worth very little. This gave rise to much gossip, and it was more than hinted that he had squandered his means and substance on a certain lady to whom he had been greatly attached. However, these little incidents were not so rare as to cause any great surprise, and the Colonel and his affairs were soon forgotten, and the world went on as usual. Colonel Ignatof had been in his grave about twelve months, when Moscow was furnished with another sensation. Although he had died poor, relatively, his nephew had got something like three thousand pounds, besides a fair amount of jewellery, some plate, books, and other odds and ends. The young fellow had never been very steady, and after his uncle's death launched out into excesses which brought him under the notice of his superiors; and he was warned that he would have to regulate his conduct a little better or he might be called upon to resign his commission, as his name was mixed up with a good many scandals, and there had been much talk about certain gambling debts he had incurred and was unable to meet. However, an unexpected and effective stop was put to his 'goings on,' and set everybody talking again.

Late one night a man was picked up near one of the gates of the Kremlin wall in a state of unconsciousness, and was conveyed by a police patrol to the nearest station-house, as the natural inference was that he was intoxicated. He was speedily identified as Captain Peter Baranoff, from cards and letters found in his pockets. Within half an hour of his admission his symptoms had become so serious as to cause alarm, and it was deemed advisable to communicate with the military authorities. No time was lost in doing this, but before any instructions could be received Baranoff collapsed, and within an hour of his admission he was dead, in spite of all the efforts made to restore him to consciousness and prolong his life.

The case, as may be supposed, surrounded with mystery as it was, caused an immense sensation. The deceased man's social position, his connection with the army, and the financial difficulties in which it was thought he was involved, removed the matter out of the sphere of an ordinary affair, and it was the 'talk of the town.' As no reason could be assigned for his premature decease, an autopsy was made, and it was then found that, as in his uncle's case, there was violent inflammation of the coats of the stomach and the intestinal track. In the stomach itself were the remains of some half-digested morsels of fish; and it was also made evident that a little while before his death the deceased had partaken freely of vodka. This led to the supposition—which was probably correct—that intoxication was accountable for the unconscious condition in which he was found; but intoxication would not account for his death. He was a young fellow of splendid physique, and none of the organs were diseased. His death, therefore, was not due to any natural cause; and after some discussion amongst the medical men, it was decided to certify that he had died from eating impure food, which, by its poisonous action, had set up inflammation, which had been much aggravated by the vodka. Of course, there was a good deal of curiosity to know where he had spent the evening, and how it was he should have been wandering alone outside of the Kremlin until he fell unconscious. The inference was that he had been revelling with friends at one or other of the numerous haunts which abound in Moscow, and which often lure young men to their destruction. Some attempt was made to trace his movements on the evening of his death; but all the attempt resulted in was that it was proved he left his quarters between six and seven. He was in private clothes, and he incidentally mentioned to a friend that he was going to the opera, and afterwards intended to sup with a lady acquaintance. He did go to the opera, but left early—that is, before ten o'clock. From that time until he was picked up unconscious later there was a blank that could not be filled in.

Strangely enough, at this time there was no suspicion of foul play. That he should die in a similar manner to his uncle was considered rather remarkable, but there the surprise ended. But within a week of the burial a sharp-eyed and thoughtful medical student, who was pursuing his studies in the great college at Moscow, addressed a few lines to the *Moscow Gazette*, in which he ventured to suggest that the doctors who examined Baranoff's body had failed in their duty in not causing a chemical analysis to be made of the contents of the deceased man's stomach; and he advanced the opinion that both Baranoff and his uncle had been wilfully done to death.

At first this idea was laughed at. It was spoken of as being 'ridiculous,' and the suspicion of foul play utterly unjustified. In a few hours, however, public opinion changed. It would be difficult to tell why, unless on the hypothesis that a new sensation was wanted. A clamour arose, and grave doubts were thrown upon the doctors' judgment. Now, in Russia public opinion has not the weight that it has in England, and the popular voice is often stifled whenever it begins to grow a little too loud. But in this case there were certain details which lent a good deal of weight to the suspicion of foul play; and in official quarters, after much discussion, it was considered advisable that some notice should be taken of it. Probably it would have been otherwise but for the seeming fact that the medical men had done their duty in a very perfunctory way, and had not been at sufficient pains to establish the accuracy of the conclusion they came to from what they saw during their scientific investigations. It was pointed out that all the symptoms exhibited by the two men were quite compatible with the suggestions of drug-poisoning; that the theory that both met their end through inadvertently partaking of stale fish was so remarkable a coincidence that it could not be regarded as a commonplace matter; and that in the interest of justice, no less than of science, some further investigation should be permitted.

In the end an official order was issued that Baranoff's body should be exhumed, and the usual means taken to test, by the aid of chemical knowledge, whether or not the deceased man came by death through an accident, through natural causes, or as the victim of foul play. In order to leave nothing to be desired in the way of research, a Professor of Chemistry, who stood at the very top of the profession, was instructed to make the analysis. This he did, with the result that he came to the conclusion that the deceased had met his death from a strong dose of black hellebore. As soon as the authorities were informed of the result of the analysis, they had Colonel Ignatof's body taken up and subjected to chemical examination. And in this instance also the Professor declared that death had been brought about by black hellebore.

At this period black hellebore was by no means a well-known poison outside the medical profession, and the average doctor was perhaps quite ignorant of the morbid symptoms it set up in the human subject when a fatal dose was administered. It is classed amongst what is known as the true narcotico-acrids, and bears the botanical name of *Helleborus niger*, and is familiar to the general public as the Christmas rose. Few people, however, who admire the beautiful rose-tinted flowers of the Christmas rose, which serve to enliven the house in the gloomy winter months, have any idea how deadly a poison can be extracted from its roots and leaves. Its active principle, according to chemists, is an oily matter containing an acid. Its effects on the human being are violent retching and vomiting, delirium, convulsions, and intense internal pains. These symptoms generally appear in from an hour to two hours after the fatal dose is swallowed, and death usually results in about six hours. If administered in alcohol or food of any kind, no suspicion is aroused on the part of the person who takes it, as the taste is quite disguised. The morbid appearances produced in the human body are inflammation of the stomach, the digestive canal, and particularly the great intestines. Poisonous fish or food of any kind almost will produce these symptoms. Therefore the medical men who certified that Colonel Ignatof and his nephew, Captain Baranoff, both died from the effects of impure fish used for soup were misled, and jumped to too hasty a conclusion. Some excuse would be found for them, however, in the fact that the effects of hellebore were not as well known then as now; at any rate, not in Russia. And as the Colonel's own dying opinion was that his illness was due to the iced fish soup he had partaken of, it was perhaps pardonable, all the other circumstances considered, that the doctors should have been put upon a false scent, and it is pretty certain that but for the medical student's letter to the *Moscow Gazette*, which sounded the alarm, no suspicion of foul play would have been aroused.

Like most vegetable poisons, hellebore is difficult to detect, and it can only be discovered in the dead body by means of the most delicate tests. The chemical Professor who was charged with the important duty of examining the remains of Ignatof and Baranoff had made toxicology an especial study, and he had given particular attention to the very large class of vegetable poisons, having travelled for this purpose in various countries. He stood at the head of his profession in Russia, and it was owing to his skill and care, and the technical knowledge he brought to bear, that he was enabled, beyond all doubt, to establish the fact that the two subjects he was charged to examine were the victims of poison.

So much having been determined, the question was mooted whether or not the poison had been administered wilfully or accidentally. The theory of accident was at once negatived. It was like an outrage on common-sense to ask anyone to believe that two men, related to each other, should each die within a year from precisely the same cause. The coincidence was too remarkable to be admitted as probable; therefore the matter resolved itself into murder—it was an ugly word, and all the incidents suggested a tragedy of no ordinary kind. The case was placed in the hands of the chief of police, who was instructed to use every means possible to unravel the mystery. An attempt was at once made to trace the movements of the two men for some hours before their death. In the Colonel's case this was not an easy matter, as he had been dead for a year; but it was discovered that Captain Baranoff called on a friend of his—a civilian named Alexander Vlassovsky, who lived in a villa just on the fringe of the town—and they went together to a café-restaurant, where they dined. After dinner they played billiards for a short time, when they separated, as Vlassovsky had an assignation with a lady. He did not know where Baranoff was going to. He did not ask him, and the Captain volunteered no information. It was proved, however, that he went to the opera, and left about ten. It was stated most positively that when Baranoff quitted the café he was in the pink of health, and in most excellent spirits. Some hours later he was found in a state of unconsciousness outside of the Kremlin walls. It followed, therefore, if the story about the café was correct—and there was no reason to doubt it—that Baranoff must have partaken of the fatal dose a short time before he was discovered, for the action of the poison is very rapid. From the time, however, of his leaving to the time he was discovered unconscious all remained a blank. Nothing could be ascertained of his movements. It was obvious that wherever he had been to, or whoever were the people he had been with, somebody had an interest in keeping his movements dark, as the efforts of the police quite failed to elicit any information. It was the same in the Colonel's case, and no one could discover where he had been to on the fatal night. Moscow is a large city, honeycombed with evil haunts; crime flourishes there to a greater extent than in any other town or city in the whole of Russia. It has been the scene of very many deeds of violence, for blackguardism is rampant, and numerous are the traps for the unwary. Its population is perhaps more varied than that of any other city of the world. Here may be seen cut-throats from the Levant; fishermen and sailors from the Baltic; Circassians, Cossacks, Tartars, Persians, Bokharians, Georgians, Greeks, and Jews of almost every nationality. It may be imagined that in such a place, and amongst such a heterogeneous collection of humanity, wickedness of every description finds a congenial soil. Notwithstanding that, Moscow is known to all Russians as

'The Holy City,' and a devout Russian, who pins his faith to the Russo-Greek Church, regards Moscow with the same veneration that a Mohammedan looks upon Mecca.

After several weeks of fruitless effort to solve the mystery in which the deaths of Colonel Ignatof and his nephew was involved, the police had to confess themselves baffled. It seemed pretty evident that both men had been cruelly done to death by the hand of an assassin. But whose was the hand that committed the deed, and the motive for it, could not be ascertained.

It was at this stage of the proceedings that a request was made to Michael Danevitch—who was then in St. Petersburg—to come through to Moscow, and endeavour to solve the mystery. He complied with the request, and at once waited upon General Govemykin, the military governor of the city, by the General's special desire.

'I want you,' said the General, 'to use every means that your skill can suggest to clear up the mystery surrounding the deaths of Colonel Ignatof and Captain Baranoff. Both these gentlemen were murdered; of that there seems to be no doubt; and the murderers must be brought to book. During the last few years a good many soldiers have lost their lives in this city by foul play, and in several instances justice has gone unsatisfied. Now two officers, men of unblemished reputation and good social position, are killed by the same means, and yet the police are unable to bring the crime home to anyone. It seems to me that it is little short of disgraceful that the police supervision of a city like this is so deficient.'

'Is it deficient?' asked Danevitch.

'Yes; otherwise, how is it officers and gentlemen can be brutally done to death and the murderers escape?'

'As far as I gather, this is no ordinary crime,' remarked Danevitch.

'Well, perhaps not; but it shows a weakness in the organization when our police fail to get the slightest clue to the perpetrator of the crime. Now, what are you going to do?'

'I don't know,' Danevitch answered, as brusquely as the General asked the question.

'If you don't know, what is the use of your taking the matter in hand?'

'Pardon me, General, but I am not a prophet, therefore I cannot foretell what I am going to do.'

'Well, no, perhaps not; but you must have some idea of the lines you intend to proceed upon.'

'I shall simply try to succeed where the police have failed.'

'And you may fail, too,' exclaimed the General, who was a little piqued by Danevitch's brusqueness.

'Oh, that is very likely,' was the answer.

'If you do, I'll take some other and more drastic means to solve the problem. Officers and men under my control shall not be done to death with impunity.'

Danevitch was not affected by this display of temper, and when the subject had been exhausted he withdrew. He recognised that the case was a difficult one, and, in view of the fact that the police had exhausted all their efforts, he was by no means sanguine, although he was of the opinion that the ordinary methods of the Russian police were very clumsy, and, in their eagerness to lay their hands on somebody, and their fossilized belief that the whole populace was ever engaged in some deep and dark conspiracy against constituted authority, they often committed the most ludicrous errors. He never hesitated to condemn the police methods of his country. He described them as inartistic, unscientific, and brutal. His outspokenness on this score made him very unpopular with the police, and they did not like him to have anything to do with cases in which they had failed. It is needless to say this did not disturb him. He had an independent mind; he worked by his own methods, and he never allowed himself to be influenced by jealousy or ill-will.

His first step in connection with Colonel Ignatof's death was to try and get hold of his private letters and papers, as he was of opinion that they might furnish him with a keynote; but he was informed that private documents of all kinds belonging to the Colonel had passed into the possession of his nephew, and when the nephew died all his papers were secured by his executor, who declined to allow them to be seen by anyone until he himself had gone through them; for, though he did not give it as his reason, he was afraid of anything becoming known that might cause a family scandal. Danevitch next sought an interview with Alexander Vlassovsky, with whom Captain Baranoff had dined on the night he met his death.

Vlassovsky was a fashionable young man, and lived in what was known as the Slobodi quarter, where most of the wealthy merchants had their villas. The business he carried on in the city was that of a stockbroker, and, judging from his surroundings and the style he kept up, he was in a flourishing way. He was a bachelor, and made no secret about it that he was fond of gaiety.

According to the account he gave, he had been acquainted with Baranoff for a long time, and had lent him considerable sums of money to enable him to keep up his extravagances; for though Baranoff's people were people of note, and exceedingly proud, they were not rich. At any rate, the young man was not able to get much from them, and his pay as a Captain was too small to enable him to uphold the position he aspired to. Of course, his financial transactions with Vlassovsky had been kept very secret, for had they become known to the military authorities, he would have got into serious trouble.

It will thus be seen that the relations between the young men were those of borrower and lender. They were not friends in the ordinary sense. Indeed, Vlassovsky remarked to Danevitch with some bitterness:

'You know, like most young officers, he was as proud as Lucifer, and seemed to think I was not his equal; though he was never averse to dine with me and drink wine at my expense.'

'Why did he come to you on the night of his death?'

'To borrow money.'

'Did you lend him any?'

'Yes.'

'How much?'

'Two hundred roubles.'

'What security did he give you for the various sums you lent him?'

'Nothing beyond his acknowledgment.'

'And you were satisfied with that?'

'Yes.'

'Why?'

'Because, if he had failed me at any time, I could have reported him to the military authorities, and that would have been his ruin.'

'But you never had occasion to do that?'

'No, certainly not.'

'Did he ever pay you back any of the money he borrowed?'

'Oh yes.'

'Where did he get the money from to pay his debts?'

'How can I tell you that? He did not make me his confidant.'

'Did he owe you much at the time of his death?'

'Yes.'

'How much?'

'Nearly ten thousand roubles.'

'That is a large sum! I suppose you will lose it?'

'Oh dear no!'

'Why? Did he die worth money?'

'His life was insured for ten thousand. I hold the policy and a letter from him to the effect that, should he die before paying me my due, I was to receive the policy money.'

'Have you any idea where he spent his last evening, after leaving you?'

'It is known that he went to the opera, because some acquaintances saw him there.'

'But after that?'

'I haven't the remotest idea.'

'Do you know nothing of his affairs of gallantry?'

'Absolutely nothing.'

'You think, however, that he had lady acquaintances?'

'I should say there isn't a doubt about it. He was wild.'

'And possibly his death was due to jealousy on the part of a rival?'

'Very possibly.'

'Did you know his uncle?'

'I did.'

'Did you accommodate him with money?'

'Yes, occasionally.'

'Was he in your debt when he died?'

'No; he paid me all he owed me a little while before his death.'

'Have you any theory to suggest with reference to the deaths of these two gentlemen?'

'None whatever.'

'Were you very much surprised when you heard of the strange way in which they both died?'

'I can't say that I was.'

'Why were you not?' asked Danevitch quickly.

'In the first place, I didn't know they had been murdered.'

'But when you did?'

'Then I thought they had made themselves obnoxious to somebody, and the somebody had put them out of the way.'

'And yet you have no idea who that somebody is?'

'No.'

Danevitch stopped his questioning at this point. As he left the house of Alexander Vlassovsky he was of opinion he had 'struck a trail'—to quote his own words—and he began to think out the ways and means of proving whether he was right or wrong.

In a semi-fashionable quarter of St. Petersburg lived a lady known generally as Madame Julie St. Joseph. She was of French origin, but had been a great many years in Russia. Her husband had carried on business in Moscow as an engraver and chromo-lithographer. He had been dead, however, a very long time, and seemed to have passed from the public mind; but it was vaguely remembered that he was almost old enough at the time of his death to have been his wife's grandfather.

Julie St. Joseph was exceedingly handsome, and at this period was about forty years of age. She might have passed, however, for being even younger, as she was remarkably well preserved, fresh-looking, bright of eye, and with an abundance of animal spirits, which seemed rather to indicate the girl than the matured woman. Much wonder was very naturally expressed that the pretty widow had remained a widow so long, for, as was well known, she had had offers of marriage innumerable, and might, had she been so disposed, have made an excellent match. But the pretty Julie was fond of gaiety and freedom. As a wealthy widow—it was universally believed that she was wealthy—she could do as she liked, and attract around her men of all sorts and conditions, and of all ages. They paid her homage. She held them, so to speak, in her hand; she could twist them round her fingers. Quarrels about her were innumerable, and more than one jealous and hot-blooded fellow had lost his life in a duel of which the bewitching Julie was the cause.

The style she elected to live in was compatible with the possession of riches. She kept up a splendid establishment; her house was sumptuously furnished; she had numerous servants, many horses. Her winter sledges were renowned for their luxurious appointments; her summer carriages were almost unique. She was a woman of the most sybaritic tastes; and every taste was pandered to and pampered. Among her servants was a Creole; he was a man of medium height, though of powerful build, and with a sullen, morose expression. He was always called Roko, but of his origin and history nothing was known. He seemed to be very strongly attached to his mistress, and always attended her wherever she went; but no man endowed with the faculty of speech could have been more silent than he was. He rarely spoke, except when compelled to answer some question; and it was rumoured that, like a faithful hound, he slept at his mistress's door, and kept watch and ward over her during the hours of night, while during the day he obeyed her slightest beck or call.

It was the beginning of the Russian New Year, and Madame Julie St. Joseph gave a ball. It was a very grand ball; everything was done on a lavish scale, and the pomp and magnificence was almost on a par with a State function. The people, however, who attended the widow's festive gathering could not lay claim to any high social position—at any rate, not so far as the ladies were concerned. The ladies who were in the habit of frequenting the pretty Julie's salons were of questionable reputations. Julie was not recognised as a person of social distinction, and in the female world some rather cruel things were said about her. The men, however, represented many grades of life: the Army, Navy, Law; the Diplomatic Service; Art, Literature, the Drama— intellectual Bohemia generally, though not a few of these men were at considerable pains to conceal the fact that they visited the charming widow, for, had it been generally known, their own women-folk might have protested in a way that would have been anything but pleasant, and they would have found themselves ostracised in those higher circles in which many of them moved. Probably Madame St. Joseph was indifferent to the opinions of her own sex, so long as she could exact homage from men; and there could be no two opinions about the power which she wielded over the sterner sex. It was, therefore, scarcely matter for wonder that the ladies of St. Petersburg should feel embittered against her. When a man is jealous, he takes a rough-and-ready means of showing his jealousy; if he has a rival, he generally 'goes for him,' and the best man wins. A woman's jealousy, on the other hand, finds expression in a different way. In her bitterness she would sully the reputation of a spotless angel, and her mother-tongue has no words strong enough wherewith to express her hatred. No wonder that the old painters, in depicting jealousy, always took a female as a model. Of course Madame Julie St. Joseph's beauty, and the power it enabled her to wield, made the women very jealous indeed; but if her female guests lacked quality, the deficiency was amply compensated for by the high standing of many of the men. She knew, and was proud of the fact, that there was hardly a man in Russia, no matter how exalted his position, that she could not have brought to her footstool had she desired to do so. Such a woman was necessarily bound to become notorious and have numberless enemies. But the widow was beautiful, she was rich, she gave grand receptions, she spent money liberally; therefore she had no difficulty in rallying around her a powerful body of adherents; and, while half St. Petersburg spoke ill of her, the other half lauded her.

Amongst the guests who attended the ball in question was a dark-skinned, somewhat peculiar-looking man, said to be a Polish Count, named Prebenski. He had a heavy moustache and beard, and wore spectacles. As he appeared to be an entire stranger to the company, the hostess took him for a time under her wing; but, as he could not or would not dance, and seemed to find irresistible attraction in the buffet, where there were unlimited supplies of vodka, as well as wines of all kinds, she left him to his own devices, and bestowed the favour of her smiles on more congenial guests. At length the Count, from the effects, apparently, of too great a consumption of strong drinks, sought a quiet nook in an anteroom, and ensconcing himself in a large chair, sank into a heavy sleep. Some time later, when the night was growing very old and the grayness of the winter dawn was beginning to assert itself, and the guests had dwindled down to a mere handful, Roko, the Creole, entered the room. Seeing the Count sleeping there, he paused for a moment as if surprised; then he shook the guest roughly, but getting no response, save a grunt, he went away, returning in a few minutes with another man. That man was Alexander Vlassovsky, who approached the Count, shook him, called him, and being no more successful in his efforts to arouse him than Roko had been, he told Roko to carry him upstairs to a bedroom. That was done, and the Count was tossed upon a bed and left there; but before half an hour had passed Vlassovsky came into the room carrying a small shaded lamp, for though it was fully daylight heavy curtains were drawn at the window.

He passed the light of the lamp over the sleeping man's eyes, shook him, called him, but as the Count remained unconscious of these efforts, the intruder placed the lamp on a small table and, seating himself in a chair by the bedside, began to search the pockets of the guest. The search resulted in the production of a miscellaneous collection of articles, which were duly returned; but at last a pocket-book was drawn forth; it was opened, and found to contain a considerable number of bank-notes, representing in the aggregate a large sum of money. These notes Vlassovsky took the liberty of transferring to his own pocket, and replacing the lightened pocket-book, withdrew.

Some hours later Count Prebenski rang the bell in his room, and in response to the summons Roko appeared, bearing a lamp. The Count eyed him for some moments in apparent astonishment, and then asked:

'Where am I?'

'In the house of Madame Julie St. Joseph.'

'What is the hour?'

'It is three o'clock.'

'In the morning?'

'No. The afternoon.' Roko drew the curtains, and revealed the bright, steel-coloured winter sky, tinged a little towards the horizon with a flush of red.

The Count seemed puzzled. He stared first at the sky, then at the Creole.

'How is it I am here?' he asked.

Roko revealed all his gleaming teeth as he grinned in reply.

'How is it I am here?' repeated the Count, peremptorily and hotly.

'Your Excellency indulged too freely in liquor, and we had to put you to bed.'

'Umph!' mused the Count; 'it was kind; now, tell me, did your mistress, Madame St. Joseph, know of my condition?'

'She did.'

'Was she angry?'

'Well, Excellency, she certainly wasn't pleased.'

'Ah! I fear I have made a bea—— a fool of myself. Give me the wherewith to put myself in a presentable condition, and I will see madam. By the way, has she risen yet?'

'Oh yes.'

'Good; as soon as I have performed my toilet, return here and conduct me to your mistress.'

Roko bowed and withdrew. In half an hour he came back again, and, followed by the Count, led the way to Madame St. Joseph's boudoir, a very comfortable little retreat, daintily furnished, cosy and bright with knick-knacks, cushions, curtains, luxurious rugs, and warmed to the high temperature beloved of Russians by means of a polished metal radiating stove. Dressed in a most elegant fur-trimmed dressing-gown, madame was stretched upon a divan. Beside her was a Moorish table, on which stood coffee and cigarettes. She was smoking as the Count entered. Without rising, she extended her delicate white hand to him, and, smiling sweetly, said:

'Pray be seated, Count. Roko, pour out some coffee. Will you take vodka or cognac with it, Count?'

The Count chose vodka, and his wants having been supplied, the lady bade Roko retire.

'I owe you an apology, madame,' began the Count. 'I forgot myself last night. It was good of you to take care of me. I am deeply indebted to you for your hospitality.'

'Oh, a mere trifle,' smiled the lady. 'My faithful slave found you asleep in a chair, and as his efforts failed to awaken you, he carried you upstairs by my orders.'

At this point in the conversation the door opened, and Vlassovsky appeared on the threshold; but seeing that madame had a visitor, he quickly withdrew.

'I am sorry to say I am the victim of a strange weakness,' answered the Count. 'I am a temperate man, but should I be tempted to indulge beyond my ordinary allowance it throws me into a sort of coma, from which I only recover after many hours of death-like sleep.'

'You are to be pitied, Count.'

'Your pity is worth having,' he answered. 'Now, tell me, madame, what penalty am I to pay for having so far forgotten myself?'

'Penalty, Count!'

'Yes. I am wealthy. Money is no object to me. I have notes. I am almost alone in the world.'

'Indeed!' exclaimed the lady, with animation, and regarding her guest with new-born interest; 'you are fortunate. I presume you are staying here temporarily?'

'Yes. I am travelling for my pleasure. When our mutual friend Trepoff was good enough to ask you to extend your courtesy to me, and sent me an invitation to your ball, I accepted it with pleasure, and was glad to leave the loneliness of my hotel; but it grieves me sorely to think that I so forgot myself.'

'Pray, Count, do not let the matter give you any concern,' said the charming widow, as she sat up and again extended her soft hand to him to kiss. 'Are you likely to remain in St. Petersburg long?'

'My stay will be regulated by the amount of pleasure I experience here. But a hotel is not the most comfortable place in the winter, and I confess I feel dull and lonely.'

The lady fixed her keen eyes upon him as she remarked:

'Indeed, I can well understand that, Count. Now, if I might venture to ask you to make my poor abode your residence during your stay in the city, it would afford me great pleasure to play the hostess. Will you accept of my hospitality?'

'Really, Madame St. Joseph, I, I——'

'Pray, no thanks or excuses, Count; the pleasure is mine, and I will endeavour at least to prevent your suffering from ennui.'

The Count rose, and warmly pressing her hand, said he was overwhelmed by her goodness, and no less enchanted with her beauty. He accepted her invitation in the spirit, in which it was given, and without losing any time would hasten to his hotel, pay his bill, and remove his things at once to madame's house. An hour later he drove up in a drosky with his luggage, and was conducted to the handsomest of the guest-chambers. That night he dined *tête-à-tête* with madame, and in the course of the dinner he told her that the previous night he managed to lose, or had been relieved of, in some way, a large sum of money. When she uttered exclamations of regret, and expressed her sympathy with him, he laughed carelessly, made light of his loss, and said that, large though the sum was, it gave him no real concern, and he would regard it as a fine he had paid for his rudeness.

The widow sighed and told him he was a fortunate man in being able to bear such a loss without feeling it.

A fortnight passed, and the Count found himself in comfortable quarters. As if desirous of monopolizing his company, the widow invited nobody to the house, and those who paid the ordinary courtesy calls she speedily dismissed; while gentlemen who had been in the habit of dropping in of an evening to play cards and sup with pretty Julie were told by Roko that she was suffering so much from the fatigues of the ball that she could see no one. One caller, Peter Trepoff, who came specially to inquire about the Count, was told that though he had been there he had departed, without saying where he was going to. All that fortnight she remained very secluded. She would not accompany the Count when he invited her to go out, and she so strongly persuaded him not to go that he yielded and remained indoors. Every fascination, every talent she possessed, she put forth and exerted to amuse and entertain him, until he was as pliable as clay in her hands. One night he had retired to rest, and had been in his room about an hour, when he heard the handle of his door move. The door was not locked; indeed, there was no key wherewith to lock it, and he had not concerned himself about it in any way. Very gently, and almost without a sound, the latch was raised and the door pushed open. Presently Roko entered on his hands and knees. He paused and listened. Certain nasal sounds seemed to indicate that the Count was sleeping very soundly. Roko carried a tiny little lantern, and he flashed a ray across the sleeper's face. Having satisfied himself that the Count was asleep, he drew from his pocket a phial containing a colourless liquid, and, approaching a night-table, on which stood a jug of barley-tea, which the Count had in his room every night, as he said it had been his custom for years always to drink barley-tea in the night-time, the Creole poured the contents of the phial into the jug, and having done that, he withdrew as stealthily as he had entered. Soon afterwards the Count rose, procured a light, and took from his portmanteau a large flask, into which he emptied the barley-tea. Then he addressed himself to sleep again, and slept the sleep of the just.

At the usual morning meal he did not put in an appearance; but he sent a request to madame, asking her to be good enough to come and see him. The request was speedily complied with. When she appeared she looked as charming and as radiant as ever. He was profuse in his apologies for having troubled her to come to his room, but pleaded as an excuse a feeling of extreme illness. She displayed great anxiety and concern, and wanted to send for a doctor; but he told her it was nothing. He thought something had disagreed with him; that was all. It would pass off. A doctor was not needed. She declared, however, that if he felt no better in an hour's time she would insist on his seeing a doctor. An hour slipped by, and he was still in the same condition, so a messenger was despatched for a doctor, who speedily put in an appearance.

To the doctor's inquiries, the patient said he believed he had eaten or drunk something which had upset him. The doctor was of the same opinion, and prescribed accordingly. In the course of the afternoon the Count said he felt somewhat better, and though the hostess tried to dissuade him from doing so, he announced his intention of going out to get a breath of fresh air. He wanted her to accompany him. That she stoutly refused to do; and when she saw he was determined to go she withdrew her opposition, and expressed a hope that he would speedily return. He assured her that he would do so. He said he was going to have a drive in a sledge on the Neva for two or three hours. Having put on his Shuba, his fur gloves, fur-lined boots, and fur cap, he took his departure.

After an absence of about three hours, he returned, and declared that he felt much better. He spent about an hour with the lady in her boudoir, then retired. She was very anxious that Roko should sit up with him, but he resolutely set his face against that, saying that there was not the least necessity for it. He was an exceedingly sound sleeper, and he was sure he would sleep as soundly as usual. About midnight his door was opened silently, as on the previous night, and once again Roko crept stealthily to the bed-table, and emptied the contents of a phial into the barley-tea. Soon after he had withdrawn the Count jumped up, poured the tea into another flask, which he produced from his portmanteau, and then lay down in the bed again until a neighbouring church clock solemnly and slowly tolled out two o'clock. Almost immediately the Count rose, and dressed himself. That done, he took from his portmanteau a revolver, and having examined it to ascertain if it was properly loaded, he lighted a lantern provided with a shutter, to shut off the light when required. Going to the door, he opened it gently, and listened. All was silent. There wasn't a sound, save that made by the wind, which whistled mournfully through the corridor. Having satisfied himself that nothing human was stirring, the Count proceeded cautiously along the corridor, descended a short flight of stairs to another corridor, along which he passed, and gained the main door that gave access to the street. He opened this door, though not without some difficulty, as there were bolts and chains to be undone, and he worked cautiously for fear of making a noise.

At last all obstacles were removed, and the heavy door swung on its hinges, letting in a blast of icy air, and revealing the brilliant stars that burned like jewels in the cloudless black sky. In a few minutes eight men filed into the house noiselessly, and the door was closed, but chains and bolts were left undone. The men exchanged a few sentences in whispers. Then, following the Count, they proceeded to the sleeping apartment of Madame Julie St. Joseph. In an anteroom, through which it was necessary to pass to reach her room, Roko, enveloped in furs, lay on a couch, locked in sleep. A shaded lamp stood on a bracket against the wall.

Four men remained in this room; the other four and the Count entered the lady's chamber. Here, again, a shaded lamp burned on a bracket, and close to it an ikon—or sacred picture—hung. The pretty widow was also sleeping. By this time the Count had undergone a strange transformation. His beard and moustache had disappeared, revealing the smooth-shaved, mobile face of Michael Danevitch, the detective. He shook the lady. With a start she awoke. The four policemen had concealed themselves; Danevitch alone was visible. It was some moments before madame realized the situation; then, seeing a strange man by her bedside, she uttered a cry, and called for Roko. He sprang up, and instantly found himself in the grip of two stalwart men, while the revolver under his pillow, which he tried to get, was seized.

'Madame Julie St. Joseph,' said Danevitch, 'get up and dress yourself.'

'What does this mean?' she asked, with a look of alarm on her pretty face, as she thrust her hand under the pillow, where she likewise had a revolver concealed. But in an instant Danevitch had seized her wrist in his powerful grasp, and one of his colleagues removed the weapon.

'It means,' he answered, 'that your career of infamy has come to an end. You are under arrest.'

A look of terror and horror swept across her face as she asked in a choked sort of voice:

'On what grounds am I arrested?'

'That you will learn later on. Sufficient for you to know that you are a prisoner. Come, rise and dress yourself.'

She recognised the hopelessness of resistance, and, of course, she understood that her faithful watch-hound Roko had been rendered powerless. She was trapped; that she knew. But it did not dawn upon her then that the Count and Danevitch were one and the same. Consequently she was puzzled to understand how her downfall had been brought about.

With a despairing sigh she rose and put on her clothes. Half an hour later she was being conveyed to the gaol with Roko, accompanied by Danevitch and three of his colleagues. The other five had been left in charge of the house. When madame had somewhat recovered her presence of mind, she assumed a bravado which she was far from feeling, and asked Danevitch airily if he knew how her guest the Count was.

'Oh yes,' answered Danevitch. 'He is perfectly well, as you may judge for yourself; for I it was who played the part of the Count so effectively.'

With an absolute scream madame bit her lip with passion, until the blood flowed, and dug her nails into the palms of her hands.

'What a fool, a dolt, an idiot I've been! But tell me, how was it Peter Trepoff asked me to invite you to the ball?'

'Peter Trepoff is my agent, madame.'

With a suppressed cry of maddening rage, the wretched woman covered her face with her hands and groaned, as she realized how thoroughly she had been outwitted.

That same night, or, rather, some hours before the widow and Roko were swept into the net which had been so cleverly prepared for them, Alexander Vlassovsky was arrested in Moscow. Danevitch learned that fact by telegraph when he went out in the afternoon. He had first begun to suspect Vlassovsky after that interview when he was making inquiries about the death of Captain Baranoff. The result was that he intercepted letters from Madame Julie St. Joseph, who had returned to St. Petersburg. She had a small house in Moscow, which she occasionally visited in order to secure victims. In Moscow, where he was well known, the wily Vlassovsky did not go near her, but he helped her as far as he could in her fiendish work. He had been very cleverly trapped by the notes which he relieved the supposed Count of. Those notes were not genuine, and when he attempted to pass them he was arrested, for Danevitch had notified the Moscow police.

Subsequent revelations brought to light that the wretched woman had been in the habit of luring men to their doom by means of her fatal beauty. She bled them of their money, her plan being to cajole them into giving her a lien on any property they might possess. This was most artfully worked by the aid of Vlassovsky, and when the victim had been securely caught, he was poisoned. The poisons were concocted by Madame St. Joseph herself, and when she could not do it herself, Roko administered the fatal dose or doses. She had picked up this man in Spanish America, where she had been for some time, and, weaving her spell about him, had made him absolutely her slave.

Vlassovsky, who, up to the time that he made her acquaintance, had been an honest, industrious man, fell under the magic of her influence, as most men did, and became her all-too-willing tool. His nature once corrupted, all scruples were thrown to the winds, and he hastened to try and enrich himself. It seemed that the miserable woman really loved him, and though he was fatally fascinated with her, he was afraid of her; and, as he confessed, his aim was to accumulate money as quickly as possible, and then flee from her and the country for ever. But unfortunately for himself, during that memorable interview following Captain Baranoff's death, he had aroused the suspicions of Danevitch, whose marvellous perceptive faculties had enabled him to detect something or another in Vlassovsky's manner, or answers to the questions put to him, which made him suspicious. For Danevitch to become suspicious meant that he would never rest until he had proved his suspicions justified or unfounded.

It need scarcely be said that with her arrest in St. Petersburg Madame St. Joseph's career came to an end. From the moment that Danevitch entered her house her doom was sealed. Believing him to be the person he represented himself to be, she begged of him to help her financially; and, seeming to yield to her entreaties, he drew up a document which purported to make over to her at his death certain estates in Poland. Of course, these estates had no existence. Having secured him, as she thought, her next step was to poison him by small doses of black hellebore, so that he might gradually sicken and die. Her devilish cunning was evidenced in every step she took. She would not appear in public with him, nor did she allow any of the visitors to her house to see him. Consequently it would not be generally known that she had associated with him. As his illness developed by means of repeated doses, she would have had him removed to a hotel, and she knew pretty well that, as in Colonel Ignatof's case, he would shrink from letting it be known that he had been intimate with her. Her cunning, however, overreached itself; she was defeated with her own weapons; Danevitch had been too much for her. The poisoned barley-tea he submitted to analysis, and the evidence against her was overwhelming. But when she found that there was no hope, she was determined to defeat justice, and one morning she was found dead in her cell: she had poisoned herself with prussic acid. The acid was conveyed to her by a warder, who was heavily bribed by one of her friends to do it. It cost him his liberty, however, for he was sent to Northern Siberia for the term of his natural life.

Roko died very soon afterwards from typhoid fever contracted in the prison, but he was faithful to the last, for never a word could be wrung from his lips calculated to incriminate the strange woman who had thrown such a spell around him. Vlassovsky was deported to Northern Siberia in company with the treacherous warder. He very soon succumbed, however, to the awful hardships he was called upon to endure and the rigours of the Arctic climate.

The number of Madame St. Joseph's victims was never determined. That they were numerous there was not the slightest doubt; and had it not been for the cleverness of Danevitch she would probably have continued to pursue her infamous career for years longer, and ultimately have passed away in the odour of sanctity. Her downfall, it need scarcely be said, caused great satisfaction in St. Petersburg and Moscow, where she had destroyed so many of her victims.

THE STRANGE STORY OF AN ATTACHÉ.

It can readily be understood that Danevitch led not only an active life, but a varied one; and the cases he was called upon to deal with revealed many remarkable phases of human nature. He never attempted to pose as a moralist, but he frequently deplored the fact that wickedness and evil should so largely predominate over goodness. He was also apt to wax indignant against the vogue to decry anything in the nature of sensation. He was in the habit of saying that life from the cradle to the grave is full of sensations, and that the inventions of the fictionist are poor, flat, and stale, when compared with the realities of existence. But this is undoubtedly the experience of everyone who knows the world and his kind. It is only the cheap critic, the bigot, or the fool, who has the boldness to deny the existence of sensation in real life, and to sneer at what he is pleased to term melodramatic improbabilities. There is no such thing as a melodramatic improbability. The only charge that can legitimately be levelled at the so-called sensational writer is his tendency to grotesque treatment of subjects which should simply be faithful reproductions from life. The curious story of young Count Dashkoff, the Russian attaché, with whom this narrative is concerned, illustrates in a very forcible way the views advanced in the foregoing lines. Indeed, as Danevitch himself says, if anyone had invented the story and put it into print, he would have raised the ire of the army of critics—the self-constituted high-priests of purity, who, being unable to improve or even equal that which they condemn, are all the more violent in their condemnation.

Count Dashkoff was a young man, a member of a very old Russian family, who had in their day wielded great power, and before the abolition of serfdom took place, had held sway over more serfs than any other family in the whole of the empire. The Count had distinguished himself in many ways. His career, up to the time of the extraordinary events about to be recorded, had been marked by brilliancy and shade. As a student and a scholar he had attracted the attention of many notable men, more particularly by his well-known and remarkable work, entitled 'The Theory of Creation,' which is conspicuous for its erudition, its deep research, and its wide grasp and clever treatment of a tremendous subject. The book is, and will ever remain, a standard, and consequently an enduring monument to the Count's ability and industry. On the other hand, he had made himself notorious by certain excesses, and a recklessness of conduct which had shocked the proprieties and outraged the feelings of those who were interested in him and hoped that he would ultimately rise to power and position. Of course, excuses were forthcoming on the grounds of his youth, and, as if trying to establish a right by two wrongs, it was urged that he had simply done what most Russian youths do who are born to high estate and have control of wealth. As a stepping-stone to the future greatness predicted for him by his friends, the Count, after a probationary course in the diplomatic service at home, was sent as an attaché to the Russian Embassy in Paris. As might be supposed, he took kindly to Parisian life. He was what is usually termed an elegant young man, with æsthetic tastes. When he first went to Paris he was about eight-and-twenty, and, apart from the advantages of youth, he had wealth, good looks, sound health, and a cheerful disposition. He enjoyed life, and showed no disposition to mortify the flesh by an austere or monastic régime. His private residence in the Champs Élysées was conspicuous for the magnificence of its appointments, and was the rendezvous of the élite of Paris society—that frivolous section which lives for no higher purpose than to live, and is attracted to wealth and luxury as bees are attracted to sugar. It seemed that this apparently fortunate young man, who could be serious enough when occasion required, was fond of attention and homage. He loved to be surrounded with a crowd of admirers, who flattered him, praised his bric-à-brac, and gorged themselves with the good things he invariably set before them. He knew, no doubt, that they were all fawners and sycophants, but, still, they made up a little world over which he ruled, and wherever he led the noodles would follow.

Two years of this sort of life passed, and then Danevitch was instructed to proceed with all haste from Russia to try and discover what had become of the Count, for he had suddenly and mysteriously disappeared, and all efforts of the Paris police and the boasted skill of the Parisian detectives had failed to reveal a trace of him. The facts of the case were as follows: In the course of the month of January the Count gave a grand ball and reception at his elegant hotel, and the event drew together the gilded youth of both sexes. These functions at the Count's residence were always marked by a magnificence of splendour and a lavish expenditure which seemed hardly consonant with his position as a mere attaché. But it must not be forgotten that he was the heir to great wealth, and represented a noble family who had ever been distinguished for the almost regal style in which they lived.

About two o'clock in the morning the Count drew an intimate friend of his—a Monsieur Eugène Peon—on one side, and told him he wanted to slip away for an hour, but he did not wish it to be known that he had gone out. He would be sure to be back in about an hour, he added. A few minutes later the concierge saw him leave the hall. He was attired in a very handsome and costly fur coat, with a cap to match; and though the weather was bitterly cold and the ground covered with snow, he wore patent-leather shoes. The concierge, who was much surprised at the fact of his master leaving the house in the midst of the revels, asked him if he wanted a carriage. To this question the Count answered curtly, and, according to the porter, angrily, 'No.' The night wore itself out. The dancers danced themselves into limpness and prostration, and began to depart. Some surprise had been expressed at the Count's absence, and various inquiries had been made about him; but it was suggested that the seductive influences of the wine-cup had proved too much for him, and he had retired. This hint or suggestion appeared to satisfy the light-headed revellers, who gave no further thought to the matter. His friend, Eugène Peon, considered it very strange that the Count should go away and remain away in such a manner, to the neglect of his guests, for he was the most punctilious host. But Peon set it down to an assignation, and thought that he had found the society of some fair one more attractive than the glitter and glare of the ballroom. The day had very well advanced before there was anything like real surprise felt at the Count's prolonged absence.

It appeared that Eugène Peon called at his friend's hotel soon after three o'clock in the afternoon, and, ascertaining that he was not at home, went down to the Embassy to inquire for him there, but to his astonishment was informed that the Count had not been there for two days. Although astonished, Peon was not uneasy. He stated that he saw no cause to be uneasy, although he had never known his friend do such a thing before, and was aware that he was most attentive to his duties. When he called again on the following morning, however, and was informed that the Count was still absent, he began then to fear that something was wrong, and he at once communicated his fears to some of the Count's close personal friends; he had no relations in Paris at all. A consultation was held, but there seem to have been divided counsels, and no steps were taken to ascertain the Count's whereabouts, though some inquiries were made of the members of the household, but all that could be elicited was that the concierge saw his master go out about two o'clock, and that he was dressed in patent-leather boots, a heavy fur coat, and a fur cap. From the tone in which he said 'No,' when asked if he wanted a carriage, he appeared to be angry; but there was no indication in his gait or speech that he was under the influence of wine. It was not until another whole day had passed that anything like real alarm had set in. The alarm by this time had reached the Embassy, and it was decided that the police should be communicated with. Strangely enough, the police did not at first attach any serious importance to the matter. They made certain inquiries in a perfunctory manner, and for some inscrutable reason—unless it was sheer, downright pig-headedness, a quality often enough conspicuous in the French police—they came to the conclusion that 'Monsieur le Comte' had been guilty of some little escapade, and would turn up very shortly. As this prediction had not been fulfilled when another twenty-four hours had elapsed, a much more serious view was taken of the young man's absence, and dark hints were let drop that he had been inveigled into one of the haunts of vice which abound in the gay city, and had been murdered. The murder theory was at once taken up; detectives were communicated with, and the theory of murder found general acceptance.

As may be imagined, a gentleman, who by reason of his position and his riches had cut a conspicuous figure in society, disappearing suddenly in this way was bound to cause a sensation, and as the Parisians dearly love a sensation and a scandal, the matter was a fruitful topic of conversation for several days, while much ink was expended over it by the journalists. But notwithstanding the publicity given to the matter, and the efforts of police and detectives, another week passed, and not a trace or sign of the missing man had been obtained.

Up to this point the Count's relatives in Russia had not been communicated with, from a desire to avoid alarm, for there were those who still hoped he would turn up again all right; but now his Russian friends in Paris regarded the affair as too serious to be longer withheld. As a preliminary, a message was at once sent asking if the Count had returned home, and almost simultaneously with the despatch of that message a courier set out for Russia with the tidings and details.

As the Count—as far as was known—had not returned to Russia, great consternation was caused amongst his friends by the report that reached them, and no time was lost in securing the services of Danevitch, who was instructed to leave for Paris without a moment's delay, and institute independent inquiries.

'I found, on arriving in the French capital,' says Danevitch, 'that by order of the Russian Ambassador all the Count's things had been sealed up and his house temporarily closed. My preliminary investigations were directed to trying to discover if there were any grounds for believing that the missing man had committed suicide. This inquiry was necessarily forced upon one— at any rate upon me, although I learnt that the possibilities of suicide had never entered the heads of the French police. And though at first they had suggested murder, they soon abandoned that idea, for no other reason, as it appeared, than that they had not been able to find his body. And in consequence of this they insisted that he had taken himself off to some other country in order to avoid the results of conduct unbecoming a gentleman and a member of the Embassy. When they were asked to give a name to his conduct, they declined, but darkly hinted at something very dreadful. I myself could find no grounds for the theory of suicide, while everyone at the Embassy, as well as all who knew him, indignantly repudiated the slur which was sought to be cast upon the young gentleman's character. I could find no one who had a word to say against his honour. That he might have had *affaires d'amour*, as the French call them, was readily admitted; but as all is considered fair in love, as in war, these matters were not supposed to reflect on the honour of a man.

'As Monsieur Eugène Peon had been very intimate with the Count, I questioned that gentleman very closely concerning his friend's movements, and elicited that he had been a pretty general lover, but, so far as he knew, the Count had formed no serious attachment to anybody. Peon could suggest no reason why the Count should have left his guests so abruptly, unless it was to keep an assignation.

'Now, it must be remembered that when he left his house it was about two o'clock on a winter morning, and, according to the concierge, he seemed angry when he went out. This seemed to me to point to two things as absolutely certain. Firstly, the Count's going out at such an hour was not premeditated. Secondly, whatever appointment he went to keep, it was not an agreeable one to him, and, being annoyed, he displayed his irritation in the sharp answer he gave the concierge. These points seemed to me of great importance, and naturally led me to an inquiry directed to finding out if one of his servants had delivered any message to him, or conveyed any letter during the evening.

'The servants had been dismissed, and it was not an easy matter to reach them all; but by persevering I succeeded in doing so, and found at last that the Count's body-servant, a Frenchman, named Auguste Chauzy, had been out all the evening, after having dressed his master, and knowing that he would not be wanted again until the morning. He returned, however, soon after midnight, and just as he was about to enter the house, a man stepped up to him hurriedly, and, putting a sealed envelope into his hand, said, "Give that immediately to your master, Count Dashkoff. Fail not to do so, as it is a matter of life and death."

'When Chauzy got into the hall, he glanced at the envelope, and saw that it simply bore the Count's name—no address; but in the left-hand corner was the French word *Pressant* (Urgent) underlined. The valet could not get near his master for some time after this, but as soon as an opportunity occurred to do so, he handed him the note. The moment the Count's eye caught the superscription, a frown settled on his face, and, with a gesture of annoyance, he thrust the letter unopened in his pocket. About half an hour later, however, the valet was informed by another servant that the Count required his fur coat and cap. They were to be placed in his dressing-room ready for him.

'I questioned Chauzy about the man who had handed him the letter in the street; but the only description he could give of him was that he seemed to be well dressed, was of medium height, and had a dark beard and moustache.'

Having brought to light the fact about the letter, Danevitch struck a keynote, as it were—and one which had not been touched upon by the French police. If that letter could have been found, it might have revealed much; but it was almost certain that if the Count did not destroy it before leaving the house he had it in his pocket when he went out. Danevitch's deduction from the letter incident was this: The Count went out owing to some communication made to him in that letter. He did not go willingly; consequently his errand was a disagreeable one, and could hardly have been to keep a love tryst. Whoever the writer of the letter was, he or she must have had some powerful hold on the Count to induce him to leave his friends and guests, and go out at two o'clock on a bitter winter morning. This line of reasoning was one which Danevitch could not avoid, for it was his wont to argue his subject from a given set of premises, and a strict regard for probabilities. He was led—and it was but natural he should be—to the conclusion that the Count's disappearance was due to conduct which had brought him in contact with unscrupulous people, into whose power he had fallen. It was clear that if he was still living he was forcibly detained somewhere or other, and was in such a position that he could not communicate with those who were so anxious about him. If this was not the case, it was hard to understand why he should have remained silent, knowing well enough the anxiety and distress his prolonged absence would cause. The other hypothesis was—the idea of suicide not being entertained—that he had been murdered. If that was the case, the motive for the murder was either revenge or robbery. It seemed almost absurd to think of robbery, for this reason: it was hardly likely that anyone would have chosen such an inopportune moment; for, at two o'clock in the morning, and entertaining a house full of guests, he would scarcely have much valuable property on his person. If he had been murdered, the crime had been prompted by feelings of revenge, and committed by someone who believed he had a deadly grievance against the young man—a grievance that could only be compensated for by the shedding of the Count's blood.

It was impossible to ignore what, on the face of it, seemed to be a fact—that the writer of the letter was personally acquainted with the Count, and possessed knowledge which placed a weapon in his hand. Of course, the Count's friends wouldn't listen for a moment to any suggestion that he had been guilty of conduct unbecoming a gentleman, and, having discovered that, Danevitch kept his views to himself; though he closely questioned Eugène Peon, who, while admitting that he had had numerous little adventures with the Count, declared that these adventures were only those which a young, handsome, and rich man would engage in, and while they might be described as foolish and reckless, they were never of a nature to reflect upon his honour. They were, in short, simply the follies and venial sins of youth, such as were common, in a greater or lesser degree, to all young men. Nothing further than this could be elicited from Peon, who appeared to be a reserved and reticent person, giving Danevitch the impression that he always had something in reserve—that he had an *arrière pensée*, and would not tell more than it suited him to tell. At any rate, he declined to suggest any theory that would account for his friend's sudden and mysterious disappearance.

'Do you not know if he had any serious love affair?' asked Danevitch with some sharpness, as he came to the conclusion that Peon was not as candid as he ought to be.

'I don't,' answered Peon emphatically.

'But surely, intimate as you were with him, you must know something of your friend's little gallantries?'

'I do not, beyond what I have told you.'

Peon gave this answer with a sharpness and decisiveness which made it clear that he would not submit to pumping, and would not be drawn on the subject of his friend's amours.

During the time that Danevitch was searching for a clue—without avail up to this stage—the Count's friends did not remain inactive. Necessarily, they were impatient, and grew more restless as the weeks sped by without bringing any tidings of the missing man. The police confessed themselves baffled, and seemed to be at a loss to suggest a feasible theory, and they urged the friends to offer a substantial reward for information that would lead to the discovery of the Count if living, and a lesser reward for his body if dead. The friends yielded, and intimated that they would pay ten thousand francs for the Count's recovery living, or five thousand for his body. The police quite believed this reward would have the desired effect, and that they would be relieved from an embarrassing situation. Of course, the human water-rats who haunt the Seine kept a very sharp look-out indeed, and every corpse that they dragged from the foul and reeking waters of the sluggish river was eagerly scrutinized in the hope that it would turn out to be the body of the missing Count. But though it was reported several times that the dead Count had been fished out of the river, the report, on investigation, proved to be false. Nor did the offer of the ten thousand francs prove more potent. Not a trace of the missing man was discovered.

This failure of the substantial reward to bring forth any tidings confirmed Danevitch in the opinion he had formed that the Count's disappearance was the result of some plot, and those engaged in it were in a position which rendered them indifferent to the reward. This did not imply that the detective considered it a certainty that the Count was living. On the contrary, he inclined to the belief that he had been murdered, but, necessarily, the murderers could not produce his body for fear of betraying themselves. In his own way, Danevitch worked away quietly and unostentatiously. He was perfectly convinced that the clue to the mystery would be found in the habits of the Count, or among some of his possessions. But the friends in Paris opposed strong objections to any exhaustive search of his effects being made, influenced thereby, no doubt, by a fear of anything being made public calculated to reflect on the missing man's honour. This supersensitiveness was annoying, and at last Danevitch applied to the relatives in Russia, and asked them to give a peremptory order for him to be allowed to go through the Count's papers. In response to this application, the Count's father came at once to Paris, and took possession of everything belonging to his son, and he and Danevitch went through the papers together. There was a mass of official correspondence and business letters, but very few private letters, except those from his parents and his near relatives, and love letters from a young lady residing in Russia. She was of high family, and well known to the Count's people, who hoped that he would ultimately make her his wife, as in every way the match was a desirable one. The letters evinced a very strong attachment on the lady's part, and were in many instances couched in warm, even extravagant, phrases of love. But there was nothing in them calculated to throw light on the mystery. She knew of her lover's disappearance, and was prostrated with grief and anxiety, so the Count's father asserted.

The result of the examination of the papers so far was very disappointing, but a small diary was found in which were some rather remarkable passages. It was not a diary of doings and events from day to day, but seemed to be the outpourings of the writer's feelings and emotions, written in a fitful and irregular manner. Those which struck Danevitch the most were as follows:

'I often wonder whether we are really free and responsible beings; whether the evil we do is the result of deliberate sinning, or whether it is due to some inward promptings which we are absolutely powerless to resist. If the latter, to what extent can we be held liable for our sins? I am sorely troubled at times with this thought, and yearn for someone to whom I could appeal with a hope of receiving such an answer as would seem to me satisfactory. The teachings of my Church do not satisfy me. The Church says that to do evil is to incur the wrath of Heaven; but if I cannot resist doing evil, is it right that I should be held responsible? Of course, the world would say that this is sophistry, but when I find myself on the one hand trying with all my might to avoid doing anything which, according to the laws of ethics and the canons of the Church, could be construed into wrong-doing, and, on the other, being drawn by some vaguely defined power, which I am too weak to resist, into doing that which I am conscious it is not right to do, I ask myself if I can really be held responsible. It seems to me that I have two distinct characters, clearly separated, and entirely antagonistic to each other. The one leads me into paths that I would fain avoid; the other causes me to weep for my frailty. I wonder if all men are constituted like this? Perhaps they are, but are less sensitive than I am.

'If a man entangles himself in a net, he may exhaust himself in his struggles to get free again, and it may even be that the more he struggles the more tightly he may enmesh himself, until he realizes the horror that he is doomed to remain powerless until death itself releases him. This is figurative language, but it is by such language that we can best convey our true meaning. It is but speaking in parables, and parables better than anything else often enable us to understand and grasp what would otherwise be obscure. Unhappily, I am entangled in a net, and I have struggled in vain to free myself. If I could undo the past, I might know true happiness once more; but that which is done is done, and though we weep tears of blood, we can never obliterate the record which is written on the tablets of memory. I wonder what the pure being in Russia, to whom I gave my heart, would say if she knew how I had wronged her. Can I ever look into her clear honest eyes again with the frank, unflinching gaze of the happy days past and gone? I fear not. Indeed, I feel that I dare not meet her again. I have dug a gulf between us, and that gulf can never be bridged. But I suffer agony of mind when I think how she will suffer when she knows my baseness, as know she must, sooner or later. It is hard to have to live two lives, as I am doing. To my friends I appear all they would believe me to be; but in the solitude of my chamber my heart bleeds as I realize how false I am.

'I have been weak, but am growing strong again. Desperation is lending me strength, in fact; and I shall burst these accursed bonds asunder. I have still youth and energy, and must make an effort to climb to higher heights. I have been walking blindly hitherto, and have missed my way, but I see it clear enough now; and a resolute and determined man, who finds himself surrounded by obstacles, should sweep them away. He who hesitates is lost; I have hesitated, but will do so no longer. Great things are expected from me, and I must not disappoint those who have placed their hopes upon me. Marie must not be allowed to keep me bound down in the gutter. It is not my place. I was destined to walk on higher heights; and since it is impossible for me to raise her, she must be cut adrift. It may seem cowardly; it may be cruel for me to do this; but it must be done, for I cannot endure the double life any longer. Is a man to suffer all his life for one false step? Am I justified in breaking the hearts of parents and betrothed? No. It must not be—shall not be. In a few weeks I shall send in my resignation, and quit Paris for ever. It will cause a nine days' wonder, but what of that? People will say I am a fool, but it won't affect me. I shall plead that I know my own affairs best, and that circumstances of a private and pressing nature necessitate my hasty return to Russia. This I am determined to do, cost what it may. I have taken

Eugène Peon into my confidence. He will help me, and satisfy the curious when I am gone.'

There was a significance in the foregoing passages which was not lost upon Danevitch. The Count gave himself away, though, of course, he never expected that any eyes but his own would read what he had written. It will be said, of course, that it was foolish for him to have committed his thoughts to paper; though it must be remembered that there are some men who seem to derive a strange pleasure in recording their evil deeds. It is a well-known fact that some of the greatest criminals have kept diaries, in which they have written the most damning evidence of their guilt. The Count's diary proved conclusively that there were certain ugly passages in his life, and two points were made clear—there was a woman in the case, and Eugène Peon knew more of the Count's affairs than he cared to own to, and confirmed Danevitch in his belief that Peon was a crafty man, and by no means carried his heart upon his sleeve.

As may be imagined, the Count's father was much cut up, as he realized that his son had been guilty of evil which was calculated to reflect upon the honour of the family, that honour of which the old man was so proud, and which he would gladly have died to shield.

Of course it became necessary now to find out who the 'Marie' referred to in the diary was; for it was obvious that she was directly or indirectly responsible for the Count's disappearance. No letters could be discovered which were calculated to throw any light on the subject, but in a small drawer of the Count's desk there was found the photograph of a young woman, and on the back, in a scrawling hand, was the following:

> 'For ever and ever thine.
> MARIE.'

The likeness was that of a singularly handsome girl of about two-and-twenty; but the handwriting was so bad it suggested that the writer was not educated.

Danevitch felt now that he was in possession of a clue—a vague one, it was true, but it was possible it might lead to very important results. Marie must be found, though he did not know at the moment how he was going to find her. Paris was a big place; Marie was a very common name. Danevitch, however, having once got on the scent, was not likely to go very far astray, and he generally found some means of bringing down his quarry at last. He was not indifferent to the self-evident fact that in this case there were no ordinary difficulties to contend against; this was proved by the large reward having failed to bring forth any information. It showed that those who were responsible for the Count's disappearance had very powerful motives for keeping their secret; and whether few or many were interested in that secret, ten thousand francs was not strong enough to tempt one of them; and it seemed as if it was not the Count's money that was responsible for his disappearance. He kept a banking account in Paris, but this had not been drawn upon since the week before he went away, when he cashed a cheque for three thousand francs. But at this stage a curious incident was brought to light, which put a new complexion on the matter altogether.

The incident was this: It appeared that the Count also kept a considerable account at the Moscow branch of the Bank of Russia. He owned a good deal of property in and about Moscow, part of it being a flourishing flax-mill, which turned over a princely revenue. His Moscow affairs were managed by an agent who had been connected with the family for nearly half a century. It was his duty to pay all money that he received into the bank without delay. Consequently, there was generally a large balance standing to the Count's credit. One day a three months' bill of exchange, purporting to be drawn on the Count by Paul Pavlovitch and Co., flax merchants, at Riga, for one hundred thousand francs, and accepted by the Count and payable at the bank in Moscow, was duly presented by an individual, who stated that he was a member of the firm. As all seemed right, the bill was paid, and a receipt given in the name of Peter Pavlovitch, who represented himself as the son of Paul. A week later the cancelled bill passed into the hands of the Count's agent, and he at once declared it to be a forgery. Pavlovitch and Co., of Riga, were immediately communicated with, and they denied all knowledge of the Count, had never had any business transactions with him, had never drawn a bill upon him, and knew nothing of Peter Pavlovitch. This was a revelation indeed, and pointed conclusively to a conspiracy. It seemed to Danevitch pretty evident that the person who forged the bill knew a good deal about the Count, and if that person could be laid hold of the plot might be unmasked. There was another thing, too, that appeared to be no less clear: the forger of the bill was acquainted with the Count's affairs, and also with Russia. The firm of Paul Pavlovitch and Co., of Riga, was an old-established firm, and there was nothing to strike a stranger as peculiar in their holding a bill of the Count's; for the Count was the owner of a flax-mill, and did business with a good many flax merchants. Nevertheless, the bank in Moscow was blamed for having been somewhat lax in paying the bill without having taken steps to satisfy themselves that the person who presented it was the person he represented himself to be. Moreover, in the business world bills of that nature were usually collected by a bank. However, the Moscow bank people defended themselves by saying that, though a little out of course, there was nothing extraordinary in a bill being presented by a member of a firm holding it.

As soon as Danevitch heard of the incident of the forged bill, he returned at once to Moscow, deeming it probable that he might there pick up some thread which would lead him to a clue. The man calling himself Peter Pavlovitch, to whom the money was paid, was described as of medium height, of muscular build, dark-complexioned, black hair, beard, and moustache, in age about thirty. He was well dressed, and the receipt he gave was written in a bold, clerkly hand. Of course, there was nothing in this description to distinguish him from thousands of others, and Moscow was a large place; but Danevitch went to work on the assumption that the man, whoever he might be, was well acquainted with the Count, and he knew a good deal of his business; that, to some extent, narrowed the inquiry, which was necessarily directed to trying to discover a person upon whom suspicion could justifiably fasten.

The Count's agent was a Pole named Padrewski. He was a man of high repute, and one in whom his employer placed the greatest confidence. He could not even vaguely identify the self-styled 'Peter Pavlovitch' from the description given, and was of opinion that he was not a resident in Moscow, though probably not a stranger. If he was not a resident in the city, it was likely enough that he sojourned there long enough to enable him to transact his business, and having possessed himself of the money, he would depart without delay. Danevitch ascertained that the bill was presented for payment about half-past ten in the morning. That argued that the person who drew the money and gave the receipt had slept in the city, and probably lodged at some café or hotel. So the detective set to work at once to make inquiries at the various hotels and lodging-houses. In Russia, as in France and Germany, every lodging-house-keeper and hotel proprietor is compelled by law to keep a register of his guests. It is therefore far easier to discover anyone who occupies temporary lodgings than it is in this country. Now, it struck Danevitch that, if the presenter of the forged bill had come to Moscow for the sole purpose of drawing the money, he would in all probability select a place near the railway-station. There were several hotels and cafés in the vicinity of the station. At all of these inquiries were made, and, at a third-rate café-restaurant, called in Russian The Traveller's Joy, it was found that a man answering the description of the one required had stayed in the house for four days, and had taken his departure by train on the same day that the bill was presented; and on that very day he had paid his account with a brand-new five hundred rouble note, receiving the change in small money. As the restaurant-keeper could not cash the note himself, he got it done at a money-changer's in the neighbourhood. The money-changer made an entry of the number of the note, and by that Danevitch was able to prove that it was one of the notes paid by the bank to 'Peter Pavlovitch.' This, of course, was an important discovery, as it conclusively proved that the man who handed the note to the landlord was the one who got the money for the forged bill. This was an important link, and another was soon discovered.

'From information received,' to quote the common police-court expression, Danevitch learnt that during the time the pseudo Peter Pavlovitch was staying at The Traveller's Joy he was visited daily by a pretty young woman, who, from her manner, style of dress, and general get-up, was supposed to be connected with the theatrical profession. Every evening Peter went out with her, then both returned together and supped, and after that went out again, and some time later Peter returned alone. The deduction from this was, assuming she belonged to the theatrical profession, that Peter took her to the theatre at night, brought her back to supper after she had done her work, and then saw her home to her lodgings. Fortunately, a very minute description of the woman was forthcoming, and from this Danevitch ultimately identified her as a Fräulein Holzstein, supposed to be of Austrian or German nationality. She was a music-hall singer, and had been fulfilling an engagement at a hall in Moscow, but had then left and gone to a place of entertainment in St. Petersburg, whither Danevitch journeyed without delay. He soon discovered the lady he was seeking, but was very cautious not to let her know that she was under surveillance. He had no difficulty in making her acquaintance, in the capacity of a man about town who enjoyed the privilege of being allowed on the stage; and on one or two occasions she deigned to accept an invitation to sup with him. He learnt from her that when her engagement terminated in St. Petersburg, as it would do in a few days, she was going to Vienna for a week, thence to Berlin for a fortnight, and after that to Paris to perform in a sensational drama at the Châtelet. Danevitch was now instinctively certain that he was on the trail, and he resolved not to lose it. Therefore, when Fräulein Holzstein took her departure from the Russian capital, he left by the same train, though she was not aware of it. He followed her to Vienna, from Vienna to Berlin, from Berlin to Paris. When she arrived at Paris she was met by a man who was at once identified from the description Danevitch had received as the man who had presented the forged bill for payment at the Moscow bank. The scent was now getting warm, but at this stage it would have been premature to have taken any steps calculated to frighten the quarry which was being so patiently shadowed. This man and woman were not the only actors in the drama, if, as was thought probable, they were in any way connected with the Count's disappearance; and Danevitch had yet to prove that there was any connection between that incident and the forged bill.

The man who had passed himself off as Peter Pavlovitch in Moscow was known in Paris as Henri Charcot, and by calling he was a theatrical and music-hall agent. He rented a small office not very far from the Châtelet Theatre; but, judging from appearances, he was not in a very flourishing way of business, although Danevitch gathered that at one time he had had an extensive connection. He had lost it, however, by inattention and shady practices. Fräulein Holzstein was, or at any rate represented herself to be, the wife of Charcot.

Another discovery was now made by the patient and watchful Danevitch. A man was in the habit of visiting the Charcots. He occupied a much higher social position than they did; but it was made evident he did not care for his visits being known to other people, for he always went at night, and invariably wore a cloak of such ample proportions that his figure was practically disguised, while a broad-brimmed, soft hat served to conceal his features. The Charcots lived in rather a poor quarter of Paris, not far from the Gare de l'Est. In this region was a very popular and much-frequented restaurant, largely patronized by the inhabitants of the neighbourhood. The Charcots invariably went there to dine. And when the strange man visited them, he generally went with them to dine or sup, as the case might be, on those occasions. They indulged in the privacy of a *cabinet particulière*, as it is called in France—that is to say, a private room.

One night the three went to the restaurant for dinner, and were shown into a snug cabinet, where a small stove dispensed a comforting warmth, for the night was excessively cold, and to protect the occupants from draught a heavy screen was drawn between the table and the window. When the coffee and cognac were placed on the table, and Madame Charcot and the two men had lighted their cigarettes, the waiter was dismissed and the door closed. Then the lady and her two companions, feeling under no restraint, freely indulged in conversation.

'Do you people intend to remain in Paris?' asked the stranger.

'Yes, I think so,' replied Charcot. 'I don't see that there is much to fear. No one suspects us, and it is not worth while giving up our business, such as it is.'

'You feel sure that your visit to Russia in connection with the bill is not known?'

'Perfectly sure. My wife and I managed the business too cleverly for suspicion to be directed against us.'

'But you mustn't forget that Michael Danevitch has got the matter in hand.'

Madame Charcot broke into a mocking laugh, as she exclaimed:

'Pooh! There is nothing to fear from Danevitch. He is a very much overrated man. All the wonderful stories that one hears about him are, I believe, invented by himself; any way, I am not afraid of him. It seems to me that it was impossible for anyone to get a clue in Russia. No, mon frère; the business has been managed too cleverly, and unless we give ourselves away we are perfectly safe.'

'I am not so sure of that,' answered the stranger musingly.

'But you've not heard or seen anything to cause you alarm, have you?' asked Charcot.

'No, no, not at all,' said the stranger, pulling his moustache and looking grave; 'but one never knows.'

'You are surely in a despondent mood, cher frère. The dinner must have disagreed with you,' madame remarked banteringly.

'The dinner was all right; but I haven't been easy in my mind for some time.'

'It's the liver, the liver, my dear boy,' Charcot remarked.

'What's the use of troubling yourself about shadows?' put in the lady. 'Haven't the Paris police used some of their best men, and yet failed to get a scent?'

'That's true,' said the stranger; 'but the affair must come to light sooner or later.'

'And what if it does?' asked madame. 'How are we to be identified with the case?'

'Not easily, if he is dead,' answered the stranger. 'The dead tell no tales.'

'Then, why in the name of common-sense should he live?' asked Madame Charcot, blowing a stream of smoke from her nostrils, and speaking with energy.

The stranger shuddered, and said:

'I'll have nothing whatever to do with his death.'

'You are chicken-hearted, man,' Charcot remarked. 'One word and an extra hundred francs to old Pierre, and every danger would be removed.'

'It might, or might not. Any way, I would rather not speak the word. The business has been bungled as it is, and instead of its proving a source of wealth to us, we only made a miserable hundred thousand francs between us, and it's hopeless to expect that we can get any more.'

'You should have played your cards better,' remarked Charcot.

'But who in the name of Satan thought that he was going to peg out as he has done.'

'Well, there is one thing we mustn't forget,' said madame; 'unless Pierre's palms are kept well greased, he'll let the cat out of the bag.'

'No, I don't think he will do that. He has already been well paid; and before I gave him the last thousand francs I made the old rascal sign a document, in which he confesses his share in the business, so that if he turns traitor I've got him on the hip. But, any way, it strikes me this is not a safe place, and I shall go abroad. No living soul suspects me, but one never knows what may happen; it's best to be on the safe side.'

'Well, you are a soldier of fortune,' said Charcot, 'and can march at an hour's notice; but we've got interests here, and unless danger really menaces, it would be folly for us to sacrifice those interests. What do you say?' turning to his wife.

'Oh, I think it's all right. If we have reason to believe there is any danger, we can clear out; but my own impression is that there is not much chance of our being suspected. Besides, we must have more money yet. Fate has been against us in that respect. We bungled in the beginning, and are paying the penalty of the error. By-and-by, however, we may be rewarded.'

'If you think so, you are much more of an optimist than I am,' the stranger remarked.

'You've always been disposed to look on the gloomy side of things,' said madame sharply. 'What is the use of meeting trouble half-way? We've played our cards, and must abide by the game. At any rate, you've done fairly well, and fortune has favoured you throughout your life. You've no just cause to grumble.'

'But suppose the game goes against us?' now asked the stranger.

'What is the use of supposing? It hasn't done so up to the present, and we've netted a fair stake.'

'But nothing nearly as much as we ought to have done.'

'That can't be helped. We've not lost, any way. But, for goodness' sake, don't mope like that. You make me miserable. We've bled our victim pretty freely, and though he has plenty more blood in him, if we cannot get it, we had better be satisfied.'

'It's tantalizing, nevertheless. Don't you think we might risk another bill here?'

'No; it would be too dangerous,' said madame.

'I would have nothing to do with it,' added her husband, 'Any attempt of that kind would betray us as sure as fate. No, no, mon cher; it can't be done.'

The stranger sighed, and resigned himself to the situation, for he was forced to admit that the arguments used against him were unanswerable.

In a little while the party broke up. The stranger embraced the woman warmly, and, shaking hands with the man, hurried away.

Charcot and his wife lingered for a while to smoke another cigarette, and for the man to consume an absinthe.

'Eugène is melancholy,' the woman remarked; 'but it's folly to weep over the milk that is lost. If matters hadn't turned out as they have done, we might all have raked in a snug little fortune. But, as it is, we haven't done so badly, and we're safe.'

'But not as safe as we should be if the Count were dead,' the husband remarked.

'That's true,' said the woman thoughtfully, while her pretty face took on a very wicked expression. 'But you know Eugène is far too sentimental. It doesn't do to be sentimental in a case of this kind. We've got ourselves to consider, and, having gone so far, it is downright folly to hesitate to take the final step, which would complete the work. What do you think?'

'I agree with you.'

'Then, you go and see Pierre, and give him a quiet hint.'

'I've a good mind to,' mused the husband.

'Don't spoil a good mind, dear.'

'But, you know, we should have to give the old rascal two or three hundred francs more.'

'And it's worth it; we can afford it. Better to pay that than allow a risk to remain that we can remove.'

'You are right—you are right, dear,' said the husband.

'And you will go and see Pierre?'

'I must consider the matter.'

'Tut, man! What does it want consideration for? We are agreed on the subject. Vacillation shows weakness. Hesitation may cost us dear. Make up your mind at once.'

'It's made up,' said the husband, after some reflection.

'And you will go?'

'Yes.'

'When?'

'To-morrow morning.'

'Good. That's a point settled, and my mind is easier.'

The man and woman now took their departure; but little did they dream that every word of the conversation which they and the stranger—who was none other than Eugène Peon—had uttered had been most carefully taken down in shorthand. Behind the screen a young man had patiently sat the whole evening, with note-book and pencil in hand. He was a trusted agent of Danevitch, who had made arrangements with the landlord of the restaurant. And thus the conspirators had been neatly trapped. Nevertheless, the story was not all learnt yet, and Danevitch considered it would have been premature to make any move or show his hand until he found out where the Count was concealed. Of course, a close watch was set on Eugène Peon's movements, so that no chance should be afforded him of slipping through the meshes of the net which was so cleverly being drawn around him and his companions in guilt. Charcot was also closely shadowed, and the next day was followed to an old house situated in the western part of Paris, outside of the barrier. It was a curious, ramshackle, tumble-down-looking building, mournful and melancholy in its ruin, and mournful and melancholy in its surroundings. At one time it had probably been the country residence of some rich person, standing in pleasant gardens, on the banks of a stream, and commanding a fine panoramic view. But that was in the long ago. The grounds were now a howling wilderness; the stream was a foul and stagnant strip of slimy water, from which protruded the decaying ribs of a half-sunk barge.

Within twenty or thirty yards were the grim and blackened ruins of a burnt-out mill that at one period had been a flourishing concern. The stream communicated with a canal a quarter of a mile away, and time was when barges came and went. The house had been the private residence of the owner of the mill, and he lived there for many years in contentment and comfort with his wife and son and daughter. Then misfortune overtook him. His daughter was accidentally drowned in the stream. Some time afterwards the son died of consumption. Then the unfortunate father gave way to dissipation, and neglected his business, with the usual result. At length the mill was destroyed by fire, and when the owner went to the insurance offices to claim the amount for which he had insured, the people refused to pay it, alleging that the fire was due to incendiarism, and a charge was laid against the unfortunate man; but he rendered it useless by drowning himself in the stream. And his widow did not long survive him; grief killed her. Then litigation ensued about the property, and as a legal heir could not be found, it fell into ruin and neglect. For many years a man named Pierre Mousson had been allowed to occupy the place, subject to the payment of a nominal rental. He was a rag-picker by calling, and a reputed miser: a low-browed, villainous-looking rascal, who had once served a term of imprisonment for nearly beating a companion to death during a quarrel about a franc, which he accused his companion of stealing from him. With that exception, there had been no charge against him. He was a big, muscular old fellow, with a suggestiveness in his appearance that he could be very dangerous in defence of himself or his belongings. His mother lived with him. She was an old woman, upwards of eighty years of age, and half imbecile.

To this place Charcot was followed by Danevitch and three French police officers, all heavily armed; and while Charcot and old Pierre were conferring together, the Russian and his companions entered, to the utter amazement of the two rascals, who were made prisoners before they could recover from their surprise. To both of them this *coup* must have been like a thunderbolt, but perhaps more particularly so to Charcot, who only the night before seemed to think he was in little or no danger. In a cellar or vault, below the level of the putrid stream, a man was discovered in a state of idiocy. He was lying on a low truckle bed, close to the damp, slimy wall, to which he was fastened by a chain and staple, and a broad leather belt round his waist. The vault was fœtid, and inconceivably horrible with filth and noisomeness, and the wretched man's feet and hands had been partly gnawed by rats. That man was Count Dashkoff, the once brilliant and handsome attaché, but now a pitiable and unrecognisable wreck. His hair was matted with slime and dirt, his beard unkempt, his eyes sunken, his face awful in its corpse-like appearance. His body was so emaciated that he was simply an animated skeleton, while the few rags that clung to his vermin-covered body scarcely sufficed to hide his nakedness.

As soon as possible, the poor fellow was removed in an ambulance to a hospital, the imbecile old woman was conveyed to an asylum, while Charcot and Pierre were hurried to prison. An hour later Eugène Peon and Madame Charcot were arrested, and before the day was out—thanks to certain letters found in Madame Charcot's possession—another man was being searched for. His name was Buhler, and he had recently acted as secretary to the Count, replacing a young man who had died. Buhler was a Russian, but had long resided in Paris. He was recommended to the Count by Eugène Peon. As was subsequently proved, Buhler had once before fulfilled the position of a secretary, but been dismissed for dishonesty. Since then he had got his living as a waiter, until he became a creature of Peon's. The strangest part of the tale has now to be told.

As most people know, the mode of procedure in France in connection with criminal cases is very different to that adopted in England. In a certain sense it partakes somewhat of the nature of the Inquisition. A functionary, who is known as a Judge of Instruction (*Juge d'Instruction*), with his assistants and clerks, subjects a suspected person to an ordeal of examination which few can pass through unscathed, unless they be absolutely innocent. The Judge is a legal man of wide experience, and generally with a very intimate knowledge of human nature. He is an adept in the art of cross-examination, and the 'suspect' must be clever indeed if he can outwit this examining Judge. Where several persons are under suspicion of complicity, they are confronted with each other, and very rarely do they fail to condemn themselves, and betray their guilt, if they are guilty, under the pitiless fire of questioning to which they are subjected. In this way the truth is brought to light, and piece by piece a story is built up. The story that was partly wrung from the prisoners in this case, and partly learnt from other sources, was as follows:

Years before the events already narrated, an Austrian named Schumacher took up his residence in Paris, with his wife and two daughters, named respectively Rosine and Anna, and a son, Fritz. The girls were at that time quite children. Schumacher, who was a cabinet-maker by trade, and his family ultimately became naturalized French subjects. As the girls grew up, they developed remarkable beauty; but this was allied to vulgar tastes and loose habits, well calculated to bring them to trouble sooner or later. At quite an early age they showed talent for the stage, and began life at a café-chantant. In the course of time Anna married a theatrical and music-hall agent named Charcot; and Rosine, who seems to have had numerous lovers, joined a theatrical company, and travelled for some time, but ultimately secured a permanent engagement at a Paris theatre. Soon after that, when she was only one-and-twenty years of age, and noted for her good looks, she made the acquaintance of Count Dashkoff. The Count was young, impressionable, foolish; the girl artful, cunning, clever. And there is no doubt she resolved to play her cards with a view to gaining a powerful influence over the Count. In this matter she was aided and abetted by her brother Fritz, though that gentleman was no longer known as Fritz.

At quite an early age Fritz had come under the notice of an old and rather eccentric lady, who sent him to school, fostered in him expensive tastes, luxurious habits, and led him to dream of future greatness. He received a good education, and spent four years—from sixteen to twenty—at the Lyceum. Unfortunately for him, his patroness died. It was then found that, though she had made a will leaving a million and a half francs to the young man, she was not worth a million sous. She had simply enjoyed a life interest in a property which produced her a handsome income, though she expended it to the last sou every year. Fritz had also taken her name of Peon, and had substituted Eugène for that of Fritz.

To find himself penniless was a great blow to his hopes and pride. His natural talents and the education he had received should have enabled him to have done well, but he hated work; he lacked energy, and so he set himself to live by his wits. He was a fascinating young fellow, with the power of attracting both men and women. When he made the acquaintance of the Count, the Count at once took to him, and Peon was far too clever to lose such an opportunity of benefiting himself; for clever as the Count was, he was rash and weak-minded in many respects, and no match for an unscrupulous adventurer like Peon, who arranged with his sister Rosine that they were to keep their relationship secret, and use every endeavour to trap the Count into a marriage. Rosine was quite equal to playing her part in this nefarious little scheme. Her fascinations proved too much for the Count, and when he found that she was deaf to all his entreaties, and proof against his costly presents, he came to the conclusion that she was a model woman, a paragon of virtue, a credit to her sex, and in an evil hour he married her. After that it did not take him long to discover what a terrible error he had made. The wife's rapacity for money, jewellery, dress, was insatiable, and her brother Eugène took good care to share her purse.

For a considerable time the Count yielded to the bleeding process tamely; and his secretary, Buhler, working in connection with Peon and Rosine, succeeded in drawing from him large sums of money. Of course, all this time the unhappy Count believed that his friend Eugène Peon was true and reliable, that Buhler was the most faithful of secretaries, and he began to yearn for some means of breaking the matrimonial bond with which he had bound himself. He found that Rosine had developed a taste for drink; he encouraged this in every possible way, and induced her particularly to consume large quantities of absinthe. The result was, she soon became a confirmed dipsomaniac; and one night, to the horror of the band of conspirators, she either threw herself into the Seine or fell in accidentally; at any rate, she was drowned. That was at a little village about twenty miles from Paris, where the Count had installed her, and where, under an arrangement with him, she lived as a single woman.

Peon, Buhler, and Anna Charcot and her husband managed to keep the news of his wife's death from the Count, and he was given to understand that she had taken herself off somewhere. A few months passed, and the conspirators felt the loss of their supplies severely. Then, in their desperation, they concocted a scheme which, for daring and wickedness, had not been surpassed for a long time. The scheme was nothing more nor less than the abduction of the Count, who was to be kept a prisoner until he secured his release by the payment of a large ransom.

The night of the ball was chosen as a fitting opportunity to put the plan into execution. Buhler wrote a letter closely imitating Rosine's handwriting. The letter stated that she had been away from Paris, but had come back seriously ill, and was then unable to leave her bed. She craved him to go and see her immediately, and promised that, if he would give her a sum of money down, she would go away and he should never hear of her again. If not, she would proclaim the following morning to all Paris that she was his lawful wife, and would also send an intimation to that effect to the Embassy. The note wound up by saying that a carriage would be in waiting not far from his house to convey him to her lodgings, and that he could easily get back again in an hour or an hour and a half.

This letter was delivered to the Count in the way that we have seen, and, unhappily for himself, he was influenced by it. He found the carriage at the spot indicated, and was driven out to the barrier to Pierre's house. Two powerful ruffians, who were to be well paid for their part of the work, had ridden on the box beside the coachman. When the destination was reached, the Count alighted, and then the lonely spot seems to have caused him to suspect that he had been brought there for some villainous purpose. He at once stepped into the carriage again, and ordered the coachman to drive him back to Paris. The two ruffians, however, seized him and dragged him out on to the road, where a desperate struggle took place. To put an end to it, one of the rascals struck the unhappy Count a violent blow over the head with a heavy stick, rendering him unconscious. He was then carried into Pierre's den.

For two days he remained insensible, and when he recovered it was found, to the horror of all the wretches concerned, that he was imbecile, but it was hoped that he would be all right in a few days. These hopes, however, were doomed to disappointment, and, being pressed for money, Buhler undertook to forge a bill, and Madame Charcot, who was then fulfilling an engagement in Moscow, was instructed to find out something of the Count's business transactions there; while Charcot went to Moscow, and, representing himself as Peter Pavlovitch, presented the forged bill at the bank and received payment for it. The money was, of course, shared by all concerned. Buhler, who seems to have been shrewder than the rest of them, having got his share, and possessed himself of such portable property of the Count's as he could lay his hands upon, took himself off somewhere, and managed to elude justice, though every effort was made to capture him.

As already stated, all this terrible story of fiendish wickedness was gradually brought to light by the Juge d'Instruction, and there was little doubt that, had Danevitch not succeeded in unravelling the plot, the unfortunate Count, who was becoming an expensive burden, and a menace to the safety of the plotters, would have been placed in a sack with a quantity of scrap iron, and deposited at the bottom of the foul and stagnant water opposite Pierre's hovel. Peon showed considerable reluctance to resort to this extreme measure, but Madame Charcot, who was less sentimental and more callous, had no scruples. She saw clearly enough that as long as the poor Count remained alive there was an ever-present danger, for if Pierre should get into trouble or die a revelation was certain. She influenced her husband to take her view of the case, and had Danevitch not stepped in when he did, murder would have been added to the other infamy. As it was, the careers of the wretches were brought to a close, and exemplary punishment was meted out to all of them. The extradition of both Charcot and his wife was demanded by the Russian Government, to answer in Russia for the affair of the forged bill—the man for having presented it and drawn the money, the woman for aiding and abetting him. But, of course, this demand was not complied with, as they had first of all to suffer punishment in France for their deeds there. After that they would be handed to the tender mercies of the Russian Government, and were destined to end their days in exile in Siberia.

For a long time Count Dashkoff remained in a pitiable state, but under tender care and treatment his health was gradually restored, though his mind was shattered beyond repair. Of course, he could not be altogether exonerated from blame for the part he had played with regard to his unhappy wife. But if he had sinned, he had also suffered, and everyone must admit that it was a terrible ending to a brilliant and what seemed a most promising career. Unhappily, neither his position, his wealth, nor his associations could save him from yielding to the fatal fascinations of vulgar beauty; and the disastrous results that followed doomed him to social extinction and a living death.

THE FATE OF VASSILO IVANOFF.

POSSIBLY very few readers of these chronicles know anything of the peculiarity—I had almost said iniquity—of the Russian law. The freeborn Briton, who in his own country may spout and write treason as long as it pleases him, and do anything that is not regarded as a legally punishable offence—and the law is very tolerant in this respect—is apt to open his eyes in astonishment when he goes on the Continent and finds himself haled to a prison-house simply because he has been jotting down some memoranda in a note-book, or mayhap has taken a snap-shot with a Kodak at a picturesque fortification which he thinks will look well in his album when he gets home. This arbitrary and high-handed proceeding is common to all parts of Europe outside of Great Britain. But though the liberty of the subject and of the foreigner is ever menaced on the Continent, and a simple indiscreet act may serve to bring the might of the law down on the luckless offender, this state of things is nothing as compared with that which prevails in Russia. It is a plain statement of fact to say that, of all the countries which boast of their civilization, Russia is the least civilized. The Russians themselves are a most hospitable people, they are clever, they make good friends and good neighbours; but their laws are antiquated, the method of government is barbarous, while the system of espionage which is in force all over the country would irritate a Briton into madness. And there is another aspect of the law, which, though it has been denied, still obtains in Russia, and that is the power of the law to keep an untried man whose guilt is not proved in prison indefinitely, and to subject him to such mental or physical torture that, to escape from it, the victim either confesses to a crime of which he is innocent or goes raving mad. To understand this, one must bear in mind that, while in our country a man is considered innocent until he is proved guilty, in Russia, as soon as ever he falls under suspicion, he is regarded as a criminal. He can then be thrown into a dungeon and kept there. If he persists in asserting his innocence, the law, if it can procure no proof one way or the other, will persist in regarding him as guilty, and will exhaust every means to overcome him, and if compelled to let him go will do so with the greatest reluctance.

This is really no exaggerated statement. A thousand and one proofs can be furnished in support of it. Danevitch, who was Russian to the backbone, was nevertheless sufficiently broad-minded to frankly admit that the laws of his native country left much to be desired. The case dealt with in this story will illustrate very forcibly what I have stated in the foregoing lines.

Vassilo Ivanoff was by profession an architect, with, as was supposed, a large and profitable connection. He was also an artist of some repute, and two or three of his pictures had found a place on the walls of the St. Petersburg

Salon. His friends sometimes rated him for devoting too much time to painting pictures that did not pay, and too little to his profession, which did pay. Ivanoff, however, was young, ardent, enthusiastic; a dreamer somewhat. He believed in himself, in his future. The world was beautiful, life was good, all men were brothers. Such in effect were his principles; but he forgot the maxim of science, which insists that theory and practice should go together. Ivanoff was a theorist, but he found it difficult to be practical. He had long been engaged to Maria Alexeyevina, who had the reputation of being one of the most beautiful young women in St. Petersburg. She was a member of an exceedingly good family, who, though poor, boasted of their noble descent. The marriage of the young couple had been delayed from time to time on the grounds that, until his financial position improved, he could not afford to keep a wife. It was a great disappointment to him, but he set to work with a will, and so far increased his business that he felt justified at last in appealing to Maria and her relatives that the marriage should be no longer delayed.

Among Ivanoff's most intimate friends was one Riskoff by name, who was said to be wealthy, and also exceedingly practical. He and Ivanoff had been to school together, and had studied at college together; but Riskoff, being considerably older than his friend, completed his studies some years before the other.

Ivanoff was in the habit of consulting Riskoff about many things, and he took him into his confidence with regard to the marriage; but Riskoff, knowing that Ivan was improvident, as well as impractical, strongly counselled him to delay the marriage. Ivanoff, however, was head-strong, Riskoff was persistent, with the result that the lifelong friends virtually quarrelled, and in the circles which they frequented it was a matter of comment that these two men, who had been like brothers, now passed each other by as if they were strangers.

Unable at last to control his feelings, Ivanoff pleaded so pathetically to Maria to consent to the marriage that she yielded, and they became man and wife. The marriage ceremony was one of those semi-grand affairs peculiar to the middle classes in Russia, and the festivities that followed were conspicuous by their magnificence and the lavish expenditure incurred. It was noted with much surprise at the time that Riskoff was not present at the wedding or the feast. It was known that there had been strained relations between the two men; nevertheless, everyone expected that Riskoff would have been invited. But, in spite of his friend's absence, Ivanoff was supremely happy; the beautiful woman for whom he would have laid down his life willingly, had she desired it, was his at last. What more could mortal man wish for? Life henceforth would know no pang. The doting couple would exist on each other's love, and not the tiniest of clouds should ever obscure the matrimonial sky. It was all very pretty. Others had thought the same thing over and over again, only to find, when the first transports of joy were past, that the married state is not quite the Elysium they believed it to be when they hastened to exchange single blessedness for wedded bliss. The blessedness is at least a known quantity, but the bliss is as often as not found to be little better than a delusive mirage. Ivanoff, however, did not concern himself about the future. With him, sufficient for the day was the evil thereof. Why think of the morrow when the to-day was so full of joy? That was his theory, and he lived up to it.

The first year of his married life, so far as was known, was a very happy one; the young couple revelled in each other's society. Their social functions were attended by people from far and near, for Maria's beauty was the talk of the town, and her husband was very happy and very proud. He believed that no such woman as his wife had ever walked the fair earth before. Romance, however, cannot last for ever, and joy must ever be evanescent in this wicked world. Vassilo Ivanoff was soon to prove the truth of this. Necessity compelled him at last to look into his affairs, and he found to his horror that he was on the verge of bankruptcy. Bills were pouring in upon him, but there was nothing in the exchequer to meet them with. It was a terrible state of matters, and to a sensitive man with a poetical temperament little short of maddening. From his ideal world he had suddenly to descend to the vulgar commonplace one, where the butcher, the baker, and candlestick-maker clamour for their little accounts; where summonses and writs run; and where brokers' men and sheriffs' officers have no bowels of compunction. It was a revelation, and a very terrible one, to Vassilo, and he had to face the fact that he was heavily in debt, with no means to meet his engagements. He could not apply to his wife's relations for assistance, for they were poor and proud, and, while unable to help him, they would not have hesitated to rate him for the disgrace he would bring upon them if his affairs should be made public, and there was every probability that such would be the case.

It was subsequently brought to light that in his distress he applied to various friends for temporary assistance; but, because they either could not or would not render it, his appeals met with no response. There is no doubt that his affairs at this stage of his career were in a very complicated state, and he realized for the first time that he was practically ruined; and to such an extent did it affect him, that one night he was seen at one of the fashionable and best-known cafés in a state of intoxication. Probably a good deal was due to his mental excitement rather than to the amount of stimulant he had imbibed, for he was a most temperate man, and rarely went to excess. Some acquaintances tried to persuade him to go home, but his excitement only increased, and he was heard to exclaim: 'It's a burning shame that I should be poor when there are thousands less worthy than I am rolling in wealth. I feel as if I could do murder on those who hoard their gold when so many are suffering for the want of common necessaries.'

This little outburst of passion and ill-will was no doubt due entirely to his condition; but it was a dangerous sentiment to give expression to in a Russian café, though, but for subsequent events, no importance would have been attached to it.

With some difficulty the unfortunate man was taken to his home, and it would appear that on the following day, when no doubt he, figuratively speaking, sat on the stool of repentance, he resolved, in his extremity, to appeal to his whilom friend Riskoff. With that intention he went to Riskoff's house, but found that he was out; and, as it was uncertain when he would return, Vassilo asked for pen and paper, and wrote a letter, in which he confessed that he had been living in a fools' paradise. But he had come to his senses, and intended to be more business-like in future. He wound up with begging Riskoff to lend him two thousand roubles, promising faithfully to repay the loan in six months' time. The following day he received this reply:

'DEAR IVANOFF,

'I confess to feeling some surprise, after the coolness there has been between us of late, that you should apply to me in your monetary difficulties for assistance. It is true I have the reputation of being a rich man, and it is highly probable that under different circumstances I would have accommodated you with this loan. But I flatly refuse to do so now. I do not consider you have treated me well. I was your warm friend at one time, and would have done anything for you; but you thought proper to trifle with that friendship, so there's an end of it. As you have made your bed, so you must lie upon it. I don't know that I am an unkindly man—indeed, I am sure I am not; but I feel angry now, and my heart hardens against you. I am truly sorry for your beautiful wife, and consider that you have done her a gross wrong in bringing her to this state of poverty. It is no use your writing to me or calling here again, as to-morrow morning I set off on my journey to visit my estates, and shall not be back for a month. I hope in the meantime you will pull through your difficulties, and that the lesson which poverty teaches will not be lost upon you.

'RISKOFF.'

It is easy to understand the effect a letter of this kind would have upon a sensitive and proud man. The refusal of his friend to help him must have been a stinging and bitter blow to Ivanoff. It appeared that for a long time he sat in moody and gloomy silence. Then he showed the letter to his wife, and it was a shock to her. Up to that moment she had not quite realized that things were as bad as they were. Allowing her feelings to get the better of her, she reproached her husband, and he made an angry retort, with the inevitable result that other harsh things were said on both sides, until the young wife, in a fit of petulance and wounded pride, hastily put on her cloak and bonnet and went off to her parents. Soon afterwards the unhappy husband also went out, and was absent for some hours. In the evening his wife returned, accompanied by her brother. She had repented her hastiness, and her people had told her that her place was at her husband's side. In the meantime he also had come back. He seemed in a much happier frame of mind, and Maria's brother witnessed a very pleasant reunion. He spent the evening with her. They had supper, and were happy. Before retiring, Vassilo told his wife that he was in funds again, and all would be well. He said the little cloud that had over-shadowed them had passed, and that henceforth they would live in clover. She asked him how he had managed to so suddenly bring about the change, but he laughingly replied that he couldn't explain just then, but would do so later on.

The next day Ivanoff rose betimes. He attended to some business matters, paid several of the most pressing claims against him, and at mid-day he and his wife lunched at a café, and in the evening they dined at their own house in company with some friends who had been invited. In the midst of the dinner the company were suddenly startled by the violent ringing of the large bell which hung at the gate. It was by no means an ordinary ringing, but suggestive of impatience and anger. The servant whose duty it was to attend to the door had not time to get down before the bell was rung a second time still more violently. The servant hurried to the door, and, flinging it open, was confronted by an important-looking official known as a Judge of Instruction, accompanied by his two legal satellites and two armed policemen.

'Is your master in?' demanded the Judge angrily.

'Do you mean Mr. Vassilo Ivanoff?'

'Of course I do. Why have you kept me so long at the door?'

'I came immediately, sir,' answered the frightened servant.

'Very well. Now, is your master in?'

'Yes.'

'Take me to him, then.'

'He is dining with some friends.'

'Blazes and thunder!' roared the official; 'what do I care whether he is dining with friends or whether he isn't? Conduct me to him. Men, follow me.'

The now speechless servant led the way to the dining-room, and close at her heels were the Judge and his men. As the intruders thus unceremoniously entered, Vassilo jumped to his feet, and his wife uttered a little cry of alarm, while the visitors looked aghast, for the presence of the Judge and the police with drawn swords was ominous.

'Sorry to disturb you,' growled the Judge gruffly.

'What do you want here?' asked Ivanoff sharply.

'I've come on business.'

'What business?'

'Very unpleasant business. I am empowered to search your house. Here is my authority.' He displayed a blue document bearing the Government seal.

Vassilo's wife had recovered her presence of mind by this time, and, going to her husband's side, she remarked:

'Oh, I suppose this is some absurd denunciation on the part of an enemy, for I am afraid that even I and my husband have enemies. But, happily for us, we never interfere in politics; we are content to lead peaceful lives.'

'It is not a question of politics,' answered the Judge, his gruff manner somewhat softening as he gazed upon the beautiful young wife and felt sympathy for her.

'Not politics!' she exclaimed, in new alarm, as she glanced at her husband's face, which had become very pale.

'No; my visit has nothing to do with politics.'

'Why are you here, then?' demanded Mrs. Ivanoff anxiously.

'I am here on very serious business indeed. Your husband is accused of—well, that is, he is suspected of murder.'

'Murder!' broke like an echo from the wife's lips, and all present started to their feet in deadly alarm, as if a bombshell had been exploded in the room.

'I am accused of murder?' gasped Ivanoff, looking dazed, as if he had received a blow on the head that had half stunned him.

'Yes, murder,' answered the Judge solemnly.

'The murder of whom?' asked the wife, a half-incredulous smile on her face.

'Mr. Riskoff.'

'Riskoff!' echoed the poor lady, as the smile gave place to a look of terror, and she fixed her eyes on her husband as if every hope she had on earth hung on the words he would next utter.

'Is he dead?' Ivanoff gasped, the dazed expression strengthening.

'Yes,' said the Judge, 'and you are charged with having murdered him.'

Ivanoff broke into a strange laugh as he exclaimed:

'This is positively absurd. Why, I was with him yesterday.'

'Yes, that fact is well known. You went to his house to see him?'

'I did.'

'No one was with him after you left him?'

'That I have no knowledge of,' moaned Ivanoff, as he passed his hand distressfully over his head from his forehead backward.

'Soon after you had taken your departure from his house he was found dead in his library.'

Poor Mrs. Ivanoff was now almost in a state of collapse, and would have fallen had not one of the ladies present caught and supported her.

The Judge had become stern and hard again. His assistants had out their note-books, and while one wrote the questions and replies in shorthand, the other took them down in longhand.

'You possessed a revolver?' asked the Judge.

'I did,' muttered Ivanoff.

'Where is it?'

'I—I lent it to—to my friend Riskoff.'

'You lent it to him!' exclaimed the Judge ironically.

'Yes.'

'Why did you lend it to him?'

'Because he asked for it.'

'Ah! very likely,' remarked the Judge, still more ironically. 'Why did he ask you for it?'

'He told me he was starting at once to visit his estates, and as he was without a revolver mine would be useful to him.'

'Why did you take your revolver to his house?'

The Judge glanced at his assistants as he asked this question, then fixed a searching glance on the suspected man's ghastly white face. Mrs. Ivanoff also gazed at her husband with staring eyes, and waited breathlessly for his answer. She had been led to a chair, and her friends were crowding round her; but with outstretched arms she kept them back, so that they might not obstruct her view of her husband, who stood motionless as a statue, save for the rapid rising and falling of his chest; and he was white as a statue, while his hands were clenched firmly together.

'Give me an answer, sir,' exclaimed the Judge angrily, as the suspected man remained dumb. 'Why did you take your revolver with you to your friend's house?'

Ivanoff was still silent. The assistants were busy writing. The Judge became more peremptory.

'Again I ask you: Why did you take your revolver to Riskoff's house?'

Ivanoff glanced nervously round the room now, and his eyes fell upon his wife. The pitiable sight she presented broke him down, and, covering his face with his hands, he burst into tears, and stammered forth, in a broken, emotional voice, the following reply:

'I went to my friend to ask him to lend me some money. I took the revolver with me, determining to shoot myself if he refused.'

'Or shoot him,' said the Judge, with a sneer.

'No, no—on my soul and before my God, no!' cried Ivanoff, raising his hands to heaven.

'Well, your friend was killed with a bullet fired from this revolver.' He produced a revolver as he spoke. 'Do you recognise it?'

'Yes.'

'Your name is engraved upon it. It was picked up on the floor of his room. Riskoff had been shot in the back of the head. The murderer, therefore, was behind him.'

A shudder ran through all present as this announcement was made. There was an exception, however. It was Mrs. Ivanoff; she sat motionless, as if she had been petrified. Her eyes were still fixed on her husband.

'Have you any money?' asked the Judge.

'Yes,' answered the wretched man.

'In notes?'

'Yes.'

'Let me see them.'

Ivanoff put his hands into his pocket, and produced a well-filled pocket-book. The Judge took it, opened it, and disclosed a packet of new notes. He examined them carefully, and consulted certain memoranda he had made in his note-book.

'Ah, this is very damning evidence!' he said at last. 'Riskoff drew from his bankers yesterday a large sum of money in notes. These notes are part of those he drew from the bank.'

Mrs. Ivanoff started to her feet now, and uttered a low moan of agony. Somebody wanted to support her, but she pushed them back, and, steadying herself with a tremendous effort, she said:

'Vassilo, what does this mean?'

'Some hideous mistake,' he murmured.

'I hope so. God grant it is so,' sobbed the unhappy lady. 'But I remember Riskoff's answer to your application for a loan. And now Riskoff is dead, your revolver is found in his house, and you are in possession of notes which he drew from his bank. Oh, my God, it's awful! It's too, too horrible! I am going mad!'

She uttered a suppressed scream, pressed her hands to her head, reeled and staggered, and fell fainting into the arms of some of her friends.

Apparently unmoved by this sad and pathetic scene, the Judge preserved his sternness and stolidity.

'So Riskoff wrote to you?' he asked.

'Yes,' answered Ivanoff in a mechanical way.

'Where is the letter?'

'I will give it to you. Come with me.'

The Judge motioned to the armed men, and they placed themselves one on either side of the suspect, while the Judge himself brought up the rear. In this order they proceeded to Ivanoff's studio, where, opening a bureau with a key he took from his pocket, he produced the letter he had received from Riskoff, wherein he point-blank refused to lend the money, and handed it to the Judge, who, having perused it, remarked:

'This is a fatal piece of evidence against you. You had better make a clean breast of the whole affair.'

By this time Ivanoff had somewhat recovered himself, and said firmly:

'I have nothing to confess. I am innocent before God.'

'Most criminals declare themselves innocent at first,' answered the Judge coldly. 'However, I have no doubt you will tell another tale before we have done with you. I charge you now with being the murderer of Mr. Riskoff, and make you my prisoner. Secure him and bring him along.'

The policemen seized the wretched man, and fastened his wrists together with a pair of handcuffs. He begged to be allowed to write two or three letters, but this request was refused, and he was taken from the house, still protesting his innocence, and without being able to take a final leave of his wife, who remained unconscious. In accordance with the mode of procedure peculiar to Russia, the suspected man was conducted to the office of the criminal prison, where he was subjected to another cross-examination, and the Judge of Instruction handed in his procès-verbal, as the French call it. The Judge, having finished his part of the affair so far, received an official receipt for his prisoner's body and left, while the prisoner himself, having been stripped of his clothing, and a prison suit allotted to him, was consigned to a secret cell, which meant that he would be kept isolated from everyone until the police had worked up sufficient evidence to secure his conviction. But in the event of their failing to do that, the prisoner himself would in all probability ultimately confess in order to be relieved from the awful horror of solitary confinement in a secret dungeon.

The case against Ivanoff seemed perfectly clear. The public condemned him from the first, for the evidence was so strong. There was the letter which Riskoff had written declining to lend the money Ivanoff had applied to him for. Yet within thirty-six hours of that letter being received, Riskoff was discovered dead in his own house. He had that very morning drawn from his bank a large sum of money. A portion of the money was found in Ivanoff's possession. Riskoff had been shot from behind. A bullet had entered the back part of the head, traversing the brain and producing instant death. The deed was done with a revolver, which was left in the room, no doubt by an oversight on the part of the slayer. The revolver was the property of Ivanoff, as proved by a little silver plate let into the butt, on which his name was engraved. On his own confession, Ivanoff had visited Riskoff. He knew that he was about to set out on a journey. He knew also that he would draw money from the bank for the purposes of his journey. Therefore, having been refused the loan he had asked for, he went to the house with the deliberate intention of killing his erstwhile friend and robbing him of his money.

Such was the construction put upon the case, and it seemed as if no one but an idiot could doubt for a moment that Ivanoff had committed the crime. And as a piece of strengthening evidence the words he had uttered in the café were raked up against him. 'It's a burning shame,' he had said, 'that I should be poor when there are thousands less worthy than I am rolling in wealth. I feel as if I could do murder on those who hoard their gold when so many are suffering for the want of common necessaries.'

All these things taken into consideration left no room to doubt that Ivanoff was a murderer. He had committed a clumsy crime, and left such tracks behind him that in a very short time the outraged law had him in its grip.

The tragedy aroused more than the usual amount of interest, as both Ivanoff and Riskoff were well known, while the prisoner's story was not without a certain romance which added to the interest. His poetical tendencies; his essays in art; his struggles; his wooing of the beautiful Maria in opposition to the sage counsels and earnest advice of his school-fellow and friend, Riskoff; his marriage; his monetary difficulties; his appeal for help to the man whose advice he had scouted—all these things afforded the general public subject-matter for discussion; they were so many chapters in an exciting tale, the end of which was murder.

As may be imagined, Mrs. Ivanoff's friends were furious, for, though poor, they were as proud as Lucifer, and felt strongly embittered against the man who had brought such disgrace into the family. Poor Maria came in for a fair amount of blame. She was told very bluntly that she had no business ever to have married such a man. These reproaches made her dreadful position still harder to bear; but when the first shock of the disclosure and the arrest had passed, she rose equal to the occasion, and startled everyone she knew by declaring her unalterable belief in her husband's innocence. This seemed to most people like flying in the very face of Providence. The accused man's guilt was so obvious that it was an outrage on intelligence to argue otherwise. But Maria Ivanoff was a young and newly-married woman. She had married for love. Her husband had always treated her with the greatest tenderness and consideration. Over and over again he had told her he worshipped the very ground she walked upon, and had done everything in his power to prove that he did not speak mere words. She believed in him; she believed in his assertion that he was innocent; and though all the world condemned him she would not. She was his wife, his loving wife, and she would try to save him. The poor woman saw clearly enough that she stood alone, and that she could expect neither sympathy nor help from anyone. Nevertheless, she was not daunted, nor was she deterred, and her first step was to seek an interview with the Minister of the Interior, or, as we should call him, the Home Secretary. It was not easy to obtain this interview, but thanks to the influence of a gentleman holding a high official position, with whom she was acquainted, she succeeded at last, and found herself face to face with the proud and pompous personage who was invested with such tremendous power that he could snatch a person from his doom even at the eleventh hour. To the Minister she pleaded, literally on her knees, for an order to visit her husband. At first the official was obdurate; but her tears, her eloquence, her distress, and perhaps, more than all, her beauty, softened him; and she left his bureau with a Government order which granted her a twenty minutes' interview with the prisoner. She flew to the gloomy prison, presented the order, and in a little while, in the presence of numerous officials, husband and wife met again; but it was in a dismal corridor, and they were separated from each other by an iron grill.

Although only little more than a week had elapsed since that cruel night when he was torn from her side, a wonderful change had taken place in him. He looked ten years older. He was haggard and ghastly, and no wonder, for he had suddenly changed the sunshine and brightness of the world for a pestiferous dungeon, far below the ground, where every movement of the prisoner was watched, where the walls were lined with felt to deaden all sound; where miasma rose up from the ground, and ooze and slime dropped from the roof; where no human voice was heard, for the stern warders were prohibited from opening their lips to a prisoner; where the food was horrible, and even the common decencies of life were not observed. No wonder that in such a place men went mad; no wonder that even in a few weeks youth and vigour were changed to tottering age.

Maria was startled and horrified. She would have thrown her arms about her wretched husband's neck, but cruel bars kept them asunder. Ivanoff iterated and reiterated again and again that he was innocent. He swore it by all that a Russian holds most sacred, and he begged with streaming eyes that his wife would use every means possible to prove his innocence and secure his release, otherwise he would in a very short time be raving mad.

When Maria Ivanoff left that awful place and got into the light again, she felt like one who had come up out of a tomb, where she had looked upon death. She knew that there was but little hope for her husband unless his innocence was made clear as day. She thoroughly believed his assertions; and she made a mental resolve that she would rest neither night nor day until she had exhausted every possible means to release him. Her friends were angry with her; everybody said it was an impossible task to prove a guilty man innocent. Her distress of mind may be imagined, not described; she told her friends she herself would go mad if somebody did not come to her assistance. Then it was that her brother, with what he intended to be the most pointed irony, said:

'You are seeking to do that which is impossible. Now, if there is a man in all Russia who can perform seemingly impossible deeds, that man is Michael Danevitch, the Government detective. Why don't you go to him? He might perform a miracle, who knows?'

Maria Ivanoff jumped at the suggestion, though it was never intended she should take it seriously. But she sought out Danevitch. She laid all the facts of the case before him. It was the first he had heard of the matter. It was the first time he had ever set his eyes on Maria. But her moving tale stirred him; her beauty won him; her tears found their way to his heart. He consoled her in a measure by a pledge that he would examine the case from every possible point of view, and communicate with her later on. Nearly a fortnight passed before she saw him again.

'There is one point, and a very curious point it is,' he said, 'that makes the evidence against the accused weak, and yet nobody seems to have noticed it.'

'What is it?' cried Maria, breathless with new hope.

'On the day that Riskoff was murdered, he drew from the bank three thousand roubles. Your husband had one thousand of this sum, according to his own statement, and the most critical investigation has failed to prove this statement false; not a rouble over and above the one thousand has been traced to his possession.'

'Yes, yes; go on,' moaned Maria, as she clasped her hands together with the emotion the detective's words begot. 'What has become of the other two thousand?'

'Ah, that is what I want to know. If your husband murdered Riskoff for the sake of the money, why did he only take one thousand roubles and leave two thousand? And if he left two thousand behind, what has become of them?'

Maria was holding her breath with that intensity of nervous emotion which one experiences when it seems as if some revelation is about to be made which means life or death to the listener. Danevitch remained thoughtful and silent. His eyes were fixed on vacancy; his lips were closely compressed; he looked absorbed and dreamy, as was his wont when he was unusually thoughtful. At last Maria could endure her pent-up feelings no longer, and in a husky voice she asked:

'What inference do you draw?'

'An inference which on the face of it seems to corroborate your husband's assertion of his innocence. Mark you, I only say it seems to do so. I do not say it does.'

Maria covered her face with her hands and wept passionately, but her tears were rather the result of hope than of despair. Her over-strained nerves were in that state when they were as liable to give way under the effects of joy as they were under the effects of sorrow. She fell on her knees at Danevitch's feet, and, clasping her hands in passionate appeal, implored him to save her husband. He raised her up, and said softly:

'I will do what I can.'

It was really remarkable that it should have been left for Danevitch to bring out that curious point about the money. All the police officials had overlooked it. They were cock-sure, for they believed that the case was so clear against the prisoner that it would not admit of a doubt. For some days after the interview with Maria, Danevitch concerned himself with endeavouring to prove if Ivanoff had had more than the one thousand roubles, but the most exhaustive inquiries, and the most rigorous search of his house, failed to get a trace of a single rouble beyond the one thousand which he had declared Riskoff had lent him, a portion of which he had paid away to his creditors. When it became known that Danevitch was engaged on the case, and that he was trying to find out what had become of the two thousand roubles out of the three thousand drawn from the bank, not only was public curiosity aroused, but to some extent opinion swung round, and sympathy was expressed for the prisoner. The police, however, were not moved, unless it was to become still more prejudiced against Ivanoff. They knew the power of Danevitch, and the influence he had in high quarters, and they were determined not to lose their prey. They therefore resorted to all the forms and pressure allowed by the Russian law to exact from the unhappy man a confession of his guilt. Beyond the facts they had already got together, they could obtain no other evidence. They knew that it was just possible those facts might fail to secure a conviction, whereas a confession wrung from the suspected man, no matter under what torture it was obtained, would be accepted without question. Such was the law in Russia.

Weeks passed, and it leaked out that the prisoner's obstinacy had at last been overcome. All that remained, therefore, to be done was to bring him up for trial, which would be a mere perfunctory business, and fix the date for his transportation. At last he appeared before the judges. The interest the case had aroused caused the court to be crowded to suffocation. When the prisoner appeared at the bar, those who had known Ivanoff previous to his arrest were shocked. They saw now an old white-haired man, with a haggard, hunted expression of face, and a wild stare in the restless eyes, as if he had suffered some tremendous mental shock. He seemed stunned, and as if he did not recognise anyone, and could not realize his position. Truly it is said of him who is sent to a Russian dungeon: 'He shall return no more to his house, neither shall his place know him any more.' The prisoner had been chained, tortured, and punished until he had become imbecile. But what of that? Was he not the slayer of a fellow-man—a scarlet-handed murderer who for the sake of a comparatively small sum of money had ruthlessly taken the life of his best friend? He himself had confessed to it, so that no one could raise up a doubt. The counsel for the prosecution seemed to have an easy task of it. He went over all the evidence that was known. Ivanoff had applied to his friend for a loan; the loan was refused, and the letter of refusal was read in court with a great flourish. Nevertheless, the prisoner went to his friend's house, taking a revolver engraved with his own name with him. What passed between them would never be known until the secrets of all hearts were revealed; but a little later Riskoff was found dead. Some distance from him was Ivanoff's revolver. The dead man had been shot with a bullet from that revolver. The bullet had gone through his brain. By an inconceivable act of folly, the prisoner left his revolver behind. It must have fallen from his hand when he was rifling the victim's pockets for the money, and he had forgotten to pick it up. Subsequently the money was found in his possession. Was ever there clearer circumstantial evidence in the world? But to make assurance doubly sure, there was the prisoner's confession, taken down from his own lips in his cell, by the Judge of Instruction; there it was for the jury to inspect, duly witnessed and attested and legalized by the great seal of the Minister of the Interior.

The prosecuting counsel sat down with the air of one who had performed a noble deed and scored a great triumph. The prisoner was silent, motionless, his eyes staring blankly into space, and his white face without any expression. Amidst a hush that was painful, the counsel for the defence—one of the ablest men in Russia—rose to his feet, and, adjusting his gown with professional gravity, said: 'I claim one of two things: either an immediate acquittal of the prisoner on the grounds of lack of condemnatory evidence, or an adjournment of the trial for a few days, when I shall be able to prove his innocence. As everyone knows, Riskoff, the murdered man, drew three thousand roubles from his bankers on the morning of his death. One thousand roubles only was traced to the prisoner. All the money was in small notes. I have here one thousand five hundred of the missing two thousand. There are witnesses present from the bank who will identify every note. We hope to regain the other five hundred shortly. These notes were not in possession of the prisoner, but of another man, the man who committed the murder, and who will yet be brought to justice. The prisoner at the bar is innocent.'

The effect of this announcement was startling and dramatic in the highest degree. Everybody seemed affected except the prisoner—he was unmoved; he continued to stare into space. There was a hasty consultation among the jury, and a hurried whispering with the Judge, who asked if it was true that Michael Danevitch had the case in hand. He was answered in the affirmative, and in the end he announced that no verdict would be given that day, but the prisoner would be put back for a fortnight.

Mrs. Ivanoff had not been present at her husband's trial. She was prostrated with illness, the result of long mental strain and intense anxiety; but a day or two before the case came on Danevitch called upon her and bade her be of good cheer, for her husband was innocent. Although she knew that Danevitch was not likely to make such a definite statement as that without warrant, she exclaimed:

'But it is rumoured that my husband has confessed the crime.'

'I have heard the same rumour,' Danevitch answered; 'but a confession that is wrung from a prisoner is not always reliable. But come, now, take heart. I told you, in the first instance, that I was much struck by the fact that only one thousand roubles could be traced to your husband. If he murdered his friend for his money, why did he not take the lot? It seemed absurd that, having committed the crime, he contented himself with one-third only of the amount he could have had. His story was that he visited Riskoff, who repented of his hastiness, and said he had written the letter of refusal when he was in a bad temper, and that had your husband not called, he was going to write an apology to him and enclose him one thousand roubles. As it was, he handed him the money, for which your husband gave a receipt as an acknowledgment that he was indebted to Riskoff to the extent of a thousand roubles. Subsequently, on Riskoff saying he was going to a gunsmith's to buy a gun and a revolver to take with him on his journey, your husband pulled his own revolver out and offered the loan of it to his friend. The offer was accepted, and soon afterwards the two men parted. On the first blush this story had the appearance of being very far-fetched, and calculated to tax one's credulity; but when I came to examine it in connection with all the circumstances, it presented itself to me as a statement of fact. Now I have no hesitation in saying that in the main, if not in actual detail, it is true.'

Mrs. Ivanoff heard this in silent thankfulness. She felt that her prayers had been heard, for night and day the poor woman had prayed that her husband might be proved innocent. Like most Russian women, she had an intense faith in the rites of her Church and the efficacy of prayer. Needless to say that after Danevitch's statement her faith was strengthened, for she knew he was not the man to express such a pronounced opinion without he had a very good foundation for it.

As he himself had said, when he came to look into the matter the case presented itself to him in a very different aspect, and the prisoner's story appeared probable. If that story was true, it necessarily followed that a third person must have been aware of the monetary transaction between the two men, and, taking advantage of the circumstances, had himself committed the crime for the sake of the two thousand roubles. It was upon that theory that Danevitch set to work. Riskoff led a bachelor life. His household consisted of two female servants and a man servant. On the morning of the crime the man had gone to the market. One of the females was an old woman who had been in the service of the family for upwards of fifty years, and had nursed

Riskoff when he was a baby; the other was a young girl of about eighteen. The old woman at the time was in bed suffering from an ulcerated foot, the result of a cut with a piece of glass on which she had inadvertently stepped. Consequently the girl—Olga was her name—was in charge of the house. She admitted Ivanoff, and very soon afterwards her master and the visitor went out, and were absent nearly an hour. Her master told her that he was going to the bank to draw some money for his journey on the morrow. The two men returned together. In about half an hour afterwards she opened the door for Ivanoff to depart. The murder was not discovered until the return of the man-servant. Then Olga went to her master's room to inquire whether he intended to dine alone that evening or whether there would be guests. On opening the door, she was horrified to find her master lying dead on the floor.

Such was Olga's story, and it seemed probable enough, but Danevitch was not satisfied. The missing two thousand roubles set him pondering deeply, and he had a private interview with the old housekeeper, and questioned her about Olga.

'Was Olga a steady girl?'

'Yes.'

'Had she a lover?'

The old woman thought not; at any rate, no one who came to the house. But did nobody visit her? Well, yes, a brother had been to see her the previous day. Her brother was called Andrey. He was a soldier stationed at Cronstadt, but was on furlough, and passed through St. Petersburg on his way to visit his parents, who resided at a place called Ladeinoe Pole, a little village lying to the north of St. Petersburg and the east of Lake Ladoga.

'Was the brother at the house on the day of the murder?'

The housekeeper did not know. She thought not. But, still, he might have been without her knowing it.

Pursuing his inquiries, Danevitch found that this soldier brother had left St. Petersburg on the night of the murder for his home. Danevitch followed him there, but found on his arrival that, his furlough being up, he had returned to Cronstadt. The parents were peasants, and, like most Russian peasants, living a miserable sort of life; but Danevitch learnt this fact, that quite recently they had been to a neighbouring market-town and purchased a horse and two cows, which made the neighbours quite envious; and, of course, such an event in so small a village was a nine days' wonder, and was much commented upon. The soldier son, who was so good to his parents, had no doubt provided them with the money. Danevitch, however, was well aware that, however dutiful and affectionate the son was, he could not save from his miserable pay a sum sufficiently large for the purchase of two cows and a horse. The pay of the Russian private is about one halfpenny a day. It is therefore impossible for him to save money. Having regard to these facts, the detective deemed some explanation imperatively necessary. But before he took his departure from the little village, it came to his knowledge that Andreyvitch, the father of Andrey, the soldier, was carrying on negotiations with a Jew—Weissmann by name—a nationalized German, for the purchase of a little plot of land in the village. Weissmann had had a mortgage on the land, had foreclosed, and was anxious to sell. At last a bargain was struck, and Andreyvitch paid one hundred roubles as earnest money. The hundred roubles was paid in notes. They formed part of the amount Riskoff had drawn from the bank. Thereupon Danevitch confronted old Andreyvitch with two armed officers of the law, and demanded to know where he got those notes from. The simple and ignorant old peasant at once answered that he had received them from his son.

'Where did the son get them from?'

The father understood that his son had found a roll of notes, and though he ought to have delivered them at the bureau of police, his strong affection for his poor old parents prompted him to commit a breach of the law by retaining the money and giving it to his father.

'Had the father any more notes?'

Yes, he had a roll of them. He produced them from a hole in the thatch of his house. They were carefully wrapped up in a piece of sheepskin to keep them from the damp. There were notes to the value of one thousand five hundred roubles. The old people had already spent about five hundred roubles in the purchase of the cows and the horse, and in clearing off certain debts. To the astonishment and terror of the old people, the notes were retained, and steps were taken to recover those that had already been paid away.

With the money in his possession, Danevitch returned to St. Petersburg, and handed it over to the defending counsel in time for him to make that dramatic *coup* in court. The next step was the arrest of Olga and Andrey. They were arrested simultaneously, though one was in St. Petersburg, the other in Cronstadt. The woman was terrified at first, but when she was confronted with the Judge of Instruction, she became sullen, and refused to answer any questions. Not so Andrey; he at once confessed that he had stolen the money, but vowed that he did not commit the murder.

'Who did commit the murder, then?'

He believed that Ivanoff did. All that he knew about it was what his sweetheart had told him; she said she had found her master shot. He was lying on the floor with a bullet-wound in the head, and on the table was a pile of bank-notes. She asked him to go to the room and take the notes, which he did.

Danevitch saw at once the discrepancies in this story. It was not at all likely that Ivanoff would have gone off leaving a large number of bank-notes on the table. So Olga and Andrey were each consigned to a secret dungeon. In the course of a week the discipline of the dungeon life had worked its effects on Olga, and with blanched lips she related the following story to the Judge of Instruction.

Her soldier lover had come to see her two days before the crime, and, unknown to her master, she had kept him in the house during those two days. On the morning of the crime, when her master and Ivanoff returned from the bank, she had to go into the room to take in some refreshments. She saw a great heap of notes on the table; she heard the conversation about the revolver, and saw Ivanoff hand his to her master. When the visitor had departed and she had closed the door upon him, she thought how easy it would be to murder the master, take his money, and let it seem as if Ivanoff had done it. Her fellow-servant was ill in bed; the man-servant was out. Her lover was at hand, and nobody knew that he was there. She hurried to him. She told him all. He was entirely under her influence. She went to her master's room again. The notes were still on the table, so was the revolver. He was busy making up his books, and did not seem to notice her. As she removed a tray containing glasses and biscuits, she secretly took away the revolver also. Then she flew to Andrey, gave him the weapon, and they returned to the room. She opened the door gently; Riskoff was sitting at the table, still writing. Andrey crept in on his hands and knees and shot him. He took the notes and the receipt given by Ivanoff to his friend for the thousand roubles, and immediately left the house. In six months' time he would be drafted into the reserve; then he and Olga would be married, and go to live with his people. Nobody would suspect them of the crime. The case was clear against Ivanoff; he would probably die, and there would be an end of it, for dead men tell no tales.

All would no doubt have turned out just as the wretches desired, had Danevitch not been brought upon the scene. The horrible story as told by Olga was corroborated in every detail, and the receipt given to Riskoff by Ivanoff was recovered. Andrey expiated his crime in the mines. Olga was sent to Northern Siberia for life. Ivanoff was released, but he was a mental wreck, and his loving and devoted wife had to place him in a lunatic asylum. Danevitch had saved him from Siberia, but could not save him from the living death to which a cruel fate had doomed him.

THE MERCHANT OF RIGA.

FERGUSON, TAUCHNITZ AND CO. were the largest firm of exporters in Riga. Their trade consisted of tallow, timber, corn, flax, hemp, flax-seed, quills, furs, etc. They had agents all over the great Russian Empire, including the far eastern and far northern parts of Siberia. The trade was principally with Great Britain, and it was said the firm employed a fleet of upwards of a hundred steam and sailing vessels, besides numerous small craft for the navigation of the Russian rivers.

Donald Ferguson, the head of the firm, was a Scotchman, naturalized in Russia, where he had lived for nearly forty years. He had married a Russian lady, by whom he had several children.

Ferguson enjoyed the distinction of being reputed one of the wealthiest merchants in Russia, and he was no less conspicuous as a prominent citizen, who had done an immense deal for his adopted country. For many years he had taken a very active part in all philanthropic movements. He had spent large sums of money in the improvement of Riga and its harbour; he had built and endowed a national hospital; had founded schools, and done much for the improvement of the lower classes, whose cause he espoused with great warmth and enthusiasm. He had earned for himself, from one end of Russia to the other, a name for fair dealing, probity, and honourable conduct. In the mercantile world he and his firm were held in the highest repute.

One night at the beginning of spring he was found lying dead in his private office at his warehouse on the quay at Riga. It was thought at first that he had died a natural death, that he had had an apoplectic seizure; but when the body came to be examined, there was conclusive evidence of his having been strangled. On each side of the throat were unmistakable signs of thumb pressure, and a post-mortem examination made it clear that strangulation had caused death. Such a prominent and well-known man could not have died in an ordinary way without his fellow-citizens experiencing a shock and being deeply affected, but when the news spread that he had been murdered it caused a profound sensation. Then there was a universal expression of regret, followed by a cry of indignation and horror, and a demand for vengeance, swift and pitiless, on the slayer of this good man. Naturally enough, the first thought was that he had been killed in order that some of his property might be carried off, but a little investigation soon put a very different complexion on the affair, and proved that the crime was mysterious, inexplicable, and remarkable. When many hours had passed, and no trace of the murderer could be got, Michael Danevitch was communicated with.

The warehouse of Ferguson, Tauchnitz and Co. was an immense block of buildings on the Grand Quay at Riga. The counting-house was in the very centre of the block, and faced the quay and the harbour. Adjoining, but at the back of the counting-house, was Mr. Ferguson's private room. This room was lighted by a large window overlooking a covered-in courtyard. On three sides of this yard were platforms provided with cranes and communicating with different floors, and it was here that carts and waggons were loaded and unloaded.

Frequently when business was very brisk, work was carried on all night at the warehouse; but the murder was committed in the early spring, when the export trade was only beginning, and the usual hour for closing up was six o'clock, and three o'clock on Saturdays. Mr. Ferguson met his death on Saturday, March 3, about seven o'clock. He was the last to leave the office, as he remained behind to close up some business he was engaged upon. It was then four o'clock, or thereabouts. He proceeded to his home on foot, being greeted on the way by many people who knew him.

His private residence was in the suburbs of Riga. His family at home consisted of his wife, two grown-up sons, and two daughters. He had two other sons, one being established in Hull as the English agent of the firm. The other travelled all over Russia, and was absent at the time of his father's death. On arriving at his home, Mr. Ferguson partook of some refreshment. He then told his wife that he had suddenly remembered something of importance he neglected to do at the office, and he would go back. He did not say what this something was.

Mrs. Ferguson asked her husband how long he was likely to be, and he answered that he would return in an hour, or an hour and a half at the outside. When he left his house it was a few minutes past five. At this time his sons were out. They arrived a little after seven, and as their father had not returned, they set off, expecting to meet him. Failing to do that, they went on to the warehouse. On arriving there they were surprised to find the main entrance door slightly ajar. They pushed it open and entered. The place was in pitch darkness, and there was unbroken silence. They naturally thought there was something wrong, otherwise the door would not have been open, but did not feel any alarm. They groped their way to their father's room. Darkness and silence there. In moving about, Donald, the elder of the two, struck his feet against something soft and yielding; he started back with a cry of horror.

'What's the matter?' asked James, the younger one.

'I don't know,' answered Donald; 'but I believe there is a body lying on the floor.'

The young man procured a light as speedily as possible. Then was revealed to them sure enough the sight of their father lying on his back, with his left leg up, and his right arm bent under his body. At first the sons thought he had fainted, but the peculiar and ghastly appearance of his face soon undeceived them, and when they touched him they had painful evidence that their worst fears were well founded. Terribly alarmed, they rushed out and sought assistance, which was soon forthcoming. The police were informed and a doctor was procured. The latter at once said that Mr. Ferguson was dead, that he had been dead about an hour. The time then was a little after eight o'clock.

'What has my father died of?' asked Donald.

'I am not prepared to say right off,' said the doctor, 'but I suggest apoplexy.'

Ferguson was a fine man. He was above medium height, well proportioned, muscular, and looked much younger than his years. His age was sixty-eight. He had gray hair, and a long flowing beard turning gray.

It was now noted by all present that the place was in great disorder. Ledgers, cash-books, and other books were lying in a confused jumble on the floor; papers and documents were scattered about in a very unbusiness-like way on the desk. A large safe was open, and its contents of papers and books had been hastily dragged out. These signs were suggestive of robbery, and the doctor was induced thereby to make a more thorough examination of Mr. Ferguson's body. For this purpose the dead man was carried into a packing-room and placed on a counter. Then the medical man noticed the marks on the neck, and having satisfied himself that he was correct, he said it was a case of murder; Ferguson had been strangled, and there were indications of great force and strength having been used. Several scratches were noticeable on the dead man's hands, and abrasions on his head, from which a little blood had flowed. These things had escaped the doctor's notice in the uncertain light, but were revealed on closer inspection. They were suggestive of a struggle, a fight for life, and this was corroborated by the way things were scattered about the room.

Other policemen were now brought in, and means were taken to ascertain to what extent robbery had been committed; but, strangely enough, on the desk was a cash-box. It was open, and contained a considerable sum of money. In the safe, so conspicuous that it could not have been overlooked by the eager eyes of a thief who had committed murder in order to rob, was a leather bag full of money. Apparently the bag had not been touched; the mouth was still tied up with tape. On Mr. Ferguson's person were many valuables, including money. It was difficult to understand how all this money should have remained untouched, if the deed of violence was the result of greed for gain. Why did the criminal, having committed murder, not avail himself of the hoard that lay to his hand? The investigators were naturally puzzled in the face of such an inexplicable state of matters.

In the meantime Ferguson's partners had been communicated with, and arrived on the scene as speedily as possible. When they had made an examination, they expressed an opinion that nothing had been taken away. That the deceased had been murdered was evident; that no robbery had been committed was scarcely less evident. Here was a problem at once.

Did the murderer enter the premises to rob, and, finding the master there, slay him, and having done this fearful deed, did he become so indifferent to his first intent as to go off without the blood-money, which was there for the taking? Having realized the extent of his crime, was he so appalled that in his eagerness to escape from the awful scene he forgot the gold? Such a thing might be possible, but it didn't seem probable. At any rate, it was hardly in accordance with the principles of debased human nature.

Mr. Tauchnitz, the second partner, who was intimately acquainted with the working of the business, and had been with Ferguson most of that day, could suggest no reason why the deceased should have gone back to the warehouse. He had never been known to do such a thing before.

As may be imagined, it was a dreadful night for the friends and relatives of the deceased; and the hour being so late when the discovery was made, the police were placed at a tremendous disadvantage. Riga is a large place. It is a populous and busy seaport, doing an enormous trade with other parts of Europe. An immense number of ships of various nationalities were lying in the harbour. As in all maritime places, there was a very rough element always prominent in the town, and after dark many shameful and brutal scenes took place. In addition to the sailors who came and went, there was always a large garrison, for the town is strongly fortified. So what with sailors and soldiers, and the nondescript hangers-on who are always to be found in their wake, law and order were not so well observed as in some other towns; and it will be understood that in the low quarters of such a place a criminal might find safe refuge from pursuing justice. In the instance we are dealing with, all the police could do was to notify the facts to their agents and spies as speedily as possible; but, necessarily, this was the work of hours; and through the long, dreary winter night—for, though nominally spring, the winter still lingered, though the ice had broken up—not much could be done. This, of course, was all in favour of the criminal. He had a big start, and unless he was absolutely a fool he would avail himself of his advantages.

The murder was supposed to have been committed about seven. The discovery was made a little after eight, but it was after nine—in fact, close upon ten—before the police really began to bestir themselves. During the time from half-past six to ten, several trains had left the town, vessels had left the harbour, and vehicles innumerable were driven forth in all directions. It will thus be seen that the murderer had many roads of escape open to him, and it could not be doubted that, if he was really desirous of saving his neck, he would avail himself of the chance he had to get clear.

That the murder was brutal could not be gainsaid; but on the face of it the crime was not one of the ordinary type. Danevitch's preliminary investigations led him to the conclusion that the motive which had prompted the deed was not robbery. That admitted—and there was evidence of it—the case was invested with a certain mystery suggestive of many things. Tauchnitz and the other partners were questioned by Danevitch as to why Mr. Ferguson had remained behind at the office on that fatal Saturday afternoon, when everybody else had gone. No satisfactory answer could be given to this question. Tauchnitz, who had been with Ferguson all the morning, declared that there was no reason whatever, as far as the business was concerned, why the ill-fated man should have stayed at the office.

'Was he in the habit of staying?'

'No.'

'Was he a methodical man?'

'Most methodical.'

'Was he given to making confidants?'

'No. He was very reticent.'

'But he bore the reputation of being straightforward, honest, upright, and just?'

'Unquestionably. He won the respect of all men. His character, so far as one knew, was without blemish.'

The members of the dead man's family spoke of him with profound sorrow and regret. He had proved himself a model husband, a kind, indulgent father, and though he was not communicative, either to his family or anyone else, no importance was attached to that. It was his nature to be somewhat silent and reserved.

Furnished with these meagre particulars, Danevitch began his work. From the first he formed the opinion that there was a deep and underlying motive for the crime, which, however, he did not consider was premeditated. And his reason for so thinking was this: A man who deliberately sets forth to slay another in cold blood generally provides himself with some lethal weapon. In this case the slayer would hardly have trusted entirely to his hands, unless he was a man of gigantic strength; for though Ferguson was well advanced in years, he was not only unusually vigorous, but unusually powerful. He was known also to be determined, resolute, fearless. Such a person was not likely to yield up his life easily. Consequently, anyone who was acquainted with him would surely have hesitated before engaging in a personal encounter. Of course it may be suggested that the murderer was an utter stranger, and knew nothing of his victim. But that was not the opinion of Danevitch, whose deductions were as follows:

Firstly, the murder was unpremeditated.

Secondly, the murderer met his victim by appointment. There were several reasons for thinking this. It was Saturday afternoon, and Ferguson had never been known to go back to the office after it was closed on Saturday afternoon before. His partners were emphatic in saying that there was nothing in connection with the business which required his personal attention at that time. No valuables having been carried off, so far as could be ascertained, and the confusion in which the papers were found, pointed to the motive being a desire on the part of the murderer to obtain possession of some document which certain circumstances and conditions, not definable at that stage, gave a greater importance to than money.

Thirdly, the victim and the murderer having failed to agree upon some point, and the former, perhaps, proving stubborn and immovable, the latter, in a sudden frenzy of passion, fell upon him, and got so much advantage in the very initial stage of the struggle that he was enabled to conquer with comparative ease, although the victim had made an effort to free himself from the death-grip.

Fourthly, the crime having been thus accomplished, and without forethought, the criminal, agitated and filled with fear and alarm, frantically turned over papers and books, and rummaged the contents of the safe, in his eager desire to find what he wanted. Finally, without discovering what he wanted to discover probably, he fled, and in his hurry and confusion forgot to close the door after him.

The foregoing was the line of reasoning that Danevitch pursued, but he kept it to himself. It was absolutely and entirely opposed to public opinion, and to the theories set forth by the police.

As is invariably the case at such times, some very wild suggestions were made; but there was a general tendency to believe that robbery was responsible for the crime, notwithstanding that nothing appeared to be missing. But public opinion did not influence Danevitch. He saw with his own eyes and thought with his own brains, and he came to the conclusion that he would probably find the key to the puzzle if he knew more of Mr. Ferguson's private life. There, of course, he was at once confronted with great difficulty. Everyone spoke well of the victim. His family believed him perfect. For Danevitch, therefore, to have breathed a word calculated to tarnish, even by suggestion, the fair fame of this merchant prince and good citizen would have been to incur odium and ill-will. But he knew human nature too well to run any such risk for the sake of a mere hypothesis. The problem, however, had to be solved if possible, and he proceeded upon his own lines to search for a tangible clue.

In taking up a case of this kind, one must ever feel in the initial stage that he is groping in the dark; but the trained mind at once begins to reason the matter out, and the very first thing sought for is a feasible and probable motive. Motive is the very keynote in all detective work, and when the motive has been more or less accurately guessed, the next stage is to try and determine who was likely to have been actuated by that motive. These remarks necessarily apply to complicated cases, where the mystery surrounding them seems impenetrable. When a man is found murdered in his house, and his valuables have been carried off, the motive is apparent enough. That is a crime of mere vulgar sordidness, and the motive is writ large. All crime is, of course, more or less vulgar, but sordidness is not always the actuating influence. Whether sordidness was or was not at the bottom of this Riga crime, it was difficult at that stage to say; but the inquirer was confronted with the remarkable fact that nothing seemed to have been stolen.

In spite of the many rumours of this, that, and the other, and the various opinions expressed, all of which were counter to his own views, Danevitch remained uninfluenced by them, and adhered to the opinion he had formed, which, as I have endeavoured to show, was based on sound reasoning. The many documents scattered about the office where the murder took place, although carefully examined by Danevitch, did not help the inquiry, as they were all business papers, and obviously had been discarded by the murderer as of no value to him. They had been dragged rudely out of the large safe, and scattered broadcast on the ground. Now, that was either the act of a madman, or of someone who was searching hurriedly for something he knew or believed to exist, and which he expected to find in the safe.

Danevitch's next step was to examine the contents of a large waste-paper basket that stood in the office. The basket was full of paper, torn and otherwise. He records that this proceeding of his was regarded as an absolutely useless one; but those who condemned it did not know what he was looking for. I have already said that, in weighing all the particulars he had gathered up so far, he formed an opinion that Mr. Ferguson had returned to his office to meet somebody by appointment. The reasons for this opinion have been set forth. One of his strong points was, having formed an opinion, which he never did until after much reflection, and a very careful examination of all details, so far as he could gather them up, he would not swerve from that opinion until he had proved it wrong; and as soon as ever he was convinced that he was in error, he was always ready to admit it.

It is strong testimony to the wonderful perseverance and patience of the man that every scrap of paper in the basket was carefully examined. Amongst the great mass he found some fragments which attracted his attention. One scrap bore the following words: 'Door at five.' It was a coarse, common enough paper, of Russian make, and the formation of the letters indicated that the writer was an uneducated person. With infinite trouble and pains he searched for the corresponding morsels of paper. And if anyone wants to know what a difficult task it was, let him fill a basket with fragments and shreds of paper, shake them well up, and then endeavour to pick out certain pieces and fit them together. No Chinese puzzle, complicated and ingenious as most of them are, was ever harder to do. But human ingenuity, coupled with exemplary patience, will accomplish much, and Danevitch at last succeeded in getting all the scraps together. Then he pasted them in their proper order on a sheet of foolscap, and was thus enabled to read the following:

'This is the last chance I shall give you. You must see me. I will be opposite your warehouse door at five on Saturday. We can then discuss the matter alone and undisturbed. You need not try to shuffle me off. If you fail to do justice to those you have wronged, I will make the whole affair public. So stay away at your peril.'

The importance of this discovery could not be overrated; and it not only gave Danevitch a clue, but proved him right in his surmises. The letter was clearly a laboured one. It was a man's handwriting, and the writer showed that he was not a practised correspondent. There were smudges and smears, and words wrongly spelt, although in the translation given above it has been deemed advisable to give the correct spelling, because in rendering it from the original into English, if the inaccuracies were retained, all sense would be lost to the reader.

It was very evident now to Danevitch that Ferguson had had a secret—the secret of some dark transaction, which placed him so far in the power of an uneducated person that he had obeyed the command to go to the office, after all was closed up for the day, in order to hold an interview with the writer, who neither dated his missive nor signed his name.

Of course Danevitch kept this discovery to himself; and he set to work with all the caution and skill for which he was famed to get some accurate and reliable information of Ferguson's disposition and his peculiarities of temperament. Everyone spoke highly of him—indeed, there seemed a general desire to belaud him, even beyond his merits, perhaps. In common phraseology, his word was considered as good as his bond. His acts were above suspicion; he was eminently respectable; he was charitable, though there was a feeling that there was a tendency to ostentation in his giving. In other words, he could hardly be ranked amongst that class of men who will not let their right hand know what their left hand gives. His marked peculiarities were an obstinately strong will, and his refusal to budge from a position he had once taken up. In this Danevitch saw a probable cause of the crime, when it was taken in consideration with the letter. The writer had not premeditated the crime, but had been exasperated into madness by Ferguson's obstinacy. This was the detective's first deduction, and as he advanced step by step it seemed to receive remarkable confirmation. Finally, as an estimate of Ferguson's character, he was regarded as a faithful and honourable husband, an affectionate father, a loyal friend. Amongst his workpeople he was looked up to with respect, if not with actual affection. He was, however, thought an exacting master, requiring the full measure of labour he bargained for; but that rendered, he could be considerate enough, and, in fact, did much for the physical and moral welfare of those who served him.

Danevitch had now reached a stage in his investigation when he could congratulate himself on having obtained a clue. It is true it was a slender one, but to such a man it was of great value. He found himself handicapped, however, by the very obvious disadvantage he would be placed in if he had ventured to suggest that there was a flaw in Ferguson's character—that he had done something or other which had placed him in the power of a person who was far below him in the social scale. Whatever the error was he had committed, it was clearly serious enough to draw him back to his warehouse after business hours, in order to have a clandestine interview with that person. As showing Danevitch's difficulty, it is worth while recording a conversation he had with Mr. Tauchnitz, who, as his name implies, was a German—a very shrewd, long-headed fellow, who held his partner in the highest estimation. Tauchnitz had been associated with Ferguson in business for a great many years, and he claimed to know and understand him better than anyone else outside his own family.

'Do you think, Mr. Tauchnitz,' Danevitch asked—'do you think that your late lamented partner had by some rash act compromised himself to such an extent with an inferior as to be completely in the power of that inferior?'

Tauchnitz looked as though a thunderbolt had suddenly fallen at his feet, and Danevitch had to repeat his question. The answer was an emphatic, 'No. Certainly not. I believe that Ferguson was absolutely incapable of anything of the kind.'

'You had the most perfect faith in him as a business man?'

'Indeed I had.'

'His business integrity was above suspicion?'

'Undoubtedly.'

'He concealed nothing from you you were entitled to know?'

'I have no hesitation in saying he did not.'

'Nevertheless, he was regarded as a reticent man.'

'About his own affairs he certainly was reticent.'

'Now, if I were to suggest he had been guilty of some dishonourable action, what would you say?'

'I should say you were doing the man a gross injustice,' replied Tauchnitz warmly.

'Had you free access to all the books and papers relating to the business?'

'Undoubtedly.'

'But is it possible that Mr. Ferguson had transactions in his office of which you knew nothing?'

'I won't admit the possibility at all,' answered Tauchnitz, waxing wroth.

'You must remember, sir,' said Danevitch severely, 'I have been instructed to try and unravel the mystery surrounding your late partner's death——'

'But I don't think you are going the right way to work,' interrupted Tauchnitz.

'That is a matter of opinion,' was the quiet rejoinder. 'But be good enough to tell me if Mr. Ferguson kept any private papers in his office?'

'Oh yes; I believe he did.'

'Ah! That is a point gained.'

'He had a large tin box,' proceeded Tauchnitz, in explanation, 'in his own room, in which he kept documents which did not relate to the business.'

'You don't know what was in that box, I suppose?'

'I haven't the remotest idea.'

'Could I have access to the box, do you think?'

'No; I am sure you could not. I have sent it away to his family.'

The opinion expressed by Mr. Tauchnitz of his partner's probity and honour was but a reflex of that which was held throughout the town—indeed, it is not too much to say throughout the greater part of Russia; for Ferguson belonged to that class of men who understand the art of getting themselves talked about. He had been wonderfully successful as a merchant, and his name was associated with so many public acts, and he had shown so much public spirit, so much enterprise, and had advocated so many measures calculated to benefit the working classes, that he had come to be regarded as a benefactor, a philanthropist.

It is interesting to dwell upon these points, because the sequel will be in the nature of a surprise. Danevitch's next step was to seek an interview with Donald, Mr. Ferguson's eldest son, who was also a partner in the business—as, in fact, all the sons were. Danevitch displayed great caution in dealing with Donald. His experience with Tauchnitz impressed him with the necessity of exercising all the diplomacy he was capable of exercising. Donald was much distressed by his father's sad end, and expressed a desire that no stone should be left unturned to bring his murderer to justice; but he evidently inherited his father's reticence, and displayed in a very marked manner the Scotch characteristic of so-called caution.

'Can you make any suggestion as to the motive for the murder?' asked Danevitch.

'It isn't for me to do that,' was the answer.

'We know that it wasn't robbery,' Danevitch said.

'I'm not so sure about that.'

'But nothing is missing.'

'As far as we know at present, nothing is.'

'Then, do you think something may have been stolen?'

'I won't express an opinion one way or the other.'

'Still, as far as one can judge, nothing was carried off.'

'So far as we can judge, that is so,' answered Donald; 'but the ways of thieves are incomprehensible.'

'Then, you think that the man who strangled your father was also a common thief?'

'I cannot say he was, and I cannot say he wasn't. We have the broad fact before us that my father was murdered. It is for you to try and find out why he was murdered.'

'I understand, Mr. Donald, that your father kept a box of private papers in his office.'

'He did.'

'Where is that box now?'

'We have it here.'

'Would you allow me to examine the papers?'

'Why?' asked Donald, evincing some surprise.

'Because it is possible—I only say it is possible—that I might find something amongst them that will help me in my inquiry.'

Something like an ironical smile flitted across Donald's face as he said:

'I don't think that is at all likely.'

'And yet, in the interest of all concerned, I should like to put it to the test. May I do so?'

'You may,' answered Donald, after a pause, 'if my mother and brother have no objections to your taking that course.'

The mother and brother being consulted, they gave their consent, subject to the two sons being present at the time of the examination. That being agreed to, the box was brought forth and opened. It was not unlike the tin boxes seen in lawyers' offices, but it was furnished with a peculiar and unusually strong lock, and as the key to fit it could not be found, the services of a blacksmith were secured, and after a great deal of trouble he got the lid open. The very first thing that Danevitch's eye fell upon was a packet, tied round with red tape, and marked in the corner very legibly, 'In the event of my death burn this packet unopened.'

By an adroit movement he seized that packet unseen by the others and slipped it into his pocket. He had a feeling that it contained the solution of the mystery, and he considered that, in the interests of justice, he was perfectly entitled to appropriate it and examine it.

It was the law of Russia, at any rate, that any papers or documents, however private, could be seized if justice was to be aided thereby. If he was mistaken in his surmise, then he would certainly carry out the dead man's request and burn the packet, and any secrets it might reveal to him would never be breathed to a living soul, and the packet once burnt, no one would be any wiser. The other papers in the box were looked through, but there was nothing found that could be of any use—nothing of a compromising character, and the sons seemed gratified and pleased.

An hour or two later, locked in his room at the hotel where he was staying, Danevitch opened the packet, and its contents revealed to him in a very short time an astounding story, and put him on the track of the murderer.

He found, as he had all along suspected, that Donald Ferguson, the upright merchant, the man of unimpeachable honour, the philanthropist, the public-spirited citizen, the defender of the weak, the faithful husband, the good father, had been very human, very weak. From the particulars furnished by the secret packet of papers, Danevitch gradually learnt the following story.

A woman named Blok had come some years before Ferguson's murder to reside in Riga. She had spent the greater part of her life in a small town in the far interior of Russia. Her husband had followed the occupation of a boatman on the Volga, being assisted by his two sons, Alex and Peter. He had two daughters, Catherine and Anna. The Blok family were held in high estimation by all who knew them. Although occupying but a comparatively humble position in the social scale, they were eminently respectable, and were regarded as hard-working, honest people. Of course, they were very poor, and were not able to make much, if any, provision for old age or accident. One day Blok and his son Alex were drowned. A steamer laden with convicts on their way to Siberia ran their boat down during a dense fog. At certain seasons of the year fogs are very prevalent on the Volga River. The breadwinner of the family being thus suddenly taken away, the Bloks found themselves without means of support. The youngest son, Peter, was then but eighteen, and unable to earn more than would suffice for his own wants. Under these circumstances, and acting on the advice of a married sister, who resided in Riga with her husband, who was a shipwright, Mrs. Blok removed to Riga with her two daughters, hoping that in the busy seaport they would all be able to find some employment.

Catherine, the younger of the two girls, was noted for her good looks. They were both pretty girls, in fact, but Catherine was exceptionally attractive. Moreover, she was bright, intelligent, and in a certain way clever. They had not been in Riga very long before they both obtained work in the firm of Ferguson, Tauchnitz, and Co. It appears that they very soon attracted the notice of Mr. Ferguson, who displayed great interest in them and improved their position very much. Six months later Anna fell seriously ill through blood-poisoning, caused by pricking her finger at the warehouse, and, in spite of the best medical advice provided for her by Mr. Ferguson, she died.

It was well known that Mr. Ferguson showed the greatest kindness to the family during their trouble, and all the expenses of the funeral were defrayed by him. Peter Blok, the only surviving son, came to Riga at this time to attend his sister's funeral, and it seemed that Mr. Ferguson took a fancy to him, and gave him employment in the warehouse, where he remained for about three months. At the end of that time he was sent on board a vessel belonging to the firm, and made several voyages, and finally he was placed in command of a river-boat employed in the Astrakhan trade.

About two years after Anna's death the Blok family, to the surprise of everyone, suddenly left Riga. The reason of their going, and the place where they were going to, were alike kept secret. For a few weeks before they went,

Catherine remained at home on the plea of ill-health. She did not seem ill, and nobody thought she was ill, consequently the astonishment of her companions was great, as may be imagined. It would appear that Catherine Blok was a somewhat remarkable girl in this way. She was exceptionally good-looking. She was far above the average peasant in intelligence. Had the opportunity been afforded, her intellectual powers would probably have enabled her to take a superior position in life—that is to say, superior to vast numbers of people occupying the same plane as herself. What is meant by this will be better understood if it is borne in mind that, as a rule, the Russian peasantry are more ignorant and more stupid, probably, than any other peasantry in the world. There are two main causes for this. The primary one is climatic; the secondary the powerful influence of the Church. The climatic conditions are a very long and terribly severe winter, which for a period ranging from seven to eight months prevents the peasant from labouring out of doors; in consequence of this he is reduced to much the same condition as hibernating animals. His winter life, in fact, is one of enforced indolence and inactivity. His house is insanitary, comfortless, and more or less filthy. His whole surroundings are calculated to debase and brutalize him. He has no intellectual enjoyments because he has no intellectual yearnings. He is content to live as his father and grandfather before him lived. What was good enough for them is good enough for him, he says. As regards the influence of his Church, that makes itself felt from his earliest years. He is taught to believe that he has no right to reason or question. Everything must be accepted in blind, implicit faith. Such education as he receives is of the most elementary character; and having inherited from his forefathers dulness of perception and a lethargic temperament, he does not concern himself about anything beyond gratifying his animal wants.

Of course, there are exceptions to all this. Among the teeming millions of Russia this must obviously be the case. The Blok family were a very notable example indeed, and Catherine was the head of them.

It presents a most interesting study in psychology—though it cannot be touched upon here except in a passing way—that Ferguson, the rich merchant, the broad-minded citizen, the respected husband and affectionate father, should have been irresistibly attracted to Catherine Blok, the very humble-born and ignorant peasant. Yet so it was, and when Catherine left Riga, she was influenced thereto by Ferguson, and her object in going was to conceal, as far as could be concealed, the fact that the merchant prince and the peasant girl had met on a common ground; and as is invariably the result under such circumstances, and in such a case, the meeting was fraught with terrible consequences to both of them.

When Mrs. Blok and Catherine left Riga, they retired to Valdai, in the Valdai Hills, in the province of Novgorod, to the south of St. Petersburg. Valdai was a very quiet, out-of-the-way place. Here the mother and daughter took up their quarters in a stone-built house, and enjoyed comfort, convenience, and luxury, which must have been very novel to them. They knew no one, and were utterly unknown; nor did they seek to be known or to know. At regular intervals, about once a month, a man visited them. He was in the habit of going to St. Petersburg. There he posted to Valdai, a distance of nearly a hundred miles. He could have gone quite close to the place by train, but he preferred the round-about way for reasons of his own. He invariably arrived at Valdai at night, and when he left he always went away early in the morning.

This sort of thing went on for something like three years. Then the visits of the man ceased, but correspondence passed between him and Catherine, who was the mother of a son about two and a half years old. The man had looked after her and her offspring, but not as liberally as he might and ought to have done. At last differences arose between them. These differences were traceable to Mrs. Blok. She thought, probably not without some justification, that her daughter had not been treated well. In the end the man exacted from Catherine a document, which was signed by herself and counter-signed by her mother. In this document, which was very artfully drawn up, and was not, it is needless to say, Catherine's composition, the man was represented as having been the victim of extortion and blackmailing, and the girl stated that it was impossible for her to fix the parentage of her son. It need hardly be said that the man who was in the habit of visiting Catherine at Valdai, and who took such extraordinary precautions to prevent his visits being known to anyone else, was Donald Ferguson, the merchant of Riga.

By means of the papers found in the packet which he took from Ferguson's private box, aided and supplemented by many and patient inquiries, Danevitch was enabled to work out the foregoing pitiable little story. During the time he was so engaged—it extended over several weeks—there was an outcry against him. He was expected to do so much; and those who ought to have known better thought he was doing so little. Of course the general public did not know that he was engaged in the business at all, and, with the pig-headedness and stupidity peculiar to a mob, they railed against the authorities, saying it was shameful that so popular, upright, and true a man as Mr. Ferguson should be strangled to death in a place considered to be so well policed and watched as Riga; and yet all the vigilance and all the cleverness of the police were powerless alike to stay the crime and to bring the criminal to justice when the crime had been committed.

'Our lives and property are not safe,' exclaimed the rabble. 'The police are supine; they are useless; they are in league with the knaves who prey upon honest citizens. If this is not so, how is it they have not brought Mr. Ferguson's murderer to book?'

This was the tone adopted by a low Radical anti-Government paper, which styled itself the organ and the mouthpiece of the people. Although as a rule it was opposed to the moneyed and privileged classes, it was pleased in this instance—because it gave it a *raison d'être* for hurling abuse at the heads of the authorities—to place Mr. Ferguson upon a pinnacle of greatness, and to speak of him almost as if he were a martyred saint. The rulers in Russia are peculiarly sensitive to, and intolerant of, criticism, and the authorities in Riga, stung by the lashings of the local organ, lunged out, so to speak, and grabbed the first person they could lay their hands on. The Russian police have a habit of doing this when driven to desperation.

In the Riga case the arrests were made so indiscriminately and fatuously that the unfortunate suspects, after enduring much misery and indignity, were set at liberty with a growl that was not unlike a curse, and the local paper hurled more thunderbolts at the heads of the police, and showed a disposition to canonize the murdered man at the expense of the authorities. During all the time that this agitation was going on, Danevitch was working slowly but surely at his task of drawing aside the curtain and revealing the mystery. But those in authority above him, in spite of his record, considered that he was fumbling in the dark, and looking for clues in impossible places. But having learnt something about Mr. Ferguson's skeleton from that packet of private papers, which was to be destroyed unopened in the event of Mr. Ferguson's death, he proceeded on his own lines. It would not be easy to give a reason that would satisfy all minds why Mr. Ferguson kept those incriminating documents; but no doubt he thought that as long as he lived the confession—if it could be so called—which he had exacted from Catherine Blok would effectually protect him against any further claims she might be inclined to make against him; because he could confront her with that document, and say, 'Look here, you acknowledge certain things. Here is your confession in black and white signed with your name. Therefore, if you don't leave me alone I will charge you with blackmailing me.'

This, of course, was the weapon of a cunning and artful man which he used to menace and subdue the ignorant, the weak and wronged woman. He knew well enough in his own mind that he dare not make that document public; for though part of the girl's statement might be believed, he would not come off scot-free, for would not people say, 'If you had nothing to fear, why did you get that confession from her?'

The first step which Danevitch took after reading the contents of the sealed packet was to learn something of the Blok family; and to that end, in the character of an old vagrant man, he visited the mother and the daughter in their retreat at Valdai. It took him some time to gather the materials for the little family history already narrated. Necessarily, before he could do that, he had to worm himself into their confidence, and he would not have succeeded in doing that had he not laid a pretended claim to occult powers, which enabled him to read the past and divine the future. With such people as the Bloks this went a long way. They, in common with their class, had a fixed belief in charms, fortune-telling and spells.

When Danevitch saw the infant son of Catherine, he exclaimed:

'Ah, that is a fine child! but alas for his future!'

'How so? What mean you?' asked the young mother in alarm.

'The child that knows not his father is ill-starred.'

'Knows not his father!' echoed Catherine, with flashing eyes, and a voice tremulous with indignation. 'How dare you say that?' she added menacingly, as she stamped her foot.

'Think you,' asked the pseudo-seer, 'that I can be deceived? I see with eyes different to yours. That child knows not his father, and never will know him, for he is dead.'

Here Catherine burst into tears, and between her sobs she exclaimed:

'It's true, it's true, it's true!'

'Of course it is,' said Danevitch, with an air of triumph.

Catherine recovered herself, and in an irascible tone said:

'No doubt you are very clever; but I doubt if you can tell me how his father died.'

Danevitch closed his eyes for some moments, and drew his hand down his face like one deeply immersed in thought. Then, suddenly starting up, he answered solemnly:

'He was done to death foully. He was strangled.'

Catherine was terribly distressed, and, sinking into a chair, she covered her face with her hands and wept bitterly.

Mrs. Blok, who was present, was indignant, and said angrily to Danevitch:

'Get you out of the house. You distress my daughter. She is an honest woman, and we do not want to hear anything more from you.'

'Be not angry, good mother,' said Danevitch. 'Your daughter questioned, and I answered.' Then, with sudden and startling abruptness, he asked, 'Where is your son?'

The mother's face grew pale, and, with evident distress and emotion, she said:

'He is dead.'

'Yes, one is; he moulders at the bottom of the Volga; but the living one, the living one, where is he?'

Mrs. Blok looked appalled, and drew back from this strange old man from whom nothing seemed hidden, and before she could answer, Catherine started up, passionate and flushed, and cried excitedly:

'Leave us, leave us! in the name of the Great Father, go! My brother is far away; hundreds of versts of sea divide him from his native land, and mayhap he will come back no more.'

'It were well for him if he stayed away,' remarked Danevitch with solemnity. 'But why grow angry with me, my child? I have sorrow for you; I have tears for you. You have been ensnared, deluded, cheated; and he who ensnared you and cheated you stood high in the estimation of men. The penalty of his folly was his life. He has paid it. For your weakness blood lies at your door, and nothing can ever wash it away.'

At these words Catherine uttered a smothered cry, and fell into her mother's arms, and Mrs. Blok, excited and enraged, screamed at him:

'Out of the house, I tell you, out of the house! You lay murder to our charge, and you lie. Go away! I command you in God's name to go.' She crossed herself as she spoke, and with her finger drew an imaginary cross between herself and the prophet of evil, murmuring as she did so: 'We are defenceless women; God shield us!'

The painful and dramatic scene affected Danevitch, and he silently withdrew; but he felt that he had got confirmation of his surmises, for as soon as he learnt the story of the family, he came to the conclusion in his own mind that the man who had deprived Ferguson of his life was Catherine's unhappy brother. The young fellow, proud-spirited and honest, flamed up at his sister's wrong, and, taking the matter in his own hands, had penned that letter to Ferguson demanding an interview. It was obvious there had been other letters written, because the writer said, 'This is the last chance I shall give you.' Who could have written that letter—which Danevitch so patiently pieced together from the shreds picked out of the waste-paper basket—if it had not been the broken-hearted brother? He knew Ferguson, he had been employed in the warehouse; and the great wrong his sister had suffered made him desperate—made him forget the social division which separated him from his sister's wronger. He went to him, not with robbery in his heart—he was too proud for that—not with murder in his heart, but to demand that the false statement which had been wrung from poor Catherine should be given up to him, and that Ferguson should recognise the claims the girl and the child had upon him.

It was easy to work out the sequel. Peter went to the office; he wanted the paper his sister had signed. He probably grew angry, and threatened his employer. The employer was obstinate, stubborn, perhaps insulting, until, stung into frenzy, the unhappy youth flew at him, and, blinded by his passion, Peter had crushed the life out of the man before he knew it. Youthful strength and fury made Peter Blok a murderer, although he may have had no wish to slay his victim. Finding, to his dismay, that death had silenced for ever the lips of his sister's betrayer, he made a frantic effort to discover the paper which he knew was in Ferguson's possession. But his search proving fruitless, he fled with remorse, no doubt, gnawing at his heart.

Danevitch says that never throughout his career did he start to hunt down a man with greater reluctance than he did in the case of Peter Blok. With the exception of Danevitch himself, no one suspected Peter, and as it had taken him some weeks to learn what he had learnt, the young fellow had got a start which would probably save him from the law's vengeance.

Danevitch, proceeding with great caution and tact, found out that Peter had been second in command of a river-boat engaged in bringing furs down from Astrakhan. The boat was one of the river fleet belonging to Ferguson, Tauchnitz, and Co. Three weeks before the crime in Riga, Peter obtained leave of absence in order to visit his mother, who was sick. As it was a long journey to where his mother was living, his lengthened absence did not arouse any suspicion. After the commission of the crime, there was every reason to believe he quitted Riga at once, and Danevitch satisfied himself that Peter had not gone to Valdai again. As he had already spent several days there with his mother and sister, had he returned he must have been noticed, for it was a small place, and a stranger was spotted immediately.

From what Danevitch had gathered during his interview, in the character of a gipsy, with Catherine and her mother, he inferred that Catherine, at any rate, if not Mrs. Blok, knew that Peter was going to see Ferguson. And from what Catherine said during the interview—'My brother is far away; hundreds of versts of sea divide him from his native land, and maybe he will come back no more'—the deduction was Peter had gone to sea. Being a sailor, he would probably experience no difficulty in obtaining a ship. And it was equally feasible to suppose that before going he wrote to his sister, telling her he was going far beyond the seas.

The most diligent and careful inquiries in Riga failed to elicit any sign that Peter had sailed from that port, and it was likely enough that he had made his way to some other port on the Baltic Sea, or else to Cronstadt. Anyway, he could not be found; and as Danevitch could not entertain a doubt that Peter had killed Ferguson, he felt bound, as a matter of duty, to circulate a description of him. This description, however, was not made public, but placed in the hands of the police and their thousand and one spies. A whole year passed, however, and no trace of Peter was obtained. The crime had died out of the public memory, though not out of that of the police. They have long memories, and thus it came to pass that one day it was announced that the supposed murderer of Donald Ferguson, the merchant of Riga, had been arrested in St. Petersburg. Although he had grown a beard and whiskers, he was soon identified as Peter Blok, and a ship's discharge upon him showed that he had come from New York to Cronstadt in an American ship.

Up to this point Danevitch had kept his knowledge of Ferguson's wrongdoing to himself, but now that Peter Blok was under lock and key he was bound to make the matter public. To the people of Riga it was like a bombshell suddenly dropped in their midst. Everywhere where Ferguson's name was known, it was a shock. At first doubts were thrown upon it; then there were open and loud expressions of disbelief; but the damning documents were produced, and could not be gainsaid. Then many sympathizers with Peter came forward when the reaction set in, and he was provided with funds for his defence; and, of course, at the trial the whole miserable story was pitilessly unfolded, until everyone knew it. It was a bitter, terrible blow to the Ferguson family. It redounds to their credit, however, that they unostentatiously made the most ample provision for Catherine and her mother, and the boy was provided for in such a way that it was not likely he would ever want, and it was stated that he was to be well educated and well brought up.

The trial of young Blok clearly proved that nearly all Danevitch's surmises and deductions were correct. The lad had heard through his mother of his sister's wrong, and from his sister herself he learnt how Ferguson, in order to save himself, had wrung from the unhappy girl that false confession, which, when she signed, she knew very little about. It was not until later that she realized how she had belied herself. Naturally that incensed her, and her brother—smarting with shame and broken pride—placed himself in communication with Ferguson, who at first tried to ignore him, until at last, threatened with exposure, he granted that interview which proved fatal to him.

When the story was all told, a revulsion of feeling in the prisoner's favour took place, and he received the mild sentence of seven years' banishment in Siberia.

THE GREAT CONSPIRACY.

COUNT OBOLENSK had resided in London for a good many years. He occupied a magnificent house in the neighbourhood of Hyde Park, where he lived in almost regal style. He kept a retinue of servants. The furnishings and appointments of his princely abode were said to be unique; and he dispensed hospitality with a lavish hand. He was known to be wealthy, to be a member of a very old and influential Russian family, and at one time to have held a high political position in his own country. Here the general knowledge of his affairs ended; but there were vague and ill-defined impressions in the public mind that he had been expelled or had fled from Russia owing to some of those political causes which in Russia count for so much, but which in most other countries, or at any rate in England, would be treated with contempt. But whatever the reasons were which had induced the Count to take up his residence in London, those who enjoyed his acquaintance and hospitality did not allow themselves to be troubled by them. In his own country he might have been regarded as little short of Satanic in his iniquity for aught that the throngs of people who attended his receptions, his at-homes and parties, knew or cared. The majority of mankind, in its concrete selfishness and gluttony, thinks little and cares less about the personal qualities of those who minister to its sensuous gratifications; what most concerns it is the quality and nature of the giver's gifts. Let these be liberal and lavish, and nothing more is asked. In Count Obolensk's case it was universally admitted that he excelled as a host, that his benevolence knew no bounds, and he dispensed charity with a cosmopolitan open-handedness which was worthy of all praise. Personally he was a handsome man, with the tact and refinement of a courtier, and the delicacy and deference of a true-bred gentleman. He was a widower, with two grown-up daughters—Catherine and Nathalia—both handsome young women; while at the head of his household, as general manageress, was an English lady, known as Mrs. Sherard Wilson, who, it was generally understood, had lived in Russia for a good many years. She was a fine-looking woman, of commanding presence and strong personality. She invariably presided at the Count's social functions, and acted as chaperon to his daughters. Of her history no one knew anything, and nobody seemed concerned about it. She was a power in the Count's household; and while she proved herself to be a woman of exceeding great tact, and one who had made the art of finesse a study, there was a tacit understanding that anyone who offended her ever so slightly could never hope to enjoy again the hospitality of the house over which she presided. Her general characteristics could be summed up thus: she was clever beyond the ordinary, well educated, a good linguist, a tasteful and excellent hostess; she was well informed, had more than a passing taste for politics, and appeared to have been acquainted with many of the leading statesmen of her time. Of them she would talk freely; about herself she was silent, and he would have been a bold man indeed who would have made the attempt to 'draw her out'; he would most certainly have come to grief. She was frequently absent from London; sometimes for a few days, at others for weeks. But where she went to, why she went, and what she did, were mysteries, and the eye of vulgar curiosity was unable to penetrate them. One thing was noted as peculiar: the Count's daughters never accompanied her.

One night at the end of January, a night that, according to Russian reckoning, was New Year's Eve, and usually celebrated with great ceremony in Russia, there was a reception at the Count's house. It was one of the few occasions when every nationality save Russian was excluded. It had been one of those trying and maddening days, peculiar to the English climate in January. A leaden sky, a choking, foggy atmosphere, a general gloominess, and a sense of that awful depression which seems to justify all the hard things said about our climate by foreigners.

However, the weather notwithstanding, there was a large gathering at the Count's house. Russians had come from France, from Germany, from Switzerland, in order to be present, and they made up a brilliant assembly. According to Russian custom, there was a religious ceremony first of all. Then followed a sumptuous repast, which included almost every known Russian dish. After that the Count and his guests retired to a large, heavily-curtained room, which, compared with other apartments in the house, was plainly furnished. It was lighted by three long windows on the east side, but each of these windows was screened by massive velvet curtains, which completely shut out the fog and the gloom, while a very handsome twelve-light gaselier, with tinted, rose-coloured shades, diffused a soft and agreeable light throughout the apartment. The floor was covered with an unusually thick carpet laid on very stout felt. Not only was this most comfortable to the feet, but it deadened sound, and the footfalls of the heaviest person walking across the room could not be heard. At one end of the room was a deep angle or recess, and placed diagonally in this recess was a large carved oak bureau or writing-desk. The entrance to the chamber was by a panelled doorway, closed by an ordinary door, masked by a second door lined with thick red felt or baize. This excluded draught as well as sound. And assuming that anyone had been prompted by curiosity or other cause to play eavesdropper, he would have needed an abnormally acute sense of hearing to have gathered any of the conversation carried on in the room. At the opposite end of the apartment—which was oblong—was another door, giving access to a small anteroom, the walls of which were lined with shelves filled with books.

On the evening in question, when the Count and his guests retired to the large chamber described, they made it evident that they wished to be free from any possibility of interruption, for the baize-covered door was locked inside, and so was its companion door. The curtains at the windows were so closely drawn that human eye could not by any possible means have discerned from the outside what was going on in the inside.

In this room the Count and his visitors remained for over two hours. They talked much, but not loudly nor excitedly. Nearly everyone smoked, until the atmosphere became heavy and thick, in spite of a large ventilator in the ceiling. But nobody seemed to mind the heat or the fœtidness. Every man appeared to be very earnest and absorbed with what was going on, and when he rolled a new cigarette, he generally did it in a preoccupied and automatic sort of way. Occasionally the host, who sat at the large desk in the recess, made notes, and read them out to the company. Sometimes what had been written was approved of; at others dissent was expressed, and discussion ensued. Then the writing would either be altered or allowed to remain as first written, according to the wishes of the majority.

It was two o'clock in the morning when the meeting broke up. Then the Count carefully locked his desk, and placed the keys in his pocket. He unlocked the doors, and led his guests to the spacious dining-room, where light refreshments were provided. A quarter of an hour or twenty minutes later a man very cautiously rose up in the recess in the room where the meeting had been held, and where he had been concealed behind the bureau or writing-desk, and, stretching his cramped limbs, he got out, crept towards the door, listened intently, and, having assured himself that the coast was clear, hurried out. At three o'clock such of the guests as were not staying in the house began to take their departure, a few in broughams, the majority in cabs, which had been waiting through the bitter night.

As most people know, the Russian New Year time is kept up with great festivity; and, hospitable though he was at all times, the Count, if possible, excelled himself on this occasion, and those who were privileged to be present went away with a feeling that they might have travelled the wide world over without meeting with such princely entertainment so delicately and gracefully dispensed. Host, hostess, and the host's daughters were always voted perfect, and very lavish praise was uttered when Mrs. Sherard Wilson was referred to, the English people particularly, who had the *entrée* to the Count's rooms during the festive gatherings, expressing their admiration in no measured terms.

At last the series of New Year receptions and entertainments came to an end, and there was a lull, which was taken advantage of by the Misses Obolensk to make their arrangements for a forthcoming ball, which they intended to give on a grand scale. The organizing of this ball was left entirely to the young ladies, as Mrs. Sherard Wilson was on the eve of departure on a journey to the Continent. The Count never concerned himself about his domestic or social arrangements; he left everything to the ladies. He was a great reader, and he wrote a good deal. Such exercise as he took he got either in his carriage or on horseback. He did not visit much, but was passionately fond of music, and went to all the principal concerts, and occasionally attended the theatres. His was a routine life; he was very regular in his habits, and one day was much like another with him. His position in every way seemed an enviable one, and apparently he lived in amity with all men. All those who knew him respected and honoured him.

About a fortnight after the gathering of Russians at his house to celebrate the New Year's Eve, Miss Nathalia Obolensk was descending the main stairway in a white satin evening dress, with a magnificent red camellia in her hair, for she was going to a grand concert with her father, and the carriage was waiting at the door. Coming after her was a liveried man-servant bearing a large tray full of tea-things, including a kettle of hot water, a silver teapot with the remains of the tea in it, a large jug of cream, and other things, that he had just brought from the drawing-room. He was a stolid, stupid-looking man, and suddenly he justified his looks by stumbling and scattering the contents of the tray over the young lady, tea, hot water, jelly, being poured over her splendid dress, to its ruin. She uttered a shrill cry of alarm, which quickly brought her father, Mrs. Wilson, and some of the other servants into the hall, and a very dramatic scene ensued. The shock to her nerves, and the realization that the mishap had not only spoilt her pretty frock, but would prevent her going to the concert, had such an effect upon Nathalia that she flew down the few remaining stairs, flung her arms about her father's neck, and fainted.

In the meantime the author of the mischief presented a very sorry spectacle. He seemed thoroughly ashamed of himself, and undecided whether to bolt at once or gather up the wreckage. Nor was his confusion and distress lessened by the torrent of abuse and passionate scolding which fell from Mrs. Sherard Wilson's lips. In the choicest of Russian she told him he was a 'dolt,' an 'idiot,' a 'fool,' a 'brute beast.'

'Leave the things, you stupid!' she exclaimed fierily. 'Ever since you entered the house, you have done nothing but make mistakes and smash things up. But it's the last chance you'll have of doing mischief here. In ten minutes you'll be out. Do you mark what I say? Ten minutes only, and if you are not out of the house, then the other servants shall kick you out.'

'If you please, my lady,' whined the man, 'I am entitled to a month's notice or a month's wages.'

'You will get neither, you blockhead!' replied the lady. 'Why, your month's wages won't pay for the things you've broken. And what business had you coming down the main staircase. It was your place to use the servants' staircase.'

'I'm very sorry,' moaned Andrey, 'and beg your pardon———'

'Sorry, you wretch! well you may be!' exclaimed the irate lady, unappeased by the culprit's penitence; 'but get out of my sight, and in ten minutes you must have left the house. Paul'—this to the head-butler—'Paul, I charge you to see the fellow is off the premises in ten minutes.'

With this peremptory command, she hastened to the reception-room, whither the Count had had his daughter conveyed. He was much annoyed, but did not allow his annoyance to find expression, as Mrs. Wilson did.

Nathalia had by this time recovered from her faint, and was bewailing her woe-begone condition, and the blighted prospects of an evening's enjoyment. Her father was urging her to go upstairs and change her dress, saying that they could still be in time for the concert, but she said it was impossible; she was too much upset, and had neither energy nor inclination to perform her toilet over again, notwithstanding that she had two maids to wait upon her. Finding that she was inflexible on this point, her father expressed a hope that she would soon regain her composure, and that he would see her at supper-time, and leaving her to the care of Mrs. Wilson, he retired to his study. In a little more than ten minutes the butler came to Mrs. Wilson and announced that Andrey had gone.

'Thank goodness!' exclaimed the lady. 'I am sure I never had such a stupid person in my service before. Whatever were you doing to engage such a dolt?'

'He came to me very well recommended, madame.'

'Then, those who recommended him ought to be ashamed of themselves; that's all that I've got to say. It's really shameful that people who call themselves honest should recommend incompetent servants in order to get them off their hands.'

'I am afraid it's frequently done, madame,' the butler remarked.

'That is no excuse.'

'I do not offer it as an excuse, madame. I agree with you that it is shameful.'

'But surely when you engaged Andrey you might have seen that he was a fool.'

'No, madame, I did not,' answered the butler with some show of wounded dignity. 'He seemed sharp enough at first. His stupidity set in afterwards. I fancy he is a little given to drink, though I've never missed anything, and have never seen him really the worse for liquor.'

'How long is it since he came here?' demanded the lady warmly.

'Just six weeks, I think.'

'That's six weeks too long. Take good care that the next man you engage knows his business.' The butler bowed and was retiring, when Mrs. Wilson called him back. 'Stay a minute. You are aware that I am leaving London to-morrow, and may be absent three or four weeks. You had better not engage anyone else until I return.'

'But, madame, we shall be short-handed, and——'

'I don't care whether you are short-handed or not. You will do as I tell you.'

Paul knew that it would be fatal to his interests to attempt to argue with his mistress when she was in a bad temper, so he made his bow and discreetly withdrew.

'Now, Nathalia,' said Mrs. Wilson, when the man had left them, 'away you go upstairs, change your dress and take your father to the concert. You know how disappointed he will be if he doesn't go, and as I am leaving to-morrow, I don't wish to see him miserable and unhappy. You know what a sensitive man he is, and though he doesn't say much, he feels the more.'

This appeal had its effect. Nathalia's ruffled feelings had smoothed down.

'Very well, I will go,' she said; 'but it's an awful nuisance having to change my things in a hurry.'

She rang for her maids, and while Mrs. Wilson gave orders that the carriage was to be kept at the door, Nathalia hurried to her room, reappearing in about twenty minutes, looking, as far as personal appearance was concerned, as if nothing had happened, though there was still an expression of worry and concern on her handsome face. Mrs. Wilson had already warned the Count not to settle himself to his reading, as he would still be able to go to the concert. He was delighted at this, for he did not like to have his plans changed, and he was waiting in the hall when his daughter came downstairs.

'Well, my dear,' he said to her in complimentary strains, 'you look charming in spite of the little contretemps. It's an ill wind that blows nobody any good, and I suppose the spoilt dress means a fresh order to your dressmaker, and a further lightening of my purse.'

He laughed pleasantly, and, following his daughter into the carriage, they drove off, and after all were in time to hear the best part of the concert.

When Mrs. Wilson and Nathalia appeared at the breakfast-table the next morning, they had both recovered from the previous evening's little annoyance. Mrs. Wilson was somewhat hasty-tempered, but she very soon got over her small outbursts, and her usual condition was a very pleasant geniality. During the breakfast, Andrey's gross stupidity was discussed and laughed at; and when the Count, with his usual generosity, said he thought that the fellow's wages should be sent to him, for, in spite of his stupidity, it was after all an accident, the lady acquiesced, and a little later she put up the amount in a packet, and instructed Paul to see that Andrey got it. Then she busied herself during the rest of the day in seeing that everything was in 'apple-pie order' previous to her departure, for whenever she was away the management of the household devolved almost entirely upon the servants. It was true there was an excellent housekeeper, and Catherine was exceedingly domesticated; besides this, she took an interest in the house. Nevertheless Mrs. Wilson was always under the impression that her absence meant disruption, and that it was impossible for things to flow smoothly while she was away. It was a pleasant little bit of conceit and did no harm, for while it gratified her it amused the others.

Dinner was unusually early that evening, for Mrs. Wilson had to catch the night mail to Dover. Her luggage—she never travelled without a considerable quantity—had previously been conveyed to the station, and, dinner over, she arrayed herself in a costly and handsome Russian fur cloak, and, in company with her maid, was driven in her brougham to Holborn Viaduct, and a first-class compartment was specially reserved for herself and her companion.

The weather was still atrocious. It was bitterly cold. There had been a drizzling rain all day long. The mud in the streets was of inky colour, and of glutinous consistency. People flitted by in the foggy atmosphere like ghosts, and not all the lights of London could relieve the gloom and depressing atmospheric effects. There were very few passengers that night; but amongst them was a man of medium height, attired in a long ulster and a seal-skin cap, the flaps of which were turned down until his face was all but hidden. He had taken a second-class ticket, and he and a young German, a commercial traveller, were the only occupants of the compartment. When Dover was reached, the rain was pouring down, the sea roared, and Channelward all was dark as Erebus. The man in the ulster, whose only luggage consisted of a hand-bag, hurried on board the small steamer, which was grinding away at the pier as the water tossed her up and down. Ensconcing himself in the shadow of the funnel, he watched the passengers as they descended the unsteady gangway; and having seen Mrs. Wilson and her maid come on board and retire to the cabin reserved for them, he dived down into the saloon and ordered supper, for he was hungry.

The crossing was an exceedingly rough one. The wretched cockleshell of a steamer which the railway company considered good enough to carry their passengers from one shore to the other was tossed about in a manner well calculated to alarm any but hardened travellers. The man in the ulster, however, was not affected. Having enjoyed a good supper, and washed it down with a pint of champagne, he produced from his case a very big and very strong-looking cigar, and lighting it, he battened his seal-skin cap down on his head and went on deck, where he remained until the steamer glided into Calais Harbour from the storm-tossed waters of the Channel. He remained until Mrs. Wilson and her maid had gone on shore. Then he followed, carrying his hand-bag. He went into the douane, had his bag examined, saw a porter deposit the lady's wraps and rugs in the first-class compartment of the carriage labelled 'Through carriage to Geneva,' and, that done, placed his own bag in an adjoining compartment, and as his second-class ticket had only been from London to Calais, he secured a first-class for Geneva, and was one of the very few passengers who travelled that dark and stormy night to the French capital of Switzerland on the shores of Lake Leman.

At the period of this story Alexander II. sat upon the throne of All the Russias. It is a matter of history now that he was one of the best-threatened monarchs who ever ruled over a so-called civilized people. His life had been attempted so many times that he lived in constant fear and dread, and the most extraordinary measures were taken for his preservation. He changed his bedroom every night; his palace was filled with soldiers; his food was cooked by special cooks, who were solemnly sworn in in accordance with the rites of their Church to protect him; nevertheless, their *chef* had to appear in the royal presence at every meal and taste all the dishes before they were served to his august master. But even then dozens of eyes watched the man's every movement, lest he might adroitly slip poison into the food. It was a terrible penalty for an Emperor to have to pay for his greatness, but, unhappily, it was a condition of things that had been familiar, more or less, to Russian rulers for a long time. Michael Danevitch was held high in the esteem of the Czar, who regarded him as one of his strongest safeguards. The famous detective's restoration to the Treasury of the stolen million roubles was a thing of the past, and was almost forgotten; but that exploit had made his reputation, and gave him an absolutely independent position as well as power. Since then he had displayed remarkable zeal and acumen. He had unearthed numerous dastardly plots, and had sent to the fortress of Peter and Paul, the prison of Schlusselburgh, and to Siberia, many desperate men, who believed that the way to freedom and reform was by the destruction of human life and the shedding of innocent blood.

It was well known throughout Russia at this time that a secret Nihilist organization existed of vast proportions, and that one of the main objects of the association was to bring about the death of the Czar. It is difficult to understand how men and women, claiming to be intelligent and reasoning beings, could come to believe that by slaying their monarch they would redress their own wrongs, real or imaginary. Everyone was aware that the moment the breath was out of the body of one Czar, another would step into his place. The cry of 'Le Roi est mort!' would be echoed back by 'Vive le Roi!'

There could be no interregnum for a single hour, unless a tremendous social upheaval took place and a republic was proclaimed. But while that is the easiest thing imaginable in France, it never has been possible in Russia; firstly, on account of the enormous extent of the country; secondly, by reason of the varied nationalities represented; and thirdly, owing to the want of anything like homogeneousness among the vast masses of people swayed by the Imperial rule. Nevertheless, to kill the Czar was the constant aim of thousands and tens of thousands of his subjects. It thus became necessary for his Imperial Majesty to take the most extreme measures for the preservation of his life. It was like a game of check and counter-check. The Nihilists watched with a thousand eyes; they plotted and planned with busy brains. But they in turn were watched; and the forces of the law were constantly at work against them. The Nihilists, however, had the best of it. They played the cleverer game. For in the army, the navy, in the law, the civil service, in all classes and ranks of society, even in the Church itself, they had their spies and agents, and those who were on the side of the Czar found all their energies, all their vigilance, taxed to avoid the mines which the others were ever ready to spring. Amongst the Czar's most devoted adherents and trusted followers was Colonel Vlassovski, who was in command of the military guard which night and day did duty at the Winter Palace, where the Emperor was then residing.

The Winter Palace of St. Petersburg is the largest residential palace in the world, with the exception of Versailles and the Vatican. Its length is four hundred and fifty-five feet, and its breadth three hundred and fifty. So spacious is its interior that as many as six thousand persons can be easily accommodated there at one time. It will be readily understood that to effectually guard a place of these stupendous dimensions from a crafty, cunning, and silent enemy, who gave no sign of his presence until he had struck his blow, was not an easy task; and the tremendous responsibility and ceaseless strain on the nerves which were inseparable from Colonel Vlassovski's position, transformed him in a few months from a comparatively young man to an old and haggard one. One day in the month of December the Colonel sent an urgent message by special courier to Danevitch, in whom he had the utmost confidence. The message was to the effect that he wished to see Danevitch immediately. The detective hurried at once to the palace, and was immediately ushered into the Colonel's private cabinet, where there were numerous telegraphic machines that placed the chief in communication with all parts of the city, and nearly every part of Russia. The Colonel temporarily dismissed his clerks and attendants when Danevitch arrived, and bolted the door so that they might be alone and free from interruption.

'I have sent for you,' he began, 'to make an investigation. Last night one of the guard in the interior of the palace, a young soldier named Vladimir, who was on duty near the Czar's apartments, was surprised by the corporal in the act of making drawings and plans of that part of the palace. He was immediately arrested, but made the most desperate efforts to destroy his papers. He was prevented, however, from doing this, and an examination proved them to be drawings to scale of certain portions of the interior of the palace. Vladimir, before he joined the army, was in an architect's office. On being questioned he grew sullen, and resolutely declined to say anything.'

'And what inference do you draw from the man's act, Colonel?'

'What inference! Why, can there be any doubt that he is a Nihilist spy?'

'Where is he now?'

'In the fortress of Peter and Paul.'

'What will be his punishment?'

'As a soldier on duty he has been guilty of treason—for it has been declared treason for any unauthorized person to make drawings or tracings of any part of a royal residence—he will therefore be summarily tried, and, if proved guilty, will be instantly shot.'

'And you think he will be proved guilty?'

'There is not a doubt about it. He was discovered making drawings of the palace without orders. When questioned, he declined to give any explanation, and his endeavours to destroy the plans showed that his motives were not innocent ones. Of course we shall try, before he is executed, to get information from him.'

'Which you will fail to do.'

'Why?'

'Because these Nihilists' agents will not betray their comrades.'

'But he will be tortured into a confession.'

'You may torture him, but he will not confess. The Nihilists are pitiless. A traitor to their cause not only destroys himself, but all those belonging to him, for the vengeance falls also on his family and connections, however innocent they may be. Vladimir knows that, and you may depend upon it that, punish him as you will, you will never wring from him a word of confession.'

'What's to be done, then?' asked the Colonel, in distress.

'Let the fellow go free. Reinstate him.'

The Colonel stared in blank amazement; then he broke into a mocking laugh, as he asked caustically:

'Have you taken leave of your senses, Danevitch, or become a fool?'

'Neither.'

'Explain, then. What do you mean?'

'A dead man cannot speak; a live one can. Put Vladimir back into his place again, and leave the rest to me. He is a key, as it were. With him you may open many doors. Kill him, and the doors will remain closed against you.'

A new light broke on the Colonel. He looked thoughtful, and for some moments remained silent; then he remarked:

'But there are a thousand difficulties now in the way of setting him free.'

'Under ordinary circumstances, yes. But in this case a stroke of the Czar's pen can do it. You are in the Emperor's confidence. Explain to him what is required, and in two hours' time Vladimir can be back in the palace again. Then he will betray himself by some act, some sign; on the other hand, all the resources of Peter and Paul will fail to wring from him a word that will be of use to us.'

The Colonel saw the force of the argument, and said that he would lose no time in procuring an interview with the Czar. That was done; result, in the course of the day Vladimir was reinstated. He had been told that on investigation the authorities were not disposed to take a serious view of his offence. He was a young soldier, and of value to the State, and another chance would be given to him. So he was severely reprimanded, and brought back to the palace, much to his own amazement. He had considered himself doomed, and his restoration to liberty puzzled him; but he was too obtuse to divine the real cause, and he did not dream how every movement of his was being watched. Some days later he justified Danevitch's prediction. Being off duty, he went into the city, and, making his way to one of the quays on the Neva, now frozen over, he met a young woman, and was seen to hand her a paper. They did not confer together long, and when they separated, the young woman was followed to her home by Danevitch. Had he been a mere subordinate of the chief of police, he would have been compelled to have reported this incident, with the result that a domiciliary visit would have been paid to the house, and as a natural corollary of that action, assuming that, as was suspected, she was in conspiracy with others, her co-conspirators would be warned, and justice might be defeated. Danevitch was aware of all this, and, like a well-trained sleuth-hound, he did not attempt to strike his quarry until he was absolutely sure of it. He knew that at the most Vladimir could be but a humble instrument; behind him and influencing him were more powerful foes to the State. These were the people he wanted to lay his hands upon. It was no use casting his net for the little fish only; it was the big ones he fished for. After witnessing the meeting between Vladimir and the young woman, Danevitch had another interview with Colonel Vlassovski, during which he informed him that Vladimir was dangerous, and should be closely watched, though care was to be taken not to allow him to suspect that he was being watched. A few days later Danevitch again went to the Colonel, and said:

'I believe I am in the way of bringing to light a great conspiracy, and I am going to leave Russia for a time.'

'But how in the world can you bring the conspiracy to light if you are out of Russia?' asked the Colonel in alarm. 'Your presence is required here if there is danger.'

'No. I can do better elsewhere. There is danger, but it does not threaten immediately. The head of the movement is not in Russia. If the head is destroyed, the tail is sure to perish. I am going to seek the head. The tail, which is here, can be trampled on afterwards.'

'Where is the head, do you think?'

'I don't exactly know. In Berlin, perhaps; in Geneva, Paris, London.'

'Ah, Geneva and London!' exclaimed the Colonel angrily. 'Those two places are responsible for much. They offer refuge to the vilest of wretches so long as they claim to be merely political offenders. Like charity, that term covers a multitude of sins, and under its protecting influence some of the most desperate and bloodthirsty scoundrels who ever walked the earth have found sanctuary.'

'True,' answered Danevitch; 'but we cannot help that. There are ways and means, however, of dragging rascals of that kind from their sanctuary. I am going to see what can be done.'

'You will keep in touch with me,' the Colonel remarked.

'Certainly I will. In the meantime, draw a closer cordon round the palace, and let no one sleep. You must not forget, Colonel, that the plots we are called upon to checkmate are hatched not in Russia, but in some of the European capitals. The poor fools who execute the work here are mere tools. We want to lay hands on the principals, the people who from a safe retreat supply the money. Stop the money, and the tools will cease to work.'

All that Danevitch urged was undeniable. The Colonel knew it. Those in power knew it. The Czar himself knew it. But hitherto the great difficulty had been to secure the principals. The prisons were full of the hirelings; hundreds and hundreds of them dragged out their miserable lives in Siberia; but still the danger was not lessened, for as long as ever money was forthcoming men and women could always be found ready and willing to pit their liberties and lives against the forces of the Government. It cannot be denied that amongst them were some, many perhaps, who were not mere hirelings, but were prompted by mistaken notions of patriotism; they were generally young people led away by false sentiments and misplaced enthusiasm. It had been found, too, that young women, for the sake of men they loved, were willing to risk all they held sacred on earth at the bidding of their lovers. They were the most pliant, the most willing tools; but they were also the weak links in the chain. They acted with less caution than men. They went to work blindly, and with a stupid recklessness which was bound sooner or later to betray them. Danevitch had a favourite theory, or saying, to the effect that, given a plot with a woman in it, all you had to do was to find out the woman, and you would discover the plot. In this case he had found out the woman. The one who met Vladimir on the quay by the Neva was a book-keeper in a general store. She shared apartments with another young woman in a poor part of the town. At night, when her duties for the day were over, she was in the habit of attending secret meetings, mostly of women, with a sprinkling of men amongst them. One of these women was a Madame Petrarna. She was an organizer and a leader. Vladimir's sweetheart was in high favour with her. Petrarna was the wife of a man who was in exile as 'a danger to the State.' He had been arrested as a suspicious personage, and though nothing was actually proved against him, he was sent to Siberia.

Having learnt so much about Vladimir's sweetheart, Danevitch devoted his attention to Petrarna. He had made the ways of Nihilists a study, and though they had their spies everywhere, he was often able to outwit them, and he succeeded in getting around him a little band of devoted agents who were ready to go anywhere and do anything at his bidding. Amongst these agents was a clever little woman, and she succeeded one night in gaining admission to a meeting over which Petrarna was presiding. The president spoke of the arrest and release of Vladimir, and how he had been able, after all, to hand to his sweetheart and their colleague certain drawings of the palace, which would be invaluable to them in their work.

This and many other things the agent learnt, and conveyed the intelligence to her employer Danevitch, whereby he was induced to go abroad to search for the head, as he had told Colonel Vlassovsky.

Weeks passed, and Danevitch was in Geneva. The weather was bitter. The winter had set in very early, and so far had been unusually severe. At this period there were something like five thousand Russians living in Geneva and its environs. The majority of these Russians were Nihilists. One night, although a black *bise* was blowing, filling the air with spiculæ of ice, and freezing to the marrow all those who ventured into the streets, various individuals—singly, in twos and threes—wended their way to an old building in a lonely side-street not far from the Gare. It was a short street, and devoted principally to warehouses, which were closed at night; consequently it was badly lighted, and after business hours practically deserted. The entrance to one of these buildings was by an arched gateway, closed with massive wooden gates, in one side of which was a small door to allow the workpeople to pass in and out when the gates were closed. On the night in question, this little door opened and shut many times; each time it opened, somebody entered after having been asked for a sign, a counter-sign, and a password. Without these none could enter. At length there were nearly fifty persons present. Then the gate was barred and guarded. In a long back upper room, the windows of which were so screened that not a ray of light could escape, a meeting was held. It was a Nihilist meeting, and the chief thing discussed was the destruction of the Czar of Russia. Reports were also read from many 'Centres,' detailing the progress that was made in what was called 'The Revolutionary Movement.' One man brought with him a great quantity of seditious literature in Russian. It had been printed by a secret press in the town. The meeting was presided over by a lady; that lady was Mrs. Sherard Wilson. She distributed a considerable amount of money among those present, and talked the most violent of language. She was a fluent and eloquent speaker, and swayed the meeting as reeds are swayed by the wind.

A long discussion followed, and many things were settled. Amongst others, the date of the 'Czar's execution' was fixed; and Mrs. Sherard announced that she would leave for St. Petersburg in a very few days to hasten the 'good cause.'

The meeting was orderly, business-like, and quiet. Every person present—man and woman—seemed terribly in earnest, and there was a grim severity in their tone and speech which argued unrelenting bitterness and hatred against the ruler of Russia and many prominent members of his council, all of whom were marked for swift and sudden death. It was midnight when the meeting broke up. Silently the people came, silently they departed; and when the last one had gone, and the door in the gate had been locked, a death-like stillness reigned in the deserted warehouse. Outside, the black *bise* roared, bringing from the lake and the surrounding hills fierce storms of hail.

A little later the door of the gate opened noiselessly, and a man, having glanced carefully up and down to see that no one was in sight, passed out, locked the door after him, and disappeared in the darkness of the night.

That man was Michael Danevitch. He had heard all that had passed at the meeting, for he had been concealed behind a pile of packing-cases, and his note-book was filled with the names, so far as he could gather them, of all those who had taken part in the proceedings.

Three days after the meeting had been held, Mrs. Sherard Wilson took her departure for Berlin, where she rested for a day and a night, and had interviews with several influential people, and at a certain bank and money-changer's in Berlin she converted an English cheque for a large amount into Russian money. She was known to the money-changer; he had cashed similar cheques before. Having completed her business, she pursued her way to Russia. At the frontier her luggage and passport were examined. There was nothing liable to duty in the former; the latter was all in order and duly viséd. The examiners at the frontier, however, failed to discover in one of her trunks a very artfully and cleverly contrived false bottom, where lay concealed not only a mass of inflammatory literature, but documents of the most damaging description. So she passed on her journey, distributing largess freely, and regarded by the officials as a lady of distinction, travelling no doubt on important business, for no one travelled for pleasure in the winter weather. Mrs. Wilson spoke French, German, Russian, and many dialects, so that she had no difficulty with regard to tongues. In the same train with her travelled a man, who was ostensibly a fur merchant, in reality her shadower—Danevitch the detective.

In due course they reached St. Petersburg, and the lady was driven to one of the principal hotels, where she engaged a suite of rooms; and when three or four days had elapsed, during which she was very active and went about much, she attended a secret meeting, held in the house of one Alexeyeff, who was a bookseller in a small way of business. In that house over sixty persons assembled, including the indefatigable Mrs. Sherard Wilson. When the last person had entered, there gradually closed around the place a cordon of heavily-armed policemen. They, again, were reinforced by a body of soldiers with loaded guns and fixed bayonets. At a given signal, when all was ready, the door of the house was burst in and the meeting, which had just got to business, was broken up in wild confusion. The people saw that they had been betrayed and were trapped. For a moment a panic seized them. Some made a bid for liberty, and rushed off, but could not get far; the cordon was too strong to be broken through. Others, with a wild despair, prepared to sell their lives and liberties dearly. But, as is well known, Continental police, and particularly the Russian police, stand on no ceremony when resistance to their authority is offered. The maudlin sentiment which we in England so often display, even when the most desperate ruffians are concerned, is quite unknown abroad. Resistance to the law generally means injury, and often death, to the resister. On the occasion in question, the police and the soldiers were all heavily armed, for they were aware that the work they were called upon to perform could not be undertaken with kid gloves on; the glittering swords and bayonets which menaced the trapped people had an effect, and what threatened to be a scene of bloodshed and death ended in a despairing surrender to the forces that were irresistible. From the moment that the police broke in upon the meeting Mrs. Sherard Wilson felt that hope had gone, and she made no attempt either to save her own liberty or arouse her followers to action.

Under a very strong escort the misguided people were conveyed to prison, and very soon it was made evident that Danevitch had brought to light one of the most desperate and gigantic conspiracies of modern times. Not only had plans been drawn up and arrangements made for killing the Czar, but many noblemen and high officials were to be killed. The conspirators were chosen from all ranks of society, and they had followers in the army and the navy, as well as in the police. That they would have succeeded in their nefarious designs there is little doubt, had it not been for the vigilance and cleverness of Danevitch. He found out that Count Obolensk, who resided in London, was supplying large sums of money to aid the work of the conspiracy. The detective therefore decided upon the bold step of taking service in the Count's household for a time. This he succeeded in doing, and on the night of the meeting recorded in the early part of this story, which was held at the Count's house, he hid himself behind the writing-desk and heard all that took place. In order to get away from the house without raising suspicion, he let the tray of china fall on the stairs as Miss Obolensk was descending. He followed Mrs. Sherard Wilson to Geneva, and was present at that other meeting, when he gained most important information, and subsequently, all unknown to her, accompanied the lady to Russia.

Investigation brought to light the fact that Mrs. Wilson was the wife of a Russian of high social position, but he had been sent to Siberia for life as a political offender. From that moment his wife became the sworn enemy of the Government and the Czar. She had previously been acquainted with Count Obolensk, and was able to exert great influence over him, and, as he was very wealthy, he proved a valuable ally. The plot failed, however, at the eleventh hour, thanks to Danevitch. How narrow had been the escape of the Emperor from a violent death was revealed at the trial of the prisoners, when it was proved that a considerable number of the officials of the palace, as well as soldiers and servants, had been corrupted, and on a given date a man was to be admitted to the palace at night, and he was to throw a bomb into the Czar's bedroom.

Simultaneously an attempt was to be made on the lives of several influential people residing outside of the palace. Desperate and terrible as all this seems, there is no doubt it would have been attempted, for the men and women who were mixed up in the plot were reckless of their lives, and terribly in earnest.

No mercy was shown to the prisoners, and the majority of them were sent to some of the most inhospitable regions of Northern Siberia, including Mrs. Sherard Wilson. To her it must have been infinitely worse than death, and it may be doubted if she ever survived to reach her destination.

THE CROWN JEWELS.

MOSCOW—or, as the natives call it, Maskva—might almost be described as a city within a city; that is to say, there is the Kremlin, and a town outside of that again. The word Kremlin is derived from the Slavonic word Krim, which signifies a fort. It is built on a hill, and is surrounded by a high turreted wall from twelve to sixteen feet thick. This wall varies from thirty to sixty feet high, and is furnished with battlements, embrasures, and gates. Within the Kremlin are most of the Government offices: the Treasury; the renowned Cathedral of St. Michael, where the monarchs of Russia were formerly interred; and the Cathedral of the Assumption of the Virgin Mary, long used as a place of coronation of the Emperors.

In the Treasury are preserved the State jewels, which, in the aggregate, are probably of greater value than any other State jewels in the civilized world. There are something like twenty crowns of such a size, splendour, and intrinsic value that each in itself is a fortune. Tradition says that one of these crowns was given by the Greek Emperor Comnenus to the great Vladimir. Some are covered with the most magnificent diamonds; others with turquoises of immense size; others, again, with rubies and pearls; the groundwork of all is solid gold, and the workmanship exquisite. Then there are sceptres of massive gold, powdered with priceless gems. There are diamond tiaras, diamond cinctures, services of gold and jewelled plate, jewelled swords. These costly treasures are preserved in a large well-lighted room of noble proportions, and to this room the public are freely admitted. It need scarcely be said that the State jewel-room of the Treasury is a source of great attraction to foreigners, and no one visiting Moscow for the first time would think of leaving the city without having paid a visit to the Treasury jewel-room. One morning, on opening the Museum for the day, there was tremendous consternation amongst the officials and attendants, when one of the guardians of the treasure-house made the discovery that no less than three crowns, two sceptres, a diamond belt and a diamond tiara were missing. The circumstance was at once reported to the keeper of the jewels—General Kuntzler. The office was generally held by a retired military officer, and was much sought after, as it was a life appointment and the salary was good. The keeper had many subordinates under him, and while they were responsible to him, he himself was held entirely responsible by the Government for the safe-guarding of the jewels. General Kuntzler had occupied the position for about two years, after long and important military service. When he heard of the robbery, he was so affected that his mind gave way, and before the day was out he shot himself.

Investigation soon made it evident that a crime of unparalleled audacity had been committed under the very noses of the Government officials, and property intrinsically valued at many thousands of pounds had disappeared. As the affair was a very serious one for all concerned, no time was lost in summoning Michael Danevitch and enlisting his services. As can readily be understood, quite apart from the monetary value of the lost baubles, the associations surrounding them made it highly desirable that every effort should be put forth to recover them; and it was impressed upon Danevitch how imperatively necessary it was to take the most active measures to get on the track of the thieves immediately, because, as everyone knew, the gold would be melted down as soon as possible, and the precious relics be thus destroyed. Amongst the crowns carried off was the one worn by the last King of Poland. It was a magnificent bauble, and was so thickly encrusted with gems that in round figures it was worth in English money something like fifty thousand pounds. It will be seen, therefore, that the loss in mere value to the State was enormous. It was, of course, as Danevitch saw clearly enough, no ordinary robbery. It must have been planned deliberately, and carried out with great ingenuity. Nor was it less obvious that more than one person had been concerned in the daring crime.

There was a prevailing impression at first that General Kuntzler must have had a share in the robbery, but Danevitch did not take that view. The unfortunate General had an untarnished record, and though his suicide was calculated to arouse suspicion, it was established by Danevitch that the poor man—fully realizing the great responsibility that rested on his shoulders—was unable to face the blame that would attach to him. It would be said that he had not exercised sufficient care, and had been careless of the safety of the priceless treasures committed to his charge. This was more than he could bear, and he ended the whole business as far as he was concerned by laying violent hands upon himself.

'I saw from the first,' Danevitch writes, 'that the guilty parties must be sought for among the ranks of those who make robbery a fine art, if one may be allowed to so express himself. Mere commonplace, vulgar minds would have been incapable of conceiving, let alone of carrying out, so daring a deed as that of robbing the State of its priceless historical baubles. It was no less self-evident to me that the affair must have been very carefully planned, and arrangements made for conveying the articles out of the country immediately, or of effectually destroying their identity. In their original condition they would practically be worth nothing to the illegal possessors, inasmuch as no man dare offer them for sale; but by taking out the gems and melting the gold the materials could thus be converted into cash. I ascertained that when the Museum was closed in the evening previous to the robbery being discovered, everything was safe.'

It appeared that it was the duty of the chief subordinate, one Maximoff, to go round the hall the last thing, after it had been closed to the public for the day, and see that everything was safe. He then reported to General Kuntzler. This had been done with great regularity. It so happened, however, that the day preceding the discovery that the jewels had been stolen was an official holiday. At stated periods in Russia there is an official holiday, when all public Government departments are closed. This holiday had favoured the work of the thieves, and some time during the forty hours that elapsed between the closing of the hall in the evening before the holiday, and the discovery of the robbery on the morning after the holiday, the jewels had been carried off.

The holiday was on a Wednesday; on Tuesday evening Maximoff made his round of inspection as usual, and duly presented his official report to his chief, General Kuntzler. According to that report, everything was safe; the place was carefully locked up, and all the keys deposited in the custody of the General, who kept them in an iron safe in his office. It was pretty conclusively proved that those keys never left the safe from the time they were deposited there on Tuesday night until Maximoff went for them on Thursday morning. During the whole of Wednesday Maximoff and the attendants were away. Maximoff was a married man, with three children, and he had taken his family into the country. Kuntzler remained, and there was the usual military guard at the Treasury. The guard consisted of six sentinels, who did duty night and day, being relieved every four hours.

'The whole affair was very complicated,' proceeds Danevitch, 'and I found myself confronted with a problem of no ordinary difficulty. I was satisfied, however, that General Kuntzler was entirely innocent of any complicity in the affair; and, so far as I could determine then, there was not the slightest ground for suspecting Maximoff. There were twelve other subordinates. They were charged with the duty of dusting the various glass cases in which the jewels were deposited, and of keeping the people in order on public days, and I set to work in my own way to endeavour to find out what likelihood there was of any of these men being confederates. It seemed to me that one or more of them had been corrupted, and proved false to his charge. Without an enemy in the camp it was difficult to understand how the thieves had effected an entrance.'

The Treasury was a large white stone building, with an inner courtyard, around which were grouped numerous Government offices. The entrance to this yard was by a noble archway, closed by a massive and ornamental iron gate. In this gateway a sentry was constantly posted. The Museum was situated in about the centre of the left wing of the main block of buildings. The entrance was from the courtyard, and the hall, being in an upper story, was reached by a flight of marble steps. To gain admission to the hall, the public were necessarily compelled to pass under the archway, and so into the courtyard. Of course there were other ways of reaching the hall of jewels, but they were only used by the employés and officials. General Kuntzler, his lieutenant, Maximoff, and four of the subordinates, resided on the premises. They had rooms in various parts of the building.

A careful study of the building, its approaches and its exits, led Danevitch to the conclusion that the thief or thieves must have reached the hall from one of the numerous Government offices on the ground-floor of the block, or from the direction of Kuntzler's apartments, and he set to work to try and determine that point. He found that one of the offices referred to was used as a depository for documents relating to Treasury business, and beneath it, in the basement, was an arched cellar, also used for storing documents. This cellar was one of many others, all connected with a concreted subway, which in turn was connected with the upper stories by a narrow staircase, considered strictly private, and used, or supposed to be used, by the employés only. The office was officially known as Bureau 7. Exit from it could be had by a door, which opened into a cul-de-sac, and was not a public thoroughfare. It was, in fact, a narrow alley, formed by the Treasury buildings and a church.

Danevitch was not slow to perceive that Bureau 7 and the cul-de-sac offered the best, if not the only, means of egress to anyone who, being on the premises illegally, wished to escape without being seen. It was true that one of the sentries always on duty patrolled the cul-de-sac at intervals; but that, to the mind of Danevitch, was not an insuperable obstacle to the escape of anyone from the building. Of course, up to this point it was all conjecture, all theory; but the astute detective brought all his faculties to bear to prove that his theory was a reasonable one.

He ascertained that the door into the cul-de-sac was very rarely used indeed, and had not been opened for a long time, as the office itself was only a store-room for documents, and days often passed without anyone going into it. Critical examination, however, revealed to Danevitch that the outer door had been very recently opened. This was determined by many minute signs, which revealed themselves to the quick and practised eyes of the detective. But something more was forthcoming to confirm him in his theory. On the floor of Bureau 7 he found two or three diamonds, and in the passage of the cul-de-sac he picked up some more. Here, then, at once was fairly positive proof that the thief or thieves had made their exit that way. Owing to rough handling, or to the jarring together of the stolen things, some of the precious stones had become detached, and by some carelessness or other a number of them had fallen unperceived to the ground; these as surely pointed the way taken by the robbers as the lion in the desert betrays his track by the spoor. This important discovery Danevitch kept to himself. He was fond of likening his profession to a game at whist, and he used to say that the cautious and skilful player should never allow his opponent to know what cards he holds.

Having determined so much, his next step was to discover, if possible, the guilty persons. It was tolerably certain that, whoever they were, they must have been well acquainted with the premises. Of course it went without saying that no one could have undertaken and carried out such an extraordinary robbery without first of all making a very careful study of every detail, as well as of every means of reaching the booty, and of conveying it away when secured. The fact of the robbery having been committed on the Wednesday, which was a Government holiday, showed that it had been well planned, and it was equally evident that somebody concerned in it was intimately acquainted with the premises and all their ramifications. The importance of the discovery of the way by which the criminals had effected their escape could not be overrated, and yet it was of still greater importance that the way by which they entered should be determined. To do that, however, was not an easy matter. The probability—a strong probability—was that those concerned had lain perdu in the building from the closing-time on Tuesday night until the business was completed, which must have been during the hours of darkness from Tuesday night to Wednesday morning, or Wednesday night and Thursday morning. In the latter case, however, the enterprising 'exploiters' must have remained on the premises the whole of Wednesday, and that was hardly likely. They certainly could not have entered on Wednesday, because as it was a non-business day a stranger or strangers seeking admission would have been challenged by the sentries, and not allowed to pass without a special permit. At night a password was always sent round to the people residing in the building, and if they went out they could not gain entrance again without giving the password. These precautions were, in an ordinary way, no doubt, effective enough; but the fact that on this occasion they had proved of no avail pointed to one thing certain, which was that the intruders had gained admission on the Tuesday with the general public, but did not leave when the Museum was closed for the night, and to another thing, not so certain, but probable, that they had been assisted by somebody living on the premises.

Altogether something like sixty persons had lodgings in the Treasury buildings, but only fourteen of these persons, including Kuntzler himself, were attached to the Museum portion. The General's apartments were just above the hall in which the Crown jewels were kept. He had a suite of six rooms, including a kitchen and a servant's sleeping-place. He was a widower, but his sister lived with him as his housekeeper. She was a widow; her name was Anna Ivanorna. The General also had an adopted daughter, a pretty girl, about twenty years of age: she was called Lydia. It appeared she was the natural child of one of the General's comrades, who had been killed during an *émeute* in Siberia, where he was stationed on duty. On the death of his friend, and being childless himself, Kuntzler took the girl, then between six and seven years of age, and brought her up. For obvious reasons, of course,

Danevitch made a study of the General's household, and so learned the foregoing particulars.

As may be imagined, the General's death was a terrible blow to his family, and Lydia suffered such anguish that she fell very ill. Necessarily it became the duty of Danevitch to endeavour to ascertain by every means in his power if Kuntzler's suicide had resulted from any guilty knowledge of the robbery. But not a scrap of evidence was forthcoming to justify suspicion, though the outside public suspected him. That, perhaps, was only natural. As a matter of fact, however, he bore a very high reputation. He had held many important positions of trust, and had been elected to the post of Crown Jewel Keeper, on the death of his predecessor, on account of the confidence reposed in him by the Government, and during the time he had held the office he had given the utmost satisfaction. An examination of his books—he had to keep an account of all the expenses in connection with his department—his papers and private letters, did not bring to light a single item that was calculated to arouse suspicion, and not a soul in the Government service breathed a word against him, while he was highly respected and esteemed by a very large circle of friends.

It was admitted on all sides that General Kuntzler was a very conscientious and sensitive man. The knowledge of the robbery came upon him with a suddenness that overwhelmed him, and, half stunned by the shock, his mind gave way, and he adopted the weak man's method to relieve himself of a terrible responsibility. That was the worst that anyone who knew him ventured to say; he was accorded a public and a military funeral, and was carried to his last resting-place amidst the genuine sorrow of great numbers of people.

'I confess that at this stage of the proceedings,' writes Danevitch in his notes of the case, 'I did not feel very sanguine of success in the task imposed upon me; and when Colonel Andreyeff, Chief of the Moscow Police, sent for me, and asked my views, I frankly told him what I thought, keeping back, however, for the time being, the discovery I had made, that the culprits had departed from the building by Bureau 7, and had scattered some diamonds on the way. The Colonel became very grave when he learnt my opinion, and paid me the compliment of saying that great hopes had been placed on me, that the reputation of his department was at stake, and if the jewels were not recovered, and the culprits brought to justice, it might cost him his position. I pointed out that I was quite incapable of performing miracles; that while I could modestly claim to have been more successful in my career than any other man following the same calling, it was not within my power to see through stone walls, or divine the innermost secrets of men's hearts.

"'But you are capable of reading signs which other men have no eyes for," exclaimed the Colonel.

"'Possibly," I answered, as I bowed my thanks for the good opinion he held of me; "but in this instance I see no sign."

"'But you are searching for one?" said the Colonel anxiously.

"'Oh, certainly I am," I responded.

'The anxious expression faded from the Colonel's face, and he smiled as, fixing his keen gray eyes on me, he remarked:

"'As long as you are still searching for a sign, Danevitch, there is hope. There must be a sign somewhere, and unless you have grown blind and mentally dull, it will not escape you for long."

'This was very flattering to my *amour propre*, and I admit that it had a tendency to stimulate me to renewed exertion, if stimulus was really needed. But, as a matter of fact, I was not just then very hopeful. Nevertheless, as I took my leave, I said that, if the problem was solvable by mortal man, I would solve it. This was pledging myself to a good deal; but I was vain enough to think that, if I failed by methods which I had made a lifelong study, to say nothing of a natural gift for my work, no one else was likely to succeed, except by some accident which would give him the advantage.'

Like most men of exceptional ability, Danevitch was conscious of his strength, but he rarely allowed this self-consciousness to assert itself, and when he did he was justified. His methods were certainly his own, and he never liked to own defeat. That meant that where he failed it was hardly likely anyone else would have succeeded. Not only had he a tongue cunning to question, an eye quick to observe, but, as I have said elsewhere, a sort of eighth sense, which enabled him to discern what other men could not discern.

After that interview with Colonel Andreyeff, he fell to pondering on the case, and bringing all the logic he was capable of to bear. He saw no reason whatever to change his first opinion, that there had been an enemy in the camp. By that is meant that the robbery could never have been effected unless with the aid of someone connected with the place, and knowing it well. Following his course of reasoning, he came to the decision that the stolen property was still within the Kremlin. His reason for this was, as he states:

'The thieves could not have passed out during the night, as they would have been questioned by the guards at the gates. Nor could they have conveyed out such a bulky packet on Wednesday, as they would have been called upon for a permit. On the other hand, if the property had been divided up into small parcels, the risk would have been great, and suspicion aroused. But assuming that the thieves had been stupid enough to carry off the things in bulk, they must have known that they were not likely to get far before attracting attention, while any attempt to dispose of the articles as they were would have been fatal. To have been blind to these tremendous risks was to argue a denseness on the part of the culprits hardly conceivable of men who had been clever enough to abstract from a sentry-guarded Government building property of such enormous value. They would know well enough that melted gold and loose gems could always find a market; but, having regard to the hue and cry, that market was hardly likely to be sought for in any part of Russia. Therefore, when reduced to an unrecognisable state, and when vigilance had been relaxed, the gold and the jewels would be carried abroad to some of the centres of Europe, where the infamous receiver flourishes and waxes fat on the sins of his fellow-men.

'In accordance with my custom in such cases,' continues Danevitch in his notes, 'I lost not a moment when I took up the case in telegraphing to every outlet from Russia, including the frontier posts. I knew, therefore, that at every frontier station and every outlet luggage would be subjected to very critical examination, and the thieves would experience great difficulty indeed in getting clear. But there was another aspect of the case that could not be overlooked, and it caused me considerable anxiety; it was this—the gems could be carried away a few at a time. A woman, for instance, could conceal about her person small packets of them, and excite no suspicion. To examine everyone personally at the frontiers was next to impossible. There was another side, however, to this view, and it afforded me some consolation. To get the gems out of the country in the way suggested would necessitate a good many journeys on the part of the culprits, and one person making the same journey several times would excite suspicion. If several people were employed in the work, they would be certain to get at loggerheads sooner or later, and the whole business would be exposed. I always made it a sort of axiom that "when thieves fall out honest men come by their due," and experience had taught me that thieves invariably fall out when it comes to a division of plunder. Of course, I was perfectly alive to the fact that it would not do to rely upon that; something more was wanted: it was of the highest importance to prevent the stolen property being carried far away, and all my energies were concentrated to that end.

'I have already given my reasons for thinking that at this stage the stolen jewels had not been removed from the Kremlin. Although there are no regular streets, as understood, in the Kremlin, there are numerous shops and private residences, the latter being inhabited for the most part by the officials and other employés of the numerous Government establishments. The result is that within the Kremlin itself there is a very large population.'

It will be seen from these particulars that the whole affair bristled with difficulties, and, given that the thieves were sharp, shrewd, and cautious, they might succeed in defeating Danevitch's efforts. One of the first things he did was to request that every sentry at the Kremlin gates should be extra vigilant, and subject passers to and fro to more than ordinary observation, while if they had reason to suspect any particular person, that person should be instantly arrested. The precautions which were thus taken reduced the matter to a game of chance. If the thieves betrayed themselves by an incautious or careless act they would lose. On the other hand, if they were skilful and vigilant the detective would be defeated; and as the stakes were very large, and to lose meant death to them (that being the penalty in Russia for such a crime), it was presumable that they would not easily sacrifice themselves. At this stage Danevitch himself confessed that he would not have ventured to give an opinion as to which of the two sides would win.

The more Danevitch studied the subject, the more he became convinced that the thieves must have been in league with someone connected with the Treasury Department. In face of the fact that false keys had been used, the theory of collusion could not be ignored; the difficulty was to determine who was the most likely person to have proved traitor to his trust. Maximoff bore a high character; General Kuntzler had reposed full confidence in him. The subordinates were also men of good repute. That, however, was not a guarantee that they were proof against temptation. Nevertheless, Danevitch could not get hold of anything that was calculated to arouse his suspicion against any particular individual. If there was a guilty man amongst them, he would, of course, be particularly careful not to commit any act, or utter any word, calculated to betray him, knowing as he did that Danevitch was on the alert.

When several days had passed, and General Kuntzler had been consigned to his tomb, Danevitch had an interview with his sister, Anna Ivanorna. She was in a state of great mental excitement and nervous prostration; and Lydia, the General's adopted daughter, was also very ill. Anna was a somewhat remarkable woman. She was a tall, big-boned, determined-looking individual, with a soured expression of face and restless gray eyes. Her manner of speaking, her expression of face, and a certain cynicism, which made itself apparent in her talk, gave one the notion that she was a disappointed woman.

'This is a sad business,' began Danevitch, after some preliminary remarks.

'Very sad,' she answered. 'It has cost my brother his life.'

'He evidently felt it very keenly,' said Danevitch.

'A man must feel a thing keenly to commit suicide, unless he is a weak-brained fool, incapable of any endurance,' she replied with a warmth that amounted almost to fierceness. After a pause, she added: 'My brother was far from being a fool. He was a strong man—a clever man.'

'So I understand. Did he make any observation to you before he committed the rash act?'

'No.'

'Yes, he did, Anna,' cried out Lydia from the couch on which she was lying, wrapped in rugs.

Anna turned upon her angrily, and exclaimed:

'How do you know? Hold your tongue. He made no observation, I say.'

Lydia was evidently annoyed at being spoken to in such a manner, and she replied with spirit, as she raised herself on her elbow:

'Don't snap at me like that, Anna. I know perfectly well. My poor father said over and over again that he had been betrayed, that there had been a traitor in the house. It was that that distracted him. He couldn't bear the thought of it.'

'And who do you suppose the traitor was?' Anna asked angrily. 'You are always thinking wrong of people.'

Lydia did not take any notice of this. She lay still, and seemed to be suffering; keen mental anguish.

'Have you any opinion how the robbery was committed?' asked Danevitch of Anna.

'No.'

'But surely you must have some idea.'

'No, I haven't.'

'Do you think it possible, now, that such a crime could have been committed without a confederate in the camp?'

'What do you mean?' demanded the woman sternly, as though she resented the bare suspicion which the question implied.

'My meaning is plain, surely. An utter stranger to the place could not have done this deed.'

'I suppose he couldn't. But whoever did it couldn't have been an utter stranger.'

'Do I understand from that that you suggest the culprit or culprits are people who were employed here?'

'No, I don't suggest that. But it stands to reason that anyone undertaking a deed of this kind would be careful to make himself acquainted with the building.'

'And how do you think he did that?'

'You know as well as I do that the place is open to the public. What is there to prevent anyone studying the place?'

'Nothing whatever, so far as the public part of it goes. But, unless with the aid of a confederate, I do not quite see how anyone could become acquainted with those parts where the public are not admitted.'

'Well, Mr. Danevitch,' said Anna, with a decisiveness which was meant to clinch the argument, 'I am not an expert like you, nor do I know anything at all about the matter, therefore don't bother me with any more questions. I am troubled enough, and have enough on my mind without this affair. I want to forget it.'

'I make every allowance for you,' replied Danevitch. 'I quite understand that your feelings are lacerated, but I thought it was within the bounds of possibility that you might be able to throw some light on the matter. However, I will not disturb you further, but take my leave.'

Anna showed him out with a sigh of relief, and she shut the door with a bang that indicated too plainly how glad she was to get rid of him. At this stage, Danevitch writes, he felt in a quandary. There were certain signs that suggested probabilities, but it was not easy to determine just then whether or not the signs were anything more than shadows, by which he might be misled. Speculation and theory were all he had to guide him, and he was only too well aware that the most astute of reasoners is apt to be misled. What necessarily concerned him was the danger of being led out of the true track by a false sign. He was not indifferent, of course, to the fact that he had made some progress—that is to say, he had determined pretty conclusively how the thieves had left the Treasury buildings when once they had secured their booty. But what was of still greater importance was to discover how they got in. Could he solve that part of the problem, he felt sure it would give him many points.

It was remarkable about Danevitch that, while he was often mistrustful about his own instincts, he seldom erred. He had made human nature so close a study that the person who, as the saying is, could have thrown dust in his eyes would have had to have been preternaturally clever. He maintained, and proved it over and over again, that the face was so certain an index to what was passing in the mind that every thought of the brain was communicated instantly to the features, which indicated it as unmistakably as a delicately-balanced needle notes the slightest current of electricity. Of course, it was necessary to understand these face-signs. That in itself is a science. Indeed, the power to understand it is a gift, and he who fully possesses it is what is termed to-day 'a thought-reader.' Danevitch did not call himself that, but he possessed the power in a marked degree, nevertheless; and no one could be indifferent to the extraordinary strength and power of his eyes. When he looked at you, you felt somehow as if he was looking right into your brain. Mr. Gladstone is said to have that peculiar eye, and it can readily be understood that anyone with guilty knowledge having to meet the piercing gaze of such an eye is almost sure to betray himself by face-signs, which to the expert are full of meaning. Danevitch had brought this study to such perfection that it proved invaluable to him, and often afforded him a clue which otherwise he would never have got. Another strong trait in his character was the persistency with which he stuck to an idea when once he had thought it out. That, again, was largely responsible for the success that attended his efforts in the art of solving criminal problems. Of course, his ideas were generally very sound ones, and the result of much cogitation. He never jumped to hasty conclusions.

The foregoing little disquisition is not out of place in view of what follows, and will certainly add to the reader's interest.

About three weeks after that interview between Danevitch and Anna Ivanorna, three men were seated in a restaurant situated in what is known as the Zemlidnoi-gorod, which, being interpreted, means 'earthen town,' and it is so called because at one time it was surrounded by an earthen rampart. This part of Moscow contains a number of drinking-places, spirit-stores, shops, cafés and restaurants. The one in which the three men were seated was a very typical Russian fifth-rate house. The ceiling was black with smoke. Flimsy and frouzy curtains hung at the windows; the floor was sanded; long, rough, wooden tables, forms, and common chairs constituted the furniture. At one end of the room was a small counter, covered with lead, on which stood sundry bottles, glasses, and plates of caviare and sandwiches; at the other end was the indispensable stove—a huge affair with a massive convoluted iron flue, that was suggestive of a boa constrictor.

The night being very cold, the three men were crowded round the stove, engaged in deep and earnest conversation. Two of the men were young; one about two or three and twenty, the other a year or two older. They were well dressed, and apparently belonged to a class not given to frequenting drinking-places of that kind. The third man was of a somewhat striking appearance. He was swarthy as a gipsy—a black beard and moustache, black eyes, black hair, cropped close to the skull. In his ears he wore small gold rings, and his style, manner, and dress proclaimed him unmistakably a seafaring man.

Presently the glazed door of the shop swung open, and a Jew tumbled in. He was heavily bearded; on his head was a small black, tightly-fitting skull-cap. He wore long boots, with his trousers, which were very baggy, tucked into the tops, and a fur-lined coat, which must have been in existence for a generation at least. He divested himself of this coat and hung it on a peg, and then ordered vodka and caviare.

The three men ceased their conversation when the stranger entered; and he, when he had finished his repast, rose, and with somewhat unsteady gait, as if he had been drinking, walked to the stove and asked if he might be allowed a seat there. The other three, with by no means good grace, made room for him. The seafaring man was smoking a very black, very strong cigar. The Jew produced from his pocket a huge pipe, and, filling it with coarse tobacco, asked the seafarer for a light, which was given. When his pipe was fairly in swing, he said to the man with the cigar:

'Unless I'm mistaken, you reek of the salt sea.'

'I suppose I do,' answered the other brusquely. 'Any way, I've been soaked with it often enough. Where are you from?'

'Constantinople.'

'So. A trader, I suppose?'

'Yes.'

'What do you trade in?'

'Anything on earth, so long as it will turn me in money.'

'Bah!' sneered one of the young men—'just like you Jew dogs. It's always money with you—money, money. It's your only prayer.'

'In that respect I'm not sure that there is much difference between the Jew dog and the grasping Christian. But I don't want to quarrel with you. I'm a stranger in the town. Will you drink at my expense?'

'Yes,' answered the three as one man.

So drink was ordered, and for a time the conversation was friendly and general, and when it flagged a little the Jew said:

'That's a curious robbery that has taken place lately.'

'What robbery?' asked one of the young men, eyeing the Jew keenly.

'The robbery of the Crown jewels.'

'Oh yes; very curious.'

'By Father Abraham!' exclaimed the Jew, with a great puffing out of his breath, 'but I should like to call some of the precious stones mine. The God of Jacob! I wonder what has become of them. They haven't caught the thieves yet, I suppose?'

'No,' was the curt answer.

'Ah! they are clever fellows; must be wonderfully clever to do such a deed. But I expect they'll be laid by the heels yet.'

'No fear,' answered one of the youngsters. 'You can depend upon it they know what they are about.'

'Ah! just so, just so,' mused the Jew—'just so. It's a clever bit of business—clever, clever; by God it is! I wonder, now, what has become of those jewels. They are worth risking body and soul for.'

'I say, stranger,' remarked the seafarer, 'you had better be careful what you say, or you may land yourself in trouble.'

'True, true, true!' moaned the Jew. 'But, God in heaven, only to think of all those precious gems! It almost turns one's brain.'

He sank into a moody silence, and stared fixedly at the stove, as though he was dreaming dreams about the gems. The other three men conversed in low tones for a little time, until the two younger ones rose up, said 'Good-night,' and left, for the hour was getting late. Then the Jew seemed suddenly to wake up from his reverie, and he asked the seafarer if he was going.

'No; I am lodging here,' was the answer.

'So. That reminds me. Landlord, can I have a bed?'

He was told he could. There was some haggling about the price to be paid, but the matter was amicably settled in the end, and the Jew invited the seafarer to have some more vodka. True to the traditions of his kind the world over, the sailor man accepted the invitation, and the two sat drinking until the landlord came to remind them it was time they retired.

The sailor was pretty far gone in his cups, and the Jew offered to assist him up the stairs to bed. With some difficulty the pair managed to mount the greasy, rickety stairs to where the sleeping chambers were, and the Jew accompanied the sailor man to his room, and then from his capacious pocket he produced a bottle of vodka, and they set to work to discuss it. Presently the Jew murmured in a maudlin way, as his thoughts still ran upon the gems:

'By Father Abraham, but it was a big haul! Why, there must have been a million roubles' worth of them.'

'Of what?' asked the skipper, who, though pretty well soaked, seemed to have his wits about him.

'The stolen jewels,' mumbled the Jew. 'I would buy every one of them at a price; I would, so help me God!'

'Now, what price would you give?'

'How could I tell—how could I tell, unless I saw them?'

The sailor man became thoughtful and silent, and the Jew sank down in a corner like a sack, mumbling incoherently guttural sentences, in which the words 'gems, jewels, gold,' predominated. Presently the sailor was overcome by his potations, and stretching himself on the bed, boots and all, was soon snoring in drunken sleep. A couple of hours later the Jew crept from the room, sought his own chamber, and was speedily sound asleep in the bed.

The next morning the two men drank their tea together, and having lighted one of his long black cigars, the sailor invited the Jew forth into the city.

'You say you are from Constantinople?' asked the sailor, as they walked together.

'Yes.'

'Do you reside there?'

'Yes.'

'In what part?'

'The Jews' quarter.'

'And, I suppose, like all your tribe, you don't know your own wealth?'

The Jew sighed dolefully.

'Alas, alas!' he exclaimed; 'by Abraham in heaven, I swear I am very poor.'

'Ah! you all say that.'

'It's true, it's true. But why do you ask?'

'Oh, nothing; only, if you had been rich, I might have put something in your way by which you could have doubled your riches.'

'What is it? What is it?' cried the Jew eagerly. 'Tell me; I can get money. Thousands, tens of thousands, millions of roubles, if needs be. But tell me what it is. I want to grow rich; I want money—want it by sackfuls. It is my dream; I worship it.'

'Ah,' grunted the sailor, with a smack of his lips, 'you are all alike. Have you any friends in Moscow?'

'No; I am a stranger. I have come to trade. I will lend money at interest on good security, or I will buy anything that I can sell again.'

The sailor became very thoughtful. He puffed away at his rank cigar like a man who was deeply absorbed, and the Jew ambled on by his side, mumbling to himself. Presently the sailor addressed him:

'Do you stay in the same lodgings to-night?'

'I do.'

'Good. I'll meet you at nine o'clock, and may be able to put something in your way. I must leave you now.'

'Count on me,' said the Jew. 'If we can do a deal together, I'll put money in your purse.'

'You bet you will! You don't suppose I'm going to serve you without serving myself. I don't love your race enough for that. It's a matter of convenience. But till to-night, adieu.'

'By the way, how are you called?'

'I am known as Captain Blok. I command a small trader doing business in the Black Sea.'

'Where is she now?'

'She is being overhauled at Azov.'

'Will you be alone to-night?'

'No. The two friends you saw last night may be with me.'

'Good. This looks like business. I will meet you without fail.'

The sailor went off, and the Jew continued his jaunt through the town. When nine o'clock came, it found him by the big stove in the restaurant. There were several other customers there, but he held aloof from them, for one had a little before called him 'a dog of a Jew,' saying he had no business to be there amongst Christians, and tried to pick a quarrel with him. As a quarter-past nine struck, Captain Blok entered. He was alone. He addressed a few preliminary remarks to the Jew, then requested that he would follow him to his bedroom.

'What is your name, Jew?' asked Blok, as he shut the door.

'Nikolai—Israel Nikolai.'

'Are you a Russian?'

'I was born in Poland, but have been trading in Constantinople and the Levant for many years.'

'You are good for a deal in a big way?'

'Yes.'

'And can be secret?'

'As the grave.'

At this point the door opened, and Blok's companions of the previous night entered. They looked at Blok inquiringly, then at the Jew suspiciously.

'He's right,' said Blok. Then turning to the Jew, he continued: 'Now look here, Israel Nikolai, you say you can command money?'

'Yes, to any extent.'

'Very well; now, we've got some stuff to sell, and we are going to take you to see it. The stuff is contraband, therefore you must be careful. And if you play us false, just as sure as God Almighty is up in heaven, your throat will be cut, and your dirty carcase will be flung into the river Maskva.'

The Jew smote his breast, and wailed out with passionate eagerness:

'Trust me—trust me! To those whom I serve, I am as stanch as steel.'

'That's right. Now, then, come with us.'

The four men descended the greasy staircase, and went forth into the street. It was an intensely dark night. A few hazy stars were alone visible in the black sky. The street-lamps in that part were very poor affairs, and gave but little light. The four proceeded for a short distance; then Blok said:

'Nikolai, before we go any further, you must let us blindfold you.'

The Jew protested, but at last yielded, and a thick scarf was bound about his eyes. Then one of the men took his hand and led him. They walked along in silence for quite half an hour, until, by the sound of flowing water, the Jew knew he was near the river. A halt was made. There was the grating of keys in a lock, a door was opened, and Israel was led forward into a passage, while the door was locked and barred. He was then taken down a flight of stairs, where the bandage was removed from his eyes, and a light was procured. He found himself in a cellar, with an arched brick roof, from which water dripped, while the floor of red brick was slimy and foul. The place was furnished with a single trestle table and a stool or two. In one corner was a large trunk, bound with cowhide. This was opened, and some bundles lifted out, placed on the table, and untied, and there were revealed to the wondering Jew heaps of precious stones, including diamonds, rubies, amethysts, pearls, sapphires, turquoises. At the sight of the gems the Jew rubbed his hands together, and his eyes glistened with almost unnatural brilliancy.

'Father Abraham!' he exclaimed. 'What wealth! what a fortune! Are they all real? Let me feel them; let me examine them.'

Blok so held the lamp that its rays were thrown full on to the heaps of gems, and the three men watched the Jew's every movement. He examined the stones carefully, picked out some of the finest, weighing them in his hands, holding them close to the light so as to see them better, then placing them in little heaps.

A full hour was spent in this way. But few remarks were made, though every now and again the Jew broke into an exclamation of delight. At length Blok asked Nikolai what he thought of them.

'Splendid! wonderful! magnificent!' was the gasped answer.

'Now, then, are you open to trade?'

'Yes.'

'Will you buy the lot?'

'At what figure?'

'A million roubles.'

The Jew started back with a look of disgust on his face.

'It is too much—too much!' he almost screamed. 'They are not worth it.'

'You lie, you dog!' put in one of the young men. 'You know they are worth a good deal more. But we want to sell them quickly, and you shall have them as a bargain for a million roubles.'

Nikolai groaned, swore, protested, declared by all the fathers that the price was outrageous, and at last, when he had exhausted himself, he wound up by offering seventy-five thousand roubles for the lot. After much haggling, the three men agreed to take the price, and Nikolai said he would go next day to the Bank of Moscow, to which he had letters, and draw the money, and it was arranged that the four men were to meet the following night outside of the restaurant, and proceed again to the cellar, where the money would be exchanged for the jewels. And Blok added:

'As soon as the bargain's completed, you had better clear out. You can travel with me to Azov, if you like, and I'll give you a cheap passage to Constantinople.'

The Jew turned to Blok, with a glance full of meaning, and replied:

'I may sail with you, but I'll send my jewels a safer way.'

The business, so far, being concluded, Nikolai was once more blindfolded. The lamp was extinguished, and they all left the house together. After going some distance, the bandage was removed from the Jew's eyes. The two young men went away, and Blok and Israel continued their walk to their lodgings.

The following morning Nikolai told Blok that he was going to the bank to arrange about the money, but that the deal would have to take place that evening in their bedroom at the café, as he would not trust himself with them in the cellar with so much money about him. To this Blok answered that the transaction would have to be arranged in the cellar, that everything would be perfectly square and fair.

Reluctantly the Jew yielded, and went away. He met the captain again in the evening at the restaurant, and Blok anxiously inquired if he had got the money, whereupon the Jew pulled from a deep pocket inside his vest a bundle of notes, the sight of which caused the captain's eyes to sparkle.

A little later they set off, being met on the route by the two young men. Nikolai resolutely declined to be blindfolded again. He said there was no necessity for it. He also warned his companions that he was well armed, and was prepared to resent any treachery. They laughed, and said he was a fool not to see that they were anxious to trade, and not likely to offer violence, which would imperil their own safety.

The house by the river was at last reached. It had formerly been a store of some sort, but had apparently long been untenanted, and was falling into decay. One of the young men had inserted the key into the lock of the door, and was about to turn it, when a whistle was blown, and almost as if it was by magic the four found themselves surrounded by armed men, who seemed to come through the earth. Before they could offer the slightest resistance, Blok and the two young men were seized and ironed, and a guard set over them. Then a police officer, the Jew, and three or four other men, entered the premises, descended to the cellar, and, having ascertained that the gems were in the trunk, they bore the trunk out, and placed it on a cart that was in readiness, and under a strong escort the stolen jewels were conveyed to the Treasury, where several high officials were waiting to receive them; and Blok and his companions realized that they had been tricked, trapped, and betrayed by the 'dog of a Jew,' who was none other than Danevitch.

He says it was one of the proudest moments of his life, for his part had been played with consummate art, and his triumph was complete. It remains now to explain how he managed to get on the track of his men, and net them so cleverly.

After his interview with Anna Ivanorna, he began to think that she could throw some light on the mystery if she liked, and he had her shadowed. He ascertained from Lydia that Ivanorna had a son about five-and-twenty. He had paid court to Lydia, but she did not like him. A few months before the robbery this young man had spent a fortnight with his mother during the temporary absence of General Kuntzler. His mother was blindly devoted to him, although he was known to be an idle, dissolute vagabond. He had been well educated, and had once held a position in the Post Office, but had been discharged for some irregularity. His name was Peter, and one night, some days after the robbery, he and his mother were seen to meet in a lonely part of the suburbs.

From that moment a close watch was kept on Peter's movements, and it was ascertained that he was associated with another young man, called Maiefski. They were always together, and in a little while were joined by Blok, who was Peter's half-cousin. The old disused store on the banks of the river was taken in Maiefski's name, ostensibly to store grain there; but little by little the gems from the stolen articles, which were ruthlessly broken up, were conveyed from a house in the Kremlin which Peter rented to the place on the river bank.

Blok had secured lodgings in the miserable restaurant in the poor quarter of the earthen city, as he hoped thereby to escape attracting any notice. At this restaurant the three rascals were in the habit of meeting. Then it was that Danevitch, being sure of his ground, assumed so successfully the rôle of the Jew.

On the night when he and Captain Blok staggered up to the latter's room, Danevitch was perfectly sober, although he assumed the gait and manner of an intoxicated person. When Blok had gone to sleep, Danevitch searched his person, and in a pocket-book found letters of a most compromising character. They seemed to show that the first idea was that the three men were to travel singly to Azov, each man carrying as many of the gems as he could without causing suspicions. They were to be deposited on Blok's vessel, and when all was ready Blok and his companions were to sail away to Constantinople, where they hoped to dispose of the gems, but if not, they were to take a journey to Persia, where precious stones could always be sold.

The appearance of the Jew on the scene altered their plans, and they thought if they could only get him to buy them their risk would be greatly lessened, and the moment they touched the money they were prepared to clear out, and seek safety in some other country. Their little scheme, however, was entirely frustrated, thanks to the cleverness of Danevitch.

At Peter's lodgings the battered gold of the stolen property was found, but ultimately the Polish crown was restored almost to its original state, and may still be seen in the museum at Moscow.

As the plot of the robbery was gradually unfolded, it was proved that Anna Ivanorna was the victim of her perfidious son. She was a weak, rather stupid woman—at any rate, where he was concerned—and she fell a victim to his wiles and wickedness. If she did not actually assist him, she shut her eyes while he made wax impressions of various keys, and on the night of the robbery she unquestionably helped him and his companion, Maiefski, who was secretly admitted. It is possible that, when Kuntzler heard of the crime, he had some suspicion that his sister knew something about it, and, unable to face the awful shame of exposure, he took his life.

Neither Maximoff nor his subordinates had anything to do with the robbery. They were all exonerated after a most exhaustive investigation, which led to the conviction of the guilty parties, who, with the exception of Anna, were sent to the Siberian mines for life. She was condemned to ten years' incarceration in the prison fortress of Schlusselburgh. That was practically a living death.

THE STRANGE STORY OF A SECRET TREATY.

'I RECEIVED orders,' says Danevitch, 'to proceed without delay to the official residence in St. Petersburg of Prince Ignatof,[A] who was then Minister of Foreign Affairs. He had the reputation of being one of the most powerful Ministers who had ever held the position in Russia. It was said of him, as it used to be said of Bismarck, that he was a man of blood and iron. He was dead to emotion; he had no nerves; he was pitiless; he was anti-everything that wasn't Russian; but he was also a born diplomatist—clever, brilliant, unscrupulous, far-seeing, polished as a rapier, and as deadly as a rapier when occasion called for it.

'Such was the common report about him, and no doubt it was, in the main, true. He was a widower, with one grown-up daughter. There was a deadly feud, however, between them, and he had disowned her, as she had chosen to marry against his will, and very much beneath her, as her father averred. Her husband was in the consular service. His name was Kasin; he was a member of a middle-class family who had made money in trade; but Kasin himself was said to be poor, and almost entirely dependent upon his salary.

'These facts were common property, and naturally it must have caused the Prince great annoyance to know that his daughter's name was in everyone's mouth, and that she was vulgarly referred to as the wife of a poor devil of a consul, who found it difficult to rub two roubles together. Caste is very strong in Russia, and the line of demarcation separating class from class is exceedingly well defined.

'The Prince was an utter stranger to me; I had heard much about him, but had never seen him. On being ushered into his bureau, I beheld a small-made, delicate-looking man, with a remarkable and striking face. The mouth was small and firm; the nose prominent; the eyes deep-set, and of exceptional brilliancy; the eyebrows were thin, but well defined; and the forehead, in proportion to the small, sharply-cut features, seemed enormous. He was slightly bald in front, and such hair as he had was turning gray. His face was clean-shaven. When his lips parted, he revealed a splendid set of teeth, absolutely without a flaw.

'As I looked upon this remarkable man, everything I had heard about his personal character seemed to me to be more than confirmed. It was impossible to study the mouth without feeling that it was capable of uttering cruel, cutting, bitter things. It was no less impossible not to understand that the small, brilliant eyes could peer into men's brains, and almost read their secret thoughts. Every line of his face, every feature, every glance, indicated an iron, a relentless, will; and when he spoke, the smooth, incisive tones confirmed this. His hands were small, well shaped, but sinewy, as were his wrists. This was no doubt due to many years' practice with the sword and the foil. He was a noted swordsman, had fought many duels, and had always succeeded in either severely wounding or killing his man. Physically and mentally he could be a deadly antagonist; one glance at him was sufficient to determine that fact, for fact it was.

'He was perusing a document as I entered. He glanced over the edge of the paper, motioned me to be seated, and went on reading.

'For ten minutes the silence was unbroken, save for the rustle of the paper as he turned over the leaves. Only a man of very pronounced characteristics could have remained silent so long under such circumstances.

'He finished his manuscript, folded it up, and placed it in a safe. Then he condescended to address me.

'"You have the reputation of being able to unravel mysteries when other men fail?" he commenced.

'I could only bow to this.

'He drew an elegant little penknife from his pocket, and began to trim his nails, but I noted that all the time his piercing eyes were fixed on me.

'"You are reliable?" was his next remark.

'It was put in the form of a question. In other men the remark might have seemed commonplace. Coming from the Prince's lips, it was full of meaning; it even covered a menace. That is to say, it carried with it the implication, "Woe betide you if you are not!"

'"If I were otherwise," I answered, "I should not occupy the position I do."

'"True," he replied. "Now, the matter in which I am going to enlist your services is a delicate one."

'He paused, and fixed his eyes upon me again, and toyed daintily with the penknife.

'"I have had to do with many delicate cases," I said.

'"Ah! And have been successful?"

'"More frequently than not."

'"You've been employed in Government business before?"

'"Yes," I answered shortly, as I felt somewhat annoyed at the manner in which he put his questions.

'"I am impressed with you," he was good enough to say.

'I returned no answer to that, merely making a very formal motion of the head.

'"Our little introduction places us *en rapport* with each other," he continued, closing the blade of his penknife with a snap. Even this remark was pregnant with meaning. It really meant that he understood me, or believed that he did. "And now I will tell you the business."

'He had been standing up to this moment, but here he seated himself, crossed his legs, and thrust his hands into his pockets. To the ordinary observer he would have appeared as the most unconcerned person in the world, but I could not fail to see that he was a master in the art of restraint. It was not difficult to determine that, beneath the cold, passionless, immobile face was tremendous anxiety, and a suppressed nervous energy, that could only be kept in subjection by extraordinary will-power.

'"A special, confidential, and trusted courier," he continued, "arrived here yesterday afternoon, and placed in my hands the draft of a secret treaty of the very greatest importance."

'Here he paused again, and looked at me in his peculiar manner, as if he was trying to thoroughly understand how I was affected by the information he was giving me. Or, on the other hand, it might have been that he had not quite made up his mind whether or not I was a fit and proper person to be entrusted with State business of such a momentous nature.

'"Pray proceed, Prince," I said, with the greatest unconcern.

'"Bah!" he muttered, almost inaudibly, allowing irritation to display itself for a brief instant. His irritation arose, I inferred, because he failed to read me as easily as he imagined he could do. Perhaps that was not quite the case, but it was something of the kind. The exclamation had scarcely left his lips when he broke into a smile—a cold, cynical smile, but full of meaning. "That draft has been stolen," he added abruptly, and watched to see what effect that announcement would have upon me.

'But I merely said:

'"I anticipated that."

'"Why?" he asked sharply.

'"By your manner, Prince."

'He smiled again, and said caustically:

'"I didn't know I was so shallow, and could be so easily fathomed. But pardon me; I had forgotten for the moment that you are a master in your craft. We shall get on together. Yes, you are clever; the draft has been stolen.

What that means you will better understand when I tell you that it may possibly plunge this country into war."

"'I recognise the seriousness of the matter, Prince," I said, "and, seeing how very serious it is, I would suggest that there should be no restraint, no reserve. If I am to be of use, I must not only have a free hand, but be trusted absolutely."

"'You are right, you are right,' he replied quickly. "But the whole business is fraught with such terrible potentialities that extreme caution is needed."

'He rose, and paced up and down for some moments, still keeping his hands in his pockets. His face betrayed no agitation, but his manner did. Nevertheless, his self-restraint was very remarkable. I waited for him to continue the conversation, and presently he stopped and faced me.

"'Ah, yes!" he said, speaking in an absorbed way. "Well, these are the particulars: The courier, who had been travelling night and day, arrived, as I have already said, yesterday afternoon, and delivered to me a draft of a treaty. Having perused it, I placed it in a despatch-box and locked the box in that safe; but, notwithstanding the precaution, it has been stolen."

"'The box?" I asked.

"'No; the treaty only."

"'When did you make that discovery?"

"'This morning."

"'At what time?"

"'Soon after eight o'clock."

'He did not proceed to give me all the particulars in narrative form, as another person might have done, but I had to drag them from him, so to speak, by question and answer.

"'Where did the courier come from, Prince?" I asked.

"'Bulgaria."

"'Was he aware of the importance of the despatches he carried?"

"'Certainly."

"'You don't doubt his honesty, I suppose?"

"'I don't see the slightest reason for doing so. He is one of the best men in the service."

"'Has he been here since?"

"'No. He was excessively fatigued with his long and trying journey, and being relieved of his responsibility, he said he should sleep for the next twenty-four hours.'"

"'I suppose you have caused a search to be made?'"

"'No,' answered the Prince, with great decisiveness; 'what was the use of doing that? The thief who steals a State document of that kind is not likely to leave much trace behind.'"

"'Of course a good many persons have access to your establishment?'"

"'Yes,—that is, to the business part of the establishment; but my official residence is private; and this bureau is sacred to myself; no one but very privileged people can enter here.'"

"'Do you suspect anyone?'"

"'No. It's a mystery.'"

"'But is it clear that, whoever the person is, he must have been well acquainted with this place?'"

"'Yes,' answered the Prince thoughtfully, as he stroked his chin.

"'He must also have known that the draft had been delivered to you?'"

"'True, true,' the Minister responded, with increased thoughtfulness.

"'That argues that he was behind the scenes; he knew a good deal of what was going on, and was particularly well acquainted with the importance of the treaty.'"

"'Obviously.'"

"'And the document has been stolen for political purposes?'"

"'Obviously, again.'"

"'Or the thief, being a traitor to his country, if he belongs to this country, was actuated by mercenary motives only, and stole the draft to sell it to our enemies?'"

'The Prince fixed his eye upon me again, and answered very slowly, and with emphasis on every word:

"'It might be so—perhaps it is so.'"

"'Very well,' I said. 'Now, Prince, I must ask you to let your mind dwell upon everyone in touch with you, and tell me if there is a single one of them against whom you might justifiably entertain some suspicion.'"

"'There is no one,' he answered, after a thoughtful pause.

"'And yet an utter stranger to the place could hardly have committed such a theft?" I suggested.

"'That seems a feasible theory."

"'You've no reason to suppose, Prince," I asked, "that the despatch-box was opened on the bare chance of its containing something of value?"

"'No. My deliberate opinion is the thief wanted that draft, and that alone. He is an enemy—a traitor; and if he can be identified the penalty of his crime will be death."

"'If your opinion is right, the thief, of course, must have known the draft of the treaty was there?"

"'Quite so."

"'Who was likely to have known it, do you think?"

'Another long pause ensued before the Prince answered. Then he said:

"'Legitimately, very few indeed. It is one of the State secrets. There are many people who come and go here, and an alert traitor might learn much. I see no sign to guide me. Clearly enough, the thief must have been in possession of certain information supposed to be known to this bureau alone, and he has availed himself of the knowledge to purloin a document of extraordinary political importance. Heaven and earth will have to be moved to stop the thief leaving the country; but, what is of more consequence, he must be prevented sending the document away, or any abstract of it."

"'That is easily said," I remarked, with a smile, for he seemed to me to be underrating the difficulties of the case.

"'And it must be done," came from him in a tone so commanding, so authoritative, so decisive, that it revealed the man in his true character. Moreover, his face wore a look of iron determination, and his eyes appeared to glow with a strange, almost unnatural, light. After a pause, he added: "You have the resources of an empire behind you—a well-organized police force, an army of spies, the telegraph system. These things, added to your own skill, should enable you to bring the miscreant to justice, and save the State secret from passing to our enemies."

'He spoke with a great deal of subdued force, and I could see that his mental anxiety was painful; and yet there was an outward semblance of calm. The extraordinary power of self-subjection which the man possessed enabled him to almost entirely hide the nervous excitement which would have entirely overcome any ordinary man.

'The situation was certainly a singularly trying one; for here was a responsible minister of the Crown, who, being entrusted with a State document of stupendous importance, had to confess to its having been stolen within twenty-four hours of its coming into his possession. There appeared to have been great carelessness somewhere, and I could see that the Prince was terribly anxious, in spite of his self-possession.

"'You say that the document was delivered to you yesterday afternoon, Prince?" I remarked, for I found it necessary to still question, in order to make clear certain points which were very necessary for my own guidance, and his natural reticence kept him from giving me every detail right off.

"'Yes," he answered shortly, as though he considered the question superfluous, for he had already told me what I now wanted repeating, but I intended that the question should lead up to others.

"'How long did the courier remain with you after he had delivered the papers into your hands?"

"'Not more than five minutes."

"'When he left did anyone else come into your bureau?"

"'No."

"'You perused the document, of course?"

"'I did. And to-day it was to have been laid before his Majesty the Emperor."

"'How long did you remain here after the departure of your courier?"

"'An hour."

"'And you are sure nobody came in during that time?"

"'Absolutely certain."

"'And are you as certain, Prince, that nobody was concealed in the room without your knowing it?"

'The question seemed to startle him, but in an instant he controlled himself again, and, with a cold smile, remarked, as he glanced round the room:

"'I am quite as certain. You can see for yourself that there is no place where a person could conceal himself."

'I had to admit that that was so.

"'If I have not misunderstood you," I went on, "when you had perused the document, you placed it in the despatch-box?"

"'I did. Both safe and box were afterwards locked. I locked them myself, and took the keys with me.'"

"'When did you discover the loss?'"

"'About an hour and a half ago.'"

"'Had the lock of the safe been tampered with?'"

"'Not at all.'"

"'It was intact?'"

"'Certainly.'"

"'And the despatch-box?'"

"'That was intact also.'"

"'Then, both safe and box must have been opened with keys that fitted them?'"

"'That is obvious.'"

"'Are there any duplicate keys in existence?'"

"'Yes; there are duplicate keys of all the despatch-boxes and all the safes in this department, but they are in possession of the Emperor himself. They are kept to guard against any possible contingency.'"

"'But presumably it would be very difficult for any unauthorized person to obtain possession of them?'"

"'I should say that the difficulties in the way are so great that we may dismiss it as being practically impossible.'"

"'That throws us back, then, on the theory that somebody must have got possession of your keys.'"

"'There, again, the difficulties are so great that I cannot think it possible. Come with me, and I will show you the safeguards that are adopted.'"

'I followed him out of the room. At the door of his bureau was an armed sentry. We traversed a long corridor. On each side were doors. At the end of the corridor another sentry was posted. We gained a large square hall, where several liveried servants stood. Two came forward, and partly drew aside the massive velvet curtains hung before the marble stairs; these stairs were covered with massive carpet, into which the feet sank.

'On the landings more liveried servants were posted. We passed along a carpeted passage to the Prince's official residence, and entered a magnificent room, and thence into a luxuriously furnished boudoir, where a lady sat alone, perusing a book. For a moment she did not notice me, as I was some little distance behind the Prince, and partly screened by the velvet portière at the door. She jumped up, and was about to throw her arms around his neck, but catching sight of me, she blushed, drew back, and said to him:

"'I did not expect you so soon.'"

"'I am engaged on some important business, Catarina,' he replied, a little brusquely. "You had better retire for a time.'"

'Without another word she withdrew. She was a young woman, about four or five-and-twenty, and one of the few I have seen whose beauty might be said to be without blemish. Complexion, features, eyes, teeth, lips, hair—the whole figure was perfect. She was ravishing—a woman for whom a man would have perilled his soul.

'From the boudoir we entered a spacious and magnificently arranged and furnished sleeping apartment. In one corner was a large cupboard. The Prince drew a peculiarly constructed key from his pocket, opened the door, and flung it back, remarking as he did so:

"'That door is of steel. In that niche in the cupboard all my keys are deposited every night. The door is then secured, and the key of the door, together with many other keys, are given into the charge of the confidential clerk, Vladimir Nicolayeff. He is an institution here, and has been in the Government service upwards of forty years.'"

"'Does he reside on the premises?' I asked the Prince.

"'He does,' was the answer; 'and you will now see how difficult it is, with all these precautions, for anyone to abstract the keys.'"

'In answer to this, I could not refrain from remarking:

"'And yet, Prince, there is the hard fact that your safe and despatch-box have been opened, and a State document stolen.'"

'He looked very thoughtful and grave as he replied somewhat sternly:

"'That is so. And what you have got to do is to endeavour to find out how they have been opened, who opened them, and where the papers have gone to. Please commence your work at once, as every hour's delay is in favour of the thief.'"

"'You must pardon me, Prince,' I remarked; 'but I have a few more questions to ask, and you must allow me to work in my own way.'"

"'Oh, certainly!' he exclaimed, a little peevishly, which somewhat astonished me, having regard to the way he had controlled himself so far; but it was another indication of the anxiety that was consuming him.

'Nor was it to be wondered at, for he himself had hinted that if this State secret was made known to the enemies of Russia it was quite within the bounds of possibility that war might ensue.[B]

'No man, much less the Prince, could have been indifferent to that, for it was an open political secret that Russia at that moment was far from being in a fit condition to take the field against a powerful foe. The signs of the times pointed to a coming conflict at no distant date, and fully aware of that, it was known, or believed, that the Prince, who was intensely patriotic, intensely ambitious, and no less intensely desirous of enormously expanding the Czar's dominions, had been making herculean efforts to consolidate the Empire, and gain the allegiance, or at least the neutrality, of certain States, without which Russia's aims might, and in all probability would, be frustrated. Bearing all this in mind, the reader will be at no loss to understand how a man like the Prince would be distressed by the danger which confronted him; for if anyone did know, he certainly did, that the internal weakness of Russia was too great just then for a responsible Minister to risk a great war.

'By further questioning the Prince, I ascertained that he had a private and confidential secretary, in addition to twelve ordinary secretaries. But not one of them was admitted to the private bureau, where for the time being the State papers were deposited, without the Prince's permission. His official business was transacted in another department, and the inner sanctum sanctorum was in a measure sacred to the Prince himself. A sentry was always posted at the door, and he had strict orders to allow no one to enter who had not special business, and who was not furnished with a pass.

'Being hedged round with these precautions, it seemed very difficult to comprehend how anyone could have gained access to the room in order to obtain possession of the precious documents. In constructing a theory, there were many points that could not possibly be overlooked. The chief of them was the all but absolute certainty that there had been a conspiracy, and a traitor and a spy was in the camp. He had known of the negotiations that were going on with respect to the treaty; he knew that the special courier was travelling post-haste to Russia; that the draft was delivered into the Prince's hands, and deposited temporarily in the Prince's safe, where all documents relating to the Prince's department—that is, political documents—requiring the Foreign Minister's close personal attention were placed for his convenience.

'In the case of a document of such paramount importance as this secret treaty, no copy of it could be made at first. This was another point the thief was obviously aware of, and it was also certain that he must have been pressed for time, or he would have made a copy of the draft himself, or extracts from it, which it was presumable might have answered all the purposes for which the document had been stolen. Such a course would not only have prevented the hue and cry being raised, but all the resources of a great Empire being put in motion against him.

'Examining the matter in this light, the question necessarily arose, Who was there who, having access to the Foreign Office, was enabled, in spite of all the stringent regulations and safeguards, to penetrate to the very centre of the temple—if one may use such an expression—and carry off a secret which was known to comparatively few people?

'This question was, of course, the crux of the whole affair, but I felt satisfied in my own mind about one thing. The guilty person was someone who knew the working of the Foreign Office, was well acquainted with the internal arrangements, and in close contact with the Prince. It need scarcely be said, perhaps, that the Prince was exceedingly anxious to prevent the matter leaking out and becoming public property. It would necessarily have caused great excitement and grave anxiety, and I agreed with him that on many grounds it was highly desirable to keep it from the public.

'There was one other point I ought to refer to, and it is a very important one; the theft was clearly committed during the night, or, at any rate, after business hours. On the first view that might seem to narrow the inquiry somewhat, though, as a matter of fact, it presented the affair in a more complex aspect; but, on the other hand, it seemed to me to point conclusively to several persons being concerned.

'In setting to work to read the riddle, I proceeded on the analytical principle, and searched, to begin with, for the motive. That seemed very apparent. Firstly, it was a secret treaty; secondly, it was framed against Turkey; thirdly, it was conceivable that it was of vital importance to Turkey to know what the treaty was likely to do, what it aimed at; therefore, somebody in the pay of Turkey, or somebody as a speculation, had stolen the document with a view to pecuniary gain.

'The latter supposition seemed to me hardly tenable—at any rate, not so likely as the idea that Turkey had her spies even in the Russian Foreign Office. I don't mean to say these spies were Turks themselves. As can be understood, it would have been next to impossible for a Turk to have gained entrance to the Foreign Office; but Turkey, of course, had her emissaries, and Russians were to be found so debased, so dead to all patriotism, so lost to every sense of honour, so mercenary, that they were ready to sell their country for the gain of gold. Of course, black sheep of this kind are numbered in every nation, therefore Russia was no exception.

'Everything pointed to the thief being a Russian, and, being a Russian, he also had some connection with the Foreign Office, a connection which gave him the right of being under the roof all night.

'It is necessary to explain that the Foreign Minister in Russia is provided with an official residence in the Foreign Office itself; that is to say, a portion of the actual building is set apart for the accommodation of himself and family and suite. An official of this kind keeps up a great deal more state than an English Minister does, and his suite and servants are generally very numerous.

'In the Prince's case, there were fewer people about him than usual, for the reason that he had no family. Nevertheless, I found that, including footmen, pages, and lower servants, there were forty persons in his *ménage*, and his domestic affairs were attended to and presided over by the lady whom he had addressed as Catarina, and whose ravishing beauty had so struck me. It is not necessary to refer to her by any other name. This lady had two private maids, and she exercised very considerable influence over the Prince's personal and domestic affairs.

'At this stage of my theorizing it seemed to me very clear that the miscreant would be found amongst the personnel of the Prince. The consideration of all the facts forced me to this, the most feasible conclusion. But I did not lose sight of the almost absolute certainty of a conspiracy, because it was hardly conceivable that one person, and one person only, would have committed such a daring act of treason; for an act of that kind was very foul treason indeed, and in Russia was punishable with death.

'Assuming that I was right with regard to my surmises, it would seem that a member of the household had been tampered with; pressure and temptation had been brought to bear upon him from outside. The temptation must have been great; heavy payment would be made; the traitor had been willing to sell his country for blood-money, and I was at pains to try and ascertain if any member of the Prince's *personnel* had given indications of being in possession of an unusual amount of money.

'I have endeavoured so far to make clear to those who may read this narrative the mental process by which I tried to lay hold of a clue. I need scarcely say that at the outset in a case of this kind one gropes in the dark. There is not a ray of light at first to guide him, and he must proceed cautiously and warily lest he go astray, and, while he is straining his eyes in one direction, his quarry is safely flying in another. Seeming impossibilities have to be reconciled with probabilities, and probabilities reduced to certainties. And when a clue, no matter how faint, has once been struck, it must be followed up patiently, intelligibly, and doggedly. There are three golden rules to be strictly observed by him who would succeed in connecting crime with its author. They are patience, silence, watchfulness.

'Human craft and human cunning are very difficult things to deal with, nor can one deal with them at all unless he is deeply read in human nature. In this instance craft of no ordinary kind had to be encountered. The criminal, to begin with, was not of the ordinary type. It was probable that up to this time he had lived a seeming virtuous life, and knowing how terrible was the penalty attaching to his wrong-doing, he would strain every nerve to prevent suspicion falling upon him. I had necessarily to consider all these little details, for they were essential to success.

'Although the Prince bore the reputation of being a cool, calculating diplomatist, who had outwitted every other diplomatist in Europe with whom he had had dealings, I found that in this matter of the stolen treaty he somewhat discredited his reputation; for he was by no means cool, and seemed unable to enter into the calculations which were necessary to a clear understanding of the course to be pursued if the mystery was to be unravelled. He had at the outset reminded me that I had the resources of an empire at my command, and he insisted on the telegraph being set instantly to work, and the police throughout the country being placed in possession of the facts. I was opposed to that course myself; I thought it was as likely as not to frustrate our efforts. But, of course, he had his own way, and he soon began to display not only irritation, but decided anger, when he found that I narrowed my search to the Foreign Office, and showed no inclination to go further afield. "It seems to me," he cried warmly, "that you are simply wasting time, and giving the enemy a chance. While you are hanging about here the traitor is making good his escape. Is it not certain that, whoever it is who stole the document, he is now hurrying to Turkey with it as fast as he can?"

'"No, Prince," I replied; "it is by no means certain that such is the case. On the contrary, I incline very strongly indeed to the belief that the traitor will be found here under this roof; that he has not stirred away, and is not likely to stir away."

'"You are wrong," he said sharply.

'"We shall see," I answered. "I admit that it is highly probable the document is being conveyed to the Turkish Government. If that is so, we cannot hope to overtake it, and another move will have to be made on the diplomatic board in order to checkmate those who have circumvented you. Your splendid skill in the game will enable you to determine the move. You may depend upon it that those who have entered into this conspiracy to convey valuable information to our country's enemy have well calculated the chances of success, and have taken means to ensure the information reaching its destination. But the key of the puzzle must be searched for here. If we find that key quickly, we may be able to prevent the information reaching the Turkish Government; but it is useless trying to do so without the key."

"'Then, you suspect someone in the department?" the Prince asked.

"'I don't suspect anyone at present," I answered.

"'What I mean to say is, you think the thief is one of the employés of the Foreign Office?"

"'I think the thief is a member of your own household, Prince."

'He looked at me in astonishment; then something like a smile of incredulity flitted across his stern face as he exclaimed, "Oh, nonsense!"

"'Why do you think it nonsense?" I asked.

"'It seems to me simply impossible that it could be so. No member of my household could have gained access to the bureau."

'At this I reminded him that, whereas in the daytime the corridors of the Foreign Office were patrolled by sentries, they were withdrawn when business hours closed, though sentries were on duty all night outside.

"'But all communication between my residence and the office is shut off at night by locked doors," he answered.

"'That only serves to show how very cunning and very clever the thief was to succeed in reaching your room and opening the safe in spite of bolts and bars," I said.

'The Prince grew very thoughtful. He seemed greatly struck by my theory, and ultimately confessed that he had not seen the matter from that point of view before. The result was he said I was to work in my own way, to follow my own lead, and to have an absolutely free hand.

"'It is a dastardly business," he exclaimed with warmth, "and even if the traitor were to turn out to be my own brother, I would not hesitate to shoot him, for nothing short of instant death would be a fitting punishment."'

Of course, all the resources peculiar to the Russian police system were utilized so far as they could be in a case of this kind. But the difficulties in the way will at once be apparent when it is borne in mind that the fact of a treaty having been stolen from the Foreign Office had to be kept as secret as possible. If the matter had leaked out, and become generally known to the public, the excitement would necessarily have been tremendous, and the objects in view—that is, the capture of the thief and the recovery of the missing document—would, in all probability, have been frustrated.

It will not be out of place here to explain that in Russia there is an armed police answering to the French gendarme; then there is a municipal police, very similar to the police of Great Britain; and lastly there is a vast army of spies, or *mouchards*, as the French call them. In this army both sexes are represented, and they overrun Russia. The three branches of the police service are not worked and controlled from one centre, owing to the vastness of the country; and this want of centralization has always been a flaw in the administration, as it is sometimes difficult to bring the various centres into complete harmony.

From these particulars, it will be gathered that a great deal must depend on individual effort, for while in the concrete the system may present weak parts and differences that are irreconcilable, in the abstract there is a unity of motion which gives the individual tremendous power, in this way: An accredited Government agent moving from point to point could demand, and would receive, every possible assistance, and the lumbering methods of the bureaucracy would be dispensed with.

In our own country we often complain very bitterly about the red-tapeism which so seriously clogs and hampers freedom of movement. But this red-tapeism of ours is nothing as compared with Russia. Russian red-tapeism is responsible for tremendous evils, and it often retards in a painful manner the administration of justice.

It will now be clear, probably, to the mind of the reader that an individual in Russia, endowed with faculties beyond the ordinary, has a chance of very signally distinguishing himself. This was certainly the case with Danevitch; and while nominally he was under the control and subject to the authorities in St. Petersburg, he was allowed a latitude and a freedom of action accorded to but few. His peculiar talents and his individuality begot him this distinction, and while it placed great responsibility on him, it left him so far untrammelled that he was enabled to exercise his independent judgment, and pursue the course which seemed to him, according to the circumstances of the hour, the right one.

After all, this was but another illustration of the fact that nothing succeeds like success. Danevitch had been singularly successful, though his success was due to talents only one remove from genius.

He has already, in his own words, made it plain that, in the case of the missing treaty, he believed, and in fact felt certain, that the culprit would be found amongst the Prince's household, though this did not prevent him availing himself of all the resources of the police department, which of course he had a right to do. But necessarily he was hampered by the secrecy it was so important to observe. What he did was to request by telegraph that the authorities in all the principal towns, seaports, and frontier stations should issue orders for a more than ordinarily strict examination of the passports and papers of people passing out of the country; that every person from St. Petersburg should be closely questioned, and should suspicion be aroused by his answers, he should be detained, and his luggage searched.

This is a measure permissible in Russia, but would not be tolerated in England. But in the vast dominion over which the Czar rules it is a necessity, and through its means many a crime has been detected and many a plot frustrated. It is right to say that the seizure of luggage is only resorted to when there is strong reason for believing that the owner is a dangerous person.

Although Danevitch took the steps indicated, he did not believe for a moment that anything would result beyond a great number of people being seriously inconvenienced, some innocent persons being arrested, and a great deal of blundering on the part of jacks in office, and of boorishness on the part of local police, who, dressed in a little brief authority, like to exercise it with all the brutal brusqueness peculiar to ignorant minds. He relied upon his own methods, and felt convinced that, if the mystery was ever to be unravelled, it could only be done by his own individual efforts. The more he dwelt upon all the details of the case as he had gathered them, the more he was convinced the guilty person would be found to be somebody who was in close communication with the Prince. Working on this basis, he classified the household under three heads for the purpose of giving his theory a somewhat practical form:

Firstly, there were the lower servants of the *ménage*.

Secondly, the upper servants.

Thirdly, the body servants of the Prince and his close personal attendants, including his secretaries, clerks, shorthand-writers, and amanuenses.

Those in the first category he dismissed from his calculations altogether, since it was so highly improbable that any one of them could have had the opportunities for committing such a crime. Obviously, in an establishment so constituted as the official residence of the Prince was, an inferior servant could not have gained access to the Prince's private rooms without running the gauntlet of many vigilant eyes, and incurring so much risk as to make it all but impossible that he could succeed.

Those who fell into the second category were not passed over without a little more consideration and a critical examination of the possibilities which were presented, when they were weighed individually and collectively. But when all this had been done, Danevitch scored them off the slate, too, and the sphere of his inquiry was so far narrowed.

In the third category there were necessarily included persons of intelligence which ranked higher than that to be found in the other two. But, as Danevitch progressed with the working out of his theory, he deemed it important to subdivide this third category, because his investigations made it clear that only a few of these individuals were so situated as to have the chance of abstracting the document.

Let it be distinctly borne in mind that the paper was in a despatch-box, locked. The despatch-box was in a safe, locked. The safe was in the Prince's private bureau, where none but the privileged were allowed to enter, and the door of which was also locked. Now, then, let it be still further remembered that the keys necessary to open the door of the safe and the despatch-box were kept in a safe in the Prince's bedroom, and the key of that safe was one of a number which every night were given into the custody of Vladimir Nicolayeff, the Clerk of the Keys.

There was another point which had to be very closely considered. It was this: the person who stole the document must have known it was there. He could not have known it was there if he had not occupied a position which enabled him to learn a good deal of what was going on; but as it could not be supposed for a moment that a Minister like the Prince would have lightly made a confidant of an inferior and irresponsible person, it was difficult to believe that the crime was the work of one individual; and here again Danevitch had to build up a theory, which he did as follows:

A was in possession of a secret that a draft treaty was being conveyed from Bulgaria to Russia, and would reach the Prince at a certain hour on a certain day, and for political or mercenary motives imparted the information to B, who, probably for political motives only, wished to make it known to the Government of the country against which the treaty was framed. B had to fall back upon C to procure the keys, without which the documents could not be carried off.

Here at once a conspiracy was suggested, and, a conspiracy admitted, it was impossible to dismiss the courier and Vladimir Nicolayeff from it. These two men, of course, represented extremes of position. The courier, whose name was Boruff, was a trusted and confidential Government officer of good birth and high social position. Nicolayeff, on the other hand, was a porter—a trusted servant, it was true, but a servant of humble origin and low rank. His services, if they had been given and used, must have been bought; that is, he had been corrupted, tempted from his allegiance by money. Next, the third or middle person had to be considered. What position did he occupy? It was not easy to answer that beyond saying it was obviously someone very close to the Prince.

Having arranged these various points, and set them forth in their order, he felt satisfied that his theory was a feasible one, and, if acted upon, was more likely to yield results than the search-for-the-needle-in-the-bottle-of-hay process of stopping people at the frontiers. At any rate, while that process was being carried out, Danevitch proceeded on his own lines, and his first step was directed to learning some particulars about Boruff.

In age the courier verged on forty. He had been in the Government service for fifteen years. Every confidence was reposed in him, and he was greatly respected. He had been engaged on courier duty for something like four years, and had made many journeys between Turkey and Russia. Formerly he had been a confidential clerk at the Russian Consulate at Smyrna.

He was a married man, and had four children, but lived apart from his family. There had been serious disagreements between him and his wife, owing, so it was stated, to his infatuation for another lady, which had led to all sorts of complications, difficulties, and domestic jars. These, of course, were purely family matters, and had not affected his Government position, as it was considered there were faults on both sides. Boruff was not well off. Such officials are poorly paid in Russia; and as he was forced to keep up two establishments, and moreover was extravagant, his resources were severely taxed.

So much did Danevitch learn of Boruff. Not much, if anything at all, to suggest a probability that Boruff had any guilty knowledge. He was a poor man; that was the worst that could be said about him. But poverty lays a man open to many temptations. Starving virtue is sorely tested when gold is jingled in its ears. It is so easy to be honest when one wants for nothing.

Such were Danevitch's reflections, and he put Boruff in his note-book, as he says, for future use if necessary. He thought it was just possible that ultimately the courier would prove one of the pieces necessary to complete the puzzle.

He next turned his attention to Vladimir Nicolayeff, a man of a totally different stamp. He was an old man—well, that is, he was close on sixty. He had been in the army, and had seen service in his youth, but, having been severely wounded, was discharged, and ultimately got employment under the Government. He had served at the Foreign Office a great many years. His position, though humble, was an important one. In his lodge in the entrance-hall all the keys not in use were kept. He also received messages and parcels, answered questions of inquirers, and pointed out the way to the different departments.

At this stage Danevitch sought another interview with the Prince, who cast a quick, keen glance at the detective, and asked curtly:

'What news?'

'None,' was the equally curt answer.

'Have you entirely failed?' asked the Prince.

'At present I can say nothing.'

'But you have got no clue?'

'No.'

A look of annoyance swept across the face of the Prince, and he shrugged his shoulders, as if in disgust.

'I suppose it is hopeless now to expect any results from your inquiries?'

'You forget, Prince,' said Danevitch, with dignity, 'it is not many hours since you instructed me in the matter. I cannot perform impossibilities.'

'True, true,' was the irritable response. 'But tell me, do you see any likelihood of being able to bring the guilt home to anyone?'

'Excuse me, Prince,' answered Danevitch firmly, 'I am not given to expressing ill-formed opinions, and, not being a prophet, I decline to run the risk of prophesying.'

'Forgive me,' said the Prince; 'I am afraid I have allowed my anxiety to blind me to common-sense. But the fact is, this loss has preyed upon my mind terribly. It is a very serious affair indeed—very serious. Moreover, it shows that there is a traitor somewhere. If we have traitors about, the State is in danger. Therefore it is imperative that this matter should be sifted to the very bottom. No time, no money, no patience, no skill, must be spared. The truth will have to be revealed.'

'I would venture to remind you, Prince,' said Danevitch, 'that the virtue of patience is one which, above all others, should be exercised in a case of this kind.'

The Prince was not indifferent to the point of the remark, and, bowing with consummate politeness, said:

'Pardon me, Danevitch; I have perhaps been hasty. You understand your art better than I do. I have no right to dictate to you. Pray proceed on your own lines.'

'Thank you,' Danevitch replied. 'We shall get on now. My object in requesting this interview is to ask who conveys your keys to Nicolayeff at night?'

'No one. It is his duty to come to me and receive them. But as it often happens that it is not convenient for me to see him myself, the keys are then given to him by my valet—a fine youth named André.'

'Did André give them to him the night before last, when the papers were stolen?'

'No; I gave him the keys myself.'

'There is no mistake about that, Prince?'

'None whatever.'

'One more question: Did you go out that night?'

'I did. I went to the opera.'

'What time did you return?'

'About two in the morning.'

'Did you note if the door of the safe in your sleeping apartment was closed then?'

'I haven't a doubt about it.'

'But you didn't try the door?'

'No.'

'Were the keys in their proper places in the morning?'

The Prince did not answer immediately. He appeared to be reflecting. At last he said:

'Yes, of course they were. I remember now taking them out of the safe myself, and handing them to my private secretary, who proceeded with me to my bureau. There is one point I forgot to tell you at our last interview. When I opened the safe in the bureau, I noticed that the lid of the despatch-box was wide open. It was that that aroused my suspicions, and led to my discovering immediately that the papers had gone.'

'But the despatch-box had been locked overnight?'

'I am certain of it.'

'So that the thief must have forgotten to close it again after abstracting the papers.'

'Precisely so.'

After this interview, Danevitch felt more than ever convinced that someone in very close personal relations with the Prince had been a party to the deed, and began to look round to see if suspicion could be justifiably entertained against any one of the inner household, so to speak. With a view to this end, he arranged the following plan with the Prince. He was to spend two days at the official residence in the character of a foreign visitor—the Prince's guest. André, the valet, was to be told off to personally attend him.

In due course Danevitch arrived. He was driven to the residence in one of the Prince's carriages, which was sent to the station to meet him. He had a certain amount of luggage, which was deposited in the handsome bedchamber allotted to him. He was a German on a secret mission, and did not understand Russian. His get-up would have deceived his own mother. He found André a smart, intelligent young man, who seemed to wear his heart upon his sleeve. There was nothing whatever in his manner or bearing which caused Danevitch to mistrust him.

The beautiful Catarina presided over the Prince's household, but never sat at his table. The detective was a little puzzled at first to understand the reason of that; and, in fact, Catarina was a kind of mystery, but in a few hours he had defined her position. Ostensibly she was his ward. She was the daughter of a very old friend of his, a military man, who had been killed on active service, and, in accordance with a solemn compact made between the two men, the Prince undertook to be a father to the orphan daughter. That was the story generally believed; at any rate, people affected to believe it. Danevitch did not. He found that Catarina had great influence over the Prince at times; but at others he seemed to treat her with coldness, even disdain, according to his mood. Danevitch came to the conclusion that Catarina was, in her way, almost as much a diplomatist as the Prince himself; but he saw signs—trifling ones, but significant to him—that whatever love or affection there was was on the Prince's side. He was sure that Catarina was not happy, but led a lonely, fretting life in that splendid palace.

Danevitch went for two days, but his visit was extended to a week. When he was taking his departure, the Prince asked him if he was any wiser than when he went.

'A little,' answered Danevitch.

'But is there anybody in my household whom you suspect?' asked the Prince with some anxiety.

'Frankly there is,' said the detective.

'Who is it?' the Minister demanded in a peremptory tone.

'Pardon me,' said Danevitch, 'for declining to answer you now. But unless I am very much mistaken, I shall be able to give you some valuable information before many days have passed.'

In less than a week Danevitch sought another interview with the Prince.

'I have a request to prefer this time,' said Danevitch after some preliminary remarks.

'What is it?' asked the Minister quickly, and possibly reading in his visitor's face that he had made a discovery.

'You have a daughter?'

'Yes,' gasped the Prince, who, in spite of his power of self-control, started at the question, and his brow clouded over.

'She is the wife of Kasin, who is the Russian Consul at Smyrna.'

A cold, cynical smile of bitterness played about the Prince's thin lips as he remarked:

'That is an open secret. But let me tell you at once, I have not seen my daughter for years, and never wish to see her again. She is an ingrate. I have cast her forth from my heart.'

The Prince betrayed the fact that, though he bore the reputation of being a man of blood and iron, and very likely justified his reputation when it came to matters of diplomacy, he had hidden springs of deep emotion and passion which were capable of being called into play.

'I do not wish to probe you, sir, nor touch upon your domestic affairs more than can possibly be helped. I have come here to request that you will influence the recall of your son-in-law from Smyrna.'

The Prince sprang to his feet, and grasped the back of his chair, and though he tried to control himself, it was evident he was greatly excited.

'Good God!' he exclaimed, 'do you mean to say that my son-in-law has had a hand in this business?'

'I mean to say nothing, sir, at present.'

'But your request carries with it an accusation. Remember the terrible responsibility of that. If Kasin has had a hand in purloining these papers he is a traitor, and the penalty is death.'

'I am aware of that, Prince.'

'The disgrace to me would be terrible. I hate him, but he is my son-in-law.'

The Prince paced up and down the room. He was strongly agitated. His pride was wounded, perhaps, as it had never been wounded before. Danevitch remained silent. He had nothing more to say then. Presently the Prince swung round on his heel, and said sternly, and threateningly:

'Remember this, Danevitch, not only is your own reputation at stake, but the honour of my family. You may risk your reputation as much as you like—it is naught to me; but, by the Virgin! be careful of my honour, or——'

He suddenly checked himself. Danevitch rose, and, with a cold bow, remarked:

'I will withdraw from this business altogether. What I have learnt shall be a locked secret with me. I wish you good-day, sir.'

'Stay!' cried the Prince. 'I apologize to you. I forgot myself, but make allowance for my feelings. I am in the wrong; you are in the right. Forgive me. This matter must go through, let the consequences be what they may. Though my daughter, my own flesh and blood, be guilty of this crime, she shall suffer. My country—Russia's interests have the first claim upon me. Pray proceed. I was the father a few minutes ago. I am Prince Ignatof, Russia's Minister for Foreign Affairs, again.'

He resumed his seat. He was the calm, cold, passionless, unemotional diplomatist once more.

'Now, then, tell me all,' he said peremptorily.

'At this hour I have nothing to tell you. I am here to prefer a request. That I have a motive in making that request, you may take for granted.'

'You want Kasin to be recalled?'

'Yes.'

'It shall be done.'

'When? Immediately.'

'Is it so urgent as that?'

'It is.'

'Good. He shall be recalled by telegraph.'

'I would request that he be commanded to leave Turkish soil in twelve hours' time, and to telegraph as soon as he is in Russia.'

'And after that?'

'And after that I will make a revelation to you.'

'So be it. In three days' time, call here again at this hour. You will find me alone, and prepared to receive your revelation.'

Danevitch took his departure. That same evening Vladimir Nicolayeff was walking along one of the principal streets. He had been dining at a café, and was making his way back to his duties at the Foreign Office. A bearded man suddenly confronted him at a corner of a street, and said:

'Nicolayeff, what was your reward for being false to your trust?'

'What do you mean?' demanded the porter angrily.

'Why do you answer my question with another? I ask how much were you paid for being false to your trust?'

Nicolayeff was agitated and confused.

'Who are you?' he demanded.

'The devil.'

'Then, betake yourself to your kingdom.'

'Not until I have done with you here. Again I ask you how much were you paid for giving up the key of Prince Ignatof's safe to the beautiful Catarina? Or was it her beauty alone that tempted you?'

Nicolayeff reeled. It almost seemed as if he was suddenly seized with palsy, and he uttered a strange, half-choked cry as he sank to the ground in a swoon. Perhaps in his superstitious mind he really thought the bearded man was the Evil One. A policeman approached. The bearded man whispered something in his ear and disappeared. The policeman blew a whistle, and assistance came. Then Nicolayeff was carried to the station, and when he recovered from the swoon he found himself a prisoner. In the meantime a message had been sent to the Foreign Office to say that the Clerk of the Keys had been picked up in the street in a swoon, and was then in custody. The message was conveyed direct to the Prince.

Three days passed, and Danevitch again presented himself at the Prince's bureau.

'Have you any news, Prince?' he asked.

'A code telegram was sent to Kasin recalling him.'

'Is he in Russia?'

'I don't know. He has not answered.'

'Ah, I suspected that would be the case.'

'I await your revelation,' said the Prince calmly.

'It is here,' answered Danevitch, as he took a letter from his pocket-book and handed it to the Prince. 'Shall I retire while you read it?'

The Prince glanced at the handwriting, and became very agitated.

'Yes,' he said, 'do. Come back in a quarter of an hour.'

As Danevitch went out, the Minister called to the sentry at the door:

'He will return in fifteen minutes. In the meantime let no one else enter at your peril.'

When Danevitch went back, he found the Prince seated at his desk. His face was almost deathly in its whiteness; but he was calm and frigid.

'You are deserving of your reputation,' he said. 'You have indeed made a revelation. How did you obtain possession of that letter?'

'I intercepted it. The writer believes, no doubt, that it is now on its way to Turkey.'

'Nicolayeff is under arrest.'

'He is.'

'See that not a moment is lost in securing Boruff.'

'That shall be done, Prince.'

'The interview can end.'

'Have you no other instructions?' asked Danevitch significantly.

The Prince understood. A pang of emotion caused his face to twitch, and he turned away. But in a few moments he was the cold, passionless man once more.

'I have no other instructions,' answered the Prince with equal significance.

'And the letter?'

'I will keep it.'

Danevitch bowed and withdrew.

The following morning, early, a closed carriage, drawn by four superb horses, left the Foreign Offices. The occupants of the carriage were Prince Ignatof and the beautiful Catarina. She was elegantly attired, and looked charming; but there was an expression of some anxiety on her face, and when she gave certain instructions to her maid, who was to sit with the driver, there was a tremulousness in her tone which was not natural to her.

The carriage was driven to one of the Prince's country estates on the great Moscow road. It was an old-fashioned mansion in the midst of pine-woods, and the extensive pine-woods round about swarmed with game, fur and feathered. The Prince often entertained large shooting-parties there, but on this occasion he had no guests. The servants in charge had been apprised of his coming, and had the mansion in readiness.

Two nights later a strange thing happened. The Prince and Catarina were together in their chamber, when a shrill scream resounded through the house. It was a woman's scream. A few minutes afterwards the Prince flung open the door, and rang his bell for assistance. He was pale and agitated. When the servants rushed up, he said, 'Your mistress has been taken suddenly ill. Attend to her,' and at the same time he ordered a man-servant to ride with all speed for a doctor from the neighbouring village, six miles away.

When the servants entered the room, they found Catarina fully dressed, lying on the bed. Her face was ashen in its hue. Her eyes seemed starting from her head. Foam was oozing from her mouth; her limbs were convulsed. The servants did what they could, but Catarina never spoke. When the doctor came, she was dead. He examined her, and said she had died from the effects of some powerful poison. There was a strange smell in the room; there was a broken glass on the floor. Before leaving the house, however, he changed his opinion, and certified that she had died from apoplexy.

Some nuns were brought from a neighbouring convent to pray and watch by the body. Three days afterwards it was quietly and unostentatiously buried in a plain grave in the little village cemetery. The Prince followed as chief mourner. An hour later he was a changed man. He seemed to have grown ten years older. About three weeks later it was officially announced in the *Gazette* and other papers that Prince Ignatof had retired from the Foreign Office by the advice of his physicians, his health having completely broken down.

Some few particulars have yet to be told. The letter which Danevitch intercepted and handed to the Prince was written by Catarina. It was addressed to Madame Kasin at Smyrna. There are reasons why the letter should not be given *in extenso*, but its substance can be indicated. The writer made it evident that Madame Kasin, who was as strongly embittered against her father as he was against her, conspired with her husband and Buroff and Catarina to obtain the information contained in the secret treaty, and sell it for a large sum of money to Turkey, to whom it was of immense value. Kasin, it appeared, had learnt that a treaty was being negotiated; and though Buroff would not undertake to purloin the document himself, he was heavily bribed to inform Catarina that he had brought it.

Between Catarina and Madame Kasin a very strong friendship existed. Catarina considered the daughter had been very badly treated. This sympathy and friendship had led to great ill-feeling between Catarina and the Prince, who had threatened to send her adrift. She undertook to abstract the document, but she went to work so clumsily that, as the saying is, she gave herself away. And her incautiousness in writing that condemnatory letter showed that she had not in her the qualities of a trickster and a thief. She told the whole miserable story in the letter, and said that she herself would convey the precious document to Smyrna. She did not mention Nicolayeff's name, but Danevitch felt certain that the Clerk of the Keys had been corrupted in order that the key of the Prince's bed-chamber safe should be procured, and to put his belief to the test he accosted the unfortunate porter in the street in the way we have seen. His intention was, if the porter betrayed himself, to place him at once under arrest. He was not prepared, however, for the sudden collapse of the wretched man, who did not long survive the shock and the disgrace.

The whole matter, of course, was hushed up as much as possible. It was deemed advisable that the details should not reach the ears of the public. It is perhaps needless to say that the Kasins, who were ready to prove traitors to their country, never again set foot on Russian soil. Danevitch confesses that he was anxious, if possible, to save the Prince the disgrace of having his own daughter arrested, hence the telegram. He was sure that telegram recalling Kasin would sound a note of alarm to him, and he would take himself off. That proved to be the case. When some months had elapsed, Buroff was quietly packed off to Siberia.

The Prince when he had sold off a large proportion of his estates, went abroad—to France, it is said—where he spent the rest of his days in strict retirement. Before leaving Russia, he erected a magnificent and costly marble monument over the grave of the beautiful Catarina, the mystery of whose death will never be solved until the secrets of all hearts are known.

HOW PETER TRESKIN WAS LURED TO DOOM.

THE FIRST ACT—THE PLOT.

THE period was the reign of Alexander II. The time, the afternoon of a day in early summer. The place, an office in the huge building in St. Petersburg known as the Palace of the Admiralty, one of the finest and most imposing structures of the kind in the world. Its principal front is more than a quarter of a mile in length, while its wings, which extend to the Neva, are nearly seven hundred feet long. In this palace an enormous number of people are employed, including many women; and here the whole business in connection with the Imperial navy is transacted.

The office referred to was a large room lighted by several long windows. Running the whole length of the room was a flat-topped mahogany desk, on which were spread a number of plans of vessels, tracing-papers, compasses, squares, pencils, and other things of a like kind usually found in the office of a draughtsman. To give the place its official description, it was 'Department H, Left Wing, Second Floor, Room 12. Imperial Yachts.'

It was under the control of a much-trusted Government servant, one Samuel Snell. That was not a Russian name, but an English one. Snell was an Englishman—a Cockney, for he was born within sound of Bow bells. He had been brought up as an engineer's designer and draughtsman, and was considered very clever. He left his native country when he was three-and-twenty, and went to Russia, induced thereto by a Russian friend in trade in London, who had taught him to speak the Russian language, and assured him that his talents would find greater appreciation and a better market abroad than at home. Samuel Snell was influenced by this, and went. He was fortunate, through his friend's influence, in speedily obtaining employment, and having marked ability, he made his way.

In the course of time he obtained naturalization; married a Russian lady, the daughter of a gentleman holding an appointment in the naval construction department; and ultimately, through his father-in-law's influence, obtained an appointment himself as assistant copyist in the Admiralty Palace. His talents soon made him conspicuous; he was singled out for gradual promotion, until at last he was placed at the supreme head of the department responsible for the building and repairs of the Imperial yachts. It was no sinecure, but an important and responsible position.

In this room, on the day and at the hour in question, two young women were seated. One had soft brown hair, bright blue eyes, a delicate complexion, and regular features. She was the daughter of Snell, and was just twenty years of age. Her name was Catherine. She was unmistakably of an English type, though born in Russia, of a Russian mother, and had never been out of the country in her life. Her companion was as unmistakably Russian; she had dark eyes, black hair, olive complexion, and was slightly older than the other girl. They were both good-looking. The brunette was called Anna Plevski. Her face indicated great strength of character. She had a strong, determined mouth; intelligence beamed from her eyes; her forehead spoke of brain-power.

Their respective positions were as follows: Catherine was a confidential clerk to her father. She had been specially trained for the work, and had held the appointment for over three years. Anna was in another department altogether. She was what was termed 'an indexer.'

The two girls were friends. They had been to school together. Anna had taken advantage of a little relaxation to slip into Room 12 to have a chat with Catherine, for she knew Mr. Snell was away; he had gone down to Kronstadt on official business. But it wasn't for the sake of a purposeless chat that Anna went to Room 12. She had a deep and dark design, as was destined to be revealed at a later stage of this strange and tragic drama. Her own department was a long way off, in another part of the huge building, and she was at some trouble to reach her friend's office by a very circuitous and round-about route, anxious, presumably, that it shouldn't be generally known that she had gone to Room 12.

'It's a beautiful day, Catherine, isn't it?' said Anna, after some preliminary greeting. 'It's a pity you and I are not rich.'

'Why?' asked Catherine, with a simple expression on her pretty face.

'Surely you don't need to ask why. If we were not mere drudges, we should be able to taste some of the pleasures of the world—go where we liked, stay as long as we liked, and enjoy ourselves generally, instead of being stewed up here when the sun is shining.'

'Well, you know, money doesn't always bring happiness, Anna, my dear,' answered Catherine.

'It may not always do so; but as sure as eggs are eggs there can be precious little happiness without it.'

'Oh, I don't know. Contentment goes a long way,' Catherine said, with some timidity, for she knew that her friend held very pronounced views, was unusually strong-minded, and had an iron will, to say nothing of an unyielding dogmatism, which occasionally, when stirred up, became objectionable, and at times offensive. In short, Anna had an aggressive spirit, and was disposed to find fault with all constituted authority.

'Contentment!' she echoed with a malicious sort of chuckle; 'how can one be contented with a lot that is hard, toilsome, and irritating? It's not pleasant to realize every hour of your life that you are only a drudge. I ask myself over and over again why wealth is so unequally distributed. Why should it be in the hands of the few, while the vast majority of mankind are the slaves of those few, and groan and sweat under the yoke of paid labour—for what? merely to keep body and soul together.'

Catherine had heard her friend express similar sentiments before, so that she was not surprised at this bluntness of speech; but as she herself did not consider she had any particular cause to complain, and as the views she held were not altogether in accordance with Anna's, she ventured to mildly express dissent from Anna's doctrine. It only seemed, however, to arouse that young woman to a more vigorous display of her feelings, and with a pepperiness that was distinctly characteristic of her, she exclaimed scoffingly:

'Well, friend Catherine, I can't help saying that I've no patience with anyone who is willing to accept stripes and lashes without a murmur. That's not my spirit. I've got brains, so have you, and yet we are forced to toil long hours every day for bare sustenance, while thousands and tens of thousands of brainless louts are rolling in riches. Ugh! It makes me mad to think of it.'

Catherine smiled prettily as she remarked:

'You seem to have been stirred up to-day, dear. Something has put you out of temper.'

'Yes; I am out of temper. I'm dissatisfied. Why, only to-day an order was issued in our department that we are to work two hours extra every day owing to pressure of work; but, as you know, the miserly Government take precious good care they won't pay us so much as an extra copeck, no matter how long we work. I say it's shameful!'

'But what's the use of fretting about it if we cannot alter it?' asked Catherine.

'But I say we can alter it. The working classes of this country are the bone, sinew, and brains of the country; yet they are kept in shackles and ground into the dust.'

'And yet, after all, Anna, talent is always recognised, and individualism will make its mark.'

'Great heavens!' cried Anna, lifting her dark eyebrows in amazement, while she looked at her friend with something like pitying contempt, 'is it possible that you can cheat yourself into the belief that that is true? You know as well as I do that talent and individualism are not worth a rap without influence to advance them. Kissing goes by favour in this world; and if you've no influence you may starve, while some idiot is pitchforked into power and authority. But, there, don't let us wrangle any more at present. Some day I shall convert you, and bring you round to my views. By the way, I see that our Little Father, the Czar, is to make a yachting cruise round the coast of Finland next month, and that his yacht, the *North Star*, is to be entirely overhauled and refitted.'

'Yes, that is so.'

'It's a very fine yacht, isn't it, the *North Star?*'

'I should think so. I've never seen it, though.'

'That's a wonder. I thought your father could have taken you on board any of the Emperor's yachts.'

'So he could, I've no doubt; though he has never done so.'

'But you have the plans of the *North Star* in this department, haven't you?'

'Oh yes.'

'I should like to see them. Would you mind showing them to me? I want to know what this grand vessel is like.'

Catherine hesitated; but failing to see that she would do any harm by complying with her friend's request, she went to a huge safe, and took therefrom a large roll of cartridge-paper, which she spread out on the desk, and kept it in position by weights at the corners. And then there was revealed to Anna a scale drawing, showing the hull, the sections, the ground-plan, and general design of the Imperial vessel, which was one of several used by his Majesty for pleasure cruises.

This particular one was then in the hands of the Admiralty for refit and overhaul, and was under orders to be at Kronstadt on the 20th of the following month; to receive the royal party, including the Czar, for a trip up the Gulf of Bothnia, and along the coast of Sweden, returning by the coast of Finland.

Anna looked at the plan attentively, critically. Indeed, she studied it; and having an excellent memory, the result of training as an 'indexer,' she was enabled to carry the whole of the plan in her mind's eye.

She would have liked to have made some notes, but did not dare do so, and so she fixed the details in her mind.

'The Little Father's apartments seem very spacious,' Anna remarked carelessly, as though she meant nothing.

'Oh yes,' said Catherine; 'but they are all to be reconstructed, and removed from the after-part of the vessel, where they are now.'

Anna's dark eyes opened wide, and her ears were all alertness.

'Indeed! Why?'

'Well, they are in the extreme stern of the ship now; and as the vessel pitches very much, they are not comfortable.'

'Then, where are the Czar's rooms to be placed?' asked Anna eagerly.

'A large deckhouse is to be constructed amidships. It will be fitted up like a little palace.'

'Ah! umph! I understand,' Anna muttered thoughtfully. 'Then I suppose that is where the rooms will be?' and she placed her finger in the centre of the plan.

'Yes.'

Catherine made a movement to remove the weights from the corners of the paper, when Anna exclaimed:

'Stop a minute. I just want to look at something. All right. Thanks. It's most interesting. I wish I were a rich person, that I could have a steam-yacht like that, and go where I liked.'

'You should marry an emperor; then you would have all you could desire,' said Catherine with a laugh, as she rolled the draft plan up and restored it to the safe.

'No; I wouldn't be an empress if I had the chance,' Anna replied tartly. 'Kings, queens, emperors, empresses, and the like, are all tyrants. There should be no crowned heads. I don't believe in 'em. They are a curse to the world.'

'Anna, you surprise me!' said Catherine with a frightened look. 'I knew you were peculiar, and held remarkable views, but I had no idea you were disloyal.'

'Hadn't you, dear?' answered Anna, with a laugh. 'Well, well, don't take me too seriously, you know. I say some queer things sometimes.'

Then, suddenly throwing her arms round her friend's neck, she kissed her on both cheeks and sped out of the room.

The scene changes. In what is known as the St. Petersburg quarter, which is situated on the north side of the Neva, is an old and lofty house, not unlike some of the old buildings in Edinburgh.

The house is let out in tenements, and there is a common stair for the use of all the tenants, who for the most part are working men, artisans, and the like. At the very top of the building, immediately under the tiles, is a long room with a slanting roof. In this room three men are at work, busily at work, though it is the dead of night. They carry on their work by lamplight.

Two are seated at a bench, which is covered with a miscellaneous lot of tools—pliers, small hammers, pincers, files, tiny saws, screw-drivers, chisels of various shapes, punches, etc. There are also sets of mathematical instruments; and before the men are carefully-prepared diagrams and drawings to scale, and to these the men make constant reference.

They are fitting together an ingenious and clever piece of mechanism in a small oblong box, lined with tin, and divided into compartments. It is a sort of clockwork arrangement they are engaged upon, and it is intended that the motive power of this mechanism shall be a noiseless spring, acting on a solid brass, notched wheel. In the rim of this wheel are forty-eight notches. The wheel can be made to revolve slowly or quickly, as may be desired. As the wheel revolves, every time a notch reaches a given point, mathematically determined, a tiny, but powerful, steel lever drops into it, and this causes a steel rod, something like a miniature shaft of a screw-steamer, to advance at right angles with the wheel towards a partition at the end of the box.

When this rod or shaft has been pushed forward a stage, the lever rises again, until the next notch is reached, when the same thing occurs, and the rod gets a little nearer to the partition, in which, immediately facing the point of the rod, is a circular hole corresponding in circumference to the rod itself, so that ultimately the rod must pass through the hole into a recess between the partition and the end of the box.

The object of this will presently be seen. The two men, who are evidently skilled mechanics of a high class, are both young. Neither of them has yet numbered thirty years.

A third man is engaged in a totally different occupation. He is an old man, tall and thin, with a grave, professional face, small, keen eyes, and a high forehead. He is dressed in a long, dark blouse, and wears a black silk skull-cap. He has a square table before him in the centre of the room; on it are retorts, crucibles, phials, mortars, and pestles.

In a retort, beneath which burns a spirit-lamp, he is compounding something from which most obnoxious vapours arise, but immediately above is a skylight, which is open to give egress to the fumes.

The man watches the retort anxiously and nervously, and every few minutes he plunges a small thermometer into the boiling liquid, and then, withdrawing it, reads by the light of an Argand lamp what the figures indicate.

At last he suddenly extinguishes the flame of the spirit, utters a sigh of relief, and straightens his aching back. As he does so, one of the two young men turns towards him, and says:

'Well, Professor, have you finished?'

'Yes, thank God, I have, and I am glad.'

It seemed like blasphemy that he should have thanked God, having regard to the deadly objects of his work. But the phrase was either uttered carelessly, or he was a fanatic who believed that what he was doing was blessed of Heaven.

Presently there were three light taps on the door. The men paused in their labours and listened. Then the Professor advanced noiselessly to the door, and gave three raps himself.

This was followed from outside by two quick raps, then two deliberate ones. Instantly on receiving this signal the professor turned the key, opened the door, and admitted a man, who wore a large cloak, which, on entering the room, he threw off, and a handsome, striking young man was revealed, with a strongly-marked face, and a well-shaped head covered with dark, curly hair.

It was a face full of intellectuality. The mouth, which was shaded by a carefully-trimmed moustache, was well shaped, but the lower jaw was heavy, and destroyed the general symmetry of the features. His eyes were almost coal-black, restless, and full of fire. They indicated an intense nervous energy.

There was something—it is really difficult to define it—about the man's whole appearance which suggested the masterful, commanding spirit—the leader of men. And when he spoke, the full, resonant voice, the rich, decisive tones, accentuated and emphasized this something, and proclaimed that he was one to be feared, to be obeyed. Peter Treskin—that was his name—was in every way a remarkable man. And even at the present day there are parts of Russia where he is referred to with sorrow, and spoken of with reverence.

Peter Treskin came of good family. He was intended for the law, and had studied hard and acquired an immense amount of general knowledge. But somehow he had been attracted to a set of malcontents, who were for revolutionizing everything and everybody.

They believed, or fancied they believed, which was much the same thing, that it was their mission to set the world right; to alter this and change that, to pull down thrones and set up their own forms of government, which would be so perfect, so just, so equitable, that every human wrong and every human sorrow would be done away with.

It was the Utopian dream of lotus-eaters; but fools have dreamed it through all time; they will go on dreaming it until time closes, and instead of ending sorrow, they will, as they have ever done, increase it manifold.

However, these men thought differently, and Peter Treskin's vanity was gratified, his ambition found a channel, his fiery disposition a means of satisfying it; and as he never played second fiddle to anyone, he was raised to a height, from which he commanded.

In other words, he became the head of a vast conspiracy which had for its object the destruction of the rulers who then ruled. In short, Peter, at the head of a mob, so to speak, opposed himself to the constituted forces of law and order.

It is true those forces were not what they might, and perhaps ought to, have been. They were stern, in many ways oppressive, in some respects unjust, and often ungenerous; but Peter Treskin's methods were not calculated to change them.

It was astonishing, however, how he was enabled to enlist clever and intellectual men of all sorts and conditions under his banner, which, figuratively speaking, was inscribed with one word of ghastly import—Revolution!

'Well, friends, how does the work go on?' he asked, as he entered the room, wiped his perspiring forehead with his handkerchief, and then, with a quick, nervous touch, rolled a cigarette and lit it.

'We've nearly finished,' answered one of the two men. 'By to-morrow night the machine will be ready.'

'Good! excellent! bravo!' said Treskin. 'And you, Professor?'

'My part is also nearly completed. It has been a dangerous operation, but will be successful.'

The man who spoke was Professor Smolski, a clever chemist, whose researches and knowledge, if properly applied, might have been of immense benefit to the world, and have earned him a niche in the gallery of worthies. But he had ranged himself on the side of the malcontents, and for the sake of his craze he was willing to sacrifice the prospects of fame, if not fortune, and to run the almost certain risk of a shameful death. Truly human nature is a mystery.

The other two men were brothers—Jews, Isaac and Jacob Eisenmann. They were born in Russia, but their parents had fled from Germany to avoid persecution, though, in flying from the hornets, they had encountered the wasps; that is to say, they had found no peace in Russia. They had been oppressed, persecuted, harried, and their offspring had vowed vengeance. Isaac and Jacob were sworn foes of the Government. They were clever mechanics, and their cleverness was used to build up a destructive instrument of death, contrived with devilish ingenuity and diabolical cunning.

These men represented a large party, which included women as well as men; but Treskin was the head, the leading light, the impelling spirit. His influence, his restless energy, his ambition, his vanity, made him one of the most dangerous men in all Russia. He seemed able by some extraordinary power he possessed of swerving men from the paths of rectitude into the tortuous ways of crime. He led women like lambs to the slaughter; he bent even strong men to his will.

Strangely enough, however, up to the time that he is brought under the reader's notice, he had managed to escape falling under suspicion. It is difficult to say what this immunity was due to; possibly some superior cunning, some extraordinary cautiousness. But whatever it was, Peter was not wanting in courage, and was quite ready to take his share of risk.

His co-conspirators now proceeded to explain to him the result of their labours and their ingenuity. The empty recess at the end of the mechanical box was to be filled with a novel preparation containing a latent explosive power of immense force. This latent power, however, could only be aroused into activity by the combination of a chemical fluid, and in order to bring this about, the mechanism had been arranged with wonderful precision and cleverness. Professor Smolski had produced the necessary fluid, and the two Jews had, between them, constructed the machinery. At the end of the rod or shaft already described a glass tube, hermetically sealed, would be attached by fitting into a socket. As the rod was advanced by the revolving notched wheel, which could be set to do its work in one hour or forty-eight, the glass tube would ultimately be thrust through the hole in the partition, where, coming in contact with an opposing rigid bar of iron, it would break, and then instantly something like a cataclysm would follow.

This, of course, only describes the machine in rough outline, and that is all that is intended to be done. Those who are curious to learn the details of the strange instrument of death and destruction will find drawings of it preserved in the police archives of St. Petersburg. It was, at the time, the most perfect and certain thing of its kind that man's devilishness had been able to create. And in some respects it is doubtful if it has been improved upon up to the present day.

Four o'clock was striking when Peter Treskin stole forth from that reeking den of evil designs, and made his way into the sweet, fresh air. Overhead the stars burned with an effulgency only seen in a Northern climate. Peace and silence reigned in the sleeping city. The clear, pellucid waters of the Neva glistened and glinted as they flowed to the sea, emblematic of the Stream of Time, which silently but surely sweeps all men into the great ocean of eternity, and obliterates even their memory.

Man's life is a little thing indeed when compared with the stupendousness of Time and Eternity. The bright stars shine, the rivers roll for ever; but man is born to-day; to-morrow he is dust and forgotten. No such feeling or sentiment, however, stirred Peter Treskin's emotion as he hurried along to his lodgings. He was elated, nevertheless, and full of a fierce, wicked joy, for his designs seemed to be going well. He had that night seen the completion, or almost the completion, of an instrument of destruction which was calculated and intended to strike terror into the hearts of tyrants, and he even believed that the hour was at hand when constituted power and authority, as it then existed, would be shattered into the dust, and from its ruins a new order of things would arise, in which he would figure as a supreme ruler.

Fools have dreamed these dreams before, and awakened with the curses of their fellow-men ringing in their ears; and then, having died a shameful death, have been thrust, unhonoured and unwept, into a nameless grave. But Treskin was not disturbed by any gloomy forebodings, and having reached his lodgings, he hurried to bed.

The scene shifts once more, and shows us Kronstadt, a busy, thriving seaport, arsenal, and naval and military town, at the head of the Gulf of Finland, exactly thirty-one miles west from St. Petersburg. The town is built on an island, and is so strongly fortified that it is called the 'Malta of the Baltic.' The greater portion of the Imperial navy assembles here, and there are armour and appliances, not only for repairing vessels, but building men-of-war. There are three great harbours. Two are used exclusively for the Imperial ships, and the third is a general harbour capable of accommodating seven hundred vessels. In the winter no trade with the outer world is carried on, owing to the ice; but during the summer months the flags of various nationalities may be seen, but by far the largest number of foreign vessels visiting Kronstadt sail under the British flag.

At this place, one summer afternoon, a man and woman arrived, and made their way to a tavern near the entrance to the general harbour. The woman was young, good-looking, very dark, but her features wore a careworn expression, and she seemed to glance about her with a nervous fear, as though she was in dread of something. The man was of middle height; he had an iron-gray beard and iron-gray hair. Judging from his grayness, he was advanced in years; but his step was firm, his eyes, which were very dark, were the eyes of youth—they were restless and full of fire. He carried a leather hand-bag, which he deposited on a chair beside him as he and the woman seated themselves at a table outside of the tavern and ordered refreshment, which was served by the tavern-keeper himself. The stranger got into conversation with the landlord, and asked him many questions.

'Where is the Little Father's yacht, the *North Star*, lying?' he asked.

'Out there, moored to that big buoy. You will see she has the Imperial flag flying.' As he spoke, the landlord pointed to the outside of the harbour, where a large steam-yacht, painted white, was moored. A thin film of smoke was issuing from her funnels, and a little wreath of steam from her steam-pipes. 'She has been outside into the roadstead this morning to adjust her compasses. I see a bargeload of stores has just gone off to her.'

'At what hour will the Imperial party arrive to-morrow?'

'They are timed, I understand, to be here at nine o'clock,' said the landlord.

'The Czar is a stickler for punctuality, isn't he?' asked the stranger.

'Yes. I understand he is seldom behind time if he can help it. Well, his Majesty will have a good trip, I hope. The weather promises to be fine. God protect him!'

'She is a fine yacht, is the *North Star*, I suppose?'

'Splendid! Magnificent! I once had the honour of going on board by the courtesy of one of the officers, who gave me an order. But she was laid up then, and partly dismantled. Now would be the time to see her, when she is all ready for the Little Father's reception. But that is impossible. No one not connected with the vessel would be allowed on board.'

The stranger smiled, as he remarked:

'I am not connected with the vessel, and yet I am going on board.'

'You are!' cried the host in astonishment. 'Impossible!'

'By no means impossible. I have official business.'

'Oh, well, of course, that's another thing. Well, I envy you.'

When the landlord had gone about his affairs, the girl said to her companion, speaking in low tones:

'You are a fool to talk about your intentions in that way. You are simply directing attention to yourself.'

'Tut! hold your tongue! What does it matter? There is nothing to fear from this thick-headed publican.'

'But you ought to be more careful—you ought indeed,' urged the girl tearfully. 'You are far too reckless. Remember the tremendous risks you are running—we are running—for if you sacrifice yourself you sacrifice me too.'

'Are you beginning to funk?' asked the man irritably.

'No. But there is no reason why the risks should be made greater than they are. We have a great task to accomplish, and every possible caution should be exercised.'

'Well, now what have I done that is wrong?' demanded the man angrily.

'You told the landlord you were going on board the yacht. It was foolish to do that. You drew attention to yourself.'

'Possibly you are right—possibly you are right,' her companion returned thoughtfully. 'It was a little bit of vanity on my part, but it slipped out. However, all will be well. Our plans are so well laid it is impossible for them to miscarry.'

'Nothing is impossible; nothing should be counted upon as certain until it is accomplished,' the girl said.

'You are a nice sort of Job's comforter. Do, for goodness' sake, keep quiet!' answered the man snappishly. He was evidently in a highly nervous state, and very irritable. 'Well, I must go. Be sure, now, that you don't stir from here until I return.'

'I understand,' said the girl. 'But, remember, the suspense will be awful. Don't be away from me a minute longer than you can help.'

He promised that he would not. Then, taking up his hand-bag, he embraced his companion and went out. Making his way down to the quay, he hired a boat, and instructed the boatman to row him to the Imperial yacht.

On reaching the vessel, he was challenged by the sentry on duty at the gangway, and he replied that he had come on official business, and had a Government order. Whereupon he was allowed to get on to the lower grating of the steps, where an officer came to him, and he produced a Government document, stamped with the official seal, and setting forth that his name was Ivan Orloff, that he was one of the naval clockmakers, and had been sent down to adjust all the clocks on board the *North Star* preparatory to the Czar's arrival. Such an order could not be gainsaid, so he was admitted on board, but an armed sailor was told off to accompany him about the ship, and show him where the various clocks were situated. There were a good many clocks, as every officer had one in his cabin.

The man came at last to the Czar's suite of apartments in the newly-constructed deckhouse. The sailor paused at the entrance to cross himself before a sacred picture that hung on the bulkhead, but Orloff pushed on, and, passing beneath costly and magnificent curtains, he reached the Czar's sleeping-cabin, which was a dream of splendour. With quick, hurried movements he took from his bag an oblong box, turned a handle on an index dial, and placed the box beneath the royal bed. He scarcely had time to recover his position, and get to a chest of drawers on which stood a superb clock, when the sailor entered, and said gruffly:

'You ought to have waited for me.'

'I'm in a hurry, friend,' said Orloff. 'I want to get my work finished and return to St. Petersburg to-night.'

As he lifted the glass shade off the clock, his hands trembled and his face was as white as marble, but the sailor did not notice it.

Half an hour later Orloff had completed his task, and took his departure, and landing once more on the quay, he made his way to the tavern and joined the girl.

'Have you succeeded?' she asked anxiously.

'Yes. But a sailor kept guard over me, and I was afraid the plan would have miscarried; I racked my brains trying to find an excuse for freeing myself from him. But fortune favoured me. He stopped to mumble a prayer before an ikon, and I seized the opportunity to get into the Tsar's bed-chamber, where I planted the machine. It is set for thirty-three hours, and will go off to-morrow night when the Tsar has retired to his couch.'

The girl looked frightened, and said nervously:

'Well, let us leave here, and get back without a moment's delay.'

'Don't worry yourself, my child; there is plenty of time. I am going to dine first.'

He ordered dinner for two and half a bottle of vodka beforehand by way of an appetizer, and, having drunk pretty freely, he and the girl strolled out while the dinner was being prepared.

It was a glorious evening. The sun was setting. The heavens were dyed with crimson fire. In the clear atmosphere the masts and rigging of the vessels stood out with a sharpness of definition that was remarkable. There was no wind. The water of the gulf was motionless.

Suddenly there was a tremendous shock as if a great gun had been fired, and in a few moments a cry arose from a hundred throats that something had happened on board the Imperial yacht. The air about her was filled with splinters of wood. Men could be seen running along her decks in a state of great excitement, and she appeared to be heeling over to the starboard side. 'Her boilers have burst,' cried the people, as they rushed pell-mell to the quay, while from all parts of the harbour boats were hurriedly making their way to the *North Star*, as it was thought that she was foundering.

THE SECOND ACT—THE UNRAVELLING OF THE PLOT.

When the explosion on board the Imperial yacht occurred, Orloff and the girl were strolling along one of the quays which commanded a full view of the harbour, and, attracted by the tremendous report, they turned their eyes seaward to behold a dense column of vapourish smoke rising upwards, and wreckage of all kinds filling the air. The girl staggered, and reeled against her companion, and he, clapping his hand suddenly to his forehead, exclaimed:

'My God! what have I done? The machine has gone off before its time. I must have set the index wrong.'

The excitement both on shore and in the harbour was tremendous, otherwise Orloff and the woman would surely have drawn attention to themselves by the terror and nervousness they displayed.

'We are lost! we are lost!' wailed the woman.

At this the man seemed to suddenly recover his self-possession.

'Peace, fool!' he muttered savagely between his teeth. 'We are not lost.'

He glanced round him anxiously for some moments; then, seeing a boat containing a solitary boatman about to put off from the quay, he said hurriedly to his companion, 'Stop here for a little while; I will return shortly.'

She was so dazed and stupefied that she made no attempt to stop him, and he hurried away, rushed down a flight of stone steps, and hailed the boatman.

After a few words of haggling and bargaining, Orloff sprang into the little craft and the boatman rowed rapidly out towards the *North Star*.

The girl waited and waited in a fever of anxiety and impatience. She paced the quay—up and down, up and down. To and fro she went. Her face was as white as bleached marble. Her dark flashing eyes bespoke the fear she felt. Her hands opened and shut spasmodically from the extreme nervous tension she felt.

All the light of day faded out of the sky. A blood-red streak did linger in the western sky for a time, but was suddenly extinguished by the black robe of Night. The girl still paced the quay, but Orloff did not return. She heard the gossip of people as they returned to the shore from the harbour, and from this she gathered that the Imperial yacht had been partially destroyed, and many lives had been lost. The prevailing opinion was that the mischief was due to the bursting of a boiler.

Unable longer to endure her misery, the girl went back to the tavern. The landlord came to her, and asked if she had been off to the wreck.

'No,' she answered. 'My husband has gone. It's an awful business, isn't it? They say the boiler of the steamer blew up, and that there have been many lives lost.'

'I heard that half the crew are killed,' said the landlord. 'God be praised that the accident occurred before our Little Father arrived! It's a Providential escape.'

'Yes,' answered the girl sullenly.

The landlord asked her if she would have dinner, as it was all ready. She replied that she would wait for her husband. She drank some vodka, however, to steady her nerves, and smoked a cigarette.

Presently she went forth again, and paced the quay, going back to the tavern after a time to learn that Orloff had not returned. It was then a little after nine. And as the last train to St. Petersburg started at half-past nine, she settled the bill at the tavern, and, taking the leather bag with her, hurried to the station and got back to town. She was full of nervous apprehension, and puzzled to account for the strange disappearance of Orloff. Had he deserted her? Had he been apprehended? The suspense was horrible. It almost drove her mad.

When the news of the disaster on board the Czar's yacht reached St. Petersburg, the consternation was tremendous, and a special train filled with Government officials, including Michael Danevitch, started at once for Kronstadt to investigate the affair on the spot.

Several bodies had been recovered and brought on shore. They were laid out in a shed on the quay. The shed was lighted by oil-lamps, and their feeble glimmer revealed a ghastly sight. The bodies were all more or less mutilated. Some were unrecognisable. There were nine altogether, including the chief officer and the chief engineer.

The captain arrived with the Government officials. He had been in town, and was to have travelled down the next day in the Emperor's suite.

In mustering his ship's company, he found that twenty-three were missing altogether. Nine of that number were lying in the shed. The rest were being searched for by boats. Several were recovered, but some drifted out with the currents and were seen no more.

Investigations soon proved that the destruction was not due to the bursting of a boiler. The boilers were intact. The cause of the disaster, therefore, was a mystery, until somebody on board, having recovered his presence of mind after the dreadful shock, referred to the visit of the Government clock-winder.

That sounded suspicious. As far as the officials knew, no one had been sent down to wind the clocks. But still, as the fellow had come furnished with Government-stamped credentials, it was probably all right.

Owing, however, to some strange oversight or stupid blunder, nothing could be ascertained then, as no one was at the telegraph-office in St. Petersburg to receive messages, and so the night wore itself out, and many hours' start was given to Orloff and his co-conspirators.

During this time Danevitch was not idle. He knew, perhaps better than anyone else, how the Emperor was encompassed round about with enemies who sought his destruction, and the wily detective smelt treason in the air.

Although it was night, Kronstadt kept awake, for people were too excited to sleep, and a messenger was despatched to St. Petersburg on an engine, whose driver was ordered to cover the distance in an hour—a fast run for Russia. The messenger was furnished with a description of Orloff—at this time it was not known that a woman had been with him; it will be remembered she did not go on board—and was told to lose not a moment in circulating that description.

Then Danevitch began inquiries on his own account in Kronstadt. From the survivors on board the yacht he ascertained at what time Orloff went on board; an hour and a half before he presented himself a train had arrived from St. Petersburg.

He had probably arrived by that train. The boatman who took him off to the yacht was found. He said the supposed clock-winder carried a black bag with him both going and coming.

After his return to the shore only two trains left for St. Petersburg. By neither of those trains did he travel, so far as could be ascertained.

The sailor who had been told off to accompany Orloff over the vessel was amongst the missing; but it was gathered that when the clock-winder had gone the sailor mentioned to some of his companions that he had been much annoyed by the stranger rushing forward to the Emperor's bed-chamber, while he (the sailor) was mumbling a prayer before an ikon (sacred picture) which hung at the entrance.

When he got into the room, he noticed that the stranger was pale and flurried, as if he had received a shock. Those who heard the story thought the sailor's imagination had run away with him, and so no importance or significance was attached to what he said.

The destructive force of the explosion on board the *North Star* had been tremendous. Not only had the whole of the Czar's rooms been completely destroyed, but a large section of the ship's decks and bulwarks had been shattered, and one of her plates started, so that the water came in so fast that the pumps had to be kept going, while preparations were made to tow her into the docks, for her own engines being damaged, they would not work.

Soon after six in the morning, the engine that had been sent to the capital returned and brought some more officials. They stated that, from inquiries made, no one by the name of Orloff had been sent down to regulate the clocks on board the Czar's yacht.

All the clocks on board the Imperial fleet were kept in order by contract, and no special warrant had been supplied to anybody of the name of Orloff.

This information made it clear that a dastardly conspiracy was at work, and it was easy to surmise that the explosion on board the yacht was premature. The intention evidently was that it should take place after the Czar had embarked; but the cowardly wretches, by some blundering, had allowed their mine to go off too soon, and though many innocent people had been sacrificed, and immense damage done to valuable property, the life of the Emperor had been spared.

It was not long before Danevitch found out that the man calling himself Orloff, and a female companion, had put up at a tavern near the quay, and the landlord gave all the information he could.

He stated that Orloff told him he was going on board the vessel, and started off for that purpose, leaving the woman behind him. He returned later, and ordered dinner, and then he and the woman went off again for a stroll.

After the explosion the woman returned alone, and hurried away by herself, taking the black bag with her, to catch the last train.

This was instructive, but it was also puzzling. It was established that the woman did go up by the last train, but not Orloff. What had become of him?

Danevitch took measures to have every outlet from Kronstadt watched. Then he set off for St. Petersburg. In reasoning the matter out, it was clear to him that several, perhaps many, persons had had a hand in the conspiracy.

The infernal machine carried on board the *North Star* by the man calling himself Orloff was hardly likely to be the work of one man. Any way, a woman was mixed up in the business.

The official document that Orloff had presented was written on Government paper, and it bore the Government seal. The officer of the *North Star* who had examined it before admitting the pseudo-clock-regulator, and who was amongst those who escaped without hurt from the explosion, testified to that.

Such being the case, and the order being written on what was known as 'Admiralty' paper, it followed that it must have been stolen from the Admiralty office. It struck Danevitch that the thief was probably a female employé in the Admiralty Palace, and that it was she who accompanied Orloff to Kronstadt.

This was a mere surmise, but it seemed feasible, and with Danevitch all theories were worth testing. Whoever it was, in the hurry of leaving the tavern at that town she had left behind her a glove.

It was a black silk-thread glove, ornamented at the back with sprigs worked in white silk. With this glove in his possession, Danevitch proceeded to the Admiralty Palace. But as soon as he arrived he learnt that Miss Catherine Snell had made a statement about Anna Plevski having visited Room 12 and requested to look at the plans of the *North Star*.

Anna was at once confronted with Danevitch. Asked where she had been the night before, she replied indignantly, 'At home, of course.'

Did she know a person named Orloff? No, she did not. Why did she go to Catherine Snell and ask her to show her the plans of the *North Star*? Simply to gratify her curiosity, nothing else. She was next asked if she had worn gloves the day previous. She replied that she had. What sort were they? Kid gloves, she answered. Had she those gloves with her? No; she had left them at home, and had come to the office that morning without gloves.

After a few more inquiries she was allowed to return to her duties, but was kept under strict surveillance, while poor Catherine Snell was suspended for dereliction of duty.

In the meantime Danevitch proceeded to Anna's lodgings, and a search there brought to light the fellow to the glove left in the tavern at Kronstadt. It had been thrown carelessly by the girl on the top of a chest of drawers. This glove was a damning piece of evidence that Anna had accompanied Orloff to Kronstadt the day before, and that established, it was a logical deduction that she had stolen the stamped paper on which he had written, or caused to be written, the order which had gained him admission on board of the *North Star*. All this, of course, was plain sailing. Catherine Snell's statement had made matters easy so far. But there was a good deal more to be learnt, a great deal to be sifted before the truth would be revealed.

When a person in Russia is suspected of crime, the law gives the police tremendous power, and there are few of the formalities to be gone through such as are peculiar to our own country; and in this instance Danevitch was in a position to do almost absolutely whatever he thought fit and proper to do.

The finding of the glove carried conviction to his mind that Anna Plevski was mixed up in this new plot for the destruction of the Emperor. So, without any ceremony, he proceeded to rummage her boxes and drawers for further evidence. The want of keys did not deter him; chisels and hammers answered the same purpose. His search was rewarded with a bundle of letters. These were hastily scanned; they were all, apparently, innocent enough; the majority of them were love letters. A few of these were signed 'Peter Treskin'; the rest simply bore the initial 'P.' There was nothing in any of these letters calculated to cause suspicion, with the exception of the following somewhat obscure passage in a letter written a few days before the explosion:

'The time is at hand when your faith and love will be put to a great test. The serious business we have in hand is reaching a critical stage, and success depends on our courage, coolness, and determination. You and I must henceforth walk hand-in-hand to that supreme happiness for which we have both toiled. We love each other. We must unite our destinies in a bond that can only be severed by death.'

Having learnt so much, Danevitch once more confronted Anna. She confessed she had a lover named Peter Treskin; they had quarrelled, however, and he had gone away; but she knew not where he had gone to, and she did not care if she never saw him again.

'Perhaps you will be able to remember things better in a dungeon,' suggested Danevitch, as he arrested Anna, and handed her over to the care of a gendarme.

She turned deathly white, but otherwise appeared calm and collected, and declared that she was the victim of a gross outrage, for which everyone concerned would be made to suffer.

Danevitch's next move was to go to Treskin's lodgings. He found that gentleman had been absent for three days. Here also a search was made for compromising papers. A good many letters from Anna Plevski were brought to light. They all breathed the most ardent love and devotion for the man; and the writer declared that she could not live a day without him, that for his sake she was prepared to peril her soul. But there were other letters—love letters—written to Treskin by a woman who signed herself Lydia Zagarin. This person not only betrayed by her writing that she was desperately, madly in love with Treskin also, but from her statements and expressions it was obvious that he had carried on an intrigue with her, and was as much in love with her as she was with him. She wrote from a place called Werro, in the Baltic provinces. Danevitch took possession of these letters, and continued his search, during which he came across a slip of paper which bore the printed heading, 'The Technical School of Chemistry, St. Petersburg.' On it was written this line: 'Yes, I think I shall succeed.—SMOLSKI.'

Apparently there was not much in this, but what there was was quite enough for Danevitch under the circumstances, and he had Professor Smolski arrested. It was a summary proceeding, but in times of excitement in Russia anyone may be arrested who may possibly turn out to be a guilty person. It is not necessary that there should be a shadow of a shade of evidence of guilt in the first instance; it is enough that there is a possibility of the police being right. But if they are wrong what does it matter? The person is released, and the police are not blamed. Danevitch, however, did not often go wrong in this respect; and in this instance, Smolski being a Professor in the Technical School of Chemistry, there were probabilities that he might be able to afford some valuable information respecting Treskin.

Smolski was one of those extraordinary types of men who, having conceived a certain thing to be right, are willing to risk fame, fortune, life itself, for the sake of their opinions. Smolski was undoubtedly a gentle, high-minded man; nevertheless he believed that the ruler of his country was a tyrant; that his countrymen were little better than slaves, whose social and political rights were ignored; that the ordinary means—such as are familiar to more liberally-governed countries—being useless to direct attention to their wrongs, violent measures were justified, and the removal of the tyrant would be acceptable in God's sight. Holding these views—and though he was a family man and one respected and honoured—Smolski had allied himself with a band of arch-conspirators, whose head was Peter Treskin. He was calm, dignified, and collected under his arrest, and when he was interrogated, in accordance with Russian law, by a judge of instruction, he frankly admitted that he had been concerned in an attempt to bring about a better form of government; but he steadfastly refused to denounce any of his accomplices. He could die bravely, as became a man, but no one should say he was a traitor.

All this would have been admirable in a nobler cause; as it was, he simply proved that he had allowed his extreme views to blind him to the difference between legitimate constitutional agitation and crime—crime that, whether committed in the name of politics or not, was murder, and an outrage against God's ordinance. Smolski, in common with most men, neglected the safe rule that letters should be destroyed when they are calculated to compromise one's honour or betray one's friends. And thus it came about that when the Professor's papers were examined, not only were Isaac and Jacob Eisenmann brought into the police net, but many others; and in a diary he had kept there was a record of his experiments with the deadly compound which was destined to blow the monarch of the Empire into eternity, but which, owing to an accident or a blunder, had failed in its object so far as the Czar was concerned, though it had cruelly cut short the lives of many hard-working and worthy men. Under any circumstances, even if the Czar had been involved in the destructive influences of the infernal machine, many others must have perished with him. Such conspirators never hesitate to destroy nine hundred and ninety-nine inoffensive people if they can only reach the thousandth against whom they have a grievance.

Piece by piece the whole story as set forth in the first part of this chronicle was put together, and the plot laid bare; but though many had been brought under the iron grip of the law, the arch-conspirator, to whose ruling spirit and genius the plot was due, was still at large, and no trace of him was at that time forthcoming; but Danevitch did not despair of hunting him down, of bringing him to his doom. And no one whose mind was not distorted could say his life was not forfeited. His whole career had been one of plotting and deceit. His commanding presence and masterful mind had given him such an influence over many of those with whom he came in contact—especially women—that he had proved himself more than ordinarily dangerous, while his reckless and cowardly wickedness in carrying the infernal machine on board the Czar's yacht, and thereby causing the sudden and cruel death of something like two dozen people, stamped him at once as a being against whom every honest man's hand should be raised.

In the meantime, while Danevitch was trying to get a clue to Treskin's whereabouts, his co-conspirators—they might truly be described as his dupes—were tried, found guilty, condemned, and executed. Smolski, the two Eisenmanns, and four others, were ignominiously hanged in the presence of an enormous crowd. Smolski met his end with a perfect resignation, a calm indifference. He firmly believed he was suffering in a good cause. He died with the words 'Khrista radi' (For Christ's sake) upon his lips. He posed as a martyr.

Anna Plevski had been cast for Siberia, but before starting upon the terrible journey, the prospects of which were more appalling than death, she would have to spend many months in a noisome dungeon in the Russian Bastile, Schlusselburgh, in Lake Ladoga.

But a circumstance presently arose which altered her fate. Danevitch had kept his eye on Lydia Zagarin, of Werro. He found she was the daughter of a retired ship-master, who had purchased a little property in the small and pleasantly-situated town of Werro. He was a widower. Lydia was his only daughter. On her father's death she would succeed to a modest fortune. Treskin had borrowed money from her, and it was probable that he had singled her out from his many female acquaintances as one to whom he would adhere on account of her money. Four months after the fateful day when the Czar's yacht was partially destroyed and many people were killed, Treskin wrote to this young woman, renewing his protestations of regard for her, and asking her to send him money, and to join him with a view to his marrying her. He gave his address at Point de Galle, Ceylon, where, according to his own account, he had started in business as a merchant. He stated that, though he had taken no active part in the destruction of the *North Star*, he happened to be in Kronstadt on the night of the crime, and as he knew he was suspected of being mixed up in revolutionary movements, he deemed it advisable to go abroad; and so he had bribed a boatman to convey him to a Swedish schooner which was on the point of leaving the Kronstadt harbour on the night of the explosion, and he bribed the captain of the schooner to convey him to the coast of Sweden. By this means he escaped. From Sweden he travelled to England; from England to Ceylon, where he had a cousin engaged on a coffee plantation.

This letter came into the hands of Danevitch before it reached Lydia. How that was managed need not be stated; but Danevitch now believed he saw his way to capture Treskin. He knew, of course, that, as a political refugee, claiming the protection of the British flag, he could not be taken in the ordinary way. The British flag has over and over again been disgraced by the protection it has afforded to wretches of Treskin's type, and it was so in this instance. To obtain his extradition was next to impossible. He was a wholesale murderer, but claimed sanctuary in the name of politics, and he found this sanctuary under the British flag.

Danevitch, however, resolved to have him, and resorted to stratagem. He visited Anna Plevski in her dungeon. She knew nothing at this time of the fate of her lover, though she did know that he had not been captured. Danevitch, by skill and artifice, aroused in her that strongest of all female passions—jealousy. He began by telling her that Treskin had deserted her in a cowardly and shameful manner on the night of the crime, and did not care whether she perished or lived. Then he laid before her Lydia Zagarin's letters to Treskin, which had been seized at Treskin's lodgings, and he watched the effect on the girl as she read them. Finally he showed her the letter sent from Ceylon.

That was the last straw. Her feelings burst from the restraint she had tried to impose upon them, and she cursed him again and again. She declared solemnly that she was his victim; that she was innocent and loyal until he corrupted her, and indoctrinated her with his revolutionary ideas. He had sworn to be true to her, and used to say they would live and die together. On the night of the crime he had persuaded her to go with him to Kronstadt, because he declared that he could not bear her to be out of his sight. They had arranged that on the morrow they were to quit St. Petersburg, and travel with all speed to Austrian soil. But not only had he basely deceived her, but treacherously deserted her. She was furious, and uttered bitter regrets that she could not hope to be revenged upon him.

In this frame of mind she was left for the time. A week later, however, Danevitch once more visited her. She was still brooding on her wrongs and her hard fate. To suffer Siberia for the sake of a man who had so cruelly deceived her and blighted her young life was doubly hard.

'Would she be willing, if she had the chance, to bring him to justice?' Danevitch asked.

Her dark eyes filled with fire, and her pale face flushed, as she exclaimed with passionate gesture that she would do it with a fierce joy in her heart, and laugh at him exultingly as he was led to his doom.

She was told that the chance would be given to her to betray him into the hands of justice. She would be set free on sufferance, and allowed to proceed to Ceylon, and, provided she succeeded in her task and was faithful to the trust reposed in her, she would, on returning to Russia, receive a full pardon, and be supplied with a considerable sum of money to enable her to live abroad if she desired it.

In setting her free, however, in the first instance, the Government intended to retain a hold upon her, and to that end her youngest and favourite brother, who was an invalid, and to whom she was devoted, had been arrested on suspicion of being mixed up with revolutionary movements. If she did not return within a fixed time, the brother would be sent to the Siberian quicksilver-mines. While she was away he would be treated with every kindness, and on her return he would be set at liberty. His fate therefore was in her hands. If she allowed the false lover to prevail over her she would sacrifice her brother. If, on the other hand, she was true to her trust, she would save her brother, gratify her revenge, and be provided for for life.

She was allowed a week in which to make up her mind; but in two days she gave her decision. She would go to Ceylon. She would lure Treskin to his doom. To prepare the way she wrote a letter to dictation. In it she stated that she had been tried and found not guilty. No sooner was she released than she had been visited by a wretch of a woman named Lydia Zagarin, who abused her fearfully for having corresponded with Treskin, whom she claimed. And in her mad passion she had disclosed his whereabouts, but vowed that she hated him, knowing that he had been false to her, and that all he wanted now was her money. Anna, however, had no such thoughts about him. She loved him to distraction, and could not live without him. She intended, therefore, to go to Ceylon; and she had managed to secure some money, which she would take to him. She was perfectly sure, she added, that he loved her, and that they would be very happy together.

This letter was duly despatched, and a fortnight later Anna set out on her strange mission, having first had an interview with her brother, though she was cautioned against telling him or any living soul where she was going to. She found him almost broken-hearted, for he declared he was as innocent of revolutionary ideas as a babe unborn; but he knew that when once a man fell into the hands of the police as a 'suspect' he had very little to hope for. Anna endeavoured to cheer him up by saying she would do all that mortal could do to prove his innocence; and as the Government had failed to substantiate their charge against her, she was sure they would not succeed in his case.

The scene changes again for the final act, and shows the beautiful island of Ceylon and the wide, sweeping bay of Point de Galle, with its splendid lighthouse, its great barrier reef, and its golden sands. Anna Plevski had landed there from a P. and O. steamer, and had been met by Treskin, who, while he declared he was delighted to see her, showed by his manner he was annoyed.

As a matter of fact, he hoped for Lydia Zagarin, but Anna Plevski had come to him instead. But there was another cause for his annoyance, as Anna soon discovered. He had a native mistress; but in a little time Anna had so far prevailed over him that he put the dusky beauty away. He had commenced in business as a commission agent and coffee merchant; but so far success had not attended his efforts. He had neither the energy, the perseverance, nor the patience necessary if one would succeed in business, so that he very eagerly inquired of Anna what money she had brought. She told him that she had not very much with her, but in a few weeks would receive a remittance. In the meantime there was enough to be going on with. She thus won his confidence. Indeed, he never for a moment suspected her mission. There was nothing whatever to arouse his suspicions. It all seemed perfectly natural and he believed that under the ægis of the British flag he was perfectly safe. So he would have been if Danevitch had not played such a clever move to checkmate him.

A little more than two months passed, during which Treskin knew nothing of the sword that swung above his head. Then Anna complained of illness. She thought Point de Galle did not agree with her; she wanted a change; she had been told that Colombo was a very pretty place; she would like to see it; and as she had received a remittance of thirty pounds they could afford the journey. He must take her there. To this he consented, and they travelled by gharry. It was the first step towards his doom. With the remittance came another letter to Anna giving her secret instructions.

Colombo was duly reached. It was the best season. The days were tranquil and brilliant. The nights were wordless poems. The third night after their arrival Anna expressed a desire to go out in a native boat on the water. The sea was motionless. It was like a sheet of glass. The night was glorious; a soft land-breeze blew, laden with rich scents. The heavens were ablaze with stars, and a dreamy languor seemed to pervade the delicious atmosphere. Accordingly, a native boat and two stalwart rowers were hired, and Treskin and Anna embarked. It was the second step towards his doom.

The boatmen pulled from the land. The calm water and tranquil night made rowing easy, and presently a little bamboo sail was hoisted, which helped the craft along. Treskin lay back in the stern and smoked; Anna sat beside him, and sang softly snatches of plaintive Russian airs.

When about five miles from the shore, they saw a small steamer creeping slowly along. She came close to the boat, and an English voice hailed her and asked if anyone in the boat spoke English.

Treskin answered. The voice then inquired if the occupant of the boat would kindly take some letters on shore. The captain of the steamer did not want to go into the port.

Treskin gladly consented, and he was asked to order his boatmen to pull alongside the steamer, which proved to be a pleasure-yacht.

Without a shadow of suspicion in his mind, Treskin did so, and he was politely invited to step on board, a ladder being lowered for that purpose. He turned to Anna, and asked her if she would go. Of course she would. So she preceded him up the ladder.

As soon as he was on the deck the gangway was closed, and a man in uniform directed him to the little saloon, where some wine and biscuits stood on the table. The engines of the steamer were started, though that did not alarm him; but in a few minutes a stern, determined man entered the cabin. He wore the uniform of a lieutenant of the Russian Navy, and had a sword at his side.

'Peter Treskin,' he said in Russian, 'you have been cleverly lured on board this boat, which is owned by a Russian gentleman, and flies the Russian flag, in order that you may be taken back to Russia to answer for your great crime.'

Treskin's face turned to an ashen grayness, and, springing to his feet, he rushed to the door, but found his exit barred by armed men. In another instant he was seized, and heavily ironed. He knew then that his fate was sealed, and his heart turned to lead with an awful sense of despair.

Steaming as hard as she could steam, the yacht rounded Point de Galle, and when about fifteen miles due east of Ceylon she suddenly stopped. A Russian gunboat was lying in wait. To this gunboat the prisoner was transferred, but Anna remained on board the yacht.

The gunboat steamed away at once, and shaped her course for Manilla, where she coaled; and that done she proceeded under a full head of steam for the sea of Japan and Vladivostock.

The yacht went in the other direction, making for the Gulf of Aden and the Red Sea, and after a pleasant and uneventful voyage she sailed by way of the Bosphorus to the Crimea. She made many calls on the way, and at every port she touched at she was supposed to be on a pleasure cruise, and Anna was looked upon as the owner's wife.

As Anna Plevski entered Russia in the west, her false lover entered it in the far east, and thence under a strong escort he was conducted through the whole length of Siberia to St. Petersburg, a distance of something like five thousand miles.

It is an awful journey at the best of times. In his case the awfulness was enhanced a hundredfold, for he knew that every verst travelled placed him nearer and nearer to his shameful doom.

He was six months on the journey, and when he reached the capital his hair was white, his face haggard and drawn, his eyes sunken. He was an old and withered man, while the terrible strain had affected his mind; but as he had been pitiless to others, so no pity was shown for him. He had brought sorrow, misery, and suffering to many a home. He had made widows and orphans; he had maimed and killed, and he could not expect mercy in a world which he had disgraced.

THE DÉNOUEMENT.

It is a typical Russian winter day. The sun shines from a cloudless sky. The air is thin and transparent, the cold intense; the snow is compacted on the ground until it is of the consistency of iron.

On the great plain outside of St. Petersburg, where the public executions take place, a grim scaffold is erected. It is an exposed platform of rough boards, from which spring two upright posts, topped with a cross-bar, from which depends a rope with a noose.

It is the most primitive arrangement. The scaffold is surrounded with troops, horse and foot. There are nearly two thousand of them; but the scaffold is raised so high that the soldiers do not obscure the view.

The plain is filled with a densely-packed crowd; but on one side a lane is kept open, and up this lane rumbles a springless cart, guarded by horsemen with drawn swords. In the cart, on a bed of straw, crouches a man, bound hand

and foot. His face is horrible—ghastly. It wears a stony expression of concentrated fear.

A priest sits with the man, and holds a crucifix before his eyes. But the eyes appear sightless, and to be starting from the head.

The cart reaches the foot of the ladder which leads to the platform. The bound man is dragged out, for he is powerless to move. He is pushed and dragged up the ladder, followed by the priest. As soon as he reaches the platform and sees the noose, he utters a suppressed cry of horror, and shrinks away.

Pitiless hands thrust him forward again, and he is placed on some steps; the noose is adjusted round his neck. No cap is used to hide his awful face. At a given signal the steps are drawn away, and the man swings in the air and is slowly strangled to death. A great cheer rises from the crowd, but it is mingled with groans.

Thus did Peter Treskin meet his doom. He lived like a coward; he died like a coward. He had talents and abilities that, properly directed, would have gained him high position, but he chose the wrong path, and it ended in a dog's death.

He well deserved his ignominious fate, and yet, even at the present day, there are some who believe he was a martyr. But these people may be classed amongst those who believe not, even though an angel comes down from heaven to teach.

THE CLUE OF THE DEAD HAND
THE STORY OF AN EDINBURGH MYSTERY

CHAPTER I.
NEW YEAR'S EVE: THE MYSTERY BEGINS.

A STRANGE, weird sort of place was Corbie Hall. There was an eeriness about it that was calculated to make one shudder. For years it had been practically a ruin, and tenantless.

Although an old place, it was without any particular history, except a tradition that a favourite of Queen Mary had once lived there, and suddenly disappeared in a mysterious way. He was supposed to have been murdered and buried secretly.

The last tenant was one Robert Crease, a wild roisterer, who had travelled much beyond the seas, scraped money together, purchased the Hall, surrounded himself with a number of boon companions, and turned night into day. Corbie Hall stood just to the north of Blackford Hill, as those who are old enough will remember.

In 'Rab' Crease's time it was a lonely enough place; but he and his brother roisterers were not affected by the solitude, and many were the curious tales told about their orgies.

However, Rab came to grief one night. He had been into the town for some purpose, and, staggering home in a storm of wind and rain with a greater burden of liquor than he could comfortably carry, he missed his way, pitched headlong into a quarry, and broke his neck.

He left the place to a person whom he described as his nephew. But the heir could not be found, nor could his death be proved. Then litigation had ensued, and there had been fierce wrangles; bitterness was engendered, and bad blood made. The place, however, remained empty and lonely year after year, until, as might have been expected, it got an evil reputation. People said it was haunted. They shunned it. The wildest possible stories were told about it. It fell into dilapidation. The winter rains and snows soaked through the roof. The window-frames rotted; the grounds became a wilderness of weeds.

At last the heir was found. His name was Raymond Balfour. He was the only son of Crease's only sister, who had married a ne'er-do-weel of a fellow, who came from no one knew where, and where he went to no one cared. He treated his wife shamefully.

Her son was born in Edinburgh, and when he was little more than a baby she fled with him and obtained a situation of some kind in Deeside. She managed to give her boy a decent education, and he was sent to Edinburgh to study law.

He seemed, however, to have inherited some of his father's bad qualities, and fell into disgrace. His mother dying before he was quite out of his teens, he found himself friendless and without resources.

His mother in marrying had alienated herself from her relatives, what few she had; and when she died no one seemed anxious to own kindredship with Raymond, whose conduct and 'goings on' were described as 'outrageous.' So the young fellow snapped his fingers at everyone, declared his intention of going out into the world to seek his fortune, and disappeared.

After many years of wandering in all parts of the world, and when in mid-life, he returned to Edinburgh, for he declared that, of all the cities he had seen, it was the most beautiful, the most picturesque.

He was a stalwart, sunburnt, handsome fellow, though with a somewhat moody expression and a cold, distant, reserved manner. He had heard by mere chance of his inheritance, and, having legally established his claim, took possession of his property.

Although nobody could learn anything at all of his affairs, it was soon made evident that he had plenty of money. He brought with him from India, or somewhere else, a native servant, who appeared to be devoted to him. This servant was simply known as Chunda.

He was a strange, fragile-looking being, with restless, dreamy eyes, thin, delicate hands, and a hairless, mobile face, that was more like the face of a woman than a man. Yet the strong light of the eyes, and somewhat square chin, spoke of determination and a passionate nature. When he first came he wore his native garb, which was exceedingly picturesque; but in a very short time he donned European clothes, and never walked abroad without a topcoat on, even in what Edinburgh folk considered hot weather.

When it became known that the wanderer had returned, apparently a wealthy man, those who years before had declared his conduct to be 'outrageous,' and declined to own him, now showed a disposition to pay the most servile homage.

But he would have none of them. It was his hour of triumph, and he closed his doors against all who came to claim kinship with him.

Very soon it was made manifest that Raymond Balfour was in the way to distinguish himself as his predecessor and kinsman, Crease, had done.

Corbie Hall was turned into a place of revel and riot, and strange, even startling, were the stories that came into currency by the vulgar lips of common rumour. Those whose privilege it was to be the guests at Corbie Hall were not people who, according to Edinburgh ethics, were entitled to be classed amongst the elect, or who were numbered within the pale of so-called 'respectable society.' They belonged rather to that outer fringe which was considered to be an ungodly Bohemia.

It was true that in their ranks were certain young men who were supposed to be seriously pursuing their studies in order that they might ultimately qualify for the Church, the Law, and Medicine.

But their chief sin, perhaps, was youth, which, as the years advanced, would be overcome. Nevertheless, the frowns of the 'superior people' were directed to them, and they were solemnly warned that Corbie Hall was on the highroad to perdition; that, as it had always been an unlucky place, it would continue to be unlucky; in short, that it was accursed.

Raymond Balfour's guests were not all of the sterner sex. Ladies occasionally graced his board. One of them was a Maggie Stiven, who rejoiced in being referred to as the best hated woman in Edinburgh.

She was the daughter of a baker carrying on business in the High Street; but Maggie had quarrelled with her parents, and taken herself off to her only brother, who kept a public-house in College Street.

He, too, had quarrelled with his people, so that he not only welcomed Maggie, but was glad of her assistance in his business.

Maggie bore the proud reputation of being the prettiest young woman in Edinburgh. Her age was about three-and-twenty, and it was said she had turned the heads of half the young fellows in the town. She was generally regarded as a heartless coquette, a silly flirt, who had brains for nothing else but dress.

She possessed a will of her own, however, and seemed determined to shape her course and order her life exactly as it pleased her to do.

She used to say that, if 'the grand folk' turned up their noses at her, she knew how to turn up her nose at them.

When she found out that a rumour was being bandied from lip to lip, which coupled her name with the name of Raymond Balfour—in short, that he and she were engaged to be married—she was intensely delighted; but, while she did not deny it, she would not admit it. It was only in accordance with human nature that some spiteful things should be said.

'It's no for his guid looks nor his moral character that Maggie Stiven's fastening herself on to the reprobate of Corbie Hall,' was the sneering comment. 'It's his siller she's thinking of. She's aye ready to sell her body and soul for siller. Well, when he's married on to her he'll sune find that it taks mair than a winsome face tae make happiness. But fules will aye be fules, and he maun gang his ain way.'

It is pretty certain that Maggie was not affected by this sort of tittle-tattle. She knew the power of her 'winsome face,' and made the most of it. She knew also that the scathing things that were said about her came from her own sex.

She could twist men round her little finger. They were her slaves. That is where her triumph came in. She could make women mad, and bring men to their knees.

Whether or not there was any truth in the rumour at this time, that she was likely to wed the master of Corbie Hall, there was no doubt at all that she was a frequent visitor there.

Sometimes she went with her brother, who supplied most of the liquor consumed in the Hall—and it was a pretty good source of income to him—and sometimes she went alone.

Scarcely a night passed that Mr. Balfour was without company; and Maggie was often there three or four nights a week. She had even been seen driving about with him in his dogcart.

It seemed, therefore, as if there was some justification for the surmise as to the probable match and the ultimate wedding.

These preliminary particulars about Maggie and the new owner of Corbie Hall will pave the way to the series of extraordinary events that has now to be described.

It was New Year's Eve. Raymond Balfour had then been in possession of his property for something like nine months, and during that period had made the most of his time.

He had gone the pace, as the saying is; and the old house, after years of mouldiness and decay, echoed the shouts of revelry night after night. There were wild doings there, and sedate people were shocked.

On the New Year's Eve in question there was a pretty big party in the Hall. During the week following Christmas, large stores of supplies had been sent out from the town in readiness for the great feast that was to usher in the New Year.

Some fifteen guests assembled in the house altogether, including Maggie Stiven and four other ladies, and in order to minister to the wants of this motley crowd, three or four special waiters were engaged to come from Edinburgh.

The day had been an unusually stormy one. A terrific gale had lashed the Firth, and there had been much loss of life and many wrecks. The full force of the storm was felt in Edinburgh, and numerous accidents had occurred through the falling of chimney-cans and pots. Windows were blown in, hoardings swept away, and trees uprooted as if they had been mere saplings.

The wind was accompanied by hail and snow, while the temperature was so low that three or four homeless, starving wretches were found frozen to death.

As darkness set in the wind abated, but snow then began to fall, and in the course of two or three hours roads and railways were blocked, and the streets of the city could only be traversed with the greatest difficulty. Indeed, by seven o'clock all vehicular traffic had ceased, and benighted wayfarers despaired of reaching their homes in safety.

The storm, the darkness, the severity of the weather, the falling snow, did not affect the spirits nor the physical comfort of the guests assembled at Corbie Hall.

To the south of Edinburgh the snow seemed to fall heavier than it did in the city itself. In exposed places it lay in immense drifts, but everywhere it was so deep that the country roads were obliterated, landmarks wiped out, and hedges buried.

In the lonely region of Blackford Hill, Corbie Hall was the only place that gave forth any signs of human life. Light and warmth were there, and the lights streaming from the windows must have shone forth as beacons of hope to anyone in the neighbourhood who might by chance have been battling with the storm and struggling to a place of safety.

But no one was likely to be abroad on such a night; and the guests at the Hall, when they saw the turn the weather had taken, knew that they would be storm-stayed at the Hall until the full light of day returned. But that prospect did not concern them.

They were there to see the old year out and the new one in; and so long as the 'meal and the malt' did not fail they would be in no hurry to go.

From all the evidence that was collected, they were a wild party, and did full justice to the stock of eatables and drinkables—especially the drinkables—that were so lavishly supplied by the host.

When twelve o'clock struck there was a scene of wild uproar, and everyone who was sober enough to do so toasted his neighbour. During the whole of the evening Balfour had openly displayed great partiality for Maggie Stiven.

He insisted on her sitting next to him, and he paid her marked attention. When the company staggered to their feet to usher in the new year, Raymond Balfour flung his arms suddenly round her neck, and, kissing her with great warmth, he droned out a stanza of a love-ditty, and then in husky tones exclaimed:

'Maggie Stiven's the bonniest lass that ever lived, and I'm going to marry her.'

About half-past one only a few of the roisterers were left at the table. The others had succumbed to the too-seductive influences of the wine and whisky, and had ceased to take any further interest in the proceedings. Suddenly there resounded through the house a shrill, piercing scream. It was a scream that seemed to indicate intense horror and great agony.

Consternation and silence fell upon all who heard it. In a few moments Raymond Balfour rose to his feet and said:

'Don't be alarmed. Sit still. I'll go and see what's the matter.'

He left the room with unsteady gait, and nobody showed any disposition to follow him. Something like a superstitious awe had taken possession of the revellers, and they conversed with each other subduedly.

Amongst them was a tough, bronzed seafaring man, named Jasper Jarvis. He was captain of the barque *Bonnie Scotland*, which had arrived at Leith a few weeks before from the Gold Coast with a cargo of palm-oil and ivory.

Jarvis, who seems to have been quite in his sober senses, got up, threw an extra log on the fire, and in order to put heart into his companions, began to troll out a nautical ditty; but it had not the inspiriting effect that he expected, and somebody timidly suggested that he should go in search of the host.

To this he readily assented, but before he could get from his seat, Maggie Stiven jumped up and exclaimed:

'You people all stay here. I'll go and look for Raymond.'

Captain Jarvis offered no objection, and no one else interposed, so Maggie hurriedly left the room. From this point the narrative of what followed can best be told in the skipper's own words.

THE STATEMENT OF CAPTAIN JASPER JARVIS.

When Maggie had gone we were six all told. The four ladies had previously gone to bed. Two out of the six were so muddled that they seemed incapable of understanding anything that was going on.

The other three appeared to be under the spell of fear. They huddled together round the fire, and all became silent.

It is curious that they should have been so affected by the scream; and yet, perhaps, it wasn't, for somehow or other it didn't seem natural at all. But the fact is, we had all been so jolly and happy, and the cry broke in upon us so suddenly, that it impressed us more than it would have done otherwise.

And then another thing was, it was difficult to tell whether it was a woman or a man who had screamed. It was too shrill for a man's cry, and yet it wasn't like the scream of a woman.

When Maggie Stiven had been gone about ten minutes—it seemed much longer than that to us—Rab Thomson, who was one of three men who sat by the fire, looked at me with white face, and said:

'Skipper, you go and look after them. I don't feel easy in my mind. I've a sort of feeling something queer has happened.'

On that I rose, saying I would soon find out, and went to the door. As I opened it I heard a sigh, and then a sort of prolonged groan, and I saw, or fancied I saw, a shadowy figure flit up the stair.

The hall was in darkness, save for the light that fell through the doorway as I held the door partly open. I'm ashamed to say it, but when I saw—if I did see it—that ghostly figure glide up the stairs, and heard the sigh and the groan, I shut the door quickly and drew back into the room.

Like most sailor men, I'm not without some belief in signs, omens, wraiths, and those kind of things; though nobody can say, and nobody must say, I'm wanting in pluck.

I've been at sea for thirty-two years, and during that time I've faced death in a thousand forms, and never had any feeling of fear. But, to be straight, I don't like anything that's uncanny. I like to be able to get a grip of things, and to understand them.

When I started back into the room, Rab Thomson rose to his feet and asked me what I'd seen. I told him I had seen a shadowy figure glide up the stairs, and had heard a sigh and a groan.

He laughed, but it wasn't a real kind of laugh. He was as white as death, and I heard his teeth chatter, and with a sudden movement he went to one of the long windows, pulled aside the heavy curtain, and, pressing his face to the glass, peered out.

I think his intention was to get out of the window and go home; but he saw what an awful night it was. The snow was still falling heavily; it was piled up against the window, and no one but a madman or a fool would have dreamed of going forth in such a storm, for it was all but certain he would have lost his life in the drifts.

Rab let the curtain fall, and, drawing back, filled himself a measure of whisky, and, tossing it off, said to me:

'Why don't you go and see what's the matter, man? Surely, you are no' frightened?'

'No,' I said, 'but you are.'

And I walked to the door again, flung it open wide, so that the light streamed forth, and as I did so I saw a woman lying huddled up on the mat at the foot of the stairs.

I recognised her at once by the dress, which was a kind of pink silk, with a lot of fluffy lace all round the neck part of it, as Maggie Stiven, and, thinking she had fainted, I rushed forward, lifted her up with ease—for I am a powerful man, and she was a lightly-built little woman—and carried her to a big chair that stood empty near the fire. As I put her in the chair I noticed that her head fell forward on to her bosom with a strange kind of limpness, and her face was of a greenish, chalky kind of hue.

I felt frightened, and called out to the others to rouse up James Macfarlane, who had been studying medicine, but had nearly finished his course, and expected to get his diploma the next session.

Jamie had stowed away too much liquor in his hold in the early part of the evening, and had foundered, so somebody had rolled him up in a rug and put him on a couch, where he had been sleeping for hours. Notwithstanding that fact, it took a long time to waken him.

In the meanwhile I chafed Maggie's hand, and Rab tried to get brandy down her throat, but it flowed out of her mouth again.

When James Macfarlane realized that something was wrong, he pulled himself together at once, and having felt Maggie's pulse, he exclaimed with a horrified expression on his face:

'My God, boys, she's dead!'

This was only a confirmation of my own fears; nevertheless, the definite assertion by one who was qualified to tell was an awful shock to us.

A little more than a quarter of an hour before, Maggie, radiant with health and spirits, and looking very bonnie—she was one of the prettiest girls I think I've ever seen—had run out of the room; and now she was there in the chair, dead.

At Macfarlane's suggestion we laid her flat on her back on the rug before the fire, and he tried to force a little brandy down her throat, but failed; and as he rose to his feet again, he said sadly:

'There's no mistake about it, boys: she's dead as a herring.'

Our first thought now was of our host. What had become of him? I and Rab, who had recovered from his fright by this time, undertook to go in search of him. We lit the swinging lamp in the hall, and, taking candles with us, went upstairs to his room; but he was not there, and there were no signs of his having been there. Then we went to the room of the black fellow, Chunda.

The door was locked, and we had to shake and hammer it pretty hard before we roused him up. As he opened the door and stood before us in his night-clothes, he looked dazed, as one does when just wakened from sound sleep.

He did not speak English, but I could manage a little Hindustani, having been much in India, and I asked him if he had seen his master lately, and he answered 'No.' I told him he must come with me and look for him, as he knew the run of the house better than I did.

He only stopped to slip on some of his clothes and wrap a heavy rug round his shoulders, for he felt the cold very much.

Then we roused up the other three house-servants and the temporary servants, who had retired soon after midnight, and we went from room to room, passage to passage; in fact, we searched the house from top to bottom, but all in vain; not a trace of our friend could we get.

Our next step was to ascertain if he had gone out. But all the doors and windows were fastened. Nevertheless, I undertook to search the grounds, and, having been provided with a horn lantern, we got the big hall door opened; but the snow had drifted against it to such an extent that a great mass of it fell into the hall.

The night was pitch-dark, the air thick with snow. I made some attempt to go forth, but sank up to my waist, and was forced to return.

We then tried the back of the house, where there was a stable-yard. The snow was pretty heavy there, but not so heavy as in the front. Two men slept over the stable. I roused them up, got the keys of the stable, and went in. Balfour kept three horses, and they were in their stalls all right.

The stable-yard gate was barred, and it was very clear no one had been out that way.

I returned to the house, half frozen and very depressed. We then consulted together, and decided that nothing could be done until daylight.

It was an awful ending to our merry meeting, and the mystery of the whole affair weighed upon us like a nightmare.

The ladies of our party, who had gone to bed soon after we had drunk in the New Year, got up and dressed themselves. In the meantime we carried Maggie Stiven's body into another room, where it was laid out on a table.

James Macfarlane's opinion was that she had died from a sudden shock of fright; and when that was taken in connection with the eldritch scream which had so startled us, and the mysterious disappearance of our host, we felt that there was something uncanny about the whole business.

The rest of the night was wearily passed. The others of our party, having been o'er fu' when they went to sleep, continued to sleep through it all, and knew nothing of the tragic ending until they awoke in the morning.

With the coming of the morning our spirits revived a little, though we still felt miserable enough. It had almost ceased to snow, but the whole country was buried, and round about the house the drift was piled up until it reached to the lower windows.

As soon as it was broad daylight we made another careful search of the house, but not a sign of Raymond Balfour could we see.

Chunda helped us in our search. He was terribly cut up, and became so ill from grief and the cold that he was obliged to go to bed.

The only reasonable theory that we could find to account for Balfour's strange disappearance was that, by some means we could not determine, he had managed to leave the house, and had perished in the snow.

As it had continued to snow all night, and at eight o'clock was still falling lightly, all traces were, of course, obliterated.

Every one of the visitors was now anxious to get away, but before anyone went, I drew up a statement which was duly signed. James Macfarlane and I then undertook to report the matter to the police in Edinburgh.

Before any of us could leave, we had to clear the snow away from the door and dig a path out. And even then it was no easy matter to get clear.

We were a sorrowful enough party, as may be imagined, and we all felt that the New Year had commenced badly for us.

The death of Maggie Stiven was a terrible business, and I confess to feeling surprised that she should have died from fright, for she was by no means a nervous girl. Indeed, I think she was as plucky as any woman I have ever known, and I was certain that if fright had really killed her she must have seen something very awful.

With reference to this, nobody, I think, liked to put his thoughts into words, but somehow we seemed to divine that each believed Satan had spirited Raymond Balfour away and frightened poor Maggie to death. Any way, the mystery was beyond our solving, and we were silent and melancholy as we straggled into Edinburgh, where armies of labourers were busy clearing the streets of snow.

It was an awful day. The cold was intense, and overhead the sky was like one vast sheet of lead. Except the labourers, few people were abroad, and those few looked pinched up, draggled, and miserable.

God knows, we were miserable enough ourselves! I know that my heart was like a stone; for I was not so wanting in sense as not to see that trouble was bound to come out of the business, and I fairly shuddered when I thought of poor Balfour's end, for it seemed impossible to hope that he was still alive.

Look at the matter whichever way I would, it was a mystery which absolutely appalled me, and it had all come about with such awful suddenness that, speaking for myself, I felt stunned.

CHAPTER II.
THE MYSTERY DEEPENS.—THE NARRATIVE CONTINUED BY PETER BRODIE, OF THE DETECTIVE SERVICE.

I WAS in Liverpool, engaged on a rather delicate matter, when I received a telegram from the chief of the police in Edinburgh, telling me to return by the next train. I wasn't at all pleased by this recall, for it was wretched weather, and the prospect of a night journey to the North was far from agreeable.

The date was January 3. During the whole of New Year's Eve there had been a violent storm, which seems to have been general all over the country. The result was a breakdown of telegraph-wires and serious interruption to traffic.

The telegram sent to me was five hours on the road; and as the 'next train' meant the night mail, I had no alternative but to bundle my traps together and start.

When we reached Carlisle a thaw had set in, and on arriving at Edinburgh I thought I had never seen Auld Reekie look so glum and dour. The streets were ankle-deep in slush.

Snow was slipping from the roofs everywhere in avalanches, necessitating considerable wariness on the part of pedestrians.

Horses panted, groaned, and steamed as they toiled with their loads through the filthy snow, and overhead the sky hung like a dun pall.

On reaching the head office, I was at once instructed to proceed to Corbie Hall to investigate a case of murder, and endeavour to trace the whereabouts of one Raymond Balfour, who, according to the statement of a Captain Jasper Jarvis, corroborated by James Macfarlane, medical student at the Edinburgh College, had mysteriously disappeared soon after midnight on January 1. The remarkably sudden and unaccountable death of Maggie Stiven necessitated a legal inquiry, and Dr. Wallace Bruce was sent to examine the body and report on the cause of death.

On removing the clothes, he noticed that the linen that had been next to the chest was slightly blood-stained, and an examination revealed a very small blue puncture, slightly to the left of the sternum, and immediately over the heart.

On probing this puncture with his finger, he felt something hard. He therefore proceeded to open the chest, assisted by a colleague, Dr. James

Simpson, the well-known Edinburgh surgeon. To their astonishment, they found the puncture was due to a thrust from a very fine stiletto, which had pierced the heart on the left side. The stiletto had broken off, and four inches of the steel remained in the wound. This, acting as a plug, had prevented outward bleeding to any extent, but there had been extensive internal hæmorrhage. There was nothing else to account for death.

The girl was exceedingly well developed, well nourished, and without any sign or trace of organic disease. As she could not have driven the stiletto into her chest in such a way herself, it was obviously a case of murder.

When I reached Corbie Hall, the country round about was still white with snow, and Blackford Hill was like a miniature Alp, although the thaw was making its influence felt.

The Hall was a curious, rambling sort of place, with every appearance of age. It was a stone building, flanked by a small turreted tower at each end. It stood in about an acre of ground that was partly walled and partly fenced round. Two cast-iron gates of good design, hung on pillars, each surmounted by a carved greyhound, admitted to a carriage-drive that swept in a semicircle to the main entrance.

Passing through the doorway—the door itself was a massive structure—I found myself in a large square, paved hall, and immediately in front a broad flight of oak stairs led up to the first landing, where there was a very fine stained-glass window.

On the left was a long dining-room, which communicated by means of folding doors with another room of almost equal dimensions.

On the opposite side of the passage, and close to the foot of the stairs, was the door of the drawing-room, which was a counterpart almost of the dining-room.

Between the banisters of the stairs and the partition wall of the dining-room, the passage was continued to a door that gave access to a passage communicating with the kitchen and back premises.

The recess underneath the stairs was used for hanging up coats, hats, and other things. From the second landing the stairs struck off at an acute angle, and rose to the second story, where there were at least a dozen rooms, large and small.

Under the guidance of Chunda, the black servant, who seemed very ill and much depressed, I made a thorough inspection of the house. As he could not speak English, we had to communicate in signs, which was rather awkward. In addition to this Indian, Mr. Balfour had kept a cook and a small girl to help her, also a housemaid. Besides these, he employed a groom and a coachman. The coachman lived over the stables at the back with his wife and daughter, a girl of eighteen, and she and her mother both assisted in the house when necessary. The groom had a room to himself above the coach-house.

I questioned each of these servants individually and apart from the others as to whether they had heard the scream alluded to by Captain Jarvis. The three women living in the house said that they heard it, but those who lived over the stables did not. The ones who heard it slept in the right-hand tower. They did not retire until after the New Year had come in. Although the master had given them some hot drink, they were quite sober when they went upstairs.

As they were in the habit of doing every night, they extinguished the hall lamp and a lamp that stood on the bracket at the top of the stairs, thus leaving that part of the house in darkness. They did not attach any importance to the scream, as they thought it was some of the visitors larking, for they had all been very frisky during the evening.

The cook, however—her name was Mary Kenway—opened her door, which commanded in perspective a full view of the corridor leading to the top of the stairs, and she saw, or thought she saw, a shadowy figure standing in this corridor near the top of the stairs. Feeling a bit nervous, she shut the door hurriedly, and said to her fellow-servants, who shared the room with her:

'One of those fools is playing at ghosts or something. Well, when the wine's in, the wit's out.'

She and her companions then got into bed, and some time afterwards were startled by a loud knocking at their door. The cook hurriedly procured a light, and on asking who was there, and being informed it was Captain Jarvis, and that he was searching for the master, who had disappeared, she slipped on her clothes and opened the door.

The temporary servants, of whom there were three, were sleeping in a room above her. They had indulged somewhat too freely, and it was a considerable time before they could be made to understand that something dreadful had happened.

With these details, and the statement of Captain Jarvis, I felt I was in a position to begin my researches.

If Captain Jarvis's statement was true, and there wasn't the slightest reason to doubt it, for it was in the main corroborated by Robert Thomson and others, the whole affair was shrouded in considerable mystery. Indeed, I think it was one of the strangest cases I ever had to do with. Maggie Stiven had been foully done to death by some subtle, deft, and treacherous assassin.

She had been struck with great force, and the breaking of the weapon showed the fury with which her murderer had done his damnable work.

The skipper's statement that when he opened the dining-room door he heard a sigh and sort of groan was compatible with the nature of the wound, for though the heart was injured, the fact of the piece of steel remaining in the wound would prevent a sudden emptying of the heart, and she might have lived after being struck five to ten minutes. The shadowy figure which Jarvis said he saw 'gliding' up the stairs was no doubt the assassin, although Jarvis— his imagination having been fired—thought it a supernatural appearance.

The cook also spoke of 'a shadowy figure,' and thought that some of the guests were 'playing at ghosts.' This independent testimony suggested that there was something curious and out of the common about the figure, and I was led to infer that the person who had done the deed was small, light of foot, and agile of movement. When he struck Maggie down he had probably been lurking in the drawing-room, the door of which, as I have already described, was just at the foot of the stairs, or he may have been concealed in the recess under the stairs. Whichever way it was, the girl had not mounted the stairs, and must have been stabbed the moment she reached the mat where the body was found, and before she had time to get her feet on the stairs to go up.

Now came the question, Why was she killed? Her going in search of Raymond Balfour was quite unpremeditated, and the assassin could hardly have known that she was coming out of the room.

Why, then, did he kill her? On the face of it, it seemed to be an unprovoked and brutal crime without any reason. But a little pondering, and a careful weighing of all the pros and cons, led me to the conclusion that the deed was not as purposeless as it seemed. If it was the result of madness, there was certainly method in the madness.

Some people expressed the opinion that Balfour himself had murdered the girl, but that opinion would not hold water.

Firstly, he himself was induced to leave the room by a scream or cry that was described as 'uncanny.' Did he arrange for that cry to be uttered in order that he might have an excuse for going out, knowing that the girl would follow him?

Secondly, if he was the slayer, why did he choose to kill the girl in his own house? for very little reflection must have shown him that to escape detection would be an impossibility.

No. It was only too evident that he did not kill Maggie Stiven, and his extraordinary disappearance led me to believe that he also had fallen a victim to the assassin. But if that was so, where was his body? It was, of course, of the highest importance that he should be discovered, dead or alive.

I caused a search to be made of the house from top to bottom. There wasn't a room missed, not a cupboard overlooked, not a recess but what was scrutinized. Every box or trunk large enough to contain a man's body was opened without result.

Every hole and corner, every chimney, every likely and unlikely place, was examined, but not a trace, not a sign, of the missing man was brought to light.

His bedroom was the largest and most important room in the house. It was panelled with dark oak panelling. The ceiling was carved wood, and there was a very large carved oak mantelpiece, which was considered a work of art. Two lattice-paned windows were in keeping with the place, which had also been furnished with a view to its character.

A massive four-post bedstead occupied one corner, and near it was an unusually large clothes-press of oak. This press was spacious enough to have held the bodies of three or four men, but Balfour's body was not there.

From this room a small door gave access to a short, narrow passage, leading to another door at the foot of a stone staircase of about twenty steps, by which the top of the tower at that end of the building was gained. From the roof of the tower a very beautiful view was obtained. I need scarcely say I critically examined the doors, the passage, the stairs, the tower itself.

The locks of both doors were very rusty, and it was evident they had not been opened for some time. In the one at the foot of the tower stairs there was no key, and it was only after considerable search that one was found to fit it. And even then the lock could not be turned until it had been well oiled.

The dust on the stone stairs was the accumulation of months, and bore not the faintest trace of footprints. It was obvious that no one had passed that way for a very long time.

Having thus exhausted the interior of the building, I now proceeded to search outside.

Skipper Jarvis declared that, when he and Bob Thomson went through the house on the night of the tragedy, they looked to every door and window, but all were properly secured, and unless Balfour had squeezed himself through a keyhole or a cranny, he could not have left the building. Nevertheless, it seemed to me that the man must have got out in some way; otherwise, if he were dead, how was it we had failed to find his body in the house? So thorough had been the search that a dead mouse could not have escaped me.

There was still a great deal of snow on the ground, especially in the hollows and ravines; but it was soft and slushy owing to the rise in temperature.

Aided by half a dozen men—mostly gamekeepers—and several dogs, we commenced systematically to examine the grounds, the country round about, the burns, the woods, but all to no purpose. Every inch of Braid Glen was gone over; what is now the Waverley curling pond was dragged; the Jordan and Braid streams examined; all the quarries in the neighbourhood—of which there are many—were looked into; the Braid Hill and all round about the Braid Hill was paced; but the result was the same. Raymond Balfour was not found.

When our failure became known, the excitement increased greatly, especially amongst ignorant and stupid people, who stoutly maintained that the master of Corbie Hall had been spirited away by the Evil One, who had also killed Maggie Stiven. These good folks failed to explain why the Evil One should have stabbed Maggie with a stiletto, and have left more than half the blade in the wound, when he might have deprived her of life so much more easily. I found that even Captain Jarvis was not without some belief in this absurd theory.

'If there is not something uncanny about the whole business, how is it you have failed to get trace of the man?' asked Jarvis, with the air of one who felt he was putting a poser which was absolutely unanswerable. 'You see,' pursued the skipper, with an insistency of tone that was very amusing—'you see, we were a bad lot. We'd just come there for an orgie, and the meat and drink that we wasted would have kept many poor wretches from starving on that awful night.'

'Do you consider that Raymond Balfour was an exceptionally wicked man?' I asked Jarvis.

'Well, no,' he answered seriously; 'I shouldn't like to say that. But he was a wild fellow.'

'What do you mean by wild?'

'Well, he was a little too fond of liquor and the ladies.'

'Have you known him long?'

'Yes, several years. I first met him in Madras. I saw a good deal of him later in Calcutta. He was a very wild boy then, I can tell you.'

'But still no worse than tens of thousands of other people?' I suggested.

'Oh no; I don't say he was,' Jarvis answered quickly, and in a way that suggested he was anxious his friend should not be painted too black.

'Now, I want you to tell me this, Captain Jarvis,' I said somewhat solemnly, as I wished to impress him with the importance of the question: 'was there any love-making between Raymond Balfour and Maggie Stiven?'

The skipper did not answer immediately. He seemed to be revolving the matter in his mind. Then, with a thoughtful stroking of his chin, he replied:

'Balfour was fond of Maggie.'

'Did he allow that fondness to display itself before others?'

'When he was a bit gone in his cups he did,' answered the captain, with obvious reluctance.

'And was she fond of him?'

'Yes—I think so'—the same reluctance showing itself.

'Did she show her partiality?'

'Sometimes.'

'Maggie wasn't considered to be very stanch to anyone, was she?'

'Well, she'd a good many admirers. She was an awful good-looking lass, you see. And lads will always run after a pretty girl.'

'That scarcely answers my question, captain,' I said. 'I want to know if she openly—that is, before others—showed that she liked Balfour better than any other body?'

'You see, Mr. Brodie, I'm not altogether competent to answer that,' said the skipper, as though he was anxious to shirk the question.

'But did she do so on the New Year's Eve, when you were all so jovial?'

'Yes.'

'How did she display her liking?'

'She sat on his knee several times. She kissed him, and he kissed her.'

'That was before the company?'

'It was.'

'Did he make any remark, or did she? I mean, any remark calculated to engender a belief that this spooning was serious, and not a mere flirtation, the result of a spree?'

'Well—I—I heard him say two or three times, "Mag, old girl, I'm going to marry you."'

'He had been drinking then, I suppose?'

'He had, a good deal.'

'And what did she reply?'

'As near as I mind, she said, "All right, old man. We are just suited to each other, and we'll make a match of it."'

'I must now ask you one or two other questions, captain. There were several men present, were there not?'

'There were.'

'They were all young men?'

'Yes.'

'And belonged to Edinburgh or its immediate neighbourhood?'

'They did.'

'Consequently they were all more or less well acquainted with Maggie?'

'Yes. I don't think there was a man there who didn't ken her. You see, in her way she was a kind of celebrity in Edinburgh. Certain folk said hard things about her, and that made her mad sometimes, so that she took a delight in just showing how she could lead the lads by the nose.'

'Now, I want you to give me an answer to this question, captain. Is it within your knowledge that out of her many admirers there was one who had been emboldened by her to think that he had the best claim upon her?'

'I couldn't say for certain; but it's likely enough.'

'Has it occurred to you to ask yourself if that favoured one was among Raymond Balfour's guests on New Year's Eve?'

The question seemed to startle Captain Jarvis. He looked at me searchingly and inquiringly, and it was some moments before he spoke, while his expression gave every indication that he fully understood the drift of my inquiry. At last he replied, hesitatingly and cautiously:

'You see, Mr. Brodie, I wasn't the keeper of Maggie's conscience. She didn't make me her confidant. Nor was I one of her favoured suitors. I'm an old married man, and she preferred young fellows.'

'You've avoided my question now,' I remarked, a little sharply, as it seemed to me he was prevaricating.

'I'm trying to think,' he said, with a preoccupied air. Then, after a pause, he added: 'I can't answer you, because I don't know. What your question suggests is that some chap who was madly jealous of her murdered her.'

'You are correct in your surmise,' I answered.

'Then, all I've got to say is this: It was impossible for anyone to have left the room and committed the crime without my being aware of it. I say again, it would have been impossible. She couldn't have been out of the room two minutes before she was struck. You see, she had even been unable to get up the stair. Her going out was quite unpremeditated; and until she jumped up from her seat, and said she would go and look for Balfour, nobody knew she was going out of the room. No, Mr. Brodie, I'm convinced that no man of that company did the deed.'

I had every reason to think that Captain Jarvis was perfectly right in his conclusions. The logic of his argument was unanswerable. I had already taken means to ascertain some particulars about every person who had been present on the fateful night, including the extra servants; and I saw nothing and heard nothing calculated in any way to justify a suspicion being entertained against any particular individual. Nevertheless, I had them under surveillance.

What I had to deal with was the broad, plain, hard fact that Maggie Stiven had been brutally and suddenly murdered, while Raymond Balfour had disappeared as effectually as if the earth had suddenly opened and swallowed him, leaving not a trace behind. If he went forth from the house after quitting his guests, where had he gone to?

The state of the country, owing to the snow, made it physically impossible that he could have travelled far on that awful night; and had he perished in the snow near the house, his body must have been discovered, so thorough had been our search.

Then, again, assuming that he had got away, there would surely have been some indication of his mode of exit—an unfastened window, an unlocked door. But the most exhaustive inquiry satisfied me there was neither one nor the other.

But if Balfour was not out of the house, he must be in the house; and if he was in the house, it was as a dead man. And where was his body?

It seemed unreasonable to suppose that a human body could be disposed of so quickly and so effectually as to leave not a trace behind.

Then, again, granting that he was murdered, who murdered him, and why was he murdered? Who raised the unearthly cry, and was it raised purposely to draw him from the room in order that he might be immediately struck down?

Such was the problem with which I was confronted, and I freely confess that at this stage I felt absolutely baffled. I saw no clue, and nothing likely to lead me to a clue; but though baffled, I was not beaten. The mystery was profound, and the whole case so strange, so startling, that I was not surprised at ignorant people attributing it to supernatural agency. It had about it all the elements of some wild, weird story of monkish superstition, lifted from the pages of a mediæval romance. It was no romance, however, no legend, but a hard, dry fact of the nineteenth century that had to be accounted for by perfectly human means.

There was one point, however, which made itself clear through the darkness. It was that the author of the deed was a person of such devilish cunning, such brutal ferocity, such crafty ingenuity, that he would occupy a niche all to himself for evermore in the gallery of criminals.

As I have already said, though I was baffled, I was not beaten, and I felt sure I should ultimately succeed in the task set me. I had in my possession the broken blade of the stiletto, and I knew that might prove of value as a clue; and having done all that it was practical to do for the moment, I set to work to define a motive for the crime, and to construct a theory that would aid me in my efforts to solve the problem.

CHAPTER III.
THE DEAD HAND SMITES.

PETER BRODIE stood very high in his profession. He had made his mark as a detective, and had solved some very complicated problems. In recalling him from Liverpool, whither he had been sent on important business, the authorities felt that if the Corbie Hall mystery was to be cleared up he was the man to do it. They saw from the first that it was a very difficult case, when all the circumstances were considered, but they were sure that Brodie was the one man likely to tackle it successfully.

It seemed as if the evil reputation of Corbie Hall was never to pass away, and after this new tragedy people recalled how Peter Crease, the drunken owner of it, and uncle of Balfour, had broken his neck in a quarry; how, following that, the gloomy house had fallen into dilapidation, until it was shunned as a haunted place. When the rightful heir turned up, they thought he would put things right; but instead of that he proved himself to be as big a reprobate as his relative had been: and now his mysterious disappearance, and Maggie Stiven's murder, realized the croakings of the wiseacres, who had said that a curse hung over the house, and that anyone who went to live in the Hall would come to grief.

Of course, the tradition that a favourite of Queen Mary's who had once lived there mysteriously disappeared, and was never heard of again, was also recalled; and the sages predicted that as that mystery was never cleared up, so would Balfour's disappearance go down to posterity as an unsolved mystery. Possibly it might have done if Peter Brodie had not brought his intellect to bear upon it.

On the fourth day after his arrival the thaw had been so thorough that the land was quite clear of snow, and a second search was made for Balfour, but it only ended in failure, as the first had done.

Brodie was now convinced that the unfortunate man had never left the house; and yet, having regard to the critical way in which it had been examined from top to bottom, it was difficult to conceive where he could be hidden. Nevertheless, Peter stuck to his guns; for as Balfour had not gone out of the house, he must be in it, and if so, time and patient search might reveal his hiding-place.

With a view to learning as much as possible about Balfour's habits, Brodie had a long talk with Chunda, Captain Jarvis acting as interpreter. The native stated that he had travelled with his master extensively through India. He had found him rather a peculiar man. He was very secretive, and given to fits of moodiness. Although Chunda was exceedingly fond of him, he did not wish to accompany him to Scotland, but yielded on the master pressing him. Now he bitterly regretted having come, for not only did he feel crushed by his master's strange disappearance, but the cold and dampness of the climate made him very ill, and he intended to leave immediately for Southampton, so as to get a ship for India, as he yearned to return to his own warm, sunny land. He was dying for the want of sun and warmth.

Asked if his master was much given to flirtations, Chunda, with flashing eyes and an angry expression in his dark face, said that he was, and he had frequently got into trouble through it.

After this interview, Brodie came to the conclusion that the motive of the crime was undoubtedly jealousy. That is to say, someone had been jealous of Balfour, someone who considered Maggie a rival.

If this was correct, the someone must be a woman—no ordinary woman, for no ordinary woman would have been capable of carrying out such a terrible revenge. Besides Maggie Stiven, there had been four other young women in the party.

One was a married woman named MacLauchlan. Her husband kept a grocer's shop in the High Street, but he and his wife didn't get on well together. He had no idea, however, that she was in the habit of visiting at Corbie Hall.

Brodie dismissed her from suspicion. He felt sure she didn't commit the deed. She was rather good-looking, but a mild, lackadaisical, phlegmatic, brainless creature, without the nerve necessary for such a crime.

Another of the ladies was Jean Smith. She was twenty years of age, and Maggie Stiven's bosom friend, and since the night of the crime had been seriously ill in bed from the shock.

A third was Mary Johnstone. Until New Year's Eve she had never met Balfour before in her life. She had gone to the Hall in company with her sweetheart, James Macfarlane, the medical student.

The fourth was Kate Thomson, cousin to Rab Thomson. She was a woman about thirty years of age, strong and well knit, but was a good-tempered, genial sort of creature. She, too, was almost a stranger to Balfour, and was engaged to be married to a man named Robert Murchison, who was factor to a Mr. Rennie of Perth.

Brodie was absolutely certain, after studying them all, that not one of these four women had done the deed. Nor was there the slightest reason for harbouring a suspicion against the female servants.

He was, therefore, puzzled, but not disconcerted, and he stuck to his theory that a jealous woman had committed the crime.

That, of course, only made the mystery more mysterious, so to speak. For who was the woman? Where did she come from? How did she get into the house? Where did she go to?

These questions were inevitable if the theory was maintained. It did not seem easy then to answer them.

As Brodie revolved all these things in his mind, he remembered that, though he had subjected the house to a very careful search, he had done little more than look into Chunda's room, the reason being that the native was ill in bed at the time.

The room adjoined Balfour's, and at one time was connected by a communicating door, but for some reason or other the door had been nailed up and papered over. While less in size than Balfour's, it was still a fairly large room, also wainscoted, and with a carved wooden ceiling. It was lighted by one window, which commanded a good view over Blackford Hill.

To this room Brodie went one evening when Chunda happened to be absent from it. It reeked with the faint, sickly odour of some Indian perfume.

On a sideboard stood a small gilt Indian idol, and various Indian knick-knacks were scattered about. As in Balfour's room, there was a massive carved oak mantelpiece, with a very capacious fireplace; and on each side of the fireplace was a deep recess.

The floor was oak, polished, and dark in colour either by staining or time. The only carpet on it was a square in the centre. A clothes-press stood in a corner. It was the only place in which a man could be concealed. Brodie opened the door, and found nothing but clothes there. The mystery, therefore, was as far from solution as ever, apparently, as now there wasn't a corner of the house that had not been examined thoroughly and exhaustively.

As Brodie was in the act of leaving the room, his eye was attracted by something glittering on the hearthstone, where the cold, white ashes of a wood-fire still remained. He stooped down and picked from the hearth a scrap, a mere morsel of cloth. It was all burnt round the edges, and was dusty with the ash; but he found on examination that it was a fragment of Indian cloth, into which gold threads had been worked; and it was these gold threads which, in spite of the dust, had reflected the light and attracted his notice.

Taking out his pocket-book, he deposited that scrap of charred cloth carefully between the leaves, then went down on his knees and subjected the ashes to critical examination, with the result that he obtained unmistakable evidence of a considerable amount of cloth having been destroyed by fire.

There were patches here and there of white, or rather gray, carbonized, filmy fragments of cobweb-like texture. As everyone knows, cloth burnt in a fire leaves a ghost-like wrack behind, that, unless disturbed, will remain for some time.

Brodie rose and fell into deep thought, and he mentally asked himself why the cloth had been burnt. It was reasonable to presume it was some portion of clothing, and if so, why should anyone have been at the trouble to consume it in the flames unless it was to hide certain evidences of guilt.

'What would those evidences of guilt be?' Brodie muttered to himself, as he reflected on the singular discovery he had made. And suddenly it seemed to him—of course, it was purely fancy—that a voice whispered in his ear:

'Blood! blood!'

Although but fancy, the voice seemed so real to him that he fairly started, and at that instant the door opened and Chunda entered. He seemed greatly surprised to find the detective in the room, and muttered something in Hindustani.

As Brodie did not understand him and could not converse with him, he made no response, but passed out, and, hurrying to Edinburgh, called on Professor Dunbar, the eminent microscopist, and asked that gentleman to place the fragment of cloth found on the hearthstone under a powerful microscope.

The Professor did as requested, and, after a careful examination, he said he could not detect anything suggestive of blood. The cloth was evidently of Indian workmanship, and the bright threads running through it were real gold.

Brodie did not return to Corbie Hall until the following day. By that time Maggie Stiven's body had been removed by her friends for burial, and he was informed by the servants that Chunda had gone out to attend the funeral. He was rather surprised at that, and still more surprised when he found, on going to Chunda's room, that the door was locked.

He hurried back to Edinburgh, and was in time to be present at Maggie's burial in the Greyfriars Churchyard, but he saw nothing of Chunda; the native was not there, and nobody had seen him. Captain Jarvis was amongst the mourners, and when the funeral was over he and Brodie left together.

'Do you know how long Chunda has been in Balfour's service?' the detective asked, as they strolled along.

'I believe a considerable time, but I don't know from absolute knowledge. As I have already told you, Balfour was a curious sort of fellow, and particularly close in regard to his own affairs. He was one of those sort of men it is difficult to get to the bottom of. You may try to probe them as much as you like, but nothing comes of it.'

'You possibly were as familiar with him as anyone,' suggested Brodie.

'Yes, I should say I was.'

'And if he had wanted a confidant, he would probably have chosen you?'

'I think it is very likely he would. So far as such a man would make a confidant of anyone, he made one of me.'

'Do you know why he brought Chunda from India with him?'

'No. What I do know is this: Chunda had been with him for some time, and when Balfour returned to Scotland, he thought he was only going to make a temporary stay here.'

'Was he fond of Chunda?'

'I cannot tell you whether he was or was not.'

'Can you tell me this: Has Chunda been in the habit of always wearing European clothes since he came to Edinburgh?'

'I don't know that. You see, I only came into port with my vessel four weeks ago. When I first called at Corbie Hall, the fellow was wearing European clothes.'

'Did you see much of Chunda on New Year's Eve?'

'He came into the room now and again. In fact, I think he was in and out pretty often. Balfour used occasionally to smoke an opium pipe, and Chunda always filled it for him.'

'How was the native dressed that night?'

'He had trousers and vest, and wore a sort of fancy Indian jacket.'

'Was there gold embroidery on it?'

'I believe there was a sort of gold thread, or something of that kind. But, really, I didn't take much notice. We were all pretty jolly, and I didn't look to see how anyone was dressed.'

'But, still, you have no doubt that Chunda did wear a jacket or robe similar to that you describe?'

'Oh yes, I'm sure about that part of the business. It was conspicuous enough.'

When Brodie parted from the skipper, he felt that he had struck a trail, although he could not make much of it just then. But it will readily be gathered that he had begun to suspect Chunda of having committed the crime.

It was difficult to understand why Chunda should have burnt his gown or jacket unless it was to destroy traces of guilt. If there was blood on his jacket, and it was the blood of one of the victims, he would know that it might prove a ghastly piece of evidence if detected; and so he had committed it to the flames as the most effectual means of getting rid of it.

Now, assuming this surmise of Brodie's was correct, it was obvious that it was not Maggie Stiven's blood, because the nature of the wound that brought about her death was such that there was only very little outward bleeding. But if Balfour, when he went upstairs to ascertain the cause of the scream, was suddenly attacked and stabbed to death by the native, was it not reasonable to suppose that he bled so profusely as to dye the garments of his murderer?

This chain of reasoning threw a new light on the affair, and Brodie, who had made up his mind that he would read the riddle if it could be read, returned once more to Corbie Hall. He learnt that Chunda had been back about half an hour, and had given the other servants to understand that he was ill and half frozen, and was going to bed. Whereupon the detective furnished himself with a lamp, and proceeded to carefully examine the stair carpet and the landings for suggestive stains, but saw nothing that aroused his suspicions. As he could not talk to Chunda, he did not disturb him, but the next morning, quite early, he went down to the Hall again in company with Jarvis.

Chunda told the skipper, in answer to questions put to him, that he had not gone out on the previous day to attend the funeral, as stated, but to make arrangements for taking his departure from the country. He could not endure the climate; it made him very ill. Besides that, he felt that he would go mad if he stayed there, for there wasn't a soul he could talk to, and his loneliness was terrible. He therefore intended to start on the following day for Southampton, and two days later would sail in a P. and O. steamer for India.

All that he had said seemed very feasible, and that he was ill and did suffer from the cold was evident.

Nevertheless, Brodie's suspicions were not allayed. It was not easy to allay them when once they were thoroughly aroused; and having reasoned the case out from every possible point of view, he had come to the conclusion that Chunda was in a position to let in light where there was now darkness if he chose to speak. That is to say, he knew something of the crime, though, of course, at this stage there wasn't a scrap of evidence against the native that would have justified his arrest. Moreover, Brodie found himself confronted with a huge difficulty in the way of making his theory fit in. If Chunda had really murdered Balfour, how had he managed to dispose of the body? That question was certainly a poser, and no reasonable answer could be given to it.

It must not be forgotten that, from the moment of the scream being first heard to the discovery of Maggie Stiven's body on the mat at the foot of the stairs, not more than half an hour at the outside had elapsed. In that brief space of time Balfour had been so effectually got rid of that there was not a trace of him. It was bewildering to try and understand how that disappearance had been accomplished, unless it was with the aid of some devilish art and unholy magic. But as Brodie had no belief in that kind of thing, he was convinced that, sooner or later, what was then an impenetrable mystery would be explained by perfectly rational, though probably startling, causes. Be that as it might, having got his fangs fixed, to use a figure of speech, he held on with bulldog tenacity, and he was not disposed to exonerate Chunda until he felt convinced that his suspicions were unfounded.

'Do you know, captain, if there are any balls of any kind in the house?' he asked abruptly of Jarvis, who looked at him with some astonishment, for the question seemed so irrelevant and out of place.

'What sort of balls?' said Jarvis, expressing his surprise by his manner and voice.

'Oh, any sort—billiard-balls, golf-balls, balls of any kind.'

'There are plenty of golf-balls. But why do you ask?'

'I want you to get two or three of the balls,' said Brodie for answer. 'Put them into your pocket, ask Chunda to accompany you into the dining-room, and make him sit down in a chair opposite to you. Engage him in conversation for a few minutes; then, suddenly taking the balls from your pocket, tell him to catch them, and pitch them to him. Do you understand me?'

Captain Jarvis stared at the detective as though he could hardly believe the evidence of his ears. Then, as he broke into a laugh, he asked:

'Do you mean that seriously?'

'Of course I mean it.'

'And what's the object?'

'Never mind the object. Do what I ask you.'

'And where will you be?'

'In the dining-room, too. But take no notice whatever of me.'

'Well, it's a daft-like sort of proceeding, any way; but I'll do it.'

Then, having procured some golf-balls, he addressed himself to Chunda in Hindustani, and in a few moments they went together into the dining-room.

Brodie followed shortly after, and, taking a book from a little shelf that hung on the wall, he threw himself on to a lounge and appeared to be reading.

In a short while Jarvis took the balls from his pocket, and, saying something to Chunda, who sat on a chair by the window, he threw one ball after another at him, and the native held forth his hands to catch them; but, not being in a playful humour, he did not cast the balls back, but very soon got up and went out, looking very much annoyed.

'Well, what does that tomfoolery mean?' asked Jarvis.

'A good deal to me. I've learnt a startling fact by it.'

The skipper would have been glad to have had an explanation, for naturally his curiosity was greatly aroused, and he couldn't conceive what the ball-throwing could possibly have indicated. But Brodie resolutely refused to satisfy him.

'You have rendered me a service,' he said. 'Now, that's enough for the present. If I succeed in fitting the pieces of this strange puzzle together, you shall know what my motive was. Rest assured I do nothing without a motive. But I am going to exact a further service from you now. I want you to stay here all night, as I myself intend to stay. Chunda talked of leaving to-morrow. He must not leave, and, if necessary, you must find some means of detaining him.'

'Do you mean to say you suspect Chunda of having committed the crime?'— his amazement growing.

'Frankly, I do.'

'Well, all I've got to say, Brodie, is this,' answered the skipper decisively: 'you are on the wrong tack.'

'How do you know I am?'

'I am sure of it.'

'Give me your reasons for being sure.'

'Why, I tell you, man,' exclaimed the skipper warmly, 'the nigger is as harmless as a kitten, and no more likely to commit a crime of this kind than a new-born baby.'

'That is simply your opinion, Captain Jarvis.'

'It is my opinion, and it's a common-sense one. You are doing the fellow a wrong. I never saw a native servant so attached to Balfour as Chunda was to his master. I tell you, Brodie, you are on the wrong scent.'

'All right, we shall see,' he said carelessly.

'But in the name of common-sense,' cried Jarvis, who was argumentatively inclined, 'if there's any reason in your suspicions, how on earth do you suppose this nigger chap got rid of Balfour? Where has he stowed him, do you think? Do you suppose he swallowed him?'

'Ah! an answer to that question is not easily framed. Perhaps before many hours have passed I may be able to tell you.'

'Do you think because he's black he's the devil, and has spirited Balfour away?' pursued the skipper, with a defiant air, for he honestly considered that Chunda was being wronged, and he was ready to champion him.

'No, I don't think so,' answered Brodie, with a smile, 'because if he had been the devil he wouldn't have committed such a clumsy crime as this.'

'Well, clumsy as it is, it's defied you,' said Jarvis, by no means satisfied or convinced.

'For the time being it has. But it won't continue to do so much longer, unless I'm very much mistaken. But it's no use continuing the argument. A man is judged by his acts, not by his words. If I am wrong, I must abide by the penalty which attaches to failure. If I am right, I shall take credit for some amount of cleverness. You will stay here to-night, won't you?'

The skipper scratched his head, and looked as though he wasn't comfortable.

'Well, upon my word! I don't know what to say. I'm not a coward, but I'm blowed if I like the idea of passing another night in this uncanny place.'

'Why?' Brodie asked with a smile.

'I should be afraid of seeing Maggie Stiven's ghost.'

'And what if you did? A ghost couldn't do you any harm.'

'Perhaps not, but I'd rather not see one.'

'Nor are you likely to, except as a product of your own heated imagination. However, to cut the matter short, you'll stay, won't you? You've got your pipe and tobacco, and I've no doubt the cook will be able to provide us with some creature comforts. We'll have another log put on the fire, and make ourselves comfortable; and, if you like, I'll give you a hand at cribbage.'

The skipper yielded, and the matter was settled.

'Before we settle down, I want you to entertain Chunda here for half an hour during my absence,' continued Brodie.

'You are not going out, are you?' asked Jarvis quickly, and with some nervousness displaying itself in his manner, indicating evidently that he did not wish to be left alone.

'Well, no, not out of the house. But you understand, Captain Jarvis, I am doing my best to unravel this mystery; you must let me act in my own way, and take such steps as I think are necessary to the end I have in view. You can aid me, and I want you to aid me; but you can best do that by refraining from questioning, and in doing exactly as I request you to do.'

'All right,' said Jarvis. 'I've nothing more to say. You must sail your own ship, whether you come to grief or whether you don't.'

'Precisely. Now, I'll send one of the servants up for Chunda, and you'll keep him engaged in talk for half an hour, or until I come back into the room. Don't talk about the crime, and don't say a word that would lead him to think I suspect him. Do you understand me?'

'Yes, of course I do.'

'And will carry out my wishes? It is most important that you should.'

'To the letter.'

The business being thus arranged, Brodie left the room, and ten minutes later Chunda entered it. Brodie was absent nearly three-quarters of an hour before he returned. There was a look of peculiar satisfaction on his face. Chunda was dismissed; and the two men, having, through the cook, secured something in the way of eatables and drinkables, satisfied their wants in that respect, and then engaged in cribbage, and continued their game until a late hour.

At last Jarvis retired. It was arranged he was to sleep in Balfour's bedroom, but Brodie said he would stow himself on a couch in the dining-room, which was warm and comfortable.

He dozed for three or four hours, and exactly at five rose, and made his way to the stable-yard, where, according to prearrangement, the groom was ready with a horse and trap, and Brodie drove rapidly into Edinburgh. He was back again soon after eight, with two constables in plain clothes, who were for the time confined to the kitchen, until their services might be required.

Jarvis did not rise until after nine. He was a good and sound sleeper, and neither ghosts nor anything else had disturbed him. He was kept in ignorance of Brodie's journey into Edinburgh.

A few minutes before ten Chunda made his appearance. He was ready to start, and he enlisted the aid of the other servants to bring his luggage down into the hall. Again Brodie requested the skipper to detain the native in conversation, while he himself went upstairs to Chunda's room, where he shut himself in and locked the door. Then he began to tap with his knuckles the wainscoted walls, going from panel to panel.

When he reached the deep recess near the fireplace, already described, he started, as his taps produced a hollow sound. He tapped again and again, putting his ear to the woodwork. There was no mistake about it. The wall there was hollow. He tried to move the hollow panel, but only after many trials and much examination did he succeed. The panel slid on one side, revealing a dark abyss, from which came a strange, cold, earthy, clammy smell.

He closed the panel, went downstairs, and told the constables the time for action had come. They filed into the dining-room, and Jarvis was asked to tell Chunda that he would be arrested on a charge of having murdered Raymond Balfour and Maggie Stiven.

If it is possible for a black person to turn pale, then Chunda did so. Any way, the announcement was like an electric shock to him. He staggered; then clapped his hands to his face, and moaned and whined.

Brodie went upstairs once more—this time in company with one of the constables. They were provided with lanterns, and when the panel in Chunda's room was opened again, the light revealed a narrow flight of stone steps descending between the walls; and at the bottom of the steps lay something huddled up. It was unmistakably a human body, the body of Raymond Balfour.

Chunda was at once conveyed to Edinburgh, and other men were sent out from the town to the house. Then the decomposed body was got up. It was Balfour, sure enough. He had been stabbed in the chest, and the heart had been pierced through.

At the bottom of the stone steps there was also found the other portion of the long stiletto.

All this, however, was not proof that Chunda had done the deed. But there was something else that was.

The dead man's right hand was tightly clenched, and when it was opened by the doctor who was called in to examine the remains, a piece of cloth was released from the death grip. It was a piece of Indian cloth, interwoven with gold threads, and identical with the scrap that Brodie had found in the ashes.

The dead hand afforded the necessary clue; it forged the last link. The dead hand smote the destroyer. It proved beyond doubt that Chunda was the murderer. He had by some means discovered the secret panel. He had inveigled Balfour into the room. There he had stabbed him. In his dying agony the wretched man had clutched at his murderer, and had torn out a piece of the gold-threaded jacket he was wearing. That jacket must have been deeply stained with blood, and Chunda had cast it upon the fire. But murder will out, and the unconsumed fragment gave the sharp-eyed Brodie the FIRST clue. The dead hand itself of the murdered man afforded the LAST.

Chunda was the murderer, or, rather, the murderess; for Chunda was a woman. Brodie had begun to suspect this from a peculiarity of voice, from the formation of her neck and shoulders, and from other signs, and his suspicions were confirmed when he resorted to the ball test.

When the balls were thrown, Chunda did not, as a man would have done, close his knees, but spread them open. A woman invariably does this when she is in a sitting posture and anything is thrown at her lap.

Chunda subsequently proved to be a woman, sure enough, and the murder was the result—as Brodie had also correctly divined—of jealousy.

The wretched creature succeeded in strangling herself before she was brought to trial, and she left behind her a paper written in excellent English, in which she confessed the crime. She declared that she was the wife of Balfour, who had espoused her in India. She represented a very old and high-caste family. Her father was a Rajah, and Balfour had been in his employ. He succeeded in winning her affections, and when he returned to his own country she determined to accompany him. He treated her very badly, and twice he attempted to poison her. His flirtation with Maggie Stiven excited her to madness, but it was, nevertheless, a very cunning madness. She had previously discovered by chance the sliding panel and the secret stairs.

On New Year's Eve she opened the panel, went to the top of the stairs, and uttered that eerie screech or scream that had so alarmed the company. She felt sure it would bring her husband to her. She told him that she had received a horrible fright in her room; that part of the wall had opened, revealing a dark abyss, from which strange noises issued. As soon as he was in the room she stabbed him with a long Indian stiletto. It then suddenly struck her that, when he didn't return, it was very likely Maggie Stiven would go in search of him. So she hurried down the stairs and hid underneath them, and as soon as Maggie appeared she sprang upon her and stabbed her with such fury that the blade of the dagger broke.

Although her husband had treated her so badly, she had yielded to his earnest entreaties to conceal her identity and continue to pass as a man. She spoke and wrote English fluently, although he had made her promise not to let this fact be known.

Such was the story she told, and there was no doubt it was substantially correct. She considered that she had managed the crime so well that suspicion would never rest upon her, and, having carried out her deed of awful vengeance, she would be able to return to her own sun-scorched land.

That she would have succeeded in this was likely enough had Peter Brodie not been brought upon the scene. He had worked out the problem line by line, and at last, when it struck him that if Balfour was murdered he must have been murdered in Chunda's room, he proceeded to examine the floor carefully on the night when he asked Jarvis to keep Chunda in conversation for half an hour. That examination revealed unmistakable traces of blood on the boards. Then it occurred to him that, as the house was an old one, it was more than likely there was some secret closet or recess in which the body had been hidden.

Chunda had evidently been well educated. In a postscript to her confession she said that, out of the great love she bore the man who had so cruelly deceived her, she had, at his suggestion, consented to pass herself off as his servant. He had assured her that it would only be for a short time, and that when he had his affairs settled, and sold his property, he would go back with her to India, and they would live in regal splendour to the end of their days.

That she loved him was pretty certain. That he shamefully deceived her was no less certain; and that love of hers, and that deception, afforded some palliation for her bloodthirsty deed of vengeance.

For some time after the double crime Corbie Hall remained desolate and lonely. It was now looked upon as a doubly-accursed place, and nobody could be found who would take it, so at last it was razed to the ground, and is known no more.

In pulling it down it was discovered that in Balfour's room was a secret panel corresponding to the one in the next room, and that the stone stairs had at one time led to a subterraneous passage, which had an opening somewhere in Blackford Glen. It had no doubt originally been constructed to afford the inmates of the house means of escape in the stormy times when the building was first reared.

THE END.

FOOTNOTES:

[A] This name is a fictitious one, for obvious reasons, but the incidents related in the story are well authenticated.

[B] This was quite true. The contingency of war was even less remote than the Prince's words suggested. As a matter of fact, it is now well known that the treaty had been formed between Russia and another country against Turkey, and had Turkey become aware of it, there is little doubt she would have flown at Russia's throat, with results less disastrous to herself than those which befell her at a later period, when the legions of Russia crossed the Pruth, and commenced that sanguinary struggle which entailed such enormous loss of life, the expenditure of thousands of millions of money, and human agony and suffering beyond the power of words to describe.

www.ingramcontent.com/pod-product-compliance
Ingram Content Group UK Ltd.
Pitfield, Milton Keynes, MK11 3LW, UK
UKHW040816280325
456847UK00003B/446